The Sword
of Venice

Also by Thomas Quinn

The Lion of St. Mark

The Sword of Venice

Book Two of
THE VENETIANS

Thomas Quinn

Thomas Dunne Books
St. Martin's Press   New York

This is a work of fiction. All of the characters, organizations, and events portrayed in this novel are either products of the author's imagination or are used fictitiously.

THOMAS DUNNE BOOKS.
An imprint of St. Martin's Press.

www.thomasdunnebooks.com
www.stmartins.com

Maps by Carolyn Chu

Library of Congress Cataloging-in-Publication Data

Quinn, Thomas, 1951–
    The sword of Venice / Thomas Quinn.—1st ed.
        p. cm.—(The Venetians ; bk. 2)
    ISBN-13: 978-0-312-31910-6
    ISBN-10: 0-312-31910-X
    1. Nobility—Italy—Venice—Fiction. 2. Venice (Italy)—History—Turkish Wars, 1453–1571—Fiction. I. Title.

PS3617.U588 S96 2007
813'.6—dc22

                                                                2007032534

First Edition: December 2007

10 9 8 7 6 5 4 3 2 1

For my mother

The Sword
of Venice

1

Scutari

1473

Chained naked, with his arms and legs spread painfully apart, he writhed in vain. He was gripped by raw fear as cold sweat ran in rivulets down his contorted face and aching ribs. Served up like a sacrificial lamb, he was defenseless. Suddenly, a finely polished, curved steel blade flashed in the stark torchlight as his merciless, hooded tormentor slowly drew it from its scabbard. He could see hatred seething in the man's wolflike eyes; a blazing yellow fire seemed to dance in each dark orb. Mortified, he pathetically attempted to beg the executioner to spare his life, but the words froze in his paralyzed throat. As the relentless blade moved steadily toward him, he tried one last time to jerk his arms and legs free, but it was no use, as the rusted iron manacles only tore deeper into the soft flesh of his wrists and ankles. He was to be castrated, like an animal.

"No!" he managed to scream as he braced his naked groin to withstand the unimaginable pain.

"Constantine." The executioner miraculously stopped and shouted his name. "Constantine!"

Suddenly, the chains fell away from his arms and legs. The man was laughing.

Constantine sat bolt upright, dripping wet, and stared at the man, disoriented.

"Paolo!"

In the dim candlelight, he could see his older cousin, standing beside his bed. A toothy grin split the short charcoal beard that wrapped around his mouth and chin. He began to laugh heartily. Embarrassed, Constantine Ziani fell back and sucked in a deep breath as he wiped the beads of perspiration from his forehead with the back of his hand. He glanced at his wrists. They were no longer bleeding and sore.

"You were having a nightmare. Now get up and get dressed. Captain-General Loredan wants to see us—now."

He struggled to comprehend Paolo's words as he awkwardly hopped on one leg, vainly trying to push the other into his tangled pants. Paolo lit an oil lamp. Constantine's frame glowed ghostlike in the flickering light that played over his muscular back and shoulders. He had no scars, unusual for a soldier. He had not yet experienced battle in his short life. The only blood he had ever drawn belonged to his sword-fighting instructor. Just twenty years old, whiskers sprouted from his face like the annoying weeds that poked through Venice's less frequented brick-paved *campi*. At just two inches shy of six feet, he was very tall. But his physical appearance and naïve optimism, not yet dimmed by life's experiences, belied his maturity. His uncompromising steel gray eyes provided the only clue that a man lived inside his youthful shell.

Constantine neither sought out nor retreated from an argument or a fight. His values reflected the Venetian ways he had been diligently taught from the time he was a child, making him wise beyond his years. Like all Venetian *nobili,* the aristocratic men who ruled Venice, his aim was to serve honorably in any capacity required by his beloved Republic and, in so doing, to merit increasingly important assignments in the future. Personal honor was more than a code; it was a religion. Men willingly died to preserve it.

"Why does he want to see *us*?"

"How should I know? A guard woke me a minute ago and said that we are to come at once."

Constantine put on a wool shirt and pulled on his stiff leather shoes. Still rubbing grit from his eyes, he followed Paolo into the fortress yard. It was dark outside; not a single star broke through the vast, black, moonless sky. Smokelike mists, driven by mountain winds, blew around them. In the distance, they could see two soldiers standing by the door to the massive keep. One held a blazing torch that seemed to ignite his haggard face.

"It must be after midnight," muttered Constantine as they walked toward them.

Suddenly, he tripped on a cobblestone, nearly losing his balance. I cannot

The Sword of Venice

leave this godforsaken place soon enough, he thought. His toe throbbed painfully as he ran a few steps to catch up to Paolo. As they reached the door, the two guards exchanged glances, and one motioned for them to follow him.

The fortress towered above Scutari, a market town nestled in the northwestern corner of Albania, fifteen miles inland from the Adriatic and at the southern end of the lake for which it was named. The Venetians had built the citadel there on a promontory that dominated the town and countryside below. They called it La Roccaforte. It was well named with its seven imposing towers and thick stone walls. Rising on steep piles of sheer gray rock, it was virtually unassailable on three sides, and the fourth was protected by a wall, in places fifty feet thick. The only gate was a massive, impenetrable iron door at the end of a long tunnel with killing slits along both sides of its entire length.

The Turks had laid siege to the fortress seven months earlier, but after finding it so strongly defended, they had wisely decided not to storm it. The Venetians had been surprised to find that the besiegers had chosen not to manhandle their vaunted artillery over the rugged Balkan Mountains to pound La Roccaforte's walls into rubble as they had in the past at Constantinople and Negropont and a score of smaller fortresses throughout Greece.

Despite the defenders' well-known inexhaustible water supply, the Turks instead hoped they could starve the garrison into submission before winter, knowing its food supply could not last forever. They could not safely advance up the Adriatic coast, toward Venice, as long as La Roccaforte remained in Venetian hands.

Finally, Constantine and Paolo were shown to a large room where Captain-General Antonio Loredan and his officers were engaged in what appeared to be a heated council of war. The guard announced them and, closing the wooden door with a thud, departed. Six men were seated around a heavy, ornately carved oak table. Loredan abruptly held up his hand, stopping the conversation, and stood to greet them.

"Lieutenant Ruzzini," he addressed Paolo, "time is short, so I will get right to the point. Just before the Turks laid siege to La Roccaforte, we inserted several spies into their camp. One has proven particularly useful. He is an Albanian merchant who provides fine goods and other, more personal pleasures to the Turkish officers. His women frequently engage these Turks in both forms of intercourse. Each day, at noon, we look for a communication from him relating what he has learned from these liaisons. Days often pass without a message, but this morning we received most disturbing news.

"It seems the sultan has finally grown impatient with his commander's

attempt to starve us out, so he has ordered him to breach the walls and assault the fortress, quickly ending the siege—something I would have done right from the start.

"We have learned that the Turks have hauled one of their largest guns overland, all the way from Istanbul. With our fleet denying them a sea route through the Adriatic, we had hoped they would not be able to drag a gun of this size over the mountains on those wretched old Roman roads, but our spy reports that it arrived two days ago. If you look out at their camp in the morning, you will see the wooden enclosure they have built, which is intended to protect the gunners from our fire when they move it up close to the wall. They have covered it with animal hides so we cannot burn it with flaming arrows."

Loredan's expression became grave. "If the Turks are able to fire that monster at close range, we are done for. Captain Cavazzo estimates it will take them only a few days to destroy a fifty-foot section of the wall. That would compel us to surrender since we estimate that they outnumber us by at least ten to one."

Constantine and Paolo exchanged glances.

"Captain-General," interrupted Paolo, "how does this spy get his messages through? A rat could not sneak into this place from the outside, through their lines."

"At noon, when the sun is directly overhead, he uses a mirror to flash his messages from the old church tower beyond their camp. The Turks never go in there, and his signals cannot be seen from below, but we can read them well enough from our towers up here. He has been feeding us information, undetected, for months."

Loredan smiled, but he could not hide the strain on his brow or the concern in his dark eyes. The great weight he bore seemed to be finally beating him down.

"And now I must tell you why I have sent for you," he said, changing his tone. "I want you both to lead a sortie out of the fortress to destroy that gun. It is our only hope."

His words took only a few seconds to utter, but their meaning was chilling, eternal. They could both be killed or worse—become playthings for the Turks to torture at their leisure.

"But how? There are thousands of Turks in that camp," asked Paolo.

"We have given that question much thought."

Cavazzo stood and cleared his throat. He walked around the table and placed his hand on Paolo's shoulder. Constantine knew that Paolo admired the older officer.

"Just after sunset tomorrow, we will lower you and a company of ten men on ropes down the outside of the western wall. By holding on to the ropes, you can safely move along the wall to the southwest corner tower, where it meets the front wall. There, you can tie yourselves together and carefully feel your way along the boulders in the darkness until you find a good place to hide. Hopefully this damned weather will clear and the half-moon will light your way. If someone loses his footing, the others can keep him from falling to his death. As a precaution, tomorrow we will post all of our crossbowmen near that spot to prevent any Turkish scouts from discovering your hiding place."

Paolo looked quickly at Constantine. He appeared to be impressed with the thought that had gone into the plan so far.

"Then," Cavazzo continued, "you will wait through the day, until just after sunset when the Turks are at their evening prayers. As a diversion, five minutes after their prayers begin, our spies will set a building on fire near the center of their camp, to draw the Turks' attention. While they are occupied with trying to put the fire out, you and your men will rush the gun, unseen in the darkness. It is only about two hundred yards from the wall and all downhill. It should take you no more than a minute or two to cover that distance but remember: you must not be discovered. Surprise is essential."

"Then"—he smiled—"you will kill any guards you find there, take powder sacks that will surely be there, fill the gun barrel, light the fuse, and then run like deer before the gun explodes—destroying it beyond repair."

"But what if they have not stockpiled the powder?" asked Paolo.

"Trust me. There will be a mountain of black powder there. They are nearly ready to begin bombarding the wall. That is why we have waited until now to attack. We wanted to ensure it *would* be there.

"When you light the fuse—keep it as short as you dare. Then run for your lives back up to the citadel. We will open the gate for you. But I warn you, any man who is left behind or unable to flee will be mercilessly killed by the Turks—or worse."

Finished, Cavazzo let his words sink in. He was obviously confident of success. It was the kind of plan you could feel good about making for someone else but the kind you worried about if your own life depended on it. Important questions ran through their minds, but before they could ask them, Loredan spoke.

"Paolo, I knew and admired your father, and, Constantine, your father is a hero and also my friend. I am not surprised they raised fine sons like you. Now you both have the privilege to emulate them, just as they did their fathers. You can choose whoever you wish to go with you. Tell Captain

Cavazzo who you want and he will arrange everything. Form your company tomorrow afternoon at four o'clock by the western wall. Now, try to get some sleep."

Constantine and Paolo finally drifted off to sleep shortly before sunrise, in their windowless room. After rising at midday, Paolo advised Cavazzo of the ten soldiers they had chosen to lead on the dangerous mission. By four o'clock, they assembled at the wall, all dressed in dark clothing. They would travel light. Each man would carry no arms or armor, other than his dagger. The only other things they would carry were food and water for the long wait the next day, hidden among the boulders. Two would also carry matches and a length of oil-soaked cord to use as a fuse to explode the gun.

An hour passed as the raiders engaged in idle talk, trying to push back the ever-present fear of the unknown that hung over them like a shroud. Suddenly, a *muezzin's* high-pitched singing broke the silence. It was time.

The twelve men filed up the stairs to the top of the wall. The soldiers there helped them to tie ropes around their waists and attach bags, filled with food and water, to straps hung around their necks. The soldiers on the wall looked at them grimly but gratefully, admiring their courage. The rumors had been true; there was going to be a sortie. They knew how dangerous it would be to leave the protection of the citadel. There were so many things that could go wrong. Most of the soldiers pitied the twelve, relieved that they had not been selected to go.

Just after the sun set behind the purple hills to the west, the raiders were lowered to the sheer cliff, a narrow line of jagged rocks barely discernible in the faint moonlight, thirty feet below. High above, on the wall, three soldiers strained to hang on to each man's rope as they walked their precious cargo, like a marionette, along the wall to a point next to the southwest corner tower, where a previously identified large flat rock provided a good landing spot.

Paolo, in the lead, used the prearranged signal and pulled hard three times on his rope. It suddenly dropped at his feet. He threw the end to Constantine, who tied it around his waist. As Paolo moved off, Constantine swung and dropped to the same spot and began searching with his feet for the flat surface. Finding it, he jerked on his rope. The end fell to his feet. He threw it to the man behind him, ten feet away, who, in turn, tied it around his waist. Within five minutes, all twelve men were tethered together, ready to begin their trek across the mass of rocks near the southwestern corner of the wall. The going was agonizingly slow in the darkness. Two hours later, cut, bruised, and exhausted, they finally found shelter under a massive boulder and, even though it was September, they prepared for the cold night on the exposed windblown promontory. Only one man was injured. His ankle was too severely sprained for him to take part in the attack.

At sunrise the men ate their food, saving only some water, and settled down for the long wait. Paolo allowed the men to talk quietly. The nearest Turk was two hundred yards away and he knew that the wind, blowing briskly from the west, would not carry their voices into the Turkish camp.

The warm autumn day crept by slowly. Most of the men tried to sleep; a few sharpened their daggers but not Paolo. He busily crawled from man to man, talking to each one. He made certain that each knew his role by having him repeat not only his own orders but those of the other men. Their only chance was to slip in undetected, quickly rig the gun to explode, and then run for their lives back up the hill to the citadel. Paolo had chosen two artillerists who would cut and light the fuse. The rest were selected for their strength and speed and, most important, for their ruthlessness. Paolo had decided to choose men who terrified even him. He had succeeded.

Constantine's admiration for his cousin approached adoration. He had always looked up to Paolo. Five years older, Paolo was the kind of man a soldier willingly followed. To such a decisive and courageous fighter, failure was unthinkable.

Constantine smiled as he watched Paolo move among the men. Finally, his circuit completed, he returned to the place where the two of them would await sunset together, in the most advanced position. As the orange half-sun sank lower on the hazy horizon behind the hills, he could feel the tension build.

"Are you afraid?" he asked Paolo.

"Yes, but not for my own life. I am afraid that if I do not make the right decisions, we will not accomplish our mission and these brave men will die for nothing."

Paolo placed his hand on Constantine's shoulder. "Are you afraid?"

"I am not sure. I would not tell this to anyone but you, Paolo, but part of me wants to watch what happens from the security of the citadel wall while the other part wants desperately to be a part of whatever happens down at the bottom of this hill."

"Well"—Paolo smiled—"just think of all of our ancestors in heaven, smiling proudly as they watch you. Their time is past; they are gone but not forgotten. They are counting on you, and now you must do as they would have done. There *is* no one else. Strange how life is, nearly a million souls in our empire and it all comes down to just us twelve, here in this place, at this moment."

Constantine smiled and thought for a long time. "Do you think we can do it, Paolo? Destroy the gun, I mean."

"I do not know. I only know that we have been sent to do it and we will die trying to do it. They can ask no more of us than that. It is in God's hands now."

Constantine nodded.

"Just remember one thing. In war, nothing ever goes according to plan. You must be prepared for anything and everything, so for God's sake, be alert and stay close to me."

Several minutes slipped by in silence. Suddenly Constantine spoke, revealing his innermost thoughts. "I was just thinking. All these years, my father has recounted his life and his experiences in war and I have eagerly listened. Then, it was easy to revel in the glories of it all. I actually used to lament that I might never know the great deeds and noble sacrifices of a soldier. I worried that I might never shout, 'For St. Mark and Venice,' as I defended Venice's honor, slaying her enemies."

He looked deep into his cousin's eyes, searching for a hint of acknowledgment.

"But now . . . that I too am a soldier, doing what my father did, I have begun to understand so much more, and I see his stories in such a different light. War is at once beautiful and terrible. Now my thoughts are not of the glories and the nobility of it all. They are, instead, of survival, seeing my mother again, old friends, the beauty of Venice. God, Paolo, I want to live."

Paolo placed his hand on Constantine's shoulder. "You think too much to be a soldier, cousin." He smiled affectionately. "Soldiering is a job, much like a gondolier's, a farmer's, or a baker's, only . . . a soldier can lose his life doing it. Worse, if you command others, you can get them killed unnecessarily if you do not know what you are doing.

"Take that yearning you spoke of for family, friends, and Venice and make that your reason to fight, to bleed, to suffer the privations of camp . . . and, perhaps, to die. What could be nobler than that?"

They looked deep into each other's eyes. Constantine was the first to speak.

"Is it like that for you?"

"It used to be," he replied wistfully, "but the veteran quickly becomes callous to war. Hard as it is to believe, once you have seen your comrades killed—their broken, lifeless bodies, where a soul once stirred, laughing and full of life, that a woman once loved, lying like garbage on the field of battle—it changes you. All that matters is the respect of your fellow soldiers and your own respect for duty and your flag. You put your head down and get through it. That is what I shall do in a few hours."

It was not the answer Constantine had hoped for. It was too simple, too stoic. "I do not think I could ever become like you . . . about war, I mean."

Paolo shook his head. "That is what I thought when I was your age. Just wait. Someday you will tell me I was right. The sooner you understand that, the better. War is hard enough without feelings. I can no longer imagine waging it any other way. I would go mad otherwise."

"Perhaps you are right," muttered Constantine. As he considered all that Paolo had said to him, he marveled even more at what his father had achieved in his life. He was a true war hero. As time passed, Constantine, huddled under the rock, slowly resolved that he would survive and return to Venice to tell his father how much he admired him and all he had learned. Now, more than ever, he wanted to be like him.

2

The Monster

A *muezzin*'s cry split the darkness. Thousands of Turks would soon be laying out their prayer mats, as they had five times daily for months, since the siege began, without incident. Not once had the Venetians ever sortied from the citadel. Only a few sentries would remain at their posts, their senses dulled by the boredom of a routine, seemingly without purpose.

Suddenly Paolo whispered loudly, "For St. Mark and Venice!" He motioned for his company to follow him as he began to climb over the few rocks between them and the path leading down the hill to the Turkish camp.

Now, armed only with their daggers and their courage, the eleven Venetians crawled from their rocky lair to the narrow path, stood up, and began to run, keeping as low to the ground as they could. It was a difficult sprint as they ran down the hill, trying to avoid tripping on wagon ruts, loose rocks, and debris. They made little noise, except for their padded footfalls on the dirt path, having carefully bound their shoes with cloth to muffle the sound. Luckily, the wind had shifted to blowing from the south, carrying what little noise they made back toward the citadel.

On they ran, charging down the hill. When they were within fifty yards of the enclosure, Paolo suddenly raised his hand, slowing them to a crouching walk. Though they could not see any guards in the dim moonlight, they dropped to the ground and crawled the last twenty yards and rolled, one after another, into a shallow ditch right in front of the high wooden palisade enclosing the gun; each man gasped to suck air into his burning lungs. Constantine looked left and right—nothing. The few Turkish guards who would not be at prayers, still on duty, were nowhere to be seen.

Finally Paolo crawled to the wooden gun enclosure and stood alongside it. The rest of the Venetians followed him. They could barely make out voices from the other side of the wooden wall. As the excitement of the run down the hill through the darkness died down, Constantine's swollen toe began to throb painfully. He wondered how he would ever make it back up the hill. Still breathing hard, he gripped his dagger and looked to Paolo for what to do next.

"We will wait here for the fire to be set," Paolo whispered.

"What if there is no fire?" hissed one of the artillerists.

Before Paolo could answer, a loud cry shattered the quiet. Soon they could hear much commotion from the camp. The sky overhead began to flicker as the fire quickly ignited the dry wooden building. Constantine's chest was pounding. For the first time in his life, he was about to face death, but even more terrifying was his fear of the unknown.

Paolo bent down and curled his fingers under the wooden gun port door and raised it an inch. Another man gripped the other side.

"On three, kill them all," whispered Paolo.

He held up one hand and motioned with his fingers—one, two, three . . .

They heaved up the door, rotating it on its axle. The Venetians burst inside with daggers drawn. Taken completely by surprise, two Turks scrambled for their weapons, but they were too late. The Venetians quickly dispatched them. Their brief cries were drowned out by the pandemonium that had broken out in the center of the camp.

Now safely inside the enclosure, seven men formed a human chain and began stuffing ten-pound sacks of black powder down the muzzle of the huge gun. The tallest, at over six feet, stood on his toes as he pushed the bags down with the giant ramrod. Constantine and Paolo stood guard while the two artillerists prepared their fuse and lit a slow-burning match, careful to shield it from the powder.

In three minutes they were finished. The great cannon's bronze muzzle was packed with powder from end to end. From the shouting, they could tell that the enemy soldiers were returning from prayers, streaming into the camp. They were desperately trying to save one of the camp's only two brothels and avert a major catastrophe.

As Paolo lit the fuse, nine of the Venetians began to file out of the gun port to run back up the hill toward the citadel. Constantine lingered, wanting to stay with his cousin.

"Run, Constantine!"

"You said to stay close. I am not leaving you."

"With your foot, you will be lucky if the Turks do not catch you. Now go!"

He was right, thought Constantine. As he crouched down and passed through the gun port, he suddenly collided with a young Turkish soldier who was running past. Before the lad realized he was a Venetian intruder, Constantine quickly plunged his dagger deep into the lad's stomach. With his mouth agape, the boy only managed a pathetic groan as he dropped to the ground, dying, his eyes wide open with surprise. Constantine pulled out his dagger and ran as fast as his swollen foot would allow. After twenty seconds, he whirled around and looked back down the hill.

Hundreds of Turks, silhouetted by the leaping flames, were trying to prevent the fire from spreading to the rest of the camp. Angry officers barked conflicting orders as frantic soldiers searched for anything that could hold water to quench the conflagration.

As Constantine walked backward up the hill, his eyes fixed on the gun port. There was no sign of Paolo. Where was he? Suddenly his cousin emerged from the gun port, backlit by the fire, and leaped over the ditch in one bound. Constantine smiled as he thought, they will not catch him!

As Constantine was about to turn and run up the hill, the Turkish camp exploded in a towering, blinding orange flash, engulfing Paolo.

"No!" screamed Constantine.

Violent shock waves knocked him to the ground, stunning him. Unseen shards of jagged wood and metal screamed past him as he lay there.

When he came to his senses, his shoulder was oozing blood around a wooden shard that protruded from the painful wound. His hair was singed and his face stung from burns and cuts made by smaller wood splinters. He struggled onto his feet and stumbled along, dazed and bleeding.

Looking back down the hill one more time, he realized that Paolo must be dead, but there was no time to cry or mourn. A score of outraged Turks were running wildly up the hill toward him, shouting and brandishing their weapons as they passed the spot where Paolo had disappeared in the flames. Constantine turned and ran for the gate, 150 yards up the hill, forgetting the pain in his toe. His lungs burned and his body screamed back at him to give up, but he ran on. As the dark wall loomed up ahead, he shouted with all his might.

"For St. Mark and Venice! For St. Mark and Venice!"

He hoped the deadly crossbowmen up above would not mistake him for a Turk. Running for his life, he turned to catch a glimpse of his pursuers. They were about fifty yards behind him. Not far to go now, he thought. Ahead of him, he could make out dark forms on the wall. Will they shoot me? he wondered. Suddenly the big iron gate began to swing open, shrieking on its rusted hinges. He dashed inside and, before the gatekeepers could slam it shut, he turned to see that a volley of invisible crossbow bolts had decimated the nearest Turks. He tumbled to the stone floor, gasping for breath with the others. They had all made it too. As Constantine lay there, thinking about his narrow escape, he realized that a man never feels more alive than when he has just cheated death.

The blast had destroyed the Turk's massive cannon. Without it, they had no way to batter down the citadel's walls. There was not enough time for them to send for another before the onset of winter. As the first autumn winds began to whistle and whine around the rocky outcropping, the Turks' morale plummeted, but their commander chose to stay and prolong the siege rather than withdraw and face his unforgiving sultan, Muhammad II. Called *Fatih,* or Conqueror, by his subjects, the sultan would surely find that his warlike appellation only added to his embarrassment: despite their vast superiority in numbers, the Turkish army had been unable to force the stubborn Venetians to surrender Scutari.

Constantine mourned Paolo's death, but what a glorious death it had been. He had sacrificed himself to ensure the gun was destroyed, waiting until a few seconds before the fuse exploded the powder before he ran to try to save himself. He had either misjudged the time remaining on the fuse or, more likely, he had stayed behind, risking certain death, to prevent some curious Turks from thwarting the gun's destruction. Constantine hoped his own death would be so noble.

He remembered Paolo's words, under the rock. In the end, Paolo had not just put his head down—he had died a hero.

After his wounds were treated, Constantine reported to Captain-General Loredan. The Venetian commander showed none of his usually stern demeanor. Instead, he threw his arms around Constantine, as if embracing a long-lost son.

"You have saved us all," he said, in front of hundreds of defenders who had congregated around the valiant raider and his company. "When we return to Venice, I shall personally present you to Doge Marcello and his *Signoria.*"

As word of their exploits spread, Constantine and his men were soon the envy of every man and woman in La Roccaforte.

Now, with the grave threat eliminated, the Venetians settled back down to the dreary life of a garrison under siege. Many of the defenders were sick, but so far, deadly plague, typhus, or dysentery had not shown their presence among them. As the last leaves dropped from the few black scarecrow-like trees and the thick morning frost greeted the rising sun, October slipped into November and still the Turks remained, too weak to attack, too strong to admit defeat.

Loredan and his lieutenants knew that they could now outlast the Turks. They estimated there were ample food supplies to sustain them until the New Year. However, they would no longer receive any information about the enemy's camp. The day after the raid, the Venetians had awakened to find their gallant spy's flayed body hanging upside down from a gibbet like a lamb's carcass in the marketplace, a hundred yards from the citadel gate, a few birds picking indifferently at his eye sockets. More than one kind of man is capable of possessing courage—even a spy, thought Constantine.

In his own life, he had only to look to the deeds of his famous father for his ideal of courage. Antonio Ziani, a respected patrician, merchant, and war hero, had fought the Turks at Constantinople and Negropont. Even Constantine's name, unique among Venetians because it was in the Byzantine form rather than the Italian Constantino, was a constant reminder that he was part of that legacy. He had been named in honor of the great city the Venetians had bravely defended more than twenty years before. Though Captain-General Loredan's praise rang pleasingly in his ears, he could not wait to bask in his father's approval for his bravery. There is no finer thing for a man than to earn the respect of a respected father.

Constantine hurried up the circular stone staircase and walked quickly down the familiar twisting dark passageway that led to Captain-General Loredan's quarters. He was hungry, like everyone else in La Roccaforte—the siege had now lasted for more than a year—but his affluent, healthy upbringing had enabled him to bear well the privations that had taken the lives of many others. Now, long past midnight, a single candle burned down to its nub provided the only light. He abruptly turned the final corner. Recognizing him, the guard nodded as he removed his hand from his sword and stepped aside. As Constantine opened the door, he wondered who would be in the room with Loredan.

In the dim light Constantine could see five shivering men huddled together, standing in the center, talking in hushed voices. Autumn had passed into winter. The room's antique oak table and chairs had been sacrificed a fortnight ago to warm the frigid room. Now, even the crude wooden chairs that had replaced them were gone, also consumed in the fire. Loredan paused and turned in his direction.

"Well, Lieutenant Ziani?"

"The rumor is true. The great cistern *is* dry," he reported, knowing the devastating effect his words would have on these men, who had given their all for so many months to defend Scutari.

Loredan squinted and slowly shook his gray head as he stared at him in disbelief. "The great cistern is dry?" He repeated the words, as though by doing so, he could change their meaning. "But it rained just three days ago. Surely some water has accumulated by now?"

"Not enough. The guards at the well already drank what little there was."

The ruinous news tore the last shred of hope from Loredan and his four exhausted officers. He had called a council of war to decide whether to accept the Turkish commander's new terms to surrender Scutari.

"Who knows about the cistern?" asked the captain-general.

"Just the guards, their commander, and now all of you," replied Constantine.

"Good, no one else must know. This must be kept a secret."

"I have already seen to that," replied Constantine.

"Good, now listen to me, all of you." Loredan's face betrayed his resignation as he turned to the others.

"Issue orders that anyone who is caught trying to leave the citadel will be summarily executed. The Turks surely have spies in our midst, as we have had in theirs. If they find out we are out of water before we meet with them tomorrow, they will withdraw their terms, knowing we cannot last longer than a day without it."

The officers cast furtive glances at each other, each thinking the same thing but not wanting to be the first to speak it. Loredan sensed their thoughts and put his arm around Constantine.

"Even a new lieutenant knows what we must do, eh, young man?"

Constantine regretted that his curiosity had made him linger too long in the room. Now the captain-general was asking for *his* opinion. Fortunately, he was accustomed to being in the presence of powerful men. He was one of *them*—a *nobile*, one of Venice's ruling oligarchy. He had nothing to fear by speaking frankly to Loredan. He knew the captain-general wanted to use his response to make a point with the others.

"I would wait until sundown tomorrow. If it rains, perhaps we can last another day or two. Everyone in the city knows the Turks are low on food, and some have already departed. Last night there were only half as many of their campfires as there were just a fortnight ago even though the weather has turned cold and, unlike us, they have plenty of wood to burn."

"And if it does *not* rain, Lieutenant Ziani? What do you suggest we do then?"

"I will tell you what we must do, Captain-General Loredan," interrupted Cavazzo. "We must pray that the pasha keeps his word about sparing the garrison if we lay down our arms. Remember what the Turks did after Negropont?"

A raw chill colder than the icy winds that blew in through the unglazed windows made them all shiver. The sultan had butchered every single man, woman, and child in Negropont after it fell, leaving only one young soldier to return to Venice to bear witness to the massacre.

Loredan slowly outstretched his hands. "What other choice do we have? Is not a quick beheading preferable to slow starvation?"

The frigid wind howled mercilessly into the room as Loredan's officers stared silently at the floor, watching a few dried leaves swirl around and pile up in one corner.

"It is decided then." Loredan turned to Constantine. "You have demonstrated coolness in the face of the enemy, young man. Tomorrow, if there is no rain, you shall be the one to bear the white flag of surrender to the Turks."

Pride and shame struggled within Constantine. It was an assignment he did not want, but what else could he do? He had been given a direct order—he had to obey it.

The old warhorse turned and gazed out the window as another fresh gust rustled his ragged beard. A thousand stars sparkled, all seeming to pay homage to the bright yellow-crescented quarter moon that dominated the cloudless ink-black night sky. It was a bad omen. It seemed as if the Turks controlled even the heavens.

"There will be no rain tomorrow. You had better make that white flag a big one, or you will surely catch a Turkish arrow before they see it." He frowned as he turned to face Constantine and the others.

"Now I want you all to go see to the needs of your men. We must keep everyone in the city quiet until the Turks have accepted our terms."

By the time Constantine returned to his post and tried to lie down and get some sleep, the sentries were already changing. It was four o'clock. Sunrise would be in less than three hours. His mind raced with so many thoughts, he could not sleep. Finally, he decided to search for something to use for a flag. It would not do for the men to see him looking for it in the morning. He would have to conceal it in his shirt until just before he was ready to leave the citadel for the Turkish camp.

E xhausted, he had finally fallen asleep shortly after finding a discarded empty grain sack to use for a flag of truce. Now awakened, he rubbed his bloodshot eyes as he emerged into the sunlight. He looked up. The sky was clear for the first time in weeks. Now it seemed that even God had abandoned Scutari's brave defenders. There would be no rain today. Although they still had a month's rations left, all was finished. It always came down to water. Who could have foreseen that the ancient cistern would go dry as a bone?

Worn soldiers went through the motions of reporting to their posts, as they had for several hundred mornings before, more fearful of their officers' badgering than a Turkish attack they knew would not come. This morning the talk was of water. By now, despite attempts to suppress the news, everyone knew the cistern was dry.

Constantine rubbed his stiff legs as he climbed the steps to the top of the wall. His chain mail felt heavy as it rubbed against his shirt. He gazed out at the Turkish camp in the distance. A few campfires still smoldered. Behind him, he could hear babies wailing as their mothers tried to suckle them from their empty breasts. With no water, they could not produce enough milk.

Suddenly someone called out his name. He looked down into the yard. Loredan was standing there with two of his subordinates. Constantine ran back down the stairs, clutching his bulging shirt so the flag concealed there would not fall out.

"Yes, Captain-General Loredan." He saluted as he stood at attention.

"Are you ready to go?"

"But it will be hours before twilight. I thought . . ."

"Nearly fifty more died last night. There is no point in prolonging the suffering of the people. With no water, there is no telling how many more will die today. Go now and find the pasha. Tell him we have fought a good fight and accept his terms, with full faith in his guarantee of safe passage. We will leave our weapons and depart the city to march to the coast, where our fleet will embark us."

The town's inhabitants, who had suffered for so long, would be left to their fate—and to the Turks, thought Constantine. The specter of it sickened him, but there was no other way. Loredan had no choice. The army had to be saved to fight another day.

"As you wish, Captain-General." He saluted smartly despite his exhaustion.

He picked up a long spear and, removing the sack from his shirt, pushed the point through it in three places, making a crude, dirty tan flag. It was the best he could do; it was not white but it was big. The Turks could not possibly confuse it with a crimson and gold Lion of St. Mark, the Venetian battle standard. But was it big enough? The Turkish archers could fire accurately at more than three hundred yards, and Constantine knew they had not had a good target for months.

He walked through the arch and into the fifty-foot-long tunnel in the wall leading to the main gate. The smell of filth and death filled his nostrils. His stomach wretched but he managed to keep down the piece of dried fish he had eaten the day before. As he reached the iron door, a guard peered through a peephole in it to be sure there were no Turks hiding outside the wall. Another fought to loosen the rusty bolts, sunk deep into the stone. The door whined on its hinges as he opened it. Sunlight stabbed Constantine's bloodshot eyes as he slipped outside into the brilliant light where, despite the frosty November morning, the bright sun made it feel warm.

He held the flag up high and waved it. Then he slowly but deliberately began to walk down the steep rock-strewn path. As he walked along, he stopped for a moment and looked back. He could see why the Turks had not tried to attack the citadel. High on the wall above him, hundreds of his comrades stood silently, watching his progress. Some fought back tears. Others were strangely relieved for it all to be over. Word had already spread that they were going to surrender. The flag he held finally confirmed the rumor once and for all. Now the defenders were gripped with fear of the Turks and what they would do once the Venetians laid down their arms.

Suddenly he saw her. It had been months since he had been outside the citadel walls in daylight. He had forgotten about the Lady of Scutari. There, next to the gate, was a sandstone bas-relief, embedded in the wall. It portrayed a mother with her child trying to suckle at her right breast, hanging on without her help. The mother's expression was lifeless, detached, uncaring. Constantine shook his head. Had the sculptor foreseen this sad day when the people of Scutari would be abandoned by the army, as this mother had abandoned her child?

He looked down at the panorama below. The Bojana River carved its way across the amber plain. There stood the bridge the Turks had thrown across it to bring supplies into their sprawling camp that ringed the base of the hill. After a few minutes' walk, he reached the place where, two months before, he and Paolo had blown up the great gun. A tear formed in the corner of his eye as he thought of his cousin. How angry Paolo would have been at the thought of surrender, especially after his ultimate sacrifice. Constantine felt ashamed, unclean; his head was down, just as Paolo said it would be.

The wooden hovels built by the Turks stood in silent rows, but the tents were gone. There was no one in sight. Where were the sentries? Suddenly, far to the southeast, a movement caught his eye. In the foothills of the mountains, he could just make out a low cloud of dust silhouetted clearly against the blue sky. High up in the citadel the angle of sight had concealed the cloud against the peaks beyond. It was the Turks. They had gone. But I must be certain, he thought. He began to run but, just as quickly, he stopped. It would be a strange twist of fate to attract a straggler's arrow now.

He walked quickly through the Turkish camp. It was abandoned all right. Constantine fell on his knees and looked up at the sea of blue sky and ivory clouds that caressed the mountaintops in the distance. God has heard our prayers. We are saved.

By the time he returned to the citadel gate, his chest was heaving from the brisk walk up the steep hill. He turned around one last time, as if doubting what his eyes had seen. The nearest Turk was at least ten miles away.

"The Turks have gone," he began to shout over and over as he waved his arms in celebration.

A minute later the great door flew open. Soldiers and citizens alike began to pour out, cheering and praising God as they ran. The wild procession snaked down the winding path with the fittest, mostly soldiers, in the lead, running all the way to the Bojana. They plunged into its frigid waters by the hundreds to quench their terrible thirst. For the first time, the Turks had besieged a city and had failed. The Venetians were victorious. Surely, they agreed, it was the hand of God alone that had saved them.

Later, an inspection of the Turkish camps revealed rotting skins of dogs and rats scattered on the floors of the huts. Only starving men would eat rats—they had run out of food. With the onset of winter only a few weeks away and the local countryside long ago stripped bare of food and forage, the first heavy rain would turn the old Roman road between Istanbul and Scutari into a quagmire. Unable to move up new supplies of food, the starving Turks finally gave up. How could they have known that, as they began their long miserable retreat that night, Scutari's defenders, out of water, had already made their decision to surrender?

The Venetian defenders lost no time preparing to leave Scutari. The single cavalry troop that still had horses shadowed the Turks for two days, long enough to confirm their retreat was not a ruse and that they would not be back before spring. By the time the cavalry returned to Scutari, the garrison had already finished packing up all their baggage.

The next morning, Antonio Loredan and his tattered but victorious army began their slow fifteen-mile trek to the coast, where the waiting Venetian fleet would transport them back to Venice. All through the siege, La Serenissima's war galleys had prevented the Turks from advancing up the Adriatic coast, bypassing the citadel, or resupplying their army by sea.

As the last company of soldiers marched out of town, Scutari's survivors flocked to their church to give thanks to God for saving them and their town. When they entered the church, they found that the Turks had destroyed the beautiful paintings and wood carvings that had adorned its walls. The people were thankful that the Turks had not burned it when they left. Nevertheless, it was an ominous portent that they intended to return.

In less than a week, the entire army, except for five hundred men left behind to garrison the citadel, was aboard the fleet and bound for Venice. Constantine could not contain his excitement as he anticipated the reunion with his family and his meeting with the doge. He thought about how different things would be compared to his father's return, twenty years before, after surviving the shattering experience of the fall of Constantinople and his year-long imprisonment by the Turks.

3

The House of Ziani

Constantine was excited, he could just make out the green tiled roof of the 325-foot-tall Campanile di San Marco, cutting through the gray sky like a dagger. Originally a lighthouse and watchtower, Venice's tallest structure had welcomed home Venetians for nearly half a millennium.

An hour later, when he first heard its far-off bells signaling to the citizens of Venice that the time for celebration was at hand, the brisk wind suddenly died down, delaying their triumphant homecoming. The fleet was becalmed. The oarsmen were forced to pull the galleys and transports from just beyond the Lido, the six-mile-long barrier island that protected Venice from the ravages of unpredictable Adriatic storms, all the way to the Bacino di San Marco, Venice's main harbor. Unlike any other European navy, Venice's used freemen to row her galleys. Employment as an oarsman was prized because everyone in the city knew it was on the sinews of these stalwart mariners that, for centuries, Venice had built her naval and commercial sea power. Her all-volunteer merchant marine and navy made Venetian ships the most sought after for first-rate shipping in peacetime and the most feared in war.

By the time the fleet finally anchored, the short December day had faded into darkness. A thousand torches illuminated the Molo and Piazza San Marco. The rows of orange flames danced in the night air, transforming the cold milky-gray harbor into liquid fire. As soon as the crew moored his ship, Constantine sprinted down the gangway and jumped, landing two-footed, onto the broad stone Riva degli Schiavoni. The Quay of the Slavs was named in honor of the many Dalmatian and Albanian seafaring men, with pirates' blood in their veins, who had crewed Venetian ships for centuries.

Thousands of people, cheering and shouting, jammed the Piazzetta, the paved area between two columns crowned by statues of the Lion of St. Mark and St. Theodore atop a crocodile, Venice's two patron saints. Throngs packed the waterfront, from the Doges' Palace back into the Piazza San Marco, Venice's sprawling central square, surrounded on three sides by its impressive public buildings.

Constantine knew his father was out there somewhere among the pushing, shoving masses, but it would be impossible to find him. Fighting to control his excitement, he decided to make his way through the piazza and walk a quarter mile farther to the Ca' Ziani, his family's stately *palazzo* on the banks of the Grand Canal—Venice's serpentine main artery, which bisected the city.

The going was excruciatingly slow as hundreds of celebrating *cittadini* recognized him as one of the heroes of Scutari, wildly congratulating him, even though very few actually knew him by name. Even if they did not smell him—he had not bathed in weeks—his chain mail and sword distinguished him as a returning soldier. Weapons were permitted in public only on special occasions. There was no need for them. Violent crime was virtually unheard of and, in nearly eight hundred years, the city had never been attacked. Her unique geography in the lagoon provided a two-mile-wide barrier of water around the entire city—twice the range of the most powerful cannon.

He shouted at anyone he recognized, asking them if they had seen his father, but no one had. As he walked farther from the tumult, the crowds finally thinned out a bit. When he turned the last corner and beheld the Ca' Ziani, he was filled with a sense of relief. He ran the few remaining yards across the narrow street and into the garden where he had loved to play as a child. Stepping up to the threshold, he took a deep breath before pushing open the ornate oak and iron door. He hoped someone would be home and that they were not all back on the Molo looking for him.

He was crestfallen—the house was as still as a crypt. He moved quickly through the large ground-floor warehouse, passing between the piles of crates and terra-cotta jars filled with expensive goods. A Venetian merchant's home was also a place of business. He stored his merchandise on the ground floor, which he used as a showroom, while the master of the house and his extended family lived in luxury on the upper floors.

Constantine bounded up the broad staircase and, reaching the third floor, crept silently down the dimly lit hallway to his parents' room. The door was ajar. Quietly entering, he could see his mother seated at the window, gazing wistfully out on a panoramic view of the Grand Canal, gloriously alight in celebration of the fleet's return. She looked beautiful, much younger than her fifty years. Sensing his presence with a mother's instinct, she turned and leaped to her feet, reaching out her arms for him.

"My son! Praise God, you have come safely back to me."

They ran to each other and embraced for a long time. She leaned her head gently against his chest, careful not to cut her face on a jagged piece of broken chain mail. Tears of joy rolled down her red cheeks as she sobbed uncontrollably. Finally, Constantine held her at arm's length and looked deeply into her eyes.

"I missed you terribly, Mother. I have so much to tell you."

"Your father will be disappointed. He wanted so to meet you at your ship."

"I looked but it was impossible to find him. The whole harbor is like *carnevale*. I have never seen such celebration."

"Were you hurt?"

"No, praise God, thankfully I am all right. A few scratches but nothing serious."

Paolo, he thought—he had to tell her about Paolo. He had thought about the difficult task so many times on the voyage home, but now he did not know how to begin. She sensed that he was reluctant to tell her something.

"Something is wrong. Tell me." She began to cry again. "Where is Paolo?"

"He is dead." A deep voice rang out from behind them.

Constantine spun around. There, in the doorway, stood his father.

"He was killed," said Antonio, as gently as he could. "He died a hero's death, saving the garrison from destruction. Paolo and Constantine are the heroes of Scutari."

Antonio had searched for Constantine for more than an hour. Now he wanted to rejoice in his son's safe return and applaud his newfound fame, but he knew from years of marriage that he first needed to mourn with his wife for her nephew.

"Tell us what happened, my son," said Antonio.

Constantine recounted the raid and all its gory details, sparing only the worst. He concealed the possibility that Paolo might have misjudged the timing of the explosion and instead told his mother and father that Paolo

had died preventing the Turks from saving their gun. With her curiosity satisfied and certain that Paolo had died a hero's death, Isabella Ziani resigned
herself to smiling tenderly as she wiped away her tears and daubed her red-
dened eyes with a small linen handkerchief.

The Zianis, like most Venetians, were not sentimental. Unlike other Italians, they ruled their emotions with pragmatism. Paolo was dead, but he had
sold his life dearly. That was the point. A man could die so easily. Plague,
drowning, bad food, or any one of a hundred diseases could kill. What mattered was not how *long* one lived, but how *gloriously* one died. Only God
could determine how long a man lived, but *how* he lived, that was his own
doing. His deeds alone determined the value of his life.

"Father, where is Seraglio?"

"He will be along soon. No doubt he is on the Molo at this very moment, listening to an account of the siege of Scutari from Captain-General
Loredan himself. You know how he always wants to learn as much as he can
about everything."

Antonio smiled just thinking about Seraglio, all three and a half feet of
him, interrogating warriors like Loredan and Cavazzo and giving them a
tougher time than the Turks had. There was no one in Venice quite like
him. He had diligently tutored Constantine, forming a close bond with the
boy. After Antonio and Isabella, Seraglio had always been the most important person in Constantine's life.

Seraglio's head was half again too large for his small body. He was unkempt and seemed to retain the aroma of his most recent meal, usually reeking of the many exotic spices he loved to eat. When he talked, he was like an
actor performing on a stage. His voice was a bit too loud, and he laughed so
heartily at his own jokes he would sometimes have to gasp to catch his
breath. He savored life more than any man Antonio had ever known.

The years Seraglio had spent as an orphan, growing up in a Byzantine
monastery, had taken a toll on his body. The other boys regularly beat him,
as boys will do to one who looks different from the rest. With his short legs,
long arms, and gnarled fingers, they called him "God's mistake." But somehow Seraglio had overcome the effect of the cruel beatings, managing to receive a first-rate education and mastering five languages. Years later, after
losing his prestigious position as interpreter to the emperor's chief architect,
he suffered the humiliation of being reduced to begging for his supper,
wasting his life away as he dragged drunken sailors into an inn in return for
food and a dry bed.

Antonio had met Seraglio during the siege of Constantinople, twenty-
one years before, and had invited him back to Venice to live. They were

complementary souls. What qualities the one lacked, the other possessed. They both recognized how seldom life permitted a man to find such a friend. Fortune had smiled on them, that day so many years before, when they had met.

Seraglio's proudest moment had come a year before, when he had officially become a Venetian citizen after residing in Venice for the required twenty years. Together, they could accomplish almost anything. As confirmation, the government had recently begun sending them on important and delicate diplomatic missions.

It was late when Seraglio finally burst into the room to welcome home his protégé. Constantine was tired but he stayed up, taking care to show Seraglio the respect he deserved, recounting every detail of the siege and answering all the questions the little man fired at him. Later, Seraglio smiled as he gently tucked a blanket around his exhausted young charge. Constantine had truly become the son he never had.

True to his promise, Captain-General Loredan arranged for Constantine to meet with the doge. The visit was brief; Niccolò Marcello was an old man. He was ill the day he had become doge in August, suffering from a persistent cough. Later, at a thanksgiving mass in mid-November to celebrate the victory, he was so weak that two of his counselors had to help him stand to deliver his shortened remarks.

The important thing was that Constantine's bravery and service to the Republic had been officially recognized by the government. Only Captain-General Loredan, the commander of the Venetians' heroic defense of Scutari, was more revered than Constantine Ziani, the man who had destroyed the Turk's great gun. Though he was one of several thousand young men who had been there, after a week he had risen from obscurity to fame. The whole city knew of his and Paolo's exploits. Now, for the first time in his life, strangers nodded and smiled at him, honoring him for his own deeds, not simply because he was Antonio Ziani's son.

4

The House of Soranzo

The Ca' Soranzo occupied its rightful place among the long rows of stately *palazzi* that lined both banks of the Grand Canal. Its ash gray stones rose triumphantly above the dark waters of the celebrated waterway. In front, a fifty-foot-long pier sheltered a clutch of rocking black gondolas, tethered to red-and-white-striped poles. Beside its two neighbors, built of lighter Istrian stone, the Ca' Soranzo looked austere. There were no stone window boxes overflowing with gaily colored red, gold, pink, and white flowers and no bright lights illuminating the large windows, as at the other grand homes, which seemed dressed for a festive *carnevale* ball. The somber Ca' Soranzo looked dressed for a funeral.

It was the perfect image of the master who lived within. Vice-Captain of the Gulf Giovanni Soranzo was among the most renowned naval heroes in Venice. He had begun his illustrious career as a *sopracomito,* the young captain of a small galley, and had risen to be one of the Republic's senior naval commanders. For more than thirty years, he had grimly fought against all foes of his beloved Venice.

A superb swordsman, Soranzo cut an imposing figure. With his iron will, he compelled men to obey rather than incur his displeasure. The eldest son of a venerable family that had built great wealth investing in trade, he was born to command. They were not merchants but bankers, who made

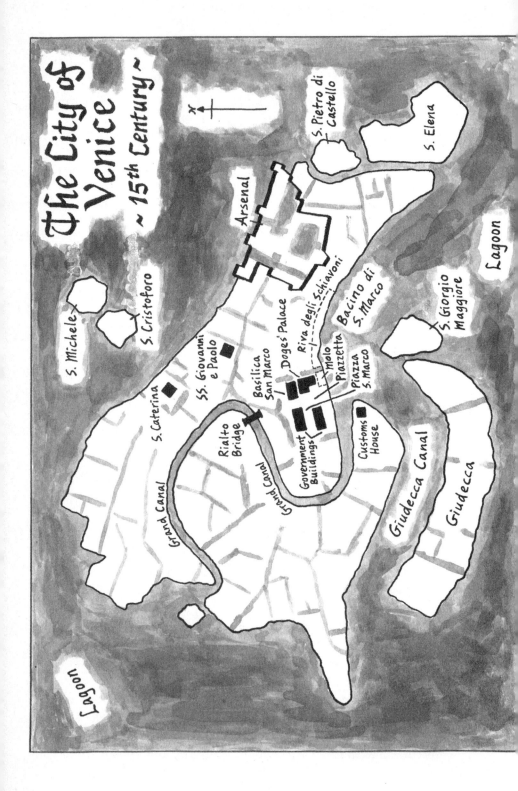

lucrative returns on their ducats for the risks they undertook. For three centuries, the House of Soranzo had been one of Venice's leading banking families. They had never failed to pay a debt or eventually collect one, and the government could always count on them to supply tens of thousands of ducats when asked to do so in time of war.

Soranzo was tall, his face dressed with a full beard, now tinted silver with age. His large head made his piercing blue eyes seem small as they dared any man to hold their gaze. He rarely smiled. What was there to be happy about? Through the years almost all the members of his immediate family had died off until all that remained were his wife, Beatrice, and his brother's son, Enrico, whom he had adopted when the boy was only eight years old, after his father had been killed fighting the Turks.

Ironically, although he was the head of a powerful banking family, Soranzo disliked business, preferring to make his mark with his sword, not his pen. He had always preferred to draw blood rather than count ducats. Soranzo left the bookkeeping to his devoted and obedient cousin Cosimo, who was eager to forgo military service and instead diligently labored over the family's accounts day and night, seven days a week.

For as long as Giovanni Soranzo could remember, his family had been at odds with the Zianis. The feud began when their grandfathers' business partnership collapsed, resulting in violent recriminations. That mutual hatred had spanned several generations, but in thirty years, he and Antonio Ziani had never fought openly. Venetian *nobili* disdained public displays of bad blood. How could they expect commoners, the *cittadini* and *popolani,* to show respect to them if they did not show it to one another?

Fortunately, as the years passed, their feuding eventually became less heated and less frequent. Both military men, lately, they would join together, supporting similar political positions in the Great Council and in the more prestigious Senate, often voting for the same hard-line measures when confronting the Turks or dealing with other important matters of state. They were both men of action and insisted on continuing the war with the Turks—no matter the cost.

Unfortunately, once a man passes his hatred on to his son, like a curse, it takes on a life of its own—even after he himself no longer hates. Sadly, years before, Enrico had learned to hate the Zianis. Now, Soranzo had begun to find that it was increasingly difficult for him to control the actions of his adopted son toward them.

A trusted friend had informed him that, only the night before, he had heard Enrico carousing with his friends in the Piazza San Marco, loudly insulting and mocking Constantine Ziani, behind his back. Soranzo knew that

Enrico was jealous of Constantine's newly won fame and that if he did not put a stop to it, Enrico would hurt his own reputation and, ultimately, the House of Soranzo's. That, he could not permit.

Giovanni Soranzo was cold and calculating and had an explosive but controlled temper. In contrast, Enrico seemed to be ruled by his emotions and was prone to rash actions instead of carefully chosen words.

Y ou sent for me?" Enrico smiled, ignorant of his father's intentions. His dark good looks reminded Soranzo of the boy's dead father.

"Sit down, son."

Soranzo's serious tone erased the grin from Enrico's face. A trace of concern crept into his eyes. Good, thought Soranzo. I must be hard on him this time.

"What have you been saying about Constantine Ziani?"

Enrico leaned back in his chair and sighed loudly to show his disdain for the question. He stared defiantly at his father before he answered.

"What have *you* heard?" He folded his arms.

Soranzo knew that when a man assumed that posture, he was trying to defend himself. He decided to teach his son a lesson he would not soon forget. He slowly rose, walked around his desk, and physically confronted him.

"Damn you, I asked you a question and I expect an answer." The fire in his eyes would have burned Enrico if the two men had been any closer.

Enrico shifted uneasily in his chair. What *did* he say? He could not remember. He recalled only that when he had seen Constantine strutting around the piazza the previous night like a cock with a flock of hens fussing over him, it had been too much for him. It had made him feel like vomiting.

"I honestly do not remember, Father. I had too much to drink last night."

"You had too much to drink, you say? That is not an answer. It is nothing more than a pathetic excuse and not worthy of a Soranzo." He shook his head. "You are jealous—jealous of Constantine Ziani's fame, envious of his exploits. So instead of emulating him, you mock him."

He looked into Enrico's dark eyes and placed a hand on his shoulder.

"Do you realize how foolish you look when you behave like that?"

Refusing to accept his father's olive branch, Enrico counterattacked. "I cannot believe you are lecturing me on my behavior toward a Ziani."

"Times change, Enrico," Soranzo interrupted him. "We are at war. We are all Venetians and we must be united in our defense of the Republic. I know you hold the Zianis responsible for your father's death, as I do, but this is not the time for Venetians to give in to internecine strife. I want you to give me your word that you will speak no more slanderous words about Constantine Ziani in public. Do you swear it?"

It is pointless to protest, thought Enrico. The old man has lost his fire. Ever since he fought at Smyrna he has been a changed man.

"Very well, you have my word. I will no longer slander him in public."

He uttered the words without a trace of emotion, conveying only that he just wanted the conversation with his father to end.

Soranzo shook his head. Simply because you have silenced a man does not mean that you have changed his mind. Enrico was becoming unmanageable. Soranzo knew it would only be a matter of time before his son committed some new sin to embarrass the family.

It was a month later. Soranzo paced nervously, careful to avoid stepping on the edge of the expensive Persian rug where it bordered the rose-colored marble floor. In his fifty-one years, he had never been a superstitious man, but he was tonight. In his wildest dreams, he had never thought that his young wife, Beatrice, would ever become pregnant. Now she had been in agonizing labor all day. It had been two hours since he had seen the physician, who had emerged from her room for some food and drink and then had returned to his work without uttering a word.

In Venice, medicine was the province of men who had studied at the great universities like those at Padua, Paris, Salerno, and in the Middle East. This physician, a Jew, was said to be the most skilled in all of Venice at delivering newborns. Soranzo had spared no expense to see to his wife's and unborn child's well-being. He knew that, according to Venetian government statistics, the first of their kind in Europe, one in three infants died at birth or succumbed within the first five years—many due to the trauma associated with birth. Mothers also died in childbirth, most often when bearing their first child.

Again, Soranzo thought that he would prefer to endure the pain of childbirth to the agony of waiting helplessly downstairs. He thought, all the pain suffered by soldiers in all the battles since time began would not equal the pain their mothers had endured to bring them into the world. Death in battle could be swift, but bearing a child rarely was.

Beatrice had experienced a relatively easy pregnancy, according to what other mothers had told her. Now she was paying the price. The physician had told them that the baby's head was not down. Instead, he or she would come with feet first—a much more difficult delivery. If the baby were small enough and his wife's birth canal large enough, he would attempt to turn the child around into the proper position, even risking breaking an arm or leg if necessary. If that did not work, the odds were against the child living, and even Beatrice's life would be endangered. The physician had rejected a cesarean delivery because Beatrice was now too weak and could not stand the loss of so much blood from that radical procedure.

Upstairs, Soranzo heard a door close. The physician appeared at the top of the stairs, bringing him to his feet in anxious anticipation.

"It is time. Your wife has lost much blood. The child is still positioned wrongly with its feet first. I must attempt to turn it now or else both mother and child will die. Fortunately, the child's foot is small and your wife has a normal-sized birth canal. These both augur well for success. It will not be long now."

He immediately turned and walked back to her bedroom, allowing no chance for questions. Soranzo remained standing, all alone, absorbing the physician's terse words—routine for him but a matter of life and death to them. Soranzo hated feeling so powerless. He was a man used to commanding and getting his own way.

The heat in the room was becoming unbearable, and the foreboding news now made him slightly nauseated. He decided to go outside and get some fresh night air.

The torturous minutes crawled by until suddenly a servant girl opened the heavy door. Awed at the sight of her master dressed in his long black robe, sternly measuring her, she became speechless—the words stuck in her throat.

"Out with it, you little fool!" spit Soranzo impatiently. "Well?"

"It is a boy. The tiniest baby boy!" she said gleefully, pressing her hands together.

Soranzo fought the urge to smile. "And my wife, does she live?"

"Yes, praise God. The physician says she will survive."

Just then another servant girl appeared behind her. She looked at her younger sister and then at her master. "The physician says you can see Signora Soranzo now."

He quickly went to her, taking great leaps up the stairs. At the top, he could hear the unmistakable sounds of a crying infant. He walked through the door, fighting to control his ragged and unfamiliar emotions.

"Signor Soranzo, I have been surprised here today." The physician approached, casually wiping his hands on a bloodstained cloth. "The baby is so small I was able to turn him without having to break any bones, but he was premature and is quite frail. Your wife is also very weak. She will need much rest, but she should recover completely."

From the start, Soranzo had worried that her frail condition might prevent her or the infant from surviving the ordeal. Obsessed with their safety, he had abstained from sexual relations with her from the day he had learned she was with child.

He lightly touched his little son's velvety white cheek and smiled down at his wife. Beatrice grimaced through her pain, but she was proud beyond words to have given her husband the greatest gift a woman could give a man—a son to carry on his name and legacy. Leaning over the baby, he kissed Beatrice on her parched, cracked lips.

"Thank you, my brave little rose," he whispered. Then he stood and turned. "And thank you," he said to the physician. "Do you need anything further?"

"No. I am finished. I left instructions with the servant girl."

Giovanni Soranzo was elated. He could not remember when he had been so happy. They had tried for years to have a child, with no result. When Beatrice had finally become pregnant, he knew that this would likely be her only pregnancy. And now he finally had a son of his own! As he walked down the stairs, he prayed that God would give him enough time to raise the boy properly, to make a true Venetian of him. Although he still felt strong and healthy, he reminded himself that he was fifty-one years old.

He walked into his library and closed the door. Pouring himself a glass of his best wine, he sank into his favorite plush upholstered chair, closed his eyes, and dreamed of all the possibilities presented to him by the birth of his new son. He would name him Carlo, a name often taken by kings.

E nrico was out in the Piazza San Marco for the first night in a month since his father had admonished him for the insulting words he had spoken about Constantine Ziani. He was determined to keep his mouth shut and stay out of trouble. His father still inspired more than a little fear in him, and Enrico did not want to challenge his authority.

He could not bear to be with his father when the baby was born. Enrico had to admit that he was jealous. At twenty-nine, one did not expect to have a new sibling. If the child survived, it would have a greater claim on his father's inheritance than he would—especially if it was a son. He prayed it would not be.

As he sat alone in one of the taverns that surrounded the huge square and slowly sipped his wine, he reflected on his life. *Why do I always seem to miss the action?* His first taste of battle was to have been at Smyrna. His father, scrupulously concerned about showing favoritism, had refused to let him serve on one of the four ships under his command. Instead, Enrico had been assigned to command a company of Marines on a galley that had run aground at the beginning of the battle, causing him to miss the fight completely, without drawing a single drop of Turkish blood. Later, as the jubilant crews were celebrating their great victory, he and his men had toiled in the ship's bilge, repairing her ruptured hull.

Recently he had served on another galley in the Adriatic, assigned to support the army defending Scutari by preventing the Turks from resupplying their army by sea. While Constantine Ziani had covered himself in glory at Scutari, Enrico had crapped his guts out, deathly ill with dysentery from the ship's putrid drinking water.

Now, back in Venice and almost thirty years old, he felt that the good things in life were passing him by, as a *carnevale* parade passes a beggar. He did not even have a woman to love him. It had been years since he had had one that he really cared about.

This night, he deliberately avoided the usual places, not wanting to engage in a conversation with his friends that would cause him to violate the promise to his father. A full moon bathed the piazza in light, making faces sparkle almost as brightly as the wine-filled glasses. Enrico was looking for something new, but he was not sure what it was.

A thousand revelers were enjoying their Saturday night, before the Sabbath, as the wine dissolved their inhibitions. Men laughed and performed while women blushed and plotted. He wondered how many secret liaisons would be consummated before the night was through? The city was still celebrating the victory at Scutari.

"Ziani," whispered Enrico to himself as he noticed a young man sitting a few tables away. Then he realized that he was mistaken. He sighed. *The bastard . . . I am seeing his face when he is not even here.* He put down his nearly empty glass.

Suddenly, just over the man's shoulder, he saw a face so perfect that he wondered why he had never before seen it in Venice. Framed by raven black hair, it glowed like an apparition in the moonlight. Her full lips pouted, as only a rich girl's could, and her eyes sparkled as she moved like a sleek galley through the swells, rocking easily from side to side. His stomach fluttered and his chest heaved. He was love-struck.

She is searching for a place to sit. He prayed she would come his way. His eyes darted to the nearby tables to see if there were any empty chairs. There were none. His table had three and she was with a single friend—another woman.

She came closer. Their eyes met.

She must have spotted my black robe. He smiled politely and nodded. She returned the favor as she floated gracefully toward him, as if she had known him all her life. *Has my luck finally changed? Perhaps, finally, I will get what I deserve.*

"Signore, are those seats free?" she asked. Her silky voice was as beautiful as her face, if that was possible. She was perfect.

"Yes, yes, please sit." He kicked back his chair and jumped to his feet. As he sat back down, in a kind of trance, he nearly missed his seat. The girls looked at each other and giggled, and then they sat too, Minerva taking pains to let Venus sit first, he observed.

"I am Enrico Soranzo," he said with a flourish.

"Your father is Vice-Captain of the Gulf Soranzo?"

"Yes, but do not worry, I will not take you prisoner tonight."

He cursed himself for making such a stupid joke.

She smiled. "I am Maria Mocenigo and this is my friend and chaperone Lucretia Vernier."

"And your father is the captain-general?" asked Enrico, slightly embarrassed.

"No, *that* would be my uncle, Pietro. *My* father is Giovanni Mocenigo. He is only a *lowly* senator, like your father."

"Since your uncle outranks my father, perhaps you will be taking me prisoner tonight." He bowed in a mock show of respect.

Clever, that is more like it.

The two girls looked at each other, but his wit elicited no laughter, not even a smile. The silence was deafening. Suddenly Enrico spotted a serving girl and called out to her. He ordered three glasses of the tavern's best wine.

Maria Mocenigo was the most stunning young woman he had ever seen. She could not have been more than twenty years old.

"Were you at Scutari?" asked Lucretia, plunging a dagger deep into his chest.

Before he could answer, Maria interrupted.

"Of course he was. All of our finest young men were there." Pushing the blade to the hilt with a devastating twist. He began to bleed confidence—profusely.

"I am a *marine*. I served on a galley with the fleet. My ship was in the squadron that protected the defenders of Scutari and brought them safely home to Venice."

Maria cast a disappointed look at Lucretia, who nodded back at her.

The table seemed to grow wider between them. The girls shifted uncomfortably in their chairs. Enrico searched for something to say—he was desperate for them to stay.

"You are very pretty . . . er . . . both of you, I mean."

His lame words trailed off into oblivion as Maria suddenly stood up and placed her full glass on the table, untouched by her magnificent lips.

"Signor Soranzo, it was very nice to make your acquaintance," said Lucretia.

Maria, already preoccupied with some young men at another table, turned and smiled at him, as an afterthought.

"Yes, thank you for the wine, Signor Soranzo."

"Perhaps we can meet again," stammered Enrico, foundering in the abrupt change in the weather. "I would like that very much."

"Yes . . . perhaps," she replied, disconnected from her words. "Good night."

As they walked away, he hoped in vain that Maria would look back at him. That would be a sure sign of her interest, he thought. His eyes followed her, hoping, praying, all in vain, until she disappeared into the night.

"A goddess," he whispered to himself. *A man could kill for a woman like her. Is it possible to love and hate a woman all at once? This night will be either the best or worst of my life—only time will tell.*

Out of earshot, Lucretia grabbed Maria's arm and quietly screeched.

"He was *so* handsome! Did you see those eyes?"

Maria pushed her hand away. "True, he *was* attractive, but there is something about him I did not like. He did not seem sorry that he was not with the rest of the men at Scutari—making excuses, instead, for his absence. I think that he is either dishonest or a coward."

E nrico was smitten. That was bad enough. But, worse, he knew Maria was not. He returned to the Piazza San Marco every night for a week, but she was not there. By the seventh night he concluded that she must be avoiding him. It only made him want her more. Unrequited love is the most exquisite torture a man can endure. It consumes him as it saps his will to think of anything or anyone else. There is only one cure for it, and that is to pursue her until she is yours.

Soon he was walking the streets near her family's *palazzo* as he tried to catch even a fleeting glimpse of her. Once, he saw her walking far ahead of him, toward her home. She was two bridges away. Though he walked faster, he could not catch her. It was as though she had eyes in the back of her head, but he was damned if he would *run* after her. That he could never do. It was then that he decided he would have to call on her at the Ca' Mocenigo if he ever wanted to see her again.

Antonio Ziani sat in his pew in the cavernous Church of San Zanipolo, a Venetian corruption of its official name, the Church of Santi Giovanni e Paolo, and contemplated the flag-draped coffin. In his moment of victory, before he could fully savor the fruits of the successful defense of Scutari, Doge Niccolò Marcello was dead. As Antonio scanned the assembled crowd of Venice's most illustrious citizens, the flower of her *nobili,* he wondered which of them would be the next doge. The election would be held in the Great Council Chamber of the Doges' Palace in two weeks. As a military man, Antonio would support Captain-General Pietro Mocenigo, the victor of Smyrna, a man he respected and trusted to lead the Republic in time of war. Mocenigo would know how to deal with the Turks.

Across the aisle, Giovanni Soranzo caught a glimpse of his old rival. Surrounded by his family, Ziani was greeting and talking to friends gathered around him. Constantine, his famous son, was by his side. Soranzo had to admit that, from accounts he had heard, young Ziani, in his first battle, had helped save Scutari and deserved the accolades he had received. He glanced at Enrico, seated next to him, and wondered what thoughts occupied his troubled mind.

While he no longer hated Antonio Ziani, he knew that Enrico still did—with a young man's passion, and that could be dangerous. He cursed himself for not finding the strength to confess to Enrico his true feelings for Ziani. Now, as he looked over at his rival again, disgusted with his own human weakness, he had to turn away.

In between greeting well-wishers and admirers, Antonio thought he saw Soranzo looking at him. For a fleeting moment, he recalled how, years before, they had been enemies. Now, as he looked contentedly at Constantine, so filled with pride, he was thankful that the trouble between their two families had finally ended.

At fifty-two, Antonio had retired from active military duty to concentrate solely on guiding the affairs of the House of Ziani. His merchant ships were reaping huge profits as they eluded Turkish warships to carry valuable cargo to and from Venice. They also brought naval stores and food back from the Republic's far-flung provinces. The government, of course, would not permit profiteering on shipments of its cargo and dictated the prices it would pay, but the danger presented by the war had enabled Antonio to charge higher rates to private shippers. When you controlled the seas, war was good for business, and the war with the Turks seemed to have no end.

5

The Letter

Pietro Mocenigo had just completed his fourth year as the longest-serving captain-general in the history of Venice. By coincidence, he had just returned from Cyprus at the time of the Doge Marcello's death. When the electors had finished voting, the sixty-eight-year-old hero of Smyrna had been elected seventieth doge to the enthusiastic approval of the Great Council and the citizens of Venice.

The new doge quickly went to work with a level of energy his two older predecessors had lacked. The whole city was astir with activities initiated by this tireless man, so accustomed to command. The attitude of the government was transformed from merely reacting to events to pursuing the initiatives envisioned by a true leader.

They are as different as two ships' captains," observed Seraglio. "Doge Tron's ship was like a galley held in the grip of a gale, tossed by waves and thrashed by the wind as he desperately tried to keep pace with events but was ultimately unable to control his ship, his sole aim being to stay afloat somehow. He feared the wind and waves. But Doge Mocenigo is like a captain whose ship is running fast with the bora winds, strong enough to increase his speed but not so strong that they overpower his firm hand on the tiller. He uses the wind to tame the sea."

"Have you forgotten Doge Marcello who served in between Doge Tron and Doge Mocenigo?" asked Antonio.

"Doge Marcello?" Seraglio laughed. "His ship had no sooner left port than it was sunk. The old man simply had the good fortune to be wearing the tiara when Scutari was successfully defended. Otherwise, he would have no legacy except having a brief audience with our young hero, Constantine, here." He winked at him mischievously.

"What time have you been summoned tomorrow to meet with Doge Mocenigo?" Constantine asked his father.

"Eight o'clock. He always was an early riser," recalled Antonio.

Antonio and Seraglio walked across the Piazza San Marco, discussing the latest news from the talks currently under way with Milan and Florence, two of the Republic's traditional and powerful rivals. Surprisingly, no one had asked the two men to participate in these important negotiations. Seraglio knew that Antonio had been disappointed that Doge Tron and, later, Doge Marcello had not even consulted with him about strategy, especially since he was a member of the Senate, the select, sixty-man body of Great Council members who were responsible for overseeing Venice's foreign policy. He wondered if he and Antonio would be sent on more diplomatic missions on behalf of the Republic, now that Antonio's old friend Pietro Mocenigo was doge.

When they entered the Sala Grimani, the doge's private audience chamber, Antonio's face broke into a broad smile that was clearly visible through his graying beard. Doge Mocenigo dispensed with formalities and welcomed him with a hearty embrace. Antonio had not only helped save him from being killed by the Turks at Smyrna, he had also helped him win the dogeship in the recent election.

"You look well, Antonio."

"And so do you"—he paused, not sure what to call his old friend— "Doge Mocenigo."

The doge turned toward Seraglio, whom he had never met. A tall man, the doge towered over the little Greek. Then he looked at Antonio.

"Permit me to introduce Seraglio, my dearest friend in the world."

"Antonio has talked about you many times—so often, I feel like I already know you. I am honored to finally make your acquaintance."

Seraglio reached out his gnarled hand and grasped the doge's. The contrast could not have been greater. Mocenigo's hand was perfectly manicured, though weather-beaten, with a large gold-encrusted ruby ring on his finger.

"So tell me, Doge Mocenigo, how have you fared in your first month as doge?" said Antonio.

He grimaced. "Allow me to thank you for helping me win the dogeship. I tell you, Antonio, sometimes I think it is easier to contend with one's foreign enemies than one's own countrymen. At least, in battle, you can always tell who your enemies are. Worse is that I had to pay dearly out of my own pocket just to win this job!"

He laughed and shook his head.

He was referring to the timeworn custom that required the doge to dispense hundreds of specially struck gold coins on his coronation day at his own expense. Further, the doge furnished his ducal apartments and paid his expenses from his own pocket.

Every jest betrays some truth. He looks a few years older already.

"Sit down, both of you, please."

The doge sat in his official chair as Antonio and Seraglio each took one reserved for visitors. Behind the doge sat his Signory, his closest advisers, dressed in crimson robes. Three *capi,* all members of the powerful Council of Ten, dressed in long black robes, were also present. They were elected for six months and forbidden to leave the doge's side during their term. These stern men were sworn to allow no one, not even his children, to be alone with the doge, thus denying him any opportunity for misdeeds. He could be alone only with his wife, the *dogaressa,* when they were in their bedchamber. The doge could open no mail and send no letters without these three overseers first inspecting it. No private meetings were allowed. The doge even had to receive their permission to leave the ducal palace for a short walk. More than anything else, this demonstrated Venice's obsession with preventing corruption or, worse, usurpation of the people's ultimate power, by anyone—even the head of state himself.

Antonio thought Doge Mocenigo looked odd wearing his *corno,* the doge's traditional soft golden brocade cap, with a single horn protruding from its rear, in place of his captain-general's hat or a gleaming bascinet. Like the other doges, he eschewed his magnificent tiara. The jewel-encrusted crown was much too heavy and ornate to be worn for anything but short periods during official state business.

"These are dangerous times for our Republic," the doge began.

Antonio and Seraglio listened intently, slowly nodding in agreement.

"Our war with the Turks has cost us scores of ships, thousands of our best fighting men, and we have lost valuable provinces in Morea and Euboea, including our naval base at Negropont, in addition to our great loss in trading privileges in Constantinople. When I became doge, I assumed we would continue our war with the sultan for another twenty years if necessary. But now we have been given a golden opportunity to end the war honorably, if only we can seize it."

Antonio detected the gleam in his old friend's eye. His heart began to race.

"I am certain you have wondered why you were not chosen to negotiate the treaties with Milan and Florence. Doge Marcello and his counselors had their reasons, to be sure, but it had nothing to do with their assessment of your skill in conducting such affairs. As it turns out, it is fortunate that you are not involved."

Antonio and Seraglio exchanged quick glances, unsure of what was to follow.

"It appears now that this triple alliance will be consummated shortly. This will give us a much needed advantage in dealing with the Turks, with our back secure."

"Do you trust the Florentines and the Milanese?" asked Antonio.

"About as much as I trust my physicians. But the terms of the treaty should hold them in check for a few years. And from the outside, it will look like our three states are *united*. That is what counts. In all my years I have learned that unity in the face of a relentless foe is essential. Predators always seek out the weak or the lone prey."

"Negotiations with our neighbors here on the Italian peninsula have not been our only initiatives. We have also been at work elsewhere."

"The Hungarians! I knew it," interrupted Seraglio, his enthusiasm getting the better of him.

Antonio and the doge smiled. The *capi* shifted in their seats, wondering how the little Greek gnome could have known.

"Better still, Seraglio," continued the doge. "We believe we have, let us say, convinced both the Hungarians *and* the Poles to declare war on the sultan."

"Do you think they can carry the fight to the Turks and actually defeat them?"

"Not alone. But we have shared some secret information with them—Uzun Hasan, the Turkoman ruler and the sultan's implacable enemy in Asia, is also going to attack him, compelling the sultan to fight a difficult two-front war."

"How did we discover Uzun Hasan's intentions?" asked Antonio.

"We did not discover them—we created them. Hasan is a much richer man today with the ten thousand ducats he has added to his treasury."

"But what can the two of us do that has not already been done?"

The doge stroked his beard and leaned forward. Every man in the room seemed to increase his interest in what the doge was about to say.

"There is more. Two days ago, I received a personal letter."

The doge opened a folio, withdrew a paper, and handed it to Antonio. An elaborate, official-looking seal was affixed at the bottom. It read in Italian:

To His Excellency,
Doge Pietro Mocenigo
of the Serene Republic of Venice—

On behalf of my stepson, the Sultan Muhammad II el Fatih, Ruler of the Ottoman Empire, Caliph of Islam and Protector of Mecca and Medina, and Caesar of the Roman Empire, I entreat you to use your great powers to bring this war between us to an end. My son is prepared to welcome to Istanbul, in good faith, a delegation from Venice, empowered by you and the Senate to negotiate a fair peace, recognizing the reality of what has passed between us and what will surely happen if a way to peace is not found. The sultan expects a response no later than thirty days from this date.

Signed,
Fatima,
Sister of Huma Hatun and Stepmother of Muhammad II
15 January 1475
Allah Akbar

Antonio carefully handed the letter to Seraglio, who quickly read it and handed it back to the doge. No one spoke as they all waited for Antonio's reaction.

"You want us to go to Istanbul and negotiate on behalf of the Republic?"

"Precisely. You saved me once, Antonio, and I am hoping you can do it again—and you have always told me that Seraglio speaks Turkish like a pasha."

"What do you think?" asked Antonio as he looked directly at Seraglio.

The little Greek shrugged his shoulders. Then he slowly stood, and though he did not reach the height of the other men who were all still seated, he held them in the palm of his hand.

"Signori, what price are you willing to pay for peace—in territory, in money, in future concessions?" Seraglio looked into the eyes of each man, searching his thoughts. Most of them confidently returned his gaze, but a few shifted nervously or looked down at the floor. Who is this man to advise us? they seemed to be thinking.

"The sultan may not even want peace. This may simply be a ploy to divide us by splitting those who want peace at any price from those who would fight on, no matter the cost," added Antonio.

"The speed of our response will give the sultan an indication of how close we are to giving in," added Seraglio as he retook his seat.

"It will not cost us anything to talk to them," observed the doge.

"Only if we are not lulled into a false sense of security by empty promises," replied Antonio.

"True," said the doge.

"I want you both to leave for Istanbul within the week and see what the Turks will offer in return for peace. Find out their price. You are empowered to enter into any terms you deem reasonable or expedient, but tell them that anything you agree to must be ratified by the Senate before it is binding on the Republic." Then his tone became grave. "And now, let us agree upon your negotiating strategy . . ."

When the meeting finally ended, Doge Mocenigo put his arm around Antonio.

"Your must be extremely proud of Constantine."

"Yes, he has made an excellent start in his service to the Republic."

The doge smiled and winked. "You must have him call on my niece, Maria Mocenigo. She is about his age and is very beautiful. They would make a perfect match."

Antonio replied, "You know how young people are these days, so strong-willed. He would probably resist, thinking I was trying to arrange a bride for him."

"I tell you, Antonio, he would not be upset with you once he laid eyes on her."

Antonio laughed. "If it is your command, I will arrange it. Who is her father?"

"My younger brother, Giovanni."

"Very well, wish me luck, Pietro." Antonio took the liberty of using the doge's Christian name as he made his exit.

As they walked home, Antonio remarked to Seraglio that, despite Mocenigo's age, he still seemed interested in the ladies. It had always been rumored that he had brought ten slave girls home with him from his raid on Smyrna. Antonio could just imagine what Isabella would have said if he had done the same thing.

Back home, when he told his wife about their mission, she was proud but sad to learn he would be gone for such a long time. She would miss him, but more, she remembered, with tears, the last time he had gone to that ill-fated city so long ago. Constantine wanted to accompany them, but

Antonio forbade it. He was still under arms and had not been discharged from the army. His wound had healed, and in a few months, hostilities would resume if peace could not be made.

The Senate had sent a discreet answer to the sultan, indicating a diplomatic mission had been dispatched and would arrive within two months. As Antonio packed for their long voyage, his mind raced. Their task would be difficult. The Turks were winning the war, but fortunately, for the first time in years, Venice had checked them at Scutari. Now was the time to make peace on the most favorable terms possible.

6

The Inn

They sailed on the *Eagle,* one of Antonio's galleys, captained by his cousin, Andrea Ziani. The trip started out well enough, but when they reached the lower end of the Adriatic, a severe winter storm struck without warning. Their ship was at the mercy of the wind and waves as the relentless easterly gale blew them far off course. It was impossible for their oarsmen to row. For three days the ship was driven west, all the way across the sea to a point just south of Brindisi, on the eastern coast of Italy. When the winds finally subsided, an inspection revealed that they had sustained considerable damage to their mainsail and rigging. Andrea informed Antonio that it would take several days to complete repairs.

The storm had driven many other ships into Brindisi, filling up all the rooms in the inns. So they hired some horses, and after searching for hours, they finally found two rooms in a large country inn, about five miles inland in the little town of Mesagne.

Antonio and Seraglio shared one room and Andrea and Bertucci, the *Eagle*'s first officer, took the other. That night, three of them dined downstairs in the crowded inn. Andrea, who was tired, stayed in his room. While they ate, Antonio noticed the other patrons were not the usual rough seafaring types who frequented the ports throughout the Mediterranean. From the looks of them, they were mostly local farmers and manual laborers. Although a few seemed to take an interest in the well-dressed strangers, they appeared harmless enough. When their dinner was finished, they returned upstairs and talked for a few minutes in Andrea's room, over a bottle of wine.

"I did not like the looks of that crowd downstairs. They have the smell of brigands, regular cutthroats," observed Seraglio. "Lock your door and keep your weapons close at hand," he said as he laid his ancient, rusty dagger on the table.

"Sometimes, Seraglio, you worry more than a woman," said Antonio.

"Perhaps, but one cannot be too careful these days. After all, this is not Venice!"

"Seraglio may be right," said Andrea. "I suggest that we each take turns sleeping while the other stands watch."

Antonio nodded. *We are on edge after the harrowing storm, but it is not a bad idea for someone to be awake just in case there is trouble.* Antonio and Seraglio soon said good night and retired to their own room. Antonio offered to take the first watch. Bertucci took the first watch in the other room. Soon Seraglio was fast asleep, but next door Andrea lay awake, restless and unable to sleep, as Bertucci sat in a chair, struggling to stay awake, exhausted after their ordeal at sea.

Just as Andrea was about to doze off, Bertucci's loud snoring broke the dark silence. Unable to sleep through the incessant noise, Andrea decided to let his older subordinate get some well-deserved sleep while he took the watch lying on his bed.

One hour passed, then another. As Andrea was just thinking about waking Bertucci to take the next watch, a tiny crack of light suddenly pierced the darkness, startling him. It began as a faint line across the wall, grew wider, and then disappeared, leaving the room pitch-black again. The light did not come from the door to the hallway, which was shut and locked. Ten minutes passed. He decided to let Bertucci sleep a little bit longer as he lay quietly in his bed, thinking about the various repairs he planned to make to the *Eagle* the next day.

I must get some sleep. As he was about to rise and wake Bertucci, he suddenly heard a faint brushing sound on the rough wooden floorboards. He sensed something moving, somewhere on the floor. Was it an animal, a cat perhaps? Or was it an intruder? He cursed himself for not heeding Seraglio's advice. His sword and dagger were on the floor, tucked under the bed. He slowly reached for them, not making a sound.

Suddenly, Bertucci grunted and gurgled. His thunderous snoring was cut short. *Someone is in the room! Have they killed poor Bertucci?* Andrea willed his eyes to penetrate the darkness but to no avail. All he could hear was the steady clicking sound at the foot of his bed as Bertucci's blood dripped onto the wooden floor.

"There is another one over there," he distinctly heard a man whisper.

"Would you kill a poor man before he can deliver to you a rich man?" asked Andrea.

There was no reply at first, but suddenly the same voice rang out.

"Who are you?"

"I am a desperate man, just like you," Andrea responded. "That fool you just killed was supposed to be guarding me, but he fell asleep."

A match lit a candle at the far end of the room, bathing the room in an eerie yellow glow. He could see a door and three faceless human forms. A fourth, Bertucci, sat dead, with his throat cut and his head thrown over the back of his chair. A pool of blood stained the floor black beneath him. Bertucci had the strange appearance of a man about to speak. One man, standing alone in the doorway, held the candle. The other two, eerily illuminated by its dim flickering light, clutching daggers in their hands, stared at Andrea as he lay on the bed. The short one began to laugh.

"And what do we have here?" he said menacingly, moving toward Andrea.

Andrea decided the man in the doorway must be the leader. He quickly determined his only chance would be to try to talk his way out of his perilous situation. His muscles tensed and his backbone pushed into the bed, as though by doing so, he could avoid the points of their daggers. As the man moved in close, pushing his blade just inches from Andrea's stomach, the tall one reached out and grabbed the other man's arm. Then the man standing in the doorway with the candle spoke.

"Do not kill him yet. Search them both first. See if this one is telling the truth."

"The dead man *was* armed." The tall one sounded surprised as he picked up Bertucci's fallen dagger from the floor, admiring the expensive weapon.

The tall man quickly relieved Bertucci's corpse of its worldly possessions and placed them on the bed next to Andrea while the short one expertly searched him. There was nothing to find; he had placed his purse with his sword and dagger.

Now the leader emerged from the darkness of the secret doorway, holding the candle up high in front of him, and walked to the foot of the bed. He was old, with an unkempt, bushy beard. The long whiskers obscured his face, except for his eyes, which blazed brightly in the candlelight. He had the look of a ravenous wolf.

Now the man who had picked the pockets of the dead first officer began to sort through their contents on the bed, inches from Andrea's feet. This immediately drew the tall man's attention like a shark smelling blood in the water. As the two thieves began to argue over the spoils of their murder, the leader scolded them for their greed. Andrea used this brief respite to consider his desperate situation.

They will surely know that Antonio and Seraglio are in the next room. Will they assail them next? Andrea knew he must somehow deceive the intruders and warn his comrades.

Finished dividing Bertucci's possessions, they turned their attention to Andrea.

The short man held his razor-sharp dagger to Andrea's throat, slightly grazing his skin for effect. The leader moved in closer. His stinking breath, emanating from his bushy beard, smelled like a public latrine as he opened his mouth, forming a toothless grin.

"Why was he not guarding you? If you were as desperate as us, you would have been in irons." He laughed. "Or at least bound up with stout cords."

The three killers were judging him. He could see it in their eyes. If he answered the wrong way, they would instantly slit his throat too.

He replied, "I have been accused of stealing from my employer. The man you killed was a policeman who was bringing me back to Venice to stand trial. He bragged that he would see me rot in prison for my crime."

"Were there any others with you?" asked the leader.

"Yes, two," Andrea responded truthfully. He was betting that they had seen Bertucci eating dinner with Antonio and Seraglio. "The short little bastard is my employer. The other one is also a policeman."

Quick glances caromed between the old man and his accomplices. Finally convinced, the leader pulled back the short man's arm, removing the blade from Andrea's bleeding throat. Then he looked intently at Andrea.

"Trying to kill a policeman can be dangerous. Before we enter his room, we must know what we will find there. What can you tell us about him and your employer?"

"My employer is a rich Venetian merchant, a *nobile*. I hate him. He has falsely accused me of stealing from him."

"How much money does he carry with him?"

"He never has less than twenty ducats in his purse."

"Twenty ducats!"

The old thief looked at his men and grinned. "The saints strike me dead if I did not predict a pretty profit tonight!" Turning back to Andrea he asked, "He is deformed—little more than a dwarf. Can he fight?"

"Of course not." Andrea struggled to laugh. "But the policeman can."

"What arms has he? We saw his sword when he was eating downstairs. Does he carry a dagger?"

"No," said Andrea quickly, sealing his fate.

He was committed now. If things went wrong, they would kill him when they found Antonio's dagger. His mind swirled with a score of scenarios he could attempt to foil the killers. He fought to remain calm and be patient.

"There is one more thing that might help. Just as this policeman was sound asleep, the other will be, too. But my employer will be awake. He is too greedy to sleep. He will be worried about his twenty ducats. He will surely be the one on guard in that room."

He hoped Antonio still slept lightly. Their lives would depend upon it!

"Well, my friend, we shall see how much you despise your employer. There is also a secret entrance to his room. This inn is well constructed for brigands, is it not?" He laughed, his slow-witted accomplices quickly joining in. "You will crawl into his room and first plunge a dagger into the sleeping policeman. Then you can cut the balls off your employer if you like."

"Or I will." One of the killers laughed moronically.

"Leave them both to me," spat Andrea. "But I have never killed a policeman before. Since he has no heart, should I slit his throat?"

"I prefer the throat cut myself. No noise. But Giacomo here prefers to gut them like pigs. Either way will do. There is so much noise downstairs, no one will hear his protests either way. Dead is dead."

The plan made, the conversation ended. The leader turned toward the secret door and motioned for Andrea to follow. He obediently complied. The two others followed him. He felt cold steel on his skin as one of the killers held the point of his dagger against Andrea's neck.

They walked silently through the passageway, guided only by the old man's single candle. After a dozen paces, they came to a small door. The leader turned toward Andrea and whispered.

"Crawl across the floor toward the bed. Do it quickly. If all goes well, we will let you go. If you make a mess of it, when it is all over, you will be part of the mess."

He motioned to one of his men. "Give him the dead man's dagger."

As the man reluctantly handed the expensive weapon to him, Andrea quickly formulated his plan. Antonio would be asleep in the bed but easily aroused. Seraglio would be in a chair in the corner, as he always was. He had not slept in a bed in the twenty years that Andrea had known the strange little man.

It was time. He crouched down, holding the dagger tightly in his right hand. The old man put the candle on the floor against the wall farther down the secret passage to diminish its light. Then he opened the door a tiny crack and waited, listening for any sounds. From somewhere in the room, they could hear Seraglio's rhythmic snoring.

Andrea carefully pushed against the door with his shoulder, slowly opening it wide enough to fit through, hoping it would not squeak and awaken Antonio too soon, while he was so close to the killers with their sharp daggers. To his amazement, it made no sound. It had been well oiled to assist in the crimes that must have been committed there often. The shutters on the windows were closed. The room was black.

He leaned forward, sliding on his belly, as Bertucci's assailants had done. The old man slowly pulled the door closed, leaving only a crack to play a faint yellow light upon the wall to guide him to his intended victim. Slithering slowly from side to side, like a viper toward its prey, he wondered if he would be alive in another minute.

Andrea could see two objects hanging over the end of the bed in the dim light—a pair of shoes. Antonio was on the bed. Andrea's heart beat hard against the floor as he crawled the remaining distance. He avoided making any noise in between Seraglio's thunderous snores, since if Antonio were awake, he would surely fall on Andrea with his sword or dagger. Andrea paused for a moment and, saying a prayer, rose up onto one knee at the foot of the bed. Antonio was motionless, still breathing deeply.

"Prepare to die!" he shouted and jumped to his feet. He violently shoved Antonio's boot and leaped backward against the far wall to avoid the slashing sword that would surely be his cousin's response.

Antonio was indeed a light sleeper. He had seen the light on the wall and had heard the intruder. With his sword in one hand and his dagger in the other, he feigned the breathing of a sleeping man while he made ready to defend himself. When he spotted the assailant on the floor, he prepared to strike with his sword as soon as the intruder was within range. Antonio knew the blow would not be mortal, weakened, as it would be, by his prone position. When his assailant jumped to his feet, Antonio's sword was already in motion, but as he swung into the blackness, he sensed his target retreating.

In that unexplainable state of slowed yet acute senses that occurs when one is in mortal danger, Antonio felt the hard push on his boot and heard the warning shout. He quickly realized that Andrea Ziani was his would-be assailant. Springing from the bed, Antonio jumped onto the floor and lunged toward the light in the doorway, his weapons slashing toward what he thought must be the real foe.

The instant he heard Andrea shout, the old man rushed through the doorway after his two accomplices. They could barely see Antonio in the darkness, but he could see them clearly, silhouetted in the candlelight. Since they were packed together tightly and slightly off balance, only the short man in front had any chance to defend himself.

Antonio's sword ripped through the air and sliced the unsuspecting assailant across his face, exploding his left cheekbone into his mouth. Never knowing what hit him, the man fell in a clump on the floor, mortally wounded. The taller man, charging behind the victim, tripped over his comrade's falling body, lost his balance, and fell forward. Antonio swung his dagger upward, missing his target, but a second downward backhanded swing of his sword slashed his assailant hard on his right shoulder. The blow drove the man to the floor but failed to dislodge the dagger, gripped tightly in his left hand.

The sudden commotion told the leader that his plan had fallen apart. He vainly tried to turn and rush back through the secret doorway, but in his panic, he could not push the door open fast enough to escape. Antonio was on him, twice plunging his dagger deep into the man's back, piercing his lungs, cutting short his scream.

Yet before Antonio could withdraw his dagger, the man he had hit in the shoulder rose and was about to stab him when Andrea dove through the air and plunged his own blade into the man's exposed back, stopping him just in time. As Antonio turned, he saw the man fall toward him, revealing Andrea behind him in the candlelight that now bathed that end of the room. The dying leader of the brigands had finally opened the door with his last bit of strength and was lying facedown across the threshold in a pool of his own blood. The whole action had taken just fifteen seconds.

"Are you hurt?" panted Andrea.

"Who were they?" asked Antonio excitedly.

"Brigands. They killed Bertucci while I was in my bed. They tried to make me kill you to save my own life."

Meanwhile, Seraglio, now fully awake, retrieved the candle and began to inspect the bodies of the three brigands. The leader was dead. The other two were dying. Andrea quickly dispatched each of them with a single slice to the throat.

"Their friends may be downstairs, wondering where they are," said Antonio hurriedly. "We will have to climb out of the window to get to our horses in the stable. When we are safely away from this place, we will talk more about what happened. There is no time now."

Andrea threw open the shutters and looked down in the moonlight. He could hear shouting from below, footsteps rushing up the stairs. They had been discovered. He jumped first, followed by Seraglio and then Antonio. As they dropped from the window, each landed on a bush that helped to break the impact of their fall.

They jumped to their feet, ran to the stable, and threw open the doors. Startled horses and donkeys whinnied and bumped in their stalls. There was no time to saddle their horses. Antonio grabbed his horse's mane and pulled himself up. Andrea did the same. Seraglio reached out his hand to Antonio, who pulled him off his feet and up behind him. Suddenly a man appeared in the doorway. He shouted and disappeared. Antonio sunk his heels into his mount's flanks, and the big gray mare surged out of the open door and galloped into the black unknown with Andrea's horse close behind him.

Turning left, they galloped away from the inn and up a grassy embankment. They could hear more shouts as people poured out of the inn as if it were on fire. Quickly Antonio turned and rode between two houses and onto the old Roman road. They circled in place to get their bearings. Antonio pointed and they took off down the road as fast as their horses could carry them. Seraglio held tightly to the folds of Antonio's cloak. As they sped toward Brindisi, they knew they had barely escaped with their lives.

The crew took three days to finish the repairs. The Neapolitan authorities never came to question them about the men who were in the inn at Mesagne. As far as they were concerned, whoever had committed that deed had performed a public service by eliminating the murderous vermin.

7

The Mission

enice was prepared to give up her territory already taken by the
Turks but still technically belonging to her in return for a perma-
nent end to hostilities. At this point, the Senate had long abandoned
any concern about what other Christian states might think about her signing a separate peace with the Turks. Those states had all selfishly remained
out of the fight while Venice had spent her blood and gold. Instead, they had
tried to usurp the Republic's dominance in Mediterranean trade rather than
help her to defeat the Turks. Now, *they* could fight the Turks.

The challenge Antonio and Seraglio faced was to negotiate from
strength without revealing that the Hungarians, Poles, and Turkomans
planned to go to war with the sultan. Their fear was that the Turks would
bargain in bad faith, using a peace treaty with Venice to achieve a temporary
pause in hostilities and consolidate their gains, only to later renew their relentless campaign to dismember the Republic.

As the *Eagle* rounded the point of land high above the Bosporus and
made her way into the Golden Horn, the city's main harbor, Antonio and
Seraglio were amazed by how much its appearance had changed. It had been
eighteen years since they had last seen Istanbul. A hundred minarets towered
above the sprawling city, and Topkapi, the sultan's magnificent new palace,
rose above the promontory along the Bosporus like a city within a city. The

sight of the old Byzantine sea walls that ringed the city brought back painful memories of the devastating siege they had endured when the city was still called Constantinople.

Negotiations began in May and dragged on into the hot summer. The lead negotiator for the Ottomans was Prince Bayezid, the sultan's eldest son. The others were the governor of Istanbul and the pasha of Anatolia, both close confidants of the sultan and veterans of the long war with Venice. At first, Bayezid obstinately refused to come to terms until Antonio grudgingly agreed to cede all of the territory lost to the Turks since the start of hostilities. By September, they had begun to hammer out a business arrangement under which the Turks would permit Venice to resume her trade with the spice-rich East through Ottoman territory, in return for paying a tax. Finally, after another long month of bargaining, the question of peace was at hand. It was time for Antonio to assert what Venice wanted in return for all their proposed concessions to the Turks.

"Prince Bayezid, you are on the verge of gaining much valuable territory, including virtually all of our possessions in the Ionian Sea. We have also agreed to a lucrative two percent tax on all Venetian goods passing through your empire. But, as I said the first day we met, all this will only be approved by the Senate in return for a guarantee of peace signed by your father, the sultan. Without that, the Senate will never agree to the terms we have negotiated."

Antonio held his breath. He wanted the prince to be the first to raise the inevitable issue of tribute, thinking it might result in a lower price for Venice to pay.

"My father is a stubborn man," sighed Bayezid. "He has fought you Venetians for more than a decade, spending a fortune to take what you have now so generously offered to let him keep. The gall of you Venetians really is remarkable. Did you think paying a bribe to Uzun Hasan would help you? His army is in retreat back across the border."

The prince exchanged confident smiles with the pasha and the governor.

"As you are subject to your Senate and Doge, I am subject to my father. Simply because I am his son, he will not expect less of me—he will expect *more*. You must help me win a reputation as a good negotiator. Otherwise, I cannot help you."

He looked sideways at his two colleagues. "Leave us."

The pasha and the governor slowly rose and walked to the far end of the room, out of earshot. Then the prince leaned forward and said softly, "In exchange for peace I must bring back to my father a proposal worthy of his consideration."

"What more do you want?" asked Antonio, not wishing to commit himself first.

"Agree to pay us twenty thousand ducats a year—for ten years. For that sum, I think I can convince him to agree to a general peace."

The prince leaned back and folded his arms, his eyes locked on Antonio, who did not answer. Meanwhile, Seraglio observed the two men across the room. Finally, Bayezid signaled them to rejoin him.

"That is a fantastic sum. You are asking us to pay nearly as much, each year, as the entire ransom we paid to release our captives after the siege of Constantinople."

"True," interrupted the pasha, a veteran of the siege, "but this time, instead of spending all that gold to repatriate some miserable, defeated soldiers to continue a war you could not win, Venice can reclaim her lucrative trade routes and live in peace with the Ottoman Empire."

Antonio let his pride get the better of him. "May I remind the pasha that I was one of those soldiers?"

"Prince Bayezid, can you please excuse us for a short while?" Seraglio broke in. "There is something we need to discuss before we can respond to your offer."

Antonio looked at him, surprised. *What is he up to now?*

They walked into the hallway, leaving the Turks whispering among themselves.

"Antonio, Bayezid's performance was an act. It was the twenty thousand ducats he was after all along. You should have seen the pasha and the governor. They knew exactly what he was going to say."

"We have no choice but to take the prince's terms back to the Senate," said Antonio, disappointed.

"But the Senate will never agree to them."

"We know that, but they do not. By the time we return to Venice and the Senate considers the offer, winter will almost be upon us. I am afraid that all we have gained with our efforts is a year's respite."

Antonio was right. The Senate voted down the sultan's offer by a margin of three to one. Venice would fight on, but if she lacked the money to pay the sultan's exorbitant annual tribute, where would she get the greater sum to pay for the ships, men, armaments, and supplies she needed to fight on against the Turks?

8

The Courtship

ntonio had invited Constantine and Seraglio to join him in his library. He was eager to tell them about a special meeting of the Great Council he had attended earlier that evening. Composed of every male member of the *nobili* at least twenty-five years of age, it was the supreme authority in Venice.

"The Doge and his councilors were just days away from putting forward another heavy tax levy to pay for war expenses. I supported the plan, but many others were opposed to the idea, given the many sacrifices we have already demanded of the people. They are near the breaking point.

"So when the doge stood and called for silence in the chamber, I was ready for a long and contentious meeting while the debate raged on. I could not have imagined that, at the very moment when our financial stability was in such dire straits, we would be presented with a new and unanticipated source of funds to meet our state obligations."

"What happened?" asked Constantine, his curiosity aroused.

Antonio shook his head. "I am still amazed at the coincidence of events. The doge reported that the great soldier of fortune and veteran of many wars, Bartolomeo Colleoni, our most celebrated *condottiere,* had died unexpectedly. To everyone's great surprise, he bequeathed to the Republic two hundred and sixteen thousand ducats in coin and more than four hundred thousand ducats worth of property on one condition only—that the government erect a statue of him in the Piazza San Marco.

Seraglio looked at Constantine. They were both dumbfounded.

"How could one man, even the great Colleoni, have amassed such a fortune?"

"It is an unimaginable sum for one man to possess," acknowledged Antonio. "The Great Council was completely befuddled," he continued. "Venice has always ensured that no individual is raised above the government. Our entire system abhors the very thought of it."

"We do not even have statues of Jesus Christ or St. Mark the Evangelist in the Piazza San Marco," observed Constantine, trying to contribute to the discussion.

"How can they possibly grant his outrageous request?" asked Seraglio. "Colleoni was not even a native Venetian. He was born in Lombardy. I have heard that once, during his thirty years as a contract soldier for hire, he even fought *against* Venice."

"That is true," said Antonio as he leaned back in his upholstered chair. "So what do you think the Great Council decided to do to solve this little problem?"

"Erect the statue in an obscure corner of the piazza," suggested Constantine.

"Never," admonished Seraglio.

Antonio laughed. "The clever council is going to erect a massive statue, the largest equestrian statue ever cast, near the Scuola of San Marco in the Campo Santi Giovanni e Paolo, in front of the church."

"Then Colleoni will have his statue in the vicinity of San Marco, only it will not be the one he desired."

"What do his relatives have to say about that?" inquired Seraglio.

"They complained bitterly but he, unfortunately, being dead, could not. The Great Council satisfied that they have adequately complied with the wishes of the great warrior, have already appropriated his money and property by official act, over the protests of his heirs. Doge Mocenigo is proving to be lucky as well as skillful."

"One could say that about the Republic, too, Antonio. By my calculation, Colleoni's fortune will finance our war with the Turks for at least another two years."

With winter approaching, Constantine was temporarily released from military duty. Neither side would initiate hostilities until the spring.

Antonio placed him in charge of the warehouse on the ground floor of the Ca' Ziani, where the family stored their vast quantities of Murano glass, leather and ironwork, jewelry and spices. Constantine also assisted his cousin, Lorenzo, in his dealings with the government procurement office at the Arsenal. The Zianis were important suppliers of iron fittings and provisions for the Venetian navy. Lastly, his father had recently paid for the Arsenal to build a new galley, the *San Marco*. Constantine never missed an opportunity to visit the dry dock where they were constructing her 130-foot-long hull. She would be one of the newest and most powerful ships ever built there.

It was November and the air had turned colder. Gone were the creamy clouds that slid effortlessly across the azure sky, broken only by the seabirds that punctuated its vastness. Even though it was midday, only a few hundred citizens were scattered around the sprawling brick-paved Piazza San Marco. In summertime there would have been several thousand, all taking a break from their daily labors. Venetians disliked the cold.

Constantine pulled his cloak up around his neck to protect himself from the chilly sea air that seemed to penetrate right to the bone. He slipped into a little shop to get warm, without noticing or caring what they sold. A few *nobili,* dressed in black robes, and highborn women, browsed the fine jewelry, neatly arranged on tables, under the attentive eyes of the proprietor and his wife. *Nobili* were required to wear simple black robes when in public. Fine clothes were permitted only on special occasions or when inside their homes. This was done so that the *cittadini* and *popolani* would not be reminded of the vast gulf that existed between them and La Serenissima's ruling families.

He recognized the owner, an overly accommodating man with a neatly trimmed beard. Constantine recalled that the owner had recently purchased some jewelry from the House of Ziani. When the man recognized him, he smiled but then gave him a strange look. *What are you doing in here?* his eyes seemed to say. *You have no need of anything I sell.*

"Signor Ziani, welcome to my humble establishment," he said ceremoniously and loud enough so everyone in the shop could hear him. "For what purpose do you honor us with your visit?"

Constantine did not know what to say. There *was* no reason, except to get warm.

Someone giggled behind him. He turned to see two young women, hunched over, with their hands covering their mouths.

"Honestly, Maria, sometimes you can be so silly," said the other girl.

The object of her scorn stood erect, removed her hand from her face, and regained her composure. She smiled at Constantine, her dark eyes fluttering. She was the most beautiful woman Constantine had ever seen. *Surely, she does not live in Venice; I would have noticed her before.*

"Signorina Mocenigo, may I recommend this bracelet? As you can see, the craftsmanship is exquisite." The owner's wife was trying hard to control her impatience.

"What is the origin of the piece?" asked Maria.

"It was made in Bavaria."

"Munich, to be precise," interjected Constantine.

"You seem very sure of yourself, Signore." Her smile disappeared.

"I should know. I sold it to this fine gentleman only last week."

Taking his cue, the merchant chimed in, "Do you know who this is?"

Every conversation in the shop ceased.

"Why, this is Signor Ziani . . . of the House of Ziani."

"Are you related to Constantine Ziani, the hero of Scutari?" asked Maria's friend.

"I am Constantine Ziani," he replied, as modestly as he could.

The two girls eyed each other, surprised at their good fortune.

Maria raised her eyes and looked boldly into Constantine's. They seemed to say, *I have been searching for you all my life, and now I have found you.*

In that instant, Constantine's world turned upside down. His life was changed forever. He was staring back into the face of the woman he could give his heart to. He smiled a toothy grin and she smiled back harder. Her friend, the shop owner and his wife, and the other patrons along with the tables filled with expensive jewelry, all faded into obscurity, leaving only the two of them.

Constantine grasped her delicate outstretched hand and softly kissed it.

"I am pleased to meet you, Signorina Mocenigo."

"And I am pleased to meet you, Signor Ziani."

So began their courtship. From that day, each would think of no other.

E nrico! I am speaking to you."

"I am sorry, what did you say?"

"Your mind has been like a ship lost at sea. What is wrong with you?"

I might as well tell him. What harm could it do? He took a deep breath and began.

"I am in love with a beautiful woman, but she does not love me. I think this must be the worst torture a man can suffer. At least if I were in a dungeon, wracked with pain, I could be comforted by a simple kindness, but with her, a simple kindness only increases my suffering by giving me false hope. She must not be capable of falling in love, or else surely she would have given her heart to me by now."

"I see," said Soranzo thoughtfully, a trace of a smile hidden beneath his beard. Of course, he thought, this explains quite a bit. "Who is this Venus?"

"I am ashamed to tell you," replied Enrico as he sunk deeper in his chair.

"Please do not tell me it is the daughter of some Arsenal worker, a *popolano*."

"Of course not." Enrico glowered at the insinuation.

"Her name is . . . Maria Mocenigo. She is the doge's niece."

"You fool. Why did you keep this from me?" Soranzo laughed—something he rarely did. "You know how close I am to her uncle. I could have helped you."

"That is just the point of it. Do you not see? I do not want your help. At least, not like that. I am nearly thirty and a member of the Great Council. This is something I must do for myself." He lowered his eyes. "What would she think of me if you intercede in this affair? She already has mocked me for not fighting the Turks at Scutari."

I swear I will never understand how his mind works. Only a fool would turn down help to land a prize like her. Soranzo had heard the doge tell of Maria's beauty and charm. If she had not been the doge's own niece, thought Soranzo, Enrico probably would have had to fight the old lecher himself for her. He struggled to keep from laughing again, knowing it would only upset Enrico more.

Soranzo placed his hand firmly on his son's shoulder and smiled, like Socrates to a young student. "What is your plan?" How will you win her love?"

I should have known it would come to this. He is going to interrogate me now, like some junior naval officer who has just joined his fleet. Oh well, nothing I have tried has worked, so perhaps I can learn something from him.

"Ever since I met her one night in the piazza, I have pursued her to no result. I have seen her a few times but only at a distance. I swear she is avoiding me." Enrico shook his head, pain and frustration written across his face. "I cannot believe I never saw her before, not even in church or at the balls I have attended over the years. I have inquired and learned that she is nearly twenty."

"You have not seen her because she was sent away to school when she was twelve. Even then, her father knew she would grow up to be a woman every man in Venice would desire. He has kept her locked away in a convent school in Padua for the last eight years. The doge objected to this, but his brother is fanatical in his desire to protect her from suitors. He told me she is not permitted to go out in public alone."

"Yes, the few times I have seen her, she was with her friend, Lucretia Vernier."

"My son, you have changed the subject to avoid it. Again I ask you, What is your plan? Do not tell me what you have done that has *not* produced the results you desire. Tell me what you are going to do *differently,* to obtain a different result."

Soranzo knew that this would be a perfect opportunity to teach Enrico something about life. A student learns best when he seeks the knowledge that matters to him most.

"I have tried everything. I have searched for her every night in the Piazza San Marco and everywhere else I would expect to see her, but she is never there. I have stood for hours outside the Ca' Mocenigo, waiting for her to come out, but she does not. My heartfelt notes go unanswered. I have tried to get to her through her friends, but she seems to have none, except Lucretia, who also avoids my overtures. Nothing has worked."

"Have you tried a frontal assault and simply walked up to her door and announced yourself and your intention to court her?"

Enrico stared at him, saying nothing.

I rarely employ this tactic in war, but in love, I have found it works well. Too much maneuvering can permit your quarry to escape. Go to the Ca' Mocenigo tomorrow and ask to see her. When her father sees it is Enrico Soranzo, he will surely invite you in. To turn you away would be an insult to me."

"I confess, I have considered this approach, but each time my mind always overrules my heart. What if she refuses to see me?"

"Then you will obtain the only satisfactory result besides winning her. You will know for certain that she is lost. Then you will devote no more valuable time pursuing her."

The day dawned bright. It was going to be one of those brilliant November days when the sun's rays colored the calm waters of the lagoon a milky gray and the autumn flowers that spilled from window boxes looked as if they had been painted by Bellini himself. It was a good omen, thought Enrico.

He bathed and splashed his body with expensive French scented oil. Then he put on his best black robe and black cloak with the scarlet piping and carefully opened the box that contained his finest hat, a special gift from his father on his twenty-fifth birthday, the day he first sat on the Great Council. He was in full battle dress for courting, he thought, but he would have preferred to be wearing his chain mail.

His father was not home. A servant told Enrico that Soranzo had risen early and gone to the Arsenal. Enrico was too nervous to eat. He decided he might as well get it over with, but first, he thought, it would be wise to buy a gift for Maria's parents.

As he walked through the maze of narrow streets and over the steep wooden bridges that spanned the canals, he clutched the paper wrapped around the fine Murano glass vase, tucked tightly under his arm. He hoped that Maria's mother would squeal when she opened it. It was magnificent and it had cost him plenty. The artisan who had made it said that it had taken him two weeks to create all the fine detail that adorned it.

He reached the last street before the Grand Canal. Strangely, his fears had subsided. More than anything, he just wanted to know where he stood. Was there a chance for him or not? His back straightened. His stride lengthened. How could he have let a woman, a girl really, put him in such a state? He would show her that he was a man. Perhaps that was what she really needed, really wanted, without realizing it.

He crossed the last bridge and turned left. There it was—the Ca' Mocenigo. It was even more magnificent than his family's *palazzo*. He eyed the front door, made of wood and iron; a menacing bronze lion held a door knocker in its mouth. Even the lion seemed to be smiling this day. He stood before the door and crossed himself. Silly, he thought, just a habit, but he would take all the help he could get. He hoped that God would answer his prayers this day.

He reached for the ring and gripped it tightly in his right hand and then slammed it hard against the lion's chest. He waited for what seemed like an eternity. Suddenly he could hear life inside. Footsteps echoed from the foyer. The door slid open, noiselessly swinging on its well-oiled hinges. A middle-aged, well-groomed man dressed in a royal blue uniform stood in the dim light inside.

"Yes, signore?"

"I am here to see Signor and Signora Mocenigo about their daughter, Maria," he said confidently, impressed with his own cool composure, which only a day before would have been impossible for him to muster.

"If you will kindly come in and wait here, I will announce you."

Why did I not do this in the first place? He cursed himself for the feeble notes he had composed and sent earlier in the week. He hoped she had not seen them.

The servant walked up the stairs and disappeared. As Enrico stood there alone, he admired the marble floor with its swirling blue and gray hues that gave the whole surface the appearance of the sea. He thought about Maria's beauty and how he longed to possess her—not only to have her but to show her off to others. He thought about what it would say to the world about him if the most beautiful woman in Venice bore his name and held his arm as they walked across the Piazza San Marco or into a *carnivale* ball in the doge's *palazzo*. What glorious moments they would be, he thought. The sound of footsteps descending the stairs interrupted his musings. It was the servant again.

"Signor Mocenigo is not at home. Signora Mocenigo will come down presently."

The two men stood silently. Enrico was not interested in starting a conversation with the servant, and the servant was not permitted to initiate one with him.

Enrico's stomach fluttered when he heard the light footsteps shuffling on the marble floor above. As they moved down the stairs, his confidence began to crumble. *Did he say Signora or Signorina?* He could not remember, but he was too proud to ask.

It was Maria's mother. She was a charming, pleasant woman who exuded kindness. Her calm demeanor immediately encouraged Enrico.

"Signor Soranzo, what a surprise it is to see you. How are your father and mother? I have heard that she has recently delivered a child—a boy, I think."

Her expression changed as she conveyed her surprise at his age. How could that woman have two children nearly thirty years apart?

"My father and mother are well. Perhaps you are unaware that they are my adoptive parents. My father died at Constantinople, and my real mother died several years ago. Giovanni Soranzo is actually my uncle."

"I am sorry," said Signora Mocenigo, without a trace of embarrassment. The silence was deafening. He suddenly remembered the gift.

"I have something for you. I hope you like it."

Enrico held out the heavy vase with both hands.

She looked at him and smiled courteously but did not reach for it.

"Signor Soranzo . . . Maria is busy right now and cannot see you."

"I see. Well then, can you please tell me when would be a good time to return?"

"Signore . . . I think . . ."

The lion's ring crashed on the other side of the door. Signora Mocenigo and the servant both looked past Enrico. The servant moved dutifully to the door and opened it as Enrico studied Maria's mother. She was blushing slightly.

"Signora Mocenigo! How are you this fine day? Is Maria ready?"

Enrico spun around to face the intruder.

"Signor Soranzo," stammered the servant, "may I introduce Signor Ziani."

Enrico's stomach hit the marble floor—Ziani.

Constantine smiled and extended his hand. Enrico instinctively reached for it, his head swimming. His fragile resolve collapsed like a proud tower blasted into rubble. *So this is why she has spurned me all this time.*

"Constantine! You are early—"

Enrico turned around again. Maria was at the top of the landing, her hand covering her mouth as she looked down at the awkward scene in the foyer below. Time stood still. Constantine's smile disappeared when he saw Maria's reaction.

"Signor Soranzo, what are you doing here?" she blurted.

Aghast, Enrico lowered his head. As his arms dropped to his sides, the heavy vase slipped from his hands. The cavernous foyer echoed with the sound of shattering glass as the rare piece exploded into a thousand tiny rainbow-colored shards on the marble floor. Maria's mother and Constantine recoiled at the spectacle. Without a word Enrico pushed past Constantine and walked through the open doorway and out into the street. As the servant slowly closed the door behind him, none of the others spoke as they tried to regain their composure. Only the servant felt any pity for the proud young man.

Slowly walking home, Enrico was despondent. With each step, he felt more violated, more victimized. As with a deep knife cut in the hand, he knew he had been grievously injured, but he could not yet feel the burning pain or see the oozing blood that would surely come. Maria's rejection had been cruel and complete. It was as if she had known he was coming and had planned the encounter to inflict the most pain on him. He had never been so humiliated in his life. He would *never* forgive her—or Ziani—for what they had done to him this day. They had stripped him of his very manhood.

Now he had a *casus belli* of his own. It cried out for revenge, louder than any other wrongs ever perpetrated upon his family by the contemptible Zianis. If his father would no longer fight them, he would.

9

The Plot

Constantine gripped the rail tightly and leaned out over the ship as far as he dared, silently taunting the choppy sea to throw spray in his face. He recoiled as a sheet of cold droplets soaked his smooth, naked cheeks, matting his hair. Wiping the salt water from his eyes with his sleeve, he thought about Maria. He missed her but he knew there would be many times in his life when he would be separated from the woman he loved. Though they were to be married in just two months, he had jumped at the opportunity to serve as an officer on one of his father's ships and the chance for adventure.

Many times before, he had tried without success to convince his father to let him go to sea, serving on a galley. Now things were different. His exploits at Scutari had enabled him to cross the threshold between youth and manhood in his father's eyes. His father had finally agreed to allow Constantine to serve as *sopracomito* on the *Eagle*. As long as they were at war with the Turks, the Venetians could ship goods only in fast armed galleys or in convoys of merchant ships protected by escorting warships.

The *Eagle*'s hold was packed with a cargo of Murano glass, Belgian lace, gold jewelry set with precious gems, and exquisite textiles. They were bound for Naples, where these articles would command a handsome price. He would have preferred to sail into the jaws of death fighting the Turks but, he thought, for a first voyage, this would do. He hoped there would be some excitement to break the monotony of the hard work.

Two weeks out of Venice, they were passing between the headland of the Amalfi Peninsula and the Isle of Capri, once home to the Roman emperor Tiberius. He could see the island's rocky white promontory towering above as they steered straight through the channel into the wide Bay of Naples and made for their destination to the northeast. The tired rowers rested on their oars, letting the sails and the fresh breeze propel the ship.

The bay was a massive prehistoric caldera, fifteen miles across. It was formed by the same subterranean forces that had created Vesuvius, the destroyer of ancient Pompeii and Herculaneum in A.D. 79. To the east, Constantine could see the volcano emitting a faint wisp of gray smoke from its slumbering cone, looming darkly against the twilight sky. To the west, the bay sparkled like diamonds in the setting sun. The sky was a palette of royal purple, burning orange, and crimson set against a field of dark blue. Up ahead, he could see lights in the distance marking the entrance to the great harbor of Naples.

The three other officers on board had accepted him, not only because his father owned the ship or even because of the fame he had won at Scutari but because he was a hard worker, faithfully completing any task they assigned to him. He acted as if he was unaware of his station, treating them with the respect a *sopracomito* should give to his superiors. They liked him. As proof, Captain Manin had invited him to go ashore with them after docking in Naples later that evening. Constantine was looking forward to his first night out with these veteran sailors. He was ready to have fun.

They docked the ship at the foot of the massive and foreboding Castel Nuovo. After leaving a few trustworthy sailors on board to guard the valuable cargo, the four officers and the rest of the crew went ashore. They would not risk an accident unloading the hold in the dark. The expectant shore party headed straight for the long line of alehouses and inns that ran along the quay.

Captain Manin, according to the ship's custom, bought the entire crew a round of ale in the nearest tavern. Then he and the officers departed, leaving the crew to revel in their debauchery—the men were expert at debasing themselves and needed no instruction from them. This separation also allowed the officers to behave like common crew members without losing the respect of their men. This way, the crew would not see that the only difference between them, when they were ashore, was the amount of silver in their pockets.

Constantine tried in vain to keep up with his three older shipmates. He was astounded by their capacity to consume drink. He decided to go easy, to avoid making a fool of himself. The others caroused until after midnight, straying some distance up the hill from the port to inns frequented by the locals, near the royal palace.

Manin abruptly pushed his chair back from the table, stood up, and loudly announced that it was time to go if they were to return to the ship ahead of the crew. It was his responsibility to count heads as the drunken sailors crawled back on board, stinking with ale and bruised and bloodied from their inevitable brawling. Walking with some difficulty back toward the docks, they spied a small tavern. Bright lights and music poured out through its open windows and doorway into the street. Corelli, one of the officers, whispered in the captain's ear. Manin stopped, turned around, and smiled.

"One more drink before we return to the ship—on me!"

The others cheered the captain and followed him inside.

They found an empty table in a corner at the back of the room and sat noisily, inviting the attention of the mostly local Neapolitan revelers. A comely young girl came over and took their order. As Constantine glanced at the others' faces in the dim light, he could see that he was the only one close to being sober.

When the maid returned, she impudently banged the large wooden tankards onto the tabletop, spilling ale all over it and onto the floor. Angered, the captain threw a coin down and scolded the girl profanely for her carelessness.

"You must be from Venice!" she hissed contemptuously as she angrily scooped up the coin with her hand.

"The way you grabbed that coin, your regular job must be in a brothel," replied Manin as the others laughed. Constantine felt slightly sorry for her. After all, she was just a young girl, not much older than Maria.

"How much for you?" Corelli slurred, adding insult to insult.

The others laughed boisterously as the girl walked quickly to the bar and began talking excitedly with some men who were standing there. Constantine could not hear what she was saying, but from her excited gestures he knew there would be trouble.

"We must learn to mind our manners when we are in a foreign port," slurred the captain as he saw a wave of anger begin to spread through the room. "There must be a dozen of them and but four of us. Do not use your daggers unless they draw first."

Slowly and unafraid, the captain rose. The others followed his lead. Then, together, they began to walk bravely toward the door. The Neapolitans formed up between them and the exit, blocking their way out. Would they move aside or fight? A small feisty man stepped forward.

"You must apologize to my sister for your insult."

"I would be delighted to, but first your sister must bring us another round of ale to replace the one she spilled," said the captain.

"Unlike you Venetians, we value our women more than our ale."

The Neapolitans were crowding closer, menacing the Venetians. There is going to be a fight, thought Constantine. No sooner had the notion entered his mind than the room erupted like Vesuvius. Arms swung wildly and tables and chairs flew through the air as men grappled and swore. The odds were thirteen against four. It was no contest. Constantine hit a man in the chin as hard as he could, but just as he turned to find another victim, his head exploded with pain. He fell to the floor, unconscious.

His first sensation when he awoke was a terrible aching in his head and ribs. He felt as though he had been trampled by a team of horses. As his senses slowly returned, the throbbing pain turned into fear. *Where am I?*

He slowly surveyed his surroundings. He was seated in a small chamber about ten feet square. It had a dirt floor and damp black stone walls, covered with slimy green moss. The low ceiling was only five feet above the floor. At the far end of his prison, a single tall, thin candle provided the only light. One of his ankles was ringed by a rusty iron manacle attached by a short chain to an ancient bolt protruding from the wall. He pulled hard on the stout chain. He would not break that. A prisoner, but alive, he wondered what had become of the others.

Except for the dried blood that encrusted the wound on his head and the angry bruises on his sides, he had suffered only minor cuts and scratches. The nasty lump told him he had been hit with a heavy object and knocked senseless, but was he in jail or was he being held for ransom? As the word entered his mind, he instinctively felt for the gold ring his father had given him. It was gone!

As the hours passed, his fear grew. To make things worse, he was famished. Finally, after what seemed like an eternity, he heard sounds up above. Then a small hatch door in the ceiling opened and a short ladder dropped down through it. A man descended, carrying a lantern, followed by a young woman.

He was about forty, powerfully built, and had the look of a man used to having his way. He had the olive skin and coal black hair of a Neapolitan. He leered like a predator at Constantine, his clear, dark eyes betraying his intelligence.

"What is your name?" he asked in a low scratchy voice.

"I am Constantine Ziani. Who are you and why are you holding me here?" The man ignored his questions. "What ship are you from? Is it the *Eagle*?"

He did not look like any of the men they had fought in the tavern. They were common workers. This man's clothes were expensive. The woman was difficult to see in the dim light, but she did not look like the careless barmaid who had caused the fight.

"Yes, my ship is the *Eagle*. What have you done with the others?"

"They are back on your ship, nursing their wounds. No doubt they are very upset that you are not with them." He turned to the young woman and laughed.

"What do you want from me?" demanded Constantine despite his circumstances.

"I have been ordered to kill you," he said icily, without a trace of emotion.

Constantine was seized with fear like none he had ever known before. *Am I to die in this stinking hole?* He jerked again on the chain that held him fast to the wall, like some animal. The man laughed coldly. He slowly slid a dagger from his belt and crawled over to where Constantine was sitting, carefully keeping just out of reach of his captive's unchained foot. Suddenly, in one quick motion, he seized Constantine by the hair and, with an assassin's skill, pulled his head back painfully and held the blade against his throat. The razor-sharp steel slit the top layer of his tender skin. Blood oozed from the long, thin cut.

"How much would your father pay to get you back, Signor Ziani?"

Terrified at first, Constantine quickly became confused. *Why is he talking about a ransom if he has orders to kill me?*

"How much do you want?" he stammered, not knowing exactly what to say but desperately trying to do anything to avoid having his throat cut.

"Would he pay one hundred ducats?"

"Yes," he replied quickly without thinking.

His captor deftly increased the pressure on his blade, widening the cut slightly. Constantine trembled from a mixture of terror and pain. He felt dizzy, nauseous.

"You answered much too quickly, signore. I think he would pay more." He withdrew the dagger and crawled around so that Constantine could better see his face.

"You will write a note to your father asking him to pay *two* hundred ducats for your ransom. I will see to it that it is given to the *Eagle*'s captain so we can be sure it gets to your father quickly. If he does not pay that sum in sixty days, you are a dead man."

Despite his fear, Constantine could not control his anger.

"So it was a ransom all along that your employer wanted?"

"No, my young friend. It was a ransom all along that I wanted. If it were not for my greed, you would already be dead. You can thank her." He motioned toward the girl. "She convinced me that I could make more by ransoming you back to your father than by taking my employer's blood money for killing you."

"Who hired you to kill me?"

"That, I cannot tell you. I will only say that you should choose your enemies back in Venice more carefully, Signor Ziani."

"You have stolen my ring. Give it back to me," ordered Constantine defiantly.

The man turned to the girl, whose face was now clearly visible in the candlelight. "What did I tell you about these Venetians?" Then he turned and suddenly slammed his fist hard into Constantine's jaw, violently knocking him against the wall.

"That is for being an ungrateful bastard! Your ring will accompany your ransom note so that the *Eagle's* captain and your father will have undeniable proof that we are holding you prisoner. That ring will probably save your life, my stupid young friend."

Defeated, Constantine leaned back against the rough stone wall and rolled his eyes. "Am I to remain here in this dungeon then? For sixty days?"

"I could give your father thirty days to pay instead, if you would like. Perhaps you would like me to ask King Ferrante if you could stay in his palace. I will see if I can arrange it." He laughed. The girl gave Constantine a sympathetic smile. Eyeing it, his captor motioned toward her.

"She will bring you food and water to keep you alive. Now write your note before the *Eagle* sails home without it." The man handed him a quill, ink, and paper. Constantine's hand was firm as he wrote a short note, never doubting that it and the accompanying ring would convince his father to pay the ransom. When he finished, he handed it to the man. After quickly whispering something to the girl, the man climbed the ladder and was gone. The girl lingered, giggling and smiling at him, and then she too climbed the ladder, lifted it, and closed the iron trap door in the ceiling with a loud bang.

The days were interminably boring. Sometimes Constantine thought he would go mad.

At first he focused on his own plight, but over time, he began to worry about Maria. *What if she thinks I am dead? Will her father call off the wedding?*

In her grief, will she fall for another man who showers her with sympathy? He could not bear the thought of losing her. He suffered through agonizing nightmares, dreaming of her loving other men. When he would awaken, alone in his stinking hole, his mind would run wild with thoughts of her infidelity. *She is just too beautiful. Another man will take her.*

He tried to divert his thoughts by playing with the insects that shared his prison until he knew all their movements and the ways they avoided or preyed on each other. His only pleasure was the twice-daily visit by the girl, when she brought him food and water and removed his waste bucket. She was strange, and though she rarely talked, he looked forward to her visits. She was his only contact with the outside world. Once, she had blurted out that her name was Estella, but when he had tried to start a conversation with her, to prolong her short visit, she remained silent. He learned nothing else of the girl or his captor. He thanked God for the single candle that burned constantly, giving him light.

Constantine often thought about who could have done this to him. He knew it was not the act of some Neapolitan brigand. Someone in Venice was involved, but who? His captor had no reason to lie to him about that. He considered whether Enrico Soranzo might be the culprit, but he rejected the thought, unable to believe that unrequited love for Maria could drive Enrico to murder a fellow *nobile*. Besides, Maria had told him that she had rejected Enrico because he was a coward.

Unable to distinguish night from day, Constantine quickly lost track of time, but he began to sense that the end was near. Finally, he heard two sets of footsteps above. Constantine's stomach tightened as he prayed silently for deliverance. The man descended the ladder, followed by Estella. Constantine could see his captor's face clearly, but it provided no clue to his fate. He hoped the man had not changed his mind about sparing his life. Or would he keep the ransom and kill Constantine anyway, obeying his employer's orders and pocketing the ransom money?

The man leered at Constantine, as he had that first and only other time they had met. Constantine clenched his teeth and resolved to have courage, no matter what.

"Your father has paid your ransom. You are free to go."

Constantine could not believe his ears.

"Now I will take you to a ship that is waiting for you in the harbor. I hope you will forgive my poor hospitality, but until now, I could afford no better." He laughed and Estella hugged him as she joined in his celebration of their newfound wealth.

After a short ride down to the harbor in a donkey cart, hidden under reeking, freshly tanned skins, Constantine was untied. Then his captor removed the blindfold.

"Go down that street and turn left at the end. The *Eagle* is there. She has come back to Naples to fetch you." With a dagger in one hand, the man extended his other, but Constantine refused it. The man's eyes narrowed as he clenched his teeth.

"I have risked my life for you, you ungrateful bastard. I was offered good money to kill you, not to set you free like this. Is this how a Venetian repays mercy?"

Constantine was confused, embarrassed. The man was right. He could be dead.

"Why did you not kill me, as you were hired to do?"

"Because you were worth more alive than dead. Like you, I too am a businessman. I have deceived my employer to make a greater profit."

"What prevented you from taking my father's money and then killing me anyway, satisfying your purse and your employer?"

"That would have been the safe thing to do. Perhaps I should have— time will tell. But it would have been a poor business decision. You see, I have doubled the profit for my labors. And, I suspect, if you ever have occasion to need the services of a shrewd man here in Naples, you will employ me." He smiled, self-satisfied, his unusually pearly teeth shining through his thick black beard. "Now that you know that I am an honorable man."

"But how would I know where to find you? I do not even know your name."

"Just go to the tavern where you were taken, only next time, mind your manners."

The man smiled as Constantine finally shook his hand. With nothing more to say, the dark Neapolitan quickly turned and climbed onto the cart in one smooth motion, swatted the donkey lightly on her rump with his stick, and slowly began to roll away. Constantine backed up a few steps, watching. Then, elated that he was alive and free at last, he turned and ran as fast as his legs would carry him down the street to the end. Looking left, he spied the *Eagle,* resting peacefully in the harbor, like an old friend, waiting to carry him home.

10

The Vendetta

"Signor Ziani! Thank God you are safe," shouted Captain Manin when he spotted Constantine running along the quayside.

"We were afraid the villains would take the ransom money and kill you anyway."

"So was I! Where is my father?" asked Constantine, out of breath as he reached the top of the wooden gangway.

"I am here, my son."

He turned to see his father standing on the deck by the cabin door, dressed in his black patrician robes, looking much older than his fifty-four years.

Constantine ran to him, threw his arms around his neck, and wept tears of joy. Seraglio, who was also there, eagerly joined in the celebration.

As they waited to sail with the afternoon tide, Antonio, Constantine, Seraglio, and Captain Manin crowded around the small table in Antonio's cabin, reconstructing what had happened.

"After the brawl," recounted Manin, "all of us were knocked unconscious and dumped in a heap near the docks. When we regained our senses, we all hurried back to the *Eagle* to gather any of the crew that could still walk and returned to the tavern, but it was closed up tight. No one was there. The next day we returned but no one knew anything. It was as though the fight had never happened. I went to the police but they were useless. That afternoon, a man delivered a ransom note with your ring wrapped inside it. I immediately sailed for Venice to report to your father what had happened."

"The *Eagle* was a week overdue," Antonio continued. "I feared you had all been lost in a storm." His voice betrayed the sadness he had felt. "All I could do was wait. Although I am a patient man, I tell you, it was agonizing. The *Falcon* was due to call on Naples two weeks after the *Eagle*. We knew that if there were any word of your fate, her captain would surely hear of it. Of course, the *Eagle* sailed from Naples before the *Falcon* arrived, so she was the first to arrive back in Venice. When I saw your ring, I knew the note was genuine. Your captor demanded a ransom of two hundred ducats. That is a lot of money, but a trifling amount when it purchases your son's life. We delivered the money to him last night."

"Father, can you describe the man you gave the money to?"

Antonio looked at Seraglio, who had actually paid the kidnapper. He described Constantine's captor in great detail.

"That was the man who kidnapped me and held me prisoner."

"How were you treated?" asked Seraglio.

"Well enough. I have never been in a prison before, and I hope I never am again." Constantine gingerly rubbed the open sores on his ankle made by the rusty shackle. "I almost went mad from boredom. If not for the daily visits from a young girl who brought me food and water, I would have gone mad." Constantine thought for a moment. "Father, when the kidnapper told the girl that the ransom had been paid, they embraced wildly. She was too young to be his lover. I think she was his daughter."

"A useful observation," said Seraglio. "What did the man say when you parted?"

"He arrogantly said he did not kill me after you paid the ransom because he wanted us to know that he was honorable, should we want to hire him in the future."

Antonio and Seraglio exchanged surprised glances.

"Do you think he was just some brigand, acting alone?" asked Antonio.

"I do not think so. He said he had been hired to kill me." Constantine shuddered.

"I see," said Antonio, stroking his beard. "I suppose he did not reveal his own identity or the identity of his employer, then."

"No, but he told me that the man who hired him was from Venice—and I believe him," Constantine added.

"Why are you so quick to believe anything such a man would say?"

"How else could someone here in Naples know that I would be on the *Eagle*?"

"But, Constantine," said Seraglio, "how would someone in Venice have gotten word to Naples ahead of the *Eagle* to let them know of your arrival in time to stage the fight in the tavern?"

"Damn!" shouted the captain as he pulled his dagger from its sheath. Seraglio quickly grabbed his arm. "Not me! Corelli, it has to be Corelli! He is the one who suggested we stop at that tavern that night."

They stormed after Manin, through the cabin door. The crew was startled by their loud shouts and headlong rush onto the deck.

"Where is Corelli?" barked the captain.

"He went ashore to find Moretti the Neapolitan," replied one of the sailors.

"Of course!" said Manin. "Corelli must have arranged the fight and kidnapping with the help of that Neapolitan villain, Moretti. We will not see either of them again."

"Captain, we have discovered the hands and arms of the plot, but the head still lurks in Venice. How many voyages did Corelli sail with you?" asked Seraglio.

"This was only his second," said the captain, eyes wide.

"The first, to commit the crime and the second, to escape," observed Antonio.

"Who was Corelli's last employer before we hired him?"

"I believe it was the House of Barozzi," said the captain.

"Barozzi, eh? Captain, if you will excuse us, there are some things I need to discuss with my son. Make certain that no one disturbs us."

"Yes, of course, Signor Ziani. I am needed here on deck to get the ship under way, since now I am without the services of a first officer."

They returned to the cabin and sat down around the table. Constantine leaned forward, listening intently for what his father was about to say.

"My son, I had always hoped that I would be able to shield you from what I am about to tell you, but events of the last two months have convinced me that I must reveal something that will change your life forever. When you emerge from this cabin, you will be hardened, forced to face life's trials in a way you could not have imagined. Your innocence has been stolen from you despite my attempts to prevent it. Forgive me, but what I am about to tell you is for your own protection. I believe the Soranzos are behind this."

Then Antonio told him the story of his great-grandfather's failed joint venture with the Soranzos that started the feud. He recounted how it had been passed down through each successive generation. He told him how Marco Soranzo had drowned and Pietro Soranzo had perished on the walls of Constantinople and how their older brother, Giovanni Soranzo, had unjustly blamed Antonio for their deaths.

He recounted how Giovanni Soranzo had threatened him and how he had attempted to ruin Antonio's reputation with the doge and the Senate. He recalled the night that he thought the vendetta had finally ended, when Captain Soranzo announced to all of Venice that he did not hold Antonio responsible for the deaths of his brothers. Finally, Antonio told Constantine about Uncle Giorgio and Vettor Soranzo at Corinth and how Vettor had contributed to Giorgio's death.

He confessed to Constantine that the real reason he had not permitted him to sail with the fleet to fight against the Turks at Smyrna was because he feared that Constantine might be forced to serve under Captain Soranzo's command. He had never trusted Soranzo. Constantine was riveted, though he periodically looked at Seraglio, who sat quietly and nodded his agreement throughout.

"I thought that, after Smyrna, Soranzo had finally put aside his vendetta against me. Apparently, I was mistaken, but I never thought he would resort to kidnapping or murder. What I want to know is whether your kidnapping was arranged without his knowledge, by Enrico, or was it something that Giovanni Soranzo ordered himself?"

"How can we find out?" asked Constantine.

"I will ask them."

Constantine and Seraglio smiled at each other. They did not know *how* Antonio would accomplish it, but they had no doubt that he *would*.

The *Eagle* made landfall, sighting the Lido late in the afternoon. Antonio ordered Captain Manin to wait until twilight before entering the channel, slowly making his way into the Bacino di San Marco, and lowering the galley's small boat. Under cover of darkness, four oarsmen rowed Antonio, Constantine, and Seraglio along the Grand Canal to the pier in front of the Ca' Ziani. As soon as they were clear of the *Eagle,* Manin, as ordered, weighed anchor and sailed east for Trieste. This would ensure that none of the crew, who had seen Constantine, could set foot in Venice until Antonio had executed his plan.

The next morning, a servant delivered a message to the Ca' Soranzo. It read:

Dear Signor Soranzo,
I would like to meet with you tomorrow to discuss an affair that, I am certain, will be of great interest to you. Please do me the honor of coming to the Ca' Ziani at midday.

Your humble servant,
Antonio Ziani

Giovanni Soranzo reread the note and threw it angrily on his desk. *I have not spoken ten words to this man in more than two years. This must have something to do with the doge's niece.* He knew Enrico was still aching for her, even though everyone knew that she was betrothed to Constantine Ziani. He called loudly for his servant. The man hurried into the room, surprised and upset by his master's uncharacteristic shouting.

"Go find my son and tell him that I require him at once."

Soranzo sat wearily in his chair, blankly staring through the window at the busy Grand Canal, shimmering below in the morning sunlight.

"God help me, what has he done now?"

E nrico entered the room confidently, the same impudence in his eyes that Soranzo had seen so many times before, ever since he was a boy. Soranzo immediately suspected, by Enrico's demeanor, that Ziani had good reason to want to speak with him.

"Why would Antonio Ziani want to see me?" He handed the invitation to Enrico, gauging his reaction as he watched him read it.

"You called me away from my meeting with Signor Barozzi for this? The way old Michele summoned me so urgently, I thought you were dying." Then Enrico looked him in the eye and said, "I have no idea."

Soranzo was becoming more exasperated by his son's intransigence.

"I can think of no reason why Ziani would want to see *me*. What have you done?"

"Father, why do you doubt me? I say again, I do not know."

Enrico parried his father's thrusting stare, his expression betraying no emotion.

Perhaps he is telling me the truth, Soranzo thought hopefully. "What could he want with me, then?"

"Perhaps he wants to invite us to his son's wedding," replied Enrico sarcastically.

Soranzo reached out for his son and gently placed a hand on his shoulder. "Do you still love her?"

"No, she is not worthy to bear the Soranzo name." Enrico smiled at his father, who returned the gesture.

"Today you will go with me to the Ca' Ziani."

A re you certain you did not see the *Eagle* in the harbor this morning?" "Yes, master. I am certain. For two hours I have asked every sailor I met if he had seen her. I went to every inn on the Quay of the Slavs and found none of her crew or anyone who had seen her. If she has returned, her crew would be here in the city. None are. I am certain. I even checked with customs. She was last here nearly a month ago."

He is a thorough man, thought Enrico. Still, he had received no news from Naples and that angered him. This man had faithfully reported to him the departures and arrivals of the Zianis' ships since the *Eagle* had originally sailed with Constantine aboard three months before. He had informed Enrico when the *Eagle* had returned and when she departed the next day with her owner aboard. Even though there had been ample time for the *Eagle* to sail to Naples and return to Venice, there was still no sign of her.

A t midday, the Soranzos went to the Ca' Ziani. A servant politely greeted them and led them to a room on the second floor. When the guests were announced, Antonio smiled and welcomed them with a polite bow.

"Signori, thank you for coming. Please sit down. I was just discussing a most distressing matter with my friend Seraglio. You *have* met before, have you not?"

They had seen each other a few times over the years. The three men all nodded, masking their thoughts behind forced smiles.

"Allow me, Signor Ziani, to introduce my son, Enrico."

Antonio smiled at the young man. He had seen him before in Great Council meetings. Constantine had also told Antonio about meeting Enrico at the Ca' Mocenigo in the most embarrassing of circumstances.

With their formal introductions completed, they sat down to talk.

Enrico stole another quick glance at the grotesque form in the corner, behind Antonio's desk. When Seraglio winked and smiled impertinently, he recoiled, as most people did when they first saw the ugly little Greek.

"Signor Soranzo," Antonio began gravely, "something terrible has happened. About three months ago, my son Constantine sailed on the *Eagle,* bound for Naples. The night they arrived there, he went missing."

Soranzo interrupted. "Has he been found? Is he safe?"

"We have since learned that someone intended to murder him." Antonio's eyes narrowed, his voice lowered, his face melted into sadness. "I would like you to help me find the man who ordered his death."

"But what can I do, Signor Ziani? I know nothing of Neapolitan criminals. I am a sailor and a banker, not a policeman."

"We suspect that two crewmen, ill-advisedly hired by the *Eagle*'s captain, arranged for his murder. One of them, a man named Corelli, the *Eagle*'s first mate, last worked for the House of Barozzi. Since you are a business associate of Signor Barozzi, I thought you could make discreet inquiries for me about this man."

Soranzo thought for a moment and then responded slowly, "I am most sorry to hear of this news, Signor Ziani." He cast a furtive glance at Enrico, but he could detect no reaction to the shocking news.

Seated quietly in the corner, Seraglio noticed that the corners of Enrico's mouth unconsciously curled upward in a nearly imperceptible expression of satisfaction.

"Have you found your son?" Soranzo asked again.

"Yes. The bastards slit his throat," replied Antonio.

As he spoke the words, he stood and stretched out his right arm, pointing straight toward the door behind the Soranzos. The two visitors turned their heads to follow his pointing finger. There, in the doorway, with his neck swathed in a thick white bandage stained crimson, stood Constantine Ziani.

The surprise was total. Enrico spun back around, his eyes accusing Antonio. "What game is this you are playing, Signor Ziani?"

"Chess, Signor Soranzo. It seems that in the House of Soranzo, the rook has taken the place of the king."

"Damn you!" shouted Enrico. "If you think my father had anything to do with whatever happened to your son, you are mad."

"Signor Ziani!" thundered Soranzo. "I can assure you that neither Enrico nor I had anything to do with this. I am insulted that you would even suggest it!"

"Giovanni, I do not think you would be involved in a business like this, but your son has vied with mine for the hand of Maria Mocenigo. He certainly had a motive for wanting to kill Constantine."

Stunned, Soranzo spun around toward Enrico. *Could it be true?* His son looked as shocked as he was. He turned back to his host. "I am sorry, Signor Ziani, but I cannot help you today."

"Very well, but take heed. If anything happens to my son—anything!—I will hold you and your son responsible."

Without uttering another word, the Soranzos walked from the room, pushing past Constantine, who had remained standing in the doorway throughout the heated exchange. As Enrico passed by, he looked straight ahead, avoiding Constantine's eyes.

Alone now, Antonio, Constantine, and Seraglio analyzed what had happened. They agreed that Enrico had probably ordered Constantine's murder. Antonio doubted that Soranzo himself was involved. Seraglio and Constantine were not so sure.

Antonio knew he could not go to the police because he had no proof that Enrico was the man behind Constantine's kidnapping, but one thing was certain: the Soranzos' long-dormant vendetta against him had flared into open warfare, and it included his son. Whether Giovanni Soranzo was an active participant or whether he had simply permitted his son to pursue the vendetta while turning a blind eye, it did not matter. It was family against family.

"We must find the man who kidnapped you and bring him back to Venice to be interrogated," said Antonio. "He will reveal the name of his employer."

It was virtually impossible to withstand the terrible tortures that the Republic employed in order to pry useful information out of witnesses.

"I will go to Naples myself," asserted Constantine. "On the day I was set free, he told me that I could find him at the tavern where I was kidnapped."

"No, that would be too dangerous. I want Seraglio to go instead. That is why I had Seraglio pay the man your ransom. He never forgets a face."

Seraglio smiled, his yellow teeth visible through his scruffy, unkempt beard.

"As you wish, but we should send some men with him for protection," said Constantine.

"He will be in the care of Captain Manin and his crew. They should return from Trieste with the *Eagle* tomorrow. This time, let us take great pains to ensure every one of those men is loyal to us."

The next day, Soranzo rose early and immediately sent for his son. The uncertainty of all that had happened tore at his conscience. When Constantine Ziani had suddenly appeared, Soranzo had been struck by the forced, disinterested expression on Enrico's face. Then, he believed that Enrico had lied to him, that he *was* involved in what had happened in Naples.

Now, he was not so sure. For his entire life, he had despised indecisiveness in others; now he had fallen victim to that same weakness in himself.

Enrico is late, as usual. It is his way of showing his lack of respect for me. He waited, his temper rising with each passing minute. Finally Enrico came, saying nothing, with utter contempt written on his face.

"I want to talk to you about what happened yesterday at the Ca' Ziani."

"Lies!" Enrico said loudly, as if a single word could end the conversation.

Soranzo stood and leaned on his desk, facing him. "Look at me." When Enrico met his father's gaze, Soranzo continued, "I raised you as my own son, loved you like my own son. I gave you every privilege a young man could desire. All I have ever wanted in return was to be proud of you, for you to be a true *nobile,* a credit to your name."

The veins in Soranzo's forehead were plainly visible, and he was trembling slightly as he struggled to control his emotions.

"Tell me the truth. Did you order Constantine Ziani's kidnapping in Naples?"

He fixed his steel gray eyes on his son and prayed for the answer he wanted so desperately to hear.

Enrico expelled a long breath, weighing his options. Slowly he rose and stuck out his forefinger, inches from his father's chin.

"What did you expect me to do? Did you really think I would just crawl away, like a beaten dog, after what that pompous bastard did to me? Did you think I was incapable of dealing with him?" He raised his voice louder. "*Yes,* if you must know, I arranged for his kidnapping. It would have worked too, if I had not chosen a rascal to carry out my orders."

His secret revealed, he stared at his father, spoiling for a fight. Soranzo dropped wearily into his chair. *At least he told me the truth.*

"Did you also order this rascal to kill him, like Ziani said?"

Enrico walked around the desk and placed his hand on his father's arm.

"I admit that I hate him, but I would never murder another Venetian."

Soranzo searched his son's soul through the window of his eyes, wanting desperately to believe him. Enrico smiled as his hostility seemed to melt.

"If I had wanted him dead, he would be. Do you doubt me? My man had him in his power. He was defenseless. What more proof do you need than that you saw him alive yesterday?" Enrico looked wronged, hurt by his father's terrible suspicions.

Soranzo thought long and hard about what he had to say next.

"Son, you must leave Venice. Ziani will make trouble for you if you stay. After all, Constantine's wife's uncle is the doge, and Antonio Ziani is also very close to him."

He reached into his desk, pulled out a paper, and began to write.

"What are you doing?"

"I am sending you to Florence to work with your cousin, Cosimo. Now that we are allied with the Florentines again, he is handling our banking there. Lorenzo the Magnificent may be the pope's banker, but Sixtus's need for florins sometimes exceeds the Medicis' willingness to accept the risk of making those huge loans. We have entered into a secret relationship with the duke to provide additional funds, from time to time, to enable him to limit his exposure to the Vatican."

"But why would the duke not simply invite one of the other powerful families in Florence to step in and provide the funds?"

Soranzo looked at his son. He still had so much to learn.

"The pope required this arrangement as a condition for the de' Medici to retain their position as the Vatican's bankers. Ever since Lorenzo accused the pope of trying to have him assassinated, they do not trust each other. Let us say that we provide a sense of security to the Holy Father by standing in the wings, ready to assume all of his financial needs if Lorenzo falters. We are like the sword of Damocles over Duke Lorenzo's head. Further, Sixtus thought that by encouraging Florence and Venice to enter into this arrangement with Milan, we might stay at peace for longer than usual."

"When do you want me to leave?"

"Tomorrow."

Enrico began to feel rejected, as he had so many times when he was growing up.

"When can I return?"

"When you swear to me that you have ended your vendetta against the Zianis.

Enrico was speechless. Defiance flowed back into his eyes. "That could be a long time—maybe forever," he hissed.

"Then I will not see you again for a long time—maybe forever."

"Tell me, father, before I take my leave. Why have you softened your hatred toward the man you always held responsible for the deaths of your brothers? How can you hate a man, encourage me to hate him too, see me bear indescribable pain and shame at the hands of that man's son and then, at the moment of decision, completely lose your nerve, as though it were all only . . . just some sort of game?"

I have been fooling myself. Enrico will never change.

"I think you should leave now."

"Not before I provide the answers that you refuse to give. I think you have grown weak because you want to protect Carlo from all of this. You are afraid he will be harmed if you come to blows with the Zianis—and Carlo means more to you than anything else in this world, certainly more than a mere adopted son like me. I have acted, all the while, thinking you would approve of my actions—even believing that you would be proud of me, for once in your life. Instead, you exile me to Florence so you can get on with raising your precious son, without me around to tell him the truth." Enrico's head shook as he reached out his hand with his fist balled tightly. "I hate you for what you have done to me. I hope you burn in hell!"

Soranzo flew into a rage. He smashed his open hand hard across his son's face, knocking him violently to the floor. Enrico slowly sat, rubbing his stinging cheek. Neither spoke, their uncompromising eyes locked. Soranzo wanted to apologize for losing his temper in a way that he had never lost it before, but he could not ask his son to forgive him, not after what he had just said.

Finally, Enrico slowly got to his feet, turned, and walked out. As he disappeared, Soranzo was filled with an overwhelming sense of failure. He thought of little Carlo. He would not fail a second time, not with his own *real* son.

11

The Evil

The finely dressed man sat at a table drinking wine with a young woman who looked half his age. They were laughing and enjoying each other's company. Anyone could see that she was enthralled by her older companion. Throughout the evening, others sat down at their table to converse with the couple. A little business was conducted. Flirtation abounded. Although the young woman was not beautiful, young men were easily attracted to her nubile body and pleasant demeanor. She had mastered the art of making them feel pleased with themselves—the essence of a woman's charm.

As the evening progressed, the packed tavern rang out with bawdy jokes and loud singing. The curious couple held court in this humble place as regally as any king and queen might in their magnificent palace. Their subjects made them the center of attention. It was another Saturday night in Naples, hot and humid. The revelers left their burdens at the door and, once inside, found their true reason for being. Each one lived two separate existences: the day was one of drudgery, tempest, and toil, but night was filled with drinking and pleasure enough to make them forget the day.

Drunk and tired, in ones and twos, the patrons began to trickle home. The weary proprietor began his nightly ritual, collecting cups, cleaning tabletops, and extinguishing the oil lamps, one by one. Seeing that another evening of revelry had come to an end, the young woman helped her older companion to his feet and, supporting his weight on her shoulder, eased him toward the door, as she had so many nights before. Saying their goodnights to the few remaining drinkers inside, they stepped out into the warm, wet night air. By now the man had straightened up, and though he was still quite drunk, he was able to walk without assistance from his constant companion.

"Wait here. I have to go back and relieve myself. I will never be able to wait until we have walked all the way home," said the young woman abruptly.

"That small bladder of yours will be the death of you," he called after her in vain as he watched her walk quickly back into the now darkened tavern. "You should get one of these!" he stammered to himself and the night as he unbuttoned the front of his pants.

"And now," he mumbled, "I will enjoy the greatest benefit of manhood. I will be finished long before you return."

He laughed as he sloppily painted an alley wall a few feet from the street, out of view of any passersby—not that there would be one at this hour, he thought, or that I would care. His daughter's incessant nagging had made him promise to observe this small sacrifice to modesty whenever he finished his evening in this manner.

Something caught his eye just as he finished. A man appeared in the alley, walked toward him, and stopped a few feet away. Despite his intoxication, he tensed up, his right hand reaching for the dagger, concealed under the folds of his cloak.

"Signor Carboni, I have been searching everywhere for you."

"Signor Corelli! I . . . I have been looking for you, too. Where have you been?"

After the initial shock of seeing the tough sailor, Carboni regained his composure. His fingers found the ivory hilt of his dagger. He wrapped his fist tightly around its smooth surface. He never saw Moretti come up behind him. The heavy club crashed down on his head before he could draw his blade, knocking him unconscious. The two men quickly carried his limp body down the alley, away from the inn, to the next street and threw it into a waiting cart. After covering it with some empty sacks, they climbed up behind the donkey and rolled away.

When Estella returned from the tavern, she looked for her father at the place where she had left him, but he was not there. *Could he have walked home without me? No, he was much too drunk to go that far by himself.* Fear came over her as she thought about the many crimes that she had seen him commit. This night, could he have been a victim of the retribution she had always feared would eventually befall him? She ran back to the tavern and enlisted the help of a few friends who had not yet gone home. They frantically searched the neighboring streets and alleyways but could find no sign of him except for his ivory-handled dagger lying on a cobblestoned alley near the tavern. There was no blood on its blade. That at least, was something to be thankful for.

When Ercolano Carboni regained his consciousness, he was lying faceup on a crude wooden table. His hands and feet were tied, and his body was bound to the table with stout cords. He was tied so tightly he found it difficult to breathe, let alone move. He could hear muffled voices, but he could not turn to see his captors. His aching head, locked in place by the cords and a U-shaped wooden block, prevented him from searching the room. He could focus only on a single oil lamp, suspended from the cracked ceiling above. He had never been tortured before in his life, but he had tortured others. Never had he trussed a victim in this strange way.

"Signor Carboni, allow me to introduce myself. I am your employer. Do you know why you are here in this most disagreeable position?" a man's voice sneered.

He could not see his questioner.

"Signore, I regret that I did not kill him. If you still want me to, I will. I swear it! I will go to Venice if I have to. May God strike me dead if I do not kill him this time!"

"And where is the ransom money you collected from his father?"

"I have been searching for Signor Corelli ever since I was paid, but I could not find him anywhere. It was as though he had disappeared. It was a fine sum too—two hundred ducats!"

"Do not insult me with your pathetic lies. Although you deserve a most painful death for your treachery, I will offer you a way to end your miserable life quickly, avoiding a slow and painful death."

Ercolano began to whimper. His captor suddenly leaned over him, pushing his face so close that Carboni could not make out his features, except for his curved lips that resembled a twisted, angry scar.

"I am going to ask you some questions. If you answer them truthfully, you will die quickly. If you do not, you will die the most horrible and painful death this side of hell. Are you prepared to speak only the truth?"

"Yes, only the truth, I swear it!"

"Does Constantine Ziani know who employed you to kidnap him?"

"No! He does not even know *my* identity—only my face."

His interrogator said nothing.

"How could I reveal your name to him when I do not even know it myself?"

"Did you tell him that I employed you to kill him, not to ransom him? Did you tell him the ransom was your idea?"

The truth always flashes in the brain just before the lie falls from the lips.

"No . . . Never did I tell him that! I swear it!"

Ercolano's lie had tripped on the truth. His employer stood erect and turned to the other unseen men in the room.

"Leave us and wait outside."

Relieved, Corelli and Moretti quickly departed, concealing their own fear.

"Please do not kill me," begged Carboni. I have a daughter . . ."

"Oh, I *am* going to kill you, Signore, and I am going to do it slowly, because you have lied to me."

"No . . . please. I beseech you. I will do anything you ask. Please," he cried.

"Your contrition is touching, but it is too late, my Neapolitan fool. I always pay my debts and to you, my friend, I owe a large one."

He reached under the bench and lifted a coarse cloth sack and placed it on Ercolano's belly. He could feel it moving. There was something alive inside.

"What are you going to do to me?"

The man ignored his question and proceeded with his work. He reached into the sack and quickly removed a small torch. Then, holding it up to the lamp, he lit it. As he brought the flame closer to Ercolano, the prisoner struggled to move with all his might, but the cords held him fast.

Suddenly the man held the flaming torch against Ercolano's immobilized hand, searing his flesh. When Ercolano screamed, the man dropped the torch on the floor and, with a swift motion, jammed a small rusted iron cylinder into his mouth with such force that he broke two of his front teeth. Now Ercolano's mouth was locked open, and try as he might, he could not expel the cylinder with his tongue. He could only utter unintelligible words as his broken mouth oozed blood. He choked and began to grow faint as he swallowed metallic-tasting blood.

Carboni was petrified now. He did not know what was to come, but he imagined that all the horrors of hell were to be unleashed. He would be paid back for all the crimes he had committed in his life. Through the fog of pain, he watched as his tormentor produced a small bottle of olive oil and slowly poured it into his open mouth through the cylinder. Carboni gulped hard to avoid choking as the oil mixed with the blood in his mouth. His mind raced as it tried to find a way to survive, but he could no longer think clearly. He resigned himself to simply pray that it would all end soon.

Finally, with his cruel eyes burning like the hot coals, Enrico Soranzo lifted the wriggling sack up by its bottom and poured its contents onto his victim's heaving chest. Ercolano, his eyes locked on the ceiling, could not see the two-foot-long shiny black and gray snake, but he could feel its slithering motions through his expensive silk shirt. Soranzo slowly lifted the small snake by its tail and displayed it to his victim. The sight of the snake's head dancing as it tried to strike him, and the menacing hiss it made so close to his face, with its foreboding forked tongue, caused him to cough and gasp as he gulped his own blood to keep from choking.

Enrico grabbed the snake just behind its head with one hand and, with the other, picked up the torch. Then he pushed the snake's head into Ercolano's gaping mouth, held wide open by the iron ring. The snake instinctively recoiled. Again Enrico pushed the serpent's head into his victim's mouth, but this time, he touched the flaming torch to the snake's tail. The fire made it jump forward as it slithered down his throat to escape the flame. Ercolano passed out. In less than a minute it was done. Repeated touches of the torch had caused the entire length of the snake to wriggle down Ercolano's well-lubricated throat, despite his unconscious choking and gagging.

The snake immediately began biting its host's innards, inflicting a burning pain as its venom began to do its work. Its small mouth and fangs worked relentlessly, striking again and again as Enrico ripped the iron ring from Ercolano's mouth. The excruciating pain quickly revived his victim.

In between spitting blood and vomit, he cried out uncontrollably, moaning unintelligible words. Ercolano could feel the serpent was inside him now, tearing at his delicate, defenseless innards. When the snake rested, the pain subsided slightly. Stripped of his dignity and his life, Ercolano finally cried out to his executioner.

"Burn in hell, you Venetian bastard!"

Enrico laughed scornfully. "You will be in hell tonight, Signor Carboni, while I am off to Florence. Now enjoy your last meal." He roared and turned toward the door, leaving his suffering victim to endure a slow and painful death. The young snake's poison would take hours to kill him.

Outside, Corelli and Moretti trembled as they peered through the open door. What kind of a man would do such things to another human being? As Enrico emerged from the room, he calmly gave them his orders, belying the horror of what he had just done.

"Late tomorrow night, take his body to the tavern and leave it. Be sure no one sees you. Then go to the usual place and wait for me. When I return, I will pay you off."

Ercolano finally died, alone, in the filthy, dimly lit room. Eventually, he had accepted the pain, but he could never overcome the image of a serpent tearing at him. In the waning minutes of his life, he had decided that there had been no point to his death. The man had killed him more to satisfy his own twisted desires than to inflict any lesson or retribution on him. He died without fearing hell—he had already met Satan.

Corelli and Moretti followed their master's instructions precisely. The next night, before the sun rose, they left Ercolano's body in the same narrow alley where they had taken him. By midday the entire neighborhood was aghast at the barbarity of the crime. The snake's head was partly visible, emerging from Ercolano's rectum. The acid from his stomach had finally burned it to death before it could wriggle its way to freedom.

12

The Funeral

The weather reflected the crowd's somber mood. Several hundred mourners lined the streets as the hearse, drawn by two horses shrouded in black, slowly wound its way through the narrow streets. Mourners walked silently behind, many weeping openly. A steady rain soaked the procession and onlookers alike, as the heavens seemed to mourn with them. After Ercolano's remains were laid to rest, they all gathered at the tavern to drown their sorrows. Distraught, Estella sat in the corner receiving condolences from friends and well-wishers, known and unknown.

As the afternoon passed into evening, she felt increasingly left out, a castoff without her gregarious father at her side. The mourners, with their expressions of grief respectfully conveyed, had reverted to happier things to talk about, leaving her to grieve alone. She had no family now that her father was gone. As she sat in the corner by herself, drinking wine, she missed him more with each glass she consumed. Suddenly she noticed a strange little man waddle through the doorway and stop, surveying the scene. In the dim light, through her wine-filled head, he looked like some otherworldly creature—not really human at all.

He seemed to be searching for someone as he craned his neck in vain. A few patrons began to eye him suspiciously. When his eyes met Estella's, he seemed to acknowledge her, and he walked purposefully toward her.

"If you please, signorina, could you tell me where I might find a young woman called Estella?" he asked politely.

"Who are you? Why do you ask?"

"I have little time. I must speak to her father."

"Why have you come? Why this day of all days?" Tears formed in her eyes.

"Are you Estella?"

She lowered her head as the tears began to flow in a torrent of grief.

I have found her, but why is she crying so?

"On the day he set Signor Ziani free, your father told him that we could find him here. I must speak to him."

Though he received no invitation, Seraglio sat down. Estella continued to cry openly. Her haggard face turned blotchy red as she tried to wipe away her tears.

"What is wrong, Estella? Why are you crying?"

Her head drooped as she shook, overcome with sobbing. Then she looked straight at him, wiping her nose with a handkerchief.

"My father is dead, murdered by a villain whose evil knows no equal!"

The unexpected news stunned Seraglio. He had traveled for weeks to come to Naples, only to find that a murderer had thwarted the sole purpose of his journey. Now, he feared, he might never find the man who had ordered Constantine's murder.

"Tell me what happened."

"Who are you, signore? Who are you to ask me such things on the day of my father's funeral?"

"I am Seraglio, a friend of Constantine Ziani. He sent me here to find you and your father. He would have come himself, but he thought it would be too dangerous."

She studied his face, searching his dark eyes as he confidently held her gaze.

"If what you say is true, how much was the ransom?"

"Two hundred ducats—a fabulous sum but well worth it."

As Estella offered her hand, Seraglio lifted it to his lips and gently kissed it. She smiled for the first time that day. She recounted the events of her father's disappearance and the discovery of his mutilated body. As she described the snake burrowed into his abdomen, Seraglio could feel anger rise inside of him, but it was tempered with fear.

"Who would kill in that way?" he said with a shiver.

"I do not know, but my father was a man from the streets, a fighter. No one could have taken him without a fight. We found his dagger, but there was no blood or any sign of a struggle. He must have known the man or men who killed him."

"Do you know the name of the man who ordered Constantine's murder?"

"No, my father never met him. But he is a rich and powerful Venetian. The man who actually employed him here in Naples is named Corelli. He is a sailor. Corelli was the officer who convinced the captain to come to the tavern the night we took him."

At the mention of Corelli's name, Seraglio's knuckles turned white as he gripped the edge of the table. The captain was right. Corelli had been the traitor.

"Do you know where this Corelli is now?"

"No. I have not seen him for months, not since before the kidnapping."

Seraglio reached across the table and held Estella's hand in his. He gazed into her sad eyes. Despite her obvious pain, they radiated defiance.

"Estella, you were kind to Constantine when he had no one to show him kindness. Let me help you now."

She pulled her hand away as her eyes narrowed in disbelief.

"My father would still be alive if he had never set eyes upon your friend. What can you do to help me now? You have brought nothing but grief to both of us."

"We can give you justice," he said with simple, disarming honesty.

"There is no justice in this world. Believe me, I know."

"Corelli can lead us to the man who killed your poor father so cruelly. I must return to Venice with the morning tide. Give us Corelli and we will give you the man behind him, the man who killed your father or ordered him killed. I am certain you have friends who would also want justice for your father. They will know how to question Corelli properly to make him talk. Send us the name of the man he excretes from his lips. That is all we ask. Leave the rest to us. Now I must leave you."

Estella raised her eyes and looked into his face. She exuded a kind of beauty, not the physical kind, but deeper, under the skin, the kind Seraglio could understand. The girl deserved justice. She smiled again for only the second time that long, sad day. They parted without saying good-bye, each knowing that someday they would meet again.

In late February, when Seraglio returned to Venice, he was surprised to learn that Doge Pietro Mocenigo had died, some said, exhausted by the concubines he had brought back with him from his Turkish raids. His successor was dour Andrea Vendramin, who, at eighty-three, was older than most doges were at the time of their election. He was a fabulously rich merchant, one of the *nuovi,* families that had recently made their fortune in trade. He quickly went to work, trying to find a way to achieve peace with the Turks while he searched for ways to shore up the Republic's finances to pay for war, in case peace overtures failed.

Constantine and Maria Mocenigo were married two months after his safe return from Naples. All of Venice's leading families attended the elaborate wedding ceremony in the Basilica di San Marco. The reception was held in the Ca' Mocenigo. Their union strengthened the Zianis' position among the *nobili* by joining two of its most important families, both *primi*— noble families of the first order. Seven hundred *nobili* were invited to what everyone agreed was the biggest social event of the year. The Soranzos never received a coveted invitation.

The dinner was superb. Maria had made sure that the cook prepared her husband's favorite food. The main course was pasta with shrimp. Italy owed a great debt to Marco Polo, the famous Venetian explorer and trader, for bringing the recipe for pasta back to Venice from China nearly two hundred years before.

Constantine poured another glass of red wine for himself and leaned suggestively on the table. His eyes caressed Maria's face. She smiled and lowered her own eyes as if, by doing so, she could evade his amorous intentions. She had sent the servants to bed after they had served the meal. They were all alone.

Constantine was twenty-two and Maria was twenty when they were married. Then, it had not seemed possible that they could fall even more deeply in love, but they had. While he enjoyed the advantages of being a member of a wealthy patrician family of merchants, Constantine hated having to be away from Venice and his pretty young wife, as his work sometimes demanded. Tonight he was enjoying his homecoming meal and looking forward to making love to his wife for the first time in nearly a month.

"Are you going to fill my glass too, Constantine?"

"But you have not yet finished the wine you have," he protested.

She lifted the delicate glass in her petite hand and raised it to her lips, slowly filling her mouth with its velvety crimson liquid. Then she slowly rose from the table and walked around it to where Constantine was sitting. She leaned over and kissed him softly on the lips. When his tongue slipped into her mouth, he could taste the warm wine as she spilled it into his own. He drank it down in a single gulp as his nose filled with the fragrant smell of her body, now so near to him.

"There," she said softly, "I have finished my wine. Now pour me another glass."

He laughed as he poured. "You will get drunk and fall asleep."

"Then perhaps we should go to bed now," she cooed.

"I was hoping you would say that," he said with an amorous smile.

She blushed and turned away from him. "Wait until I have been upstairs for a few minutes. Then come to bed. I have a surprise for you."

As he waited alone in the candlelight, he imagined Maria lying naked on their bed. He could almost feel the breeze from the open window gently wafting across their bodies as they locked in their first embrace. He was more aroused now than on their wedding night. He recalled the night with mixed emotions. He had been delighted to find that she was a virgin, but things had not gone well. Her maidenhead was thick and he had hurt her. She had been unable to go on. Fortunately, he had drunk so much wine that night that he just rolled over and fell fast asleep. The next morning had been different. They had consummated their marriage twice. Since that day, she seemed to enjoy it more each time they made love. Now she likes it more than I do, he mused to himself. He decided that he had waited long enough. It was time to go upstairs.

Picking up the half-full bottle and the two empty glasses, he walked across the room and down the broad hallway. He could see light coming from under the slightly opened bedroom door. He stopped in the hallway and put the bottle and glasses down on a small wooden table and quickly removed his shoes and robe. Then, naked, he filled the two glasses and, with one in each hand, walked unabashedly into the room.

Maria was lying there, looking just as he had imagined. She was naked, except for a golden necklace lined with jewels, throwing off brilliant sparkles that danced around the plastered walls in the flickering candlelight. The open window filled the room with the fragrant scents of flowers and the lilac tree that grew just below their window. She was smiling coyly, like a cat about to be scratched, filled with languorous anticipation.

He walked to the bed and sat down next to her. Handing her a glass, he raised his and gently touched the rim of her glass.

"I salute the most beautiful woman in Venice."

"I drink to the *second* most handsome man in Venice."

"Will I always be second to that father of yours?" he complained. Then, after carefully placing his glass on the floor, he leaned over and kissed her hard on the mouth.

"Tell me you love me more than anyone else," he demanded.

She let her empty glass drop onto the bed and then, raising her arms in the air, she beckoned him to embrace her. Sliding his arm under her neck as he kissed her, he began to shift his legs to the space between hers. Suddenly, her body stiffened. He pulled away to see what was wrong. Her face was sad.

"What is wrong, my love? Why do you invite me to your breast and then become sad when I begin to make love to you?"

"Oh Constantine, I can no longer hide it from you. There is another in your place," she whispered with a pained look.

The words hit him like a mace. His mind searched for something to say—a protest. She began to giggle and then broke into gleeful laughter. He was annoyed.

"Really, Maria, sometimes I think you enjoy hurting me," he said angrily.

"I am sorry, my dear, but I did not know how to tell you my news any other way. I am going to have your baby—in November. My mother says it will be a son because he is kicking in my womb already."

He was speechless. He rose up onto his knees and gently placed his two hands on her firm belly, as white as Carrara marble but infinitely softer to the touch. As he gently rubbed her skin, he could not feel any movement inside.

"Are you certain you are with child?" he asked incredulously.

"Of course I am. Women know these things. I can feel him moving inside of me."

"Oh Maria, can you forgive me for doubting your fidelity? It is just that you made me afraid. I love you so much. I could never abide your loving another man."

"You will never have to. I love only you—and him, of course," she said as she delicately patted her stomach.

"Does this mean we can no longer make love until after he is born?" he lamented.

"Well, just this once," she said with a vixenlike grin as she rose up and kissed him long and passionately.

With their lips still pressed together and arms entwined, they both fell onto the bed, laughing.

"Careful, you hurt my lip," she said as their teeth bumped. She soon forgot her complaint as he made her feel like the most beautiful, most adored woman in the world.

Her mother was not quite right. *Two* sons were born to them—and a month early. Mother and children recovered from the trauma of birth quickly. Constantine and Maria Ziani had begun their little family in grand style.

Constantine had always thought of himself as wealthy—he had every reason to. He lived in the family *palazzo* with its fine view of the Grand Canal. Someday, the Ca' Ziani would belong to him, the sole heir to the House of Ziani, but it was not until his two sons were born that he truly felt rich, so blessed by God. He would do anything for them, loving them as no father had ever loved his sons.

13

The Collapse

The white morning sun peered over the shimmering hillside, its blinding rays still bearable to the eye for a few moments longer. The lush, undulating green hills gently fell away to meet the thin strip of sand that divided the land from the cool waters of the lagoon. Off in the distance, about a quarter of a mile up from the shoreline, a weathered white-washed farmhouse nestled into a cleft in the earth alongside the silver ribbon of a meandering stream. Its terra-cotta roof glowed reddish brown in the light. Neat fences surrounded the kitchen garden where tomatoes and peppers hung heavy on the vine. Alongside it, in another enclosure, a cow and some goats had already begun to stir at the dawning of the new day.

The farmer stepped carefully through his fields of grain, his mind immersed in the beauty of what he had created with his own hands and with the help of God, as golden wheat buds fluttered all around him in the morning breeze.

So far, the summer had been warm and not too wet. The crops had responded by growing with abundance. He could not remember when he had seen his fields so robust. Even though the yield would mean much back-breaking work, he looked forward to the harvest that would begin in less than a month. He would be able to provide for his family and have a surplus of wheat to sell in Marghera, where it would be shipped to Venice, across the lagoon. His father and his forebears had farmed this land for as long as anyone could remember. It was among the most prized in the Veneto. Except for life itself, good land was the greatest of God's gifts.

He called and waved to his little son who was playing in the distance. The boy was his pride and joy, even more than his precious fields. He was only six, but he was already helping with the chores and showing great intelligence. The man smiled as he watched his son jump over the stream, not quite clearing its waters and soaking his sandals. The boy looked sheepishly at his father and then, forgetting his failure, leaped back across, clearing it as he rolled, laughing, in the tall grass.

As he was about to reach the crest of the ridge, the farmer suddenly remembered that he had forgotten to light the morning fire. He turned abruptly and walked quickly down the hillside, carefully retracing his steps through the wheat. The boy, sensing his father's purpose, stopped his stream jumping and, running along its low bank, scampered toward the cozy little farmhouse to playfully reach it before him.

When the man was a short distance from the house, he saw a wisp of white smoke curling skyward from the chimney as it disappeared into the vast blue sky. She had already lit the fire. The door opened and his pretty wife emerged, her long hair flowing in the light breeze. As the three members of the little family came together, they all smiled at each other. It had been more than two years since the Turks had come. They had burned the house but, forewarned, he and his wife and son had sought refuge in Venice. Since then, he had rebuilt the house and purchased new livestock. Life was finally good again.

The captain eyed his sleeping men. Desertion and disease had claimed a quarter of them on the long campaign. Still, his company was about twenty strong. They were the hearty ones. How strange it is, he thought, to see them motionless. When awakened, they were terrifying. He was thankful they were fighting *with* him and not *against* him. He felt the sense of power any leader feels when such strength is at his command. As he carried the leather saddle over to his horse, he gently kicked one sleeping man lying near his path, waking him instantly.

"I am going to see what is over that ridge. Wake the others and break camp. I will return in a few minutes."

The captain lifted his foot in the stirrup and, in one fluid motion, expertly mounted. Then he aimed his powerful black horse at the ridge to his right and cantered out of the camp as the men he left behind began to stir, cursing the new day.

It had been four months since the campaign began. The men were tired and hungry and in a foul mood. They had fought their last skirmish a week ago. Now, with the rest of the Bulgar cavalry, they had fanned out over the countryside, far outdistancing the slower Turkish regular infantry, in their search for food. There was little risk of encountering enemy soldiers now. The main Venetian army had sought the protection of their fleet and sailed for Venice after the fall of Scutari. The countryside, unscathed by war, was now laid bare for the taking, like a defenseless virgin girl.

As he crested the ridgeline, far in the distance he could see a prosperous farm, nestled in the valley. A thin wisp of smoke, barely visible, betrayed that it was still inhabited. *How slowly word travels among those uninitiated to the horrors of war.* Back in his hometown on the shores of the Black Sea, he could still remember that day when he was a boy, the first time the Sipahis came. An ironic smile curled his lip as he turned his mount around and trotted back to camp. He never thought he would be fighting *with* the Turks after they had killed his mother and father that day.

T he farmer kissed his wife good morning and added some more wood to the fire.

"Son, go down to the shoreline and gather some driftwood," he said.

Without a word, the boy picked up a basket and ran from the house, down through the fields until he disappeared over the low ridge that separated them from the beach below.

He held his wife and amorously kissed her again. This would be a good time to make love, he thought, as he pulled her away from the table and made his intentions known. She smiled back at him with a look that told him she needed convincing.

"No, there is not enough time," she protested softly. "He will be back soon."

"He will take a long time to fill his basket this morning," he replied. "The tide will be coming in, and it will be hard to find wood on the beach. Are you more afraid that it will take too long?" He laughed.

He let her break free from his embrace, and she ran out through the open door. He pulled off his shirt, to give her a head start, and then, throwing it into the air, he ran out after her. It took a moment for his eyes to adjust to the bright light. Suddenly he stopped.

She was standing there, facing him, with her eyes closed and a languorous smile on her face. Her nightgown was lying on the ground at her feet. Her naked bronzed body glistened in the morning light. Aroused and wanton, she beckoned him with her arms and hands. She could not see the men riding down the ridge behind her.

"Bella!"

With a mother's instinct, she instantly sensed that something was terribly wrong. The terror in her husband's face made her turn around. She screamed instinctively as she ran to him and threw her arms around his neck. She looked at him, her eyes wide open.

"Matteo!"

"He will be safe. Get dressed, quickly," he said as they ran inside the house. "I will see what they want."

Gian took down his axe from above the door and placed it next to him, out of sight. Then he said a short prayer and stepped outside to bravely face the intruders.

The mounted soldiers looked like *stradiotti*. They were spread out in a single line abreast. Their big horses trampled the ripe wheat underfoot as they slowly made their way toward the house. He could tell that they were irregulars. They wore no uniforms. He thanked God they were not Turks, but he did not recognize the flag that one man carried as it fluttered in the morning breeze. He had never seen one like it before. He stepped into the middle of the doorway.

"You look hungry," Gian called out boldly.

The leader, clothed in a fine suit of chain mail, pulled up his horse about twenty feet away. The image of power, he stared down at the farmer. Gian felt raw fear course through his body. He hoped Matteo would linger at the beach, as he usually did.

"Water the horses," snapped the captain to his men in his native language. Then he dismounted and faced Gian.

"Have you seen soldiers?" he asked in broken Italian. Gian could not place the accent, but he knew it was Slavic. Damned *Schiavoni!*

"No," Gian replied as he shook his head, trying desperately to cloak his fear in all the calm courage he could muster.

"Eat, please," said Bella as she bravely burst through the doorway with a large basket filled with bread she had baked the day before. She moved quickly among the mounted soldiers, handing a generous piece to each. They ate ravenously as the others waited impatiently for their piece.

"Are these all the animals you possess?" asked the captain as he pointed to the cow and goats.

"Yes," nodded Gian, long past caring that they might be plundered. *Perhaps we can satisfy them with our livestock and bread. If only they will just take what they want and leave us in peace.* Bella, now finished with the riders near the captain, moved to some that had returned from watering their horses in the stream by the side of the house. Gian tensed as she disappeared behind the captain's horse, blocking his view.

"Have you seen any Turks?" asked Gian.

"Turks?" replied the captain as he turned to look back at his men, who grinned back with near toothless smiles. "He wants to know if we have seen any Turks."

The men burst into laughter as the captain turned back toward Gian.

"Would you offer food to Turks?" Gian thought he heard him say.

He fumbled for the right words to answer the menacing question when suddenly he sensed some commotion behind the captain. As the horse began to saunter sideways, he could see Bella trying to pull her arm away from a big, hairy soldier who gripped her tightly by her wrist.

"A piece of bread will not satisfy my hunger this morning." He laughed lewdly.

The other soldiers began to laugh too as they leaned forward on their horses to get a better view of the action. Bella began to whimper, turning white with terror. He was hurting her.

"Please, take what you want but leave us in peace. I do not care who wins this war. Please . . ." His words stuck in his throat as the hairy soldier crashed his free hand down hard on Bella's cheek. With his other hand he lifted her onto his horse like a broken toy. Still conscious, she screamed at him to let her go. He threw her writhing, kicking body over the neck of his horse as she vainly struggled to escape. Then pushing his big hand against her bare buttocks to hold her in place, he kicked his heels into the sides of his mount and galloped back up the hill. All but a few of the other soldiers chased after him, laughing and shouting vulgar insults as they rode hard to catch up and join in.

Gian turned to run back into the house for his axe. Suddenly, white-hot pain seared through him, driving him to the ground. An arrow's shaft protruded from the wound deep in his back. Gian's eyes began to grow heavy. Through the fog he could feel men stepping over him and running into the house. He could smell the moist earth in his nose as Bella's beautiful face flashed like an apparition in his mind. He could not comprehend why the grass crackled and burned as he struggled to see his son jumping over the cool stream and rolling in the lush green grass.

The cavalry, some Turks but mostly Bulgars and other assorted undisciplined mercenaries, sought only spoils—they did not fight for a cause.

They had ridden north, up the Adriatic coast, inundating the land like the watery tendrils of a great flood, swirling and flowing around every hamlet and town. Now, as they headed west, no one in the Veneto, Venice's most prosperous province, was safe from their depredations.

The Turkish army was still far away in Albania. The sultan knew he could not cross the two miles of sea that ringed Venice without first defeating her navy, and the city was beyond the range of his largest guns. A full-scale invasion was out of the question. So, on they came, plundering, raping, and burning, until they had ringed the lagoon. There they remained until Venice's *terra firma* lands had been thoroughly laid to waste. Only two years before, the Turks had pillaged these same lands. Then, it was only a large raid. This time, it was far worse. The Republic, further weakened by the loss of her territories and constant interruptions to her shipping, moved her entire army to the safety of the city of Venice, completely abandoning her *terra firma* lands to the marauders.

Antonio stood with his family on the roof of the Ca' Ziani, transfixed, peering out over the lagoon at *terra firma*, visible in the distance. Normally, the *liago,* their luxurious rooftop garden, was a sanctuary, overflowing with colorful flowers and manicured topiaries, carefully nurtured by their master gardener, one of the best in the city. It had always been a place filled with fond memories, where they had entertained friends with fine wine and lavish meals. Often Antonio and Seraglio would sit there, where the air was fresh, above the city, and talk for hours under the broad crimson-and-white awning Antonio had specially made to shade them from the hot Mediterranean sun. But this day, all that was forgotten.

Antonio held his hand to shield his eyes and squinted to better see across the shimmering water. The glare would have made it difficult to pick out the towns dotted along the coast, were it not for the columns of black smoke that marked each one. Like funeral pyres, they snaked skyward, ugly blots despoiling the glorious blue sky. Thick black roiling columns towered above the towns, while thin gray shorter wisps marked the locations of villages and farms. In all, he counted more than fifty that were burning.

"There, Seraglio, over there is Mestre, and there is Marghera and to the left, further along, is Fusina. Years ago our family owned a large farm there."

"Be glad you sold it," observed the always practical Seraglio.

"All in flames," Constantine sighed, shaking his head. "How could all this have happened? What destruction."

"It happened because the sultan is bent on our destruction," replied his father. "We cannot defeat him on land, and he cannot defeat us at sea, so he has decided to choke off our commerce and deny us food by laying waste to our *terra firma* lands."

"And," added Seraglio, "he wants to terrorize us into thinking that the only safe place in the world, for a Venetian, is here in Venice."

"He has certainly convinced me. I cannot stay up here another minute. It is too upsetting," interrupted Isabella.

She turned and disappeared into the stairwell leading down to the top floor of the Ca' Ziani, tears still falling from her eyes.

Constantine was thankful that Maria had already gone downstairs to the twins.

A ragged armada of overloaded boats slowly made its way across the lagoon, their occupants seeking refuge in Venice.

"They have begun removing the buoys from the lagoon," said Andrea, Antonio's cousin and his most trustworthy ship captain.

When threatened, the Venetians always removed the buoys that marked the deep channels through the shallow lagoon into the city, to prevent a seaborne invasion. Without them, only veteran Venetian ship captains, working from memory, could navigate the infamously narrow, twisting passages through the shallows.

"The Turks would never try to engage our battle fleet," observed Constantine.

Antonio, after surveying the burning towns and villages, turned away. A pained expression hung heavily from his eyes and mouth.

"It is as if we are looking at all this through some giant window. The sight of all this destruction is too much to bear. Just look at all those towns and farms, churches and public buildings—some of them required decades to build. At least when the Hungarians came, they did not burn the churches, but this . . ." He shook his head.

"Look," said Seraglio, motioning around them. "Today is the Sabbath and nearly every rooftop in Venice is filled with people, all watching the same terrible sights. It is exactly what the Turks want—to demoralize us. And what do we see? It depends. Some of us gaze, as through a window, feeling a sort of detached guilt. We observe the destruction of our countrymen and their homes, from the sanctuary of our own, protected from invasion. It is the same way we would observe a burning city from a ship riding safely in the harbor. After a while, you must look away, for you can do nothing.

"But others see as through a looking glass. They ask, Is all this a harbinger of Venice's future? Is this the first chapter in the story of her final destruction?

They are asking, Could this happen to us too here in Venice, impregnable Venice? How do you see it, Constantine? Do you peer through a window or see a reflection in a looking glass?"

Constantine had been listening carefully and thought before he spoke.

He looked at Antonio. "I see through a window, like my father. Once the Turks have plundered and destroyed everything, they will withdraw. Then we will rebuild. It is simple, but it is the truth. And you, Seraglio?"

"I think this is the beginning of the end of our war with the Turks. I am convinced that we must have peace, no matter the cost. Only then can we rebuild our economy and achieve, in time, ultimate victory."

"But how can we accomplish that?" asked Constantine, surprised.

Seraglio winked.

"What we cannot win by the sword we will win through negotiation— war carried on by other means. The Turkish artillery and Venetian galleys are each powerful, but we have the ultimate weapon. No country on earth possesses our resources and capabilities to obtain the kind of information required to secure a decisive advantage in negotiations."

Antonio smiled and continued where Seraglio left off.

"Andrea heard rumors from a reliable source in Alexandria that the sultan is no longer so popular with his army. His soldiers and officers, veterans of his many wars, are pressing him for reforms that would transfer wealth to them from landowners. Blind obedience—the glue that has held the Ottoman Empire together for years—has hardened and dried. They no longer fear him. These raids are a further sign that the sultan's power has been weakened. He has as much need to end this war as we do."

"But how can we know that?" asked Constantine, incredulous.

"In the old days he never would have permitted his troops to pillage without claiming his own share in person," said Antonio. "Now, while they take everything that is not nailed down, he is far away, back in Istanbul, oblivious to their depredations. The only question that remains is whether the Great Council and the doge are ready to propose terms to the sultan. What do you think, Seraglio?"

"I have been wondering about that myself. After all this, they should be, but I am afraid it will take one more disaster before they can finally bury their pride and ask the sultan for terms. They will be concerned that if we sign a separate peace with the Turks, we will be reviled by the rest of the Christian world as traitors to the cross."

Constantine flinched. "Even though the rest of the Christian world has done nothing to help us fight all the time we have waged this terrible war alone?"

"Always remember, son, those with the power make the rules. The pope and the kings of France and Spain and the Holy Roman Emperor will conveniently use our capitulation against us, to gain advantage for themselves."

"I would not even be surprised to see Pope Sixtus lay an interdict upon Venice if we sign a separate peace," chimed in Seraglio, shaking his head in disgust.

"For now, we must leave no stone unturned to acquire information that will aid us in negotiating a favorable peace treaty," said Antonio.

The columns of black smoke had risen so high, they began to topple over onto one another, filling the sky with a sooty gray cloud. It would take a long time for the survivors to recover but not so long for yet another calamity to befall the Republic.

Soon after the marauders departed, leaving a devastated *terra firma* in their wake, it was obvious that the overcrowded city of Venice, teeming with refugees from the invasion, had lost her fight to maintain a tenuous hold on her sanitary conditions. In normal times, she required all visitors to be quarantined before allowing them access to the city. The *lazzaretto,* as it was called, had been instituted to prevent another outbreak of the Black Death that had decimated Venice and the rest of Europe in 1348.

Shortly after several ships had arrived from Sicily bearing Genoese survivors of the Mongol siege of Kaffa, in the Crimea, hundreds began to exhibit symptoms of a strange illness. It was the same affliction the defenders of Kaffa had suffered after the Mongols catapulted the decomposing bodies of their dead over the city walls and into the midst of the Genoese. The Mongol camp had been so decimated by the disease that they were forced to raise the siege and go home. The long, hot summer that year seemed to exacerbate the problem. In that single year, three-fifths of the city's population perished. At its peak, more than seven hundred people were dying in Venice every day.

Now, so many people sought refuge in the city that the *lazzaretto* was ignored and the delicately balanced sanitary system was overwhelmed. Within a few weeks, the plague struck. While there were far fewer deaths during this outbreak than a century before, still, thousands died in a few weeks. One was the old and feeble Doge Vendramin. He had served for less than three years.

On May 14, on the eleventh ballot, the Great Council elected as his successor Giovanni Mocenigo, the brother of Doge Pietro Mocenigo and Constantine Ziani's father-in-law. His coronation celebration was uncustomarily subdued. The new doge chose to invest funds normally earmarked for the festivities to offset a portion of the huge debt the government owed from financing its protracted war against the Turks. His civic-minded gesture drove home to all how dire Venice's situation had become.

14

The Peace

A ntonio was not surprised when he received a summons from the new doge. He was a senator, one of the sixty-man body comprised of Great Council members, responsible for overseeing La Serenissima's foreign policy. He was also one of the new doge's staunchest supporters, so it was logical that Mocenigo would consult him. Antonio had, of course, known Mocenigo's brother Pietro for many years, but he had come to know Giovanni even more intimately by virtue of Constantine's marriage to Giovanni's daughter. Antonio found the new doge to be courageous and wise, and though he had been thrust by events into an impossible position, Antonio believed that Giovanni Mocenigo was the right man for the job.

Antonio sat alone in his library, thinking, as he gazed through the tall tracery windows at the shimmering waters of the Grand Canal, already crowded with hundreds of boatmen intent on delivering their goods to a thousand places at the start of a new day. The Senate, doubled in size for crucial matters of state by the *zonta*, to one hundred and twenty members, had voted decisively the day before to finally sue for peace with the sultan. Antonio was pleased that the doge had agreed to his unusual request that Seraglio, a *cittadino,* also be invited to the special meeting later that day.

As if on cue, the door opened—it was Seraglio. He waddled across the floor and climbed up onto his chair. As they reached for the breakfast of fruit, bread, and dried fish, prepared for them by the servants, Antonio began to speak.

"Yesterday the Senate concluded that Venice will face default and ruination if the war continues, and we voted to begin negotiations. This morning you and I have been summoned by the doge. He is going to ask us to play a part in all this."

Seraglio stopped eating, looked up at his mentor, and slowly shook his head. "Surrender? I never thought I would live to see this day."

"Yes, surrender. There is no other word for it. The longer we fight on, the weaker will shall become. We have no other options."

When they entered the Doges' Palace, they were ushered immediately to the Sala del Collegio. There, they found the doge and his *Signoria* waiting. They took two chairs, obviously intended for them, the only two visitors in the room. In addition to the doge, flanked by his six counselors clad in scarlet robes, this small group of some of the Republic's leading *nobili* included the Ten, the secret power behind the power in Venice. No major decision was made without their knowledge. They were the constitutional safeguard that ensured Venice would never be corrupted or fall from internal treachery. As Antonio scanned the familiar faces, he could see that some wore the haggard mask of defeat, but the others still looked grimly determined to make the best of the situation.

"Last night," the doge began, "we unanimously agreed that we must begin our quest for peace with the sultan at once. We also decided, unanimously I might add, that you shall be the one responsible for undertaking this negotiation."

The doge paused to let the impact of his words sink in. Antonio and Seraglio exchanged glances. There was no need to speak. They each knew what this meant. The fate of the Republic would be in Antonio's hands, and one of them would be tied behind his back owing to Venice's weak bargaining position. Seraglio did not envy his friend's situation. He remembered the intransigence displayed by the Turks, led by the sultan's son Bayezid, when they had negotiated unsuccessfully with them in Istanbul.

Unanimous he says, thought Antonio. All decisions made by the *Signoria* were *publicly* announced as unanimous, as a matter of policy. The Venetians knew that the best way to avoid undermining their own strength and determination to resist Turkish aggression was to be united in the face of it. They would never allow an enemy sworn to destroy them to learn that they were divided internally. That could be fatal.

"Signor Ziani, we chose you because you know the Turks as well as anyone in Venice. We also know that you are a patriot who has always placed the Republic's interests above his own. Our goal is simple. If we cannot retain our territorial possessions lost to the Turks in this damned war, at least we can restore our trading privileges that the Turks have withheld from us. As one of the Republic's leading merchants, there is no one in Venice who knows more about what needs to be done in this respect than you."

"What have our diplomats and spies learned?"

The doge turned to one of the Ten and nodded. The man stood.

"Our ambassador in Alexandria has reported that, as we thought, the Sultan Muhammad did not send his regular troops to pillage the Friuli countryside last year because he feared they might rebel. We have learned that he is losing his grip on his army, from which he derives his power to rule."

"Who was the ambassador's source? How do we know we can rely upon this report to be true?"

The man smiled broadly, his teeth plainly visible through his thick chestnut beard.

"Our ambassador heard of it from the sultan's ambassador to Egypt, and he heard it from Prince Bayezid, the sultan's own son."

This was momentous news and confirmed the rumors. If the sultan's troops were restless, he could not press home his advantage and continue the war indefinitely. There might be some weakness in the Turks' negotiating position that Antonio could exploit.

"When do you want me to leave for Istanbul? Have we already made peace overtures to the sultan?"

"Yes, we have, but surprisingly, the negotiations will take place here in Venice."

Antonio was surprised, but Seraglio almost fell out of his chair. Protocol dictated that the party in the superior position hosted peace negotiations. If the sides were equal in strength, a neutral site was typically chosen.

"Has the sultan indicated who will be his representative?"

The man in the black robe, still standing, responded. "His name is Abdullah Ali, the sultan's foreign minister. Do you know him?"

"We have met before."

N ew Year's Day 1479 dawned unseasonably warm. Antonio had arranged for the Sala dello Scrutino, the counting room, in the Doges' Palace, to be used for the negotiations. Located on the third floor, it was the place where ballots were counted in ducal elections and where important committees met. It was secure, having by necessity very thick walls to prevent eavesdropping.

Abdullah Ali was scheduled to arrive incognito in mid-January. Bad weather delayed him until the last week of the month. His delegation was immediately escorted to a nearby inn on the Riva degli Schiavoni, owned by the government and reserved for high-ranking visiting foreign dignitaries. The government was careful to ensure that the city was unaware of the negotiations taking place.

A s Antonio and Seraglio sat waiting in the counting room, they heard a flurry of footsteps indicating their guest had arrived. A guard opened the door.

"Abdullah Ali, Foreign Minister of the Ottoman Empire, and his party, await you."

Antonio nodded and the guard dutifully disappeared.

Seraglio smiled at his friend. "Let us get down to business."

Again the door opened and in walked the representatives of the Ottoman Empire in all their worldly power.

First was the pasha of Anatolia. Antonio and Seraglio remembered him from the unsuccessful peace negotiations in Istanbul. He was unremarkable but possessed the traits most highly valued by the sultan—loyalty and frugality. He was utterly dependable and scrupulous to a fault. He would be tough. There was no acknowledgment from him that he remembered having spent months locked in a steaming room, arguing with Antonio and Seraglio a few years before.

Next was a diminutive man with a turban so large that he seemed to bend under its weight. His keen eyes, darting and measuring, revealed his intellect. His complexion was so dark that it was difficult to read his facial expressions. Presently, both of them bowed as a large man, larger than Antonio had remembered him, burst through the door like a bora, the violent winter wind that whipped the Adriatic into a fury.

"When I heard it was you that I would negotiate with, I could not decide whether your doge has made my job easier or more difficult."

Abdullah Ali embraced Antonio, kissing him on both cheeks. Then he placed his hands on Seraglio's shoulders and laughed loudly.

"Unfortunately, my old wound prevents me from embracing you, too. I am afraid if I bent that low, I would be unable to rise. Time corrupts the body before the mind."

"Your Italian is much improved," observed Seraglio.

"And I trust your ability to speak truth, that greatest of all languages, has not diminished," Ali fired back with a laugh. "In any event, I plan to return to Istanbul within the week. Our relative positions are obvious. We simply need to formalize with the pen what events have made a reality with the sword."

The three men shared a laugh while Ali's two comrades stood by awkwardly. Ali introduced the pasha and the other man, Karamani Muhammad, the commander of the sultan's army in Albania and a man intimately familiar with the relative military strength of the two parties. He had come, no doubt, to obtain useful information in case the negotiations failed. A cunning man, he was an excellent choice by the sultan.

If Antonio and Seraglio were put at ease by Abdullah Ali's congenial greeting, he soon dispelled any hope they had that he would be reasonable to deal with.

"In the interest of time, I will make the sultan's position perfectly clear," he began. "All your former territories that we currently control will be ceded permanently to the Ottoman Empire with no compensation for them due the Republic of Venice.

"You are hardly capable of taking them back from us. Face facts—they are lost forever." Ali winked at Antonio. "We stole them from you fair and square, eh, Signore?"

He continued without waiting for Antonio's response.

"The sultan also requires an indemnity payment of one hundred thousand ducats. In return, the sultan will guarantee peace to Venice and all her territories for a period of ten years. I told you, Signor Ziani, that this would be straightforward." His full black beard danced as he thrust his lower jaw forward, scowling for effect.

Antonio had expected these draconian terms. The Turks thought of themselves as invincible. Even Scutari had finally fallen to them.

"Foreign Minister Ali, you have made the sultan's position quite clear, but I must draw your attention to several points that complicate the matter."

Ali cast a quick glance at Karamani, then at the pasha.

"If we agree to your terms, you will add many jewels to the sultan's crown—Euboea, hundreds of smaller Ionian islands, Albania, and, of course, most of the Peloponnese. In return, all we get is a piece of paper with a promise, sealed by the sultan's *tughra*." Antonio stood and leaned on his fists, placing his face near Ali's.

"I must have more than a promise, something tangible to give the Senate, the doge, and his *Signoria*. Sadly, the level of trust that exists between you and me does not extend to our respective governments."

Ali rose slowly, his face flushed, trying to control his anger.

"Your request ignores the weakness of your position, Signor Ziani. If the war goes on, what do you Venetians think will happen? Do you think your friends in the Christian world will come to your aid? I will tell you what they will do. They will do just what they have always done. They will steal your business while you bleed and spend."

Seraglio remained quiet, barely able to suppress his urge to chime in.

"We have spent too much blood and money to suffer this sort of humiliation," Antonio responded. "You have offered us nothing to compensate us for the pain we will suffer at the hands of other Christian states if we sign a separate peace with you. They will regard us as traitors."

"And they will be justified, but at least you will be traitors who are free," interrupted the pasha. "That is more than the Bulgars, the Macedonians, and the Wallachians can say as we occupy their lands. Our only terms to them were to agree to be absorbed into our empire."

"So, you Venetians need a reason to justify your capitulation then?"

"Precisely."

Ali thought for a moment, but not long enough to convince Antonio and Seraglio that he was forming a new thought in his mind—he was acting.

"The sultan has reluctantly permitted me to offer an inducement if you will agree to peace without further delay. He will allow the Republic of Venice to reestablish a *bailo* in Istanbul with full trading privileges." He smiled like a wolf to a lamb.

Antonio looked at Seraglio, wondering what was next.

"Hard as it may be for you Venetians to understand, the sultan has always been a reasonable man. As proof, he has empowered me to offer to you a monopoly on trade with the Ottoman Empire. With the additional income you will generate from this, as the only Christian state permitted access to Ottoman ports and territory, you should easily be able to pay an additional twenty thousand ducats at the beginning of each year to show your appreciation for this great advantage he has given you." Ali grinned through his thick beard.

"With this arrangement, those Christian states you spoke of will clearly understand why you signed a separate peace, and you will be able, in turn, to offer them preferential treatment in Ottoman trade, according to how little trouble they each cause you. The sultan does not care how much you charge them to carry their goods."

Antonio and Seraglio had studied the value of this eventuality while preparing for the negotiations. Venice's Bureau of State Statistics had calculated for them that this trade would be worth at least seventy-five thousand ducats annually. Antonio could feel the excitement course through his body. He was about to respond to Ali when Seraglio suddenly slammed his fist onto the table, making everyone else in the room jump with surprise.

"Twenty thousand! For that paltry sum the sultan can keep his damned monopoly. Do you think the Venetian merchant fleet will carry only Venetian goods? How else will the sultan rebuild his war-ravaged economy? What Christian port will allow a single one of his ships past its breakwater?"

Antonio jumped in.

"Abdullah Ali, I apologize for my friend's harsh words. He is not as schooled in diplomatic protocol as you and I, but his point is well taken. If you will halve the tribute—and that is certainly what it is—to ten thousand ducats annually and make the payment due at the *end* of the year, instead of at the beginning, I think I can convince the Senate, the doge, and his *Signoria* to agree to your terms. By delaying our annual payment to the year's end, we will have the security of knowing the sultan will forfeit ten thousand ducats if he ever breaks the treaty."

The Turks exchanged glances. Things were moving too quickly. Karamani looked especially worried. Antonio had only to explain the terms to the Senate and let the debate begin. Abdullah Ali and his two colleagues had to convince the sultan to accept the terms, and he could be a difficult and unforgiving master.

"You have given us much to consider. Let us meet at the same time tomorrow and you shall have your answer."

With the day's negotiations ended, the Turks returned to their comfortable but sequestered accommodations.

A ntonio informed Doge Mocenigo and his closest advisers of the progress he had made. They told him to proceed with drafting the document for their approval in the event that the Turks accepted. If they did not, he was to offer more tribute but all payments in arrears to better guarantee that the sultan would honor his own peace terms.

The next morning, Antonio and Seraglio rose early to plan how they would execute these instructions.

"Seraglio, two questions still concern me. First, how will we justify our acceptance of the Turk's peace offer to the rest of the Christian world? Second, how will we keep from being dragged into a war against the Turks by Milan or Florence, with whom we have alliances that predate the peace we are about to sign with the Turks?"

His friend thought for a moment. Then his face lit up as his thick black eyebrows danced on his wrinkled forehead.

"What if we tell Ali that we do not want language in the treaty that would restrict either of us from breaking the peace?" Seraglio grinned smugly, self-satisfied with his creative solution.

"Why do you say that?" asked Antonio.

"Because if we want it, the Turks will think it is bad for them and oppose it. Once the treaty is signed, we can tell our allies in Milan and Florence that the terms of the treaty prevent us from waging war on the Turks."

Twenty thousand Arsenal workers, awakened at six o'clock by the sonorous tolling of Il Marangone, the giant bell in the Campanile di San Marco, had already made their way through the city to the sprawling shipyard by the time the Turks arrived.

"For men who have lost nearly every battle for the last twenty years, you Venetians certainly drive a hard bargain," began Ali.

"Have you forgotten the times we defeated you on the sea?" corrected Antonio. "Without control of the seas, you could never defeat us."

Ali became silent, disdain on his face. "We will need to agree upon a schedule for formally transferring control of all the possessions you will cede to us. Further, we will need to draft the terms under which Venice will be permitted to trade in our territories. Of course, despite the annual payment of ten thousand ducats, you will still have to pay the customary two percent tax on all goods that pass through our territory."

"Of course, but there is one more consideration we must discuss. Foreign Minister, we have treaties with other states that compel each to come to the aid of the other if attacked. To avoid upsetting these states, I suggest we do not announce any language that makes clear our peace shall last for ten years."

The Turks looked at each other, shifting uncomfortably in their chairs.

"That will not do," interjected Karamani. "The sultan would never agree to it."

"He is right, signore. We must make public the details of the peace. How else can we prevent our overzealous sea captains from taking Venetian ships as prizes or yours from taking ours?"

Antonio expelled a long breath and looked at Seraglio.

"This will give the doge and his counselors much pause."

"I am afraid, signore, that I must insist. The sultan needs guarantees that you Venetians can be trusted, too. A publicly announced treaty is not easily violated without incurring the distrust of others—even Christian states."

"Very well, I will have the terms drafted for you to take back to Istanbul. Our ambassador in Alexandria will advise yours when the Senate has ratified the treaty. Let this day, the twenty-fourth of January, 1479, be a day forever celebrated by both of our peoples as the day reason prevailed and our long and costly war was finally ended."

As the guard closed the door behind them, Antonio fell heavily into his chair and threw his head back, relieved. He had gained Venice the best terms possible. While she had ceded to the Turks possessions that they had already won, he had restored her trade in the eastern Mediterranean and, equally important, had crafted terms that he hoped the pope and the rest of the Christian West would loudly decry but ultimately do nothing about as Venetian ships once again carried the riches of the East to every European port.

It did not take long for the sultan to test the Venetians' willingness to abide by the treaty. The following year, he invaded the Italian mainland, landing a force in the Kingdom of Naples, at Otranto, on the southeastern Adriatic coast.

Even the Venetians cringed, however, when the Turks made the place, barely a week's journey overland from Rome, the largest slave market in the Mediterranean; they sold Christian men, women, and children there like common cattle. Many in Italy feared a large-scale attack by the sultan to follow up his success at Otranto, but it was not to be. Two months later, the sultan instead attacked the main fortress on the island of Rhodes. For 170 years it had been the possession of the Order of the Knights of St. John—the Knights Hospitaller—and the seat of the order's Grand Master, currently Pierre d'Aubusson.

Antonio went to the Piazza San Marco an hour early and, to clear his head, slowly strolled around its vast expanse. It was a warm June day. Hundreds of Venetians were out enjoying the sunshine. Twenty minutes before the Senate meeting was scheduled to begin, he entered the Doges' Palace, walked up the broad staircase to the third floor, and entered the chamber. He was surprised to see that so many of his colleagues were already there, huddled in groups of three and four, hotly debating the reasons why the special meeting had been called.

The room was not as large as the cavernous Great Council Chamber but was no less ornate. It could easily accommodate more than two hundred men, seated on seven long benches perpendicular to a raised dais where the doge, his *Signoria,* and other assorted officials presided. The room was lit by a bank of huge windows along the far side and decorated with large paintings by old Venetian masters that filled the available space on each wall and ceiling.

Black-robed *nobili* nervously awaited the arrival of the doge and his *Signoria,* who had met in advance. Everyone had been stunned by the rumors that had been sweeping the city all morning—that the Ottoman sultan Muhammad II had died unexpectedly. If that was true, his death could profoundly affect Venice and her fortunes. In her entire eight-hundred-year history, he had proven to be La Serenissima's most implacable foe.

When Doge Giovanni Mocenigo and his entourage entered the room, all but one of the sixty senators was in his seat. That one was old Dolfin, a real Turk hater who, Antonio heard, had died just the day before. Antonio would not have been surprised to see his corpse sitting in his usual spot on this momentous night. Even death itself could not have made him miss this.

The doge, dressed in his formal gold brocaded robe and *corno,* took his seat. He was the only one allowed to wear his hat in the chamber. Next, his six counselors, dressed in scarlet robes that signified they were the procurators of each of the city's six *sestieri,* took their places. High court judges, senior administrators, and leading military officers completed those in attendance.

Realizing that the doge had arrived, the people in the room quickly quieted down. Every pair of eyes was riveted on the doge, searching for a clue to what he was about to relate. Knowing him well, Antonio thought he detected a trace of a smile in the pronounced wrinkles at the corners of his eyes.

Slowly the sixty-two-year-old doge stood erect and stretched out his arms. "I bring you news from our *bailo* in Istanbul. Sultan Muhammad II is dead."

Antonio and every other man in the room jumped to his feet, cheering wildly in one unified, tumultuous roar. The doge gladly permitted the rare break in decorum. He knew it would be impossible to restore order prematurely. It was a victory twenty years in the making, won by God, not man. Finally, as the raucous celebration subsided and most of the senators retook their seats, the doge continued.

"The sultan has two sons, Bayezid, the eldest, and Cem. We do not yet know which will be the new sultan or what course he will pursue toward Venice or the Christian West, but we believe this presents us with a golden opportunity to renegotiate our treaty with the Turks."

Most in the crowd nodded. This was indeed blessed news.

"With the Senate's agreement, we will send a representative to Istanbul to congratulate the new sultan and to discuss our peace arrangement. If history is any teacher, we can expect much disarray in Istanbul for the next few months. We will strike quickly at a time when the new sultan is looking to avoid problems and seeking allies to consolidate his accession to the sultanate."

One of the Ten rose and was quickly recognized by the doge.

"Did the *bailo* report what caused the sultan's death?"

"No, he died while planning to go and personally lead another attack on Rhodes, but there is speculation that in recent years Muhammad had lost favor with other powerful men in his court. Recently his vizier, Karamani Muhammad Pasha convinced him to allow his Sipahi officers to take valuable parcels of land from rightful owners to generate more tax income. The Janissaries objected. So, of course, did the original landowners, many of whom were clerics. This strife resulted in his two sons choosing sides in the court struggle. Now we shall see which faction proves to be dominant."

The doge looked over at Antonio and smiled.

"I now place before the Senate a proposal to have Signor Antonio Ziani go to Istanbul immediately to congratulate the new sultan. Surely one of the two aspirants to the sultanate will have murdered his brother by the time our representative arrives, in the finest traditions of the Ottoman Empire."

The room erupted in laughter. How differently the Venetians chose their doge.

Antonio's excitement was tempered by his knowledge of Bayezid. Melancholy, stubborn, and superstitiously religious, he would be hard to deal with. If Bayezid became sultan, a likely outcome since he was the eldest son, Antonio was doubtful he would easily give up the gains won in the previous negotiation. But if Cem were still alive, the Venetians could use him as a lever to pry concessions out of Bayezid.

S eraglio looked at his old friend and smiled. Antonio was fast asleep at his desk, his head thrown back in his chair. He had worked through the night, long after Seraglio had retired, laboring to finish preparations for their upcoming voyage to Istanbul to meet with the new sultan, Bayezid II. Three days earlier, they had received word that Bayezid had outbribed his younger brother, Cem, securing the support of the powerful Janissaries and assuring his accession to the sultanate.

Seraglio studied the deep lines in Antonio's weathered face, partially obscured by his full beard. His once sharp features showed signs of puffiness. He had never before seen him look so old. He reached out and gently shook his friend.

Antonio stirred; his eyes fluttered open.

"I bring news," said Seraglio, barely able to contain his excitement.

"What is it?" replied Antonio as he rubbed his temples and smiled back.

"More details from the Porte," as the Ottoman capital was now referred to. "This note arrived from the doge just a few minutes ago."

As Seraglio handed it to him, Antonio could see that it bore the personal seal of the *capi,* who were required to read and approve any written communication by the doge before it was sent. He broke the seal and carefully read it.

"We have learned that Cem, the sultan's younger brother, eluded Bayezid's assassins and slipped away to Rhodes. It seems that he had made a prior agreement with the Knights' Grand Master, Pierre d'Aubusson. In exchange for a large sum, he obtained d'Aubusson's guarantee of safe passage and has placed himself under the Grand Master's protection."

"What?" Antonio interrupted himself. "I cannot believe that the Grand Master would agree to such an arrangement."

"There must be more to it than meets the eye," countered Seraglio.

Antonio kept reading. He began to chuckle. He looked up from the paper and laughed out loud—something he rarely did anymore.

"The old fox! After he welcomed Cem to the island, the Grand Master placed him under house arrest. Then he sent his ambassador to the Porte and informed Bayezid that if the Turks did not end their designs on his island, he would provide Cem with enough money to bribe the Janissaries into placing him on the throne."

Seraglio whistled. "It would seem that Cem made a good bargain."

"Not exactly." Antonio smiled. "There is still more. Our ambassador in Rome has reported that d'Aubusson's second in command met with the pope last week."

Now it was Seraglio's turn to interrupt.

"That can mean only one thing," he asserted confidently. "While Cem celebrates the wisdom of his decision to seek the protection of the Knights, anticipating a long life of luxury, d'Aubusson has other plans."

"Yes, it is the ambassador's opinion that after relieving Cem of most of his gold, in return for a promise of protection, the Grand Master is not yet satisfied. Now he is negotiating with the pope to turn Cem over to the Holy Father for safekeeping."

"No doubt for another large sum in return," observed Seraglio. "And because Cem is a Muslim, the poor bastard cannot even obtain an indulgence in return for his money from the Holy Father. He will probably spend the rest of his life in some dark, stinking dungeon."

"Whatever Cem's problems may be, this is great news for Venice and for us."

Antonio grabbed his friend by the shoulders and squeezed him. "No doubt the pope, with Cem in his possession, will use him to cow the new sultan into turning away from his designs on the West. Better still, there is now no need for us to go to Istanbul!"

A ntonio was right. After paying a large fee to the Knights, the pope took possession of Cem and handed him over to the King of Naples. The unfortunate would-be sultan would spend the rest of his life in a Neapolitan prison. Unable to avoid the threat of his brother's return, Bayezid would wait years before finding the courage to contemplate resuming hostilities toward the West.

The following month, the *bailo* in Istanbul reported that the new sultan had canceled the annual payment of ten thousand ducats and cut in half the 2 percent tax on Venetian trade in Ottoman lands.

15

The Ferrara War

The long war with the Turks was finally over. Venice was at peace.
Now she began to methodically rebuild her shattered economy as
her resourceful merchants and shrewd financiers shifted their efforts
back to trade.

When the Turks invaded Apulia and took Otranto, Venice stood by and
did nothing, emulating her neighbors who, for decades, had stood idly by as
Venice fought the Turks alone. The pope and the King of Naples, whose
territory the Turks had taken, beseeched Venice to help them, but she would
not, coldly citing the terms of her treaty, which prevented her from doing
so. More than anything, Venice, sorely weakened in strength and now in
reputation, needed time to recover. But how much would her Italian neighbors give her, furious as they were at the separate peace she had signed with
the Turks? Exhausted, Venice was more vulnerable than she had been in
centuries.

The morning dawned bright and sunny, warm enough for Antonio to
take his breakfast in the seclusion of his rooftop garden. He had invited
Constantine and Seraglio to join him there. Despite his beard, the fresh salt-
laced sea breeze made his face tingle. It was cool, but Antonio preferred to

be outside and had insisted on eating in the garden despite the chilly early spring air. His servant, trembling from the cold, had wiped the dew from table and chairs, careful not to question his master's decision.

Seraglio joined him, interested to hear what had happened in the Senate the night before, even at the cost of shivering through breakfast. His joints ached now, and his hands and feet always seemed to be stiff. As he watched the first bees of the season humming from flower to flower, he looked out over the rooftops at the Campanile di San Marco with its pale emerald roof tiles to the blue-gray Adriatic on the horizon.

Constantine emerged from the stairwell, smiling. "My boys are getting smarter every day. You would not believe how they converse—just like young men," he said, every inch a proud father.

Seraglio grinned back. "I remember when you were eight years old. You asked a thousand questions each day. Which is the more inquisitive?"

"Honestly, Seraglio, I cannot say. Sebastiano asks more questions, but Tommaso asks the more thoughtful ones."

"They complement each other well," observed Antonio. "You must always ensure they remain close and learn to depend upon each other."

"Father, I think it is time for you to begin teaching them about our Venetian heritage. They are old enough to understand now."

Constantine was referring to an old family tradition. The Zianis had always relied upon the finest tutors to educate their children in language, mathematics, science, literature, music, and religion but had always reserved for themselves the task of inculcating their young with Venetian history and values. This included an understanding of the government and what it meant to be born a *nobile*. Unfortunately, Constantine's grandfather had died before he was born. His father had seen personally to this important portion of his education. Now he wanted to take advantage of his father's vast experience to help shape his sons into men, Venetian merchants of the first order.

"Yes, Constantine, it *is* time, and I have been looking forward to it."

Antonio welcomed the opportunity to ensure his progeny would increase the fortunes of the House of Ziani, as he had always tried to do. He saw his life as an extension of his forbears'. Through him, they had attained a sort of immortality, as he would through Constantine, Sebastiano, and Tommaso. He hoped he would live a long time, long enough to complete the important work that still remained.

"So, Antonio, what happened at the Senate meeting last night?" asked Seraglio.

"We have been at peace with the Turks for less than two years. In that time, we have made great strides in replenishing our treasury with taxes gleaned from our rebuilt commerce. But now, I am afraid, the specter of war looms once again."

"The rumors are true, then?" interrupted Seraglio.

"Yes, the perfidious Duke Ercole of Ferrara has decided to repay our loyalty with ingratitude. After we supported him when his nephew, Niccolò, tried to usurp his dukedom, he now brazenly defies us in return."

"The Estes are a spirited family," observed Seraglio as he turned to Constantine. "Ercole's father, Niccolò III, had so many women there is a saying in Ferrara: 'On both sides of the Po they are all Niccolò's sons.'" Once he even named his bastard son Leonello, Ercole's half brother, as his successor."

"Spirited, perhaps, but without honor," interjected Antonio. "Listen to the latest news from Ferrara."

Antonio took a long drink of wine from his glass, carefully replacing it on the white linen tablecloth before he continued.

"Three months ago we began receiving reports that, after buying his salt exclusively from us for the last seventy years—at fair prices too, I might add—Ercole ordered salt pans to be built at the mouth of the Po. As you know, pans are built in the late winter and harvested after the summer sun bakes the vast fields of salt, removing the water, creating about a thousand tons per pan.

"When we protested, he informed the Senate that his obligation to purchase salt only from Venice was ended." Antonio was becoming agitated. "Then, last month he increased the tension between us by contesting our border delineation. Now we hear he has induced a local vicar to excommunicate a Venetian consul in the Polesine, even ignoring the wishes of his own bishop! It is as though he is daring us to declare war."

"Antonio, I believe that is exactly what he wishes. All of Italy knows we are in a weakened state after our long war with the Turks. For years Ferrara has been a semi-independent state at the pleasure of Venice. So long as the duke purchased his salt from us and behaved, we allowed him to rule, unmolested. Now he thinks the Republic's power is in decline, and he is casting us off like old shoes."

"Ercole is renowned as a lover of the arts—hardly a warlike duke. Someone else's hand is behind his sudden change," said Antonio, rubbing his head as he thought.

"Perhaps the pope?" interjected Constantine, betraying his unfamiliarity with Italian politics.

"I would hardly think so," replied Antonio. "No, this is the work of his father-in-law, King Ferrante of Naples. He is paying us back for our failure to support him against the Turks, when they took Otranto. Now that the sultan has died and the Turks have abandoned their toehold in Italy, he is free to come at us."

"Hmm. That makes sense, but Ferrante is not powerful enough to convince Duke Ercole to risk a fight with us. Someone else must be in league with them," said Seraglio.

"I agree. The doge thinks it is Duke Lorenzo de' Medici of Florence. He wants to weaken us so that he can continue to be Rome's banker, a lucrative role that we had to abandon while we were at war with the Turks."

"What will we do?" asked Constantine. "Will we fight?"

"What do you say?" Seraglio liked to challenge his protégé whenever he could.

"I fear if we do not fight, all of Italy will think the old lion has lost his teeth. True, men like me will have to take up arms, but, yes, I believe we must fight. Our honor and our reputation are at stake. I shall volunteer at once."

Antonio looked at his son, who was so full of fight. Once he was like that, too. He thought back to when Venice had decided to go to Constantinople's aid against the Turks in 1453. At thirty, Antonio had been only a little older than Constantine was now. Then, he had volunteered to fight, too.

Now he was more familiar with the ways of the world. Then, he believed that glory was something old men had invented to encourage young men to fight the wars they themselves had started. Now he believed that glory was the reward for winning, not the reason for fighting. But this time, Constantine was right. If Venice wanted respect, she *had* to fight. The upstart duke had to be put in his place. The question was, Who was behind him? Was it Lorenzo de' Medici, Duke of Florence, or Ludovico Sforza, Regent of Milan? Perhaps it was both of them—and what about the pope? What hand did Sixtus have in all this?

"Seraglio, Girolamo Riario, the pope's nephew, is at this very moment here in Venice, on one of his trips to acquire art. I think it is time for me to talk to him, but first I will talk with the doge."

Antonio's meeting with the doge confirmed his suspicions. The entire diplomatic service, spies, and even the Ten were called into action to determine the extent of the new threat facing the Republic. It was clear that someone was behind Duke Ercole's blustering public defiance of his erstwhile benefactor, Venice. Doge Mocenigo and his counselors agreed that Antonio should discreetly meet with Girolamo and determine the pope's interest in the matter. Who would he support if it came to war?

Antonio decided to invite Girolamo to the Ca' Ziani to avoid any chance of their conversation being overheard. Only the day before, a man was arrested for spying for Ferrara as he sat talking to Arsenal workers in one of the taverns near the great shipyard. Antonio knew he could not be too careful.

At eight o'clock, Lord Riario arrived and was ushered into the Ca' Ziani's well-appointed library, where Antonio conducted all of his official business. They ate a fine dinner of venison and broiled fish, followed by wine and sweet pastries.

The Venetian palate, always partial to salt, which was plentiful due to the Republic's perpetual monopoly on that essential commodity, had grown accustomed to sugar only after the Crusaders brought it back from the East—one of the many influences of the Islamic world on the West. The recent war with the Turks had choked off trade in the sweet substance, forcing Venetians to rely almost exclusively upon honey. Now, with the war over, all the Venetians, especially the bakers and children, were again enjoying the pleasing sweet taste of sugar.

A layman, Girolamo Riario, Pope Sixtus IV's nephew, had no designs on the papacy. His avoidance of the spiritual made him the ideal emissary for his uncle, who sent him to conduct secular affairs. Sixtus made him Captain of Castel Sant'Angelo, Lord of Imola and Forlì, two papal territories. And to increase Girolamo's status among Italian nobility, the pope even arranged his marriage with the beautiful fourteen-year-old Catherine Sforza, the illegitimate but accepted daughter of the murdered Duke Galeazzo Sforza of Milan. Throughout Italy, embarrassing rumors even persisted behind closed doors that Girolamo himself was actually sired by Sixtus.

Antonio would not underestimate this man. He had the pope's ear and had already been involved in enough intrigues for a man twenty years older. He had learned his craft from the master, old Sixtus himself. One such intrigue had almost succeeded.

In 1478 the failed Pazzi Conspiracy to murder Florence's Duke Lorenzo and his brother Giuliano de' Medici, while they attended mass on Easter Sunday, had as its design to put Girolamo on the throne as duke. Giuliano was assassinated but Lorenzo survived. The wrathful duke rounded up the conspirators, who were horribly tortured, revealing details of the plot. Every member of the Pazzi family was hunted down and killed. Under torture, some implicated the pope, although there was never any real proof of his direct involvement. After Lorenzo hanged one plotter, the archbishop of Pisa, and threw another, Girolamo's eighteen-year-old brother, Cardinal

Raffaele Riario, in prison, Sixtus excommunicated Lorenzo and laid an interdict on Florence. To say that relations had been stormy between the papacy and Florence was an understatement.

He is tall but very heavy, thought Antonio, as he looked across the table at his guest; his build was typical of men who owed their wealth and status to others. He had a beardless face, framed by long brown hair that flowed down to his shoulders, setting off his self-assured, somewhat arrogant demeanor. His thick lips, broad nose, and sad eyes, set deep within dark circles, made him look older than his thirty-nine years. He was well educated but unacquainted with the affairs of common men.

"I prefer the food here in Venice to anywhere else. Certainly it is far superior to that served in Rome." Riario spilled some half-chewed vegetables from his half-opened mouth, wiped his face with a cloth, and belched loudly as he reached for his glass of wine.

Antonio smiled politely. "We do not rely so heavily on the tomato as you do in the south. We also use spices as they were intended, not too much and not too little."

"Well said, Signor Ziani." His guest paused for a moment and then put down his knife and fork, perhaps to cool them off, thought Antonio, careful not to smile, even under cover of his beard.

"The invitation you sent said that you had business to discuss. Would it have something to do with the Duke of Ferrara?" He smiled, showing his full set of pearly white teeth, a rare sight in a man of his age.

"Is the Holy Father aware that the duke is building salt pans in the Polesine, in violation of our long-standing agreement with him?"

Girolamo's smile disappeared.

"He is aware that forces are at work to further weaken La Serenissima's strength here in Italy. After your refusal to help him and the King of Naples expel the Turks, he learned two things. The first is that Venice thinks only of herself and is not concerned with Christendom. Second, and more damaging to your reputation, your help was not necessary. We were able to rid the Apulian coast of the Turks without the use of your fleet." He swiped his hand through the air in a dismissive gesture.

Antonio ignored the invitation to argue, knowing he could not win. He decided to employ his favorite tool—silence.

It was so quiet, the only sounds were the gentle slapping of water in the Grand Canal against the stones that bound it and the calls of a few gondoliers still at work after dark. Girolamo shifted in his chair uneasily.

"Surely you know how disappointed my uncle was. He has always had a soft spot in his heart for Venice. It hurt him deeply, to say nothing of his embarrassment, when you Venetians refused his personal request to send men and ships."

More silence.

"Why do you remain silent?"

"I am trying to decide if you actually mean what you are saying. Or do you simply think I am foolish enough to believe your ridiculous assertions?"

Girolamo slapped his thigh and laughed. "The Holy Father asked me to admonish you a bit before we throw you a bone. He does not want you Venetians to take his good graces for granted." He pushed his empty plate to the side and leaned forward.

"Signor Ziani, ever since that bastard in Florence accused the Holy Father of complicity in the Pazzi Conspiracy and threw my brother Raffael in prison, my uncle has been spoiling for revenge. If we join forces now, we can each settle a score. Duke Ercole's behavior is merely a symptom of a disease that has infected all of Italy."

"What disease do you speak of, Lord Girolamo?"

"I speak of arrogance. The Duke of Ferrara has been bitten by the same dog that has bitten the Dukes of Florence and Milan. That dog lives in Naples. I speak of Ferrante, Ercole's father-in-law, who seems to control his every action these days."

Girolamo stood and leaned on the table, his face flushed crimson.

"We are facing a conspiracy of idiots who actually believe that they are our equals. There are no greater powers in all of Italy than the Serene Republic of Venice and the Holy Catholic Church. All that business with the Turks made us both appear to be—how should I say it?—impotent. Now these rascals band together, little more than common brigands, as they seek to cast off their yokes forever."

"Yokes, Lord Girolamo? What yokes do you speak of?"

"Surely you are not serious? I am speaking of the Church's control of their hearts and minds and your control of their fortunes with your dominance in salt, shipping, and a hundred other desired goods."

He sat down, breathing heavily, never moving his eyes from his host.

"We have confirmed that Milan, Florence, Naples, and Bologna have entered into a secret treaty with Duke Ercole to come to his defense if he is attacked by Venice."

It is time to ask him the question that matters most.

"If Venice attacks the Duke of Ferrara, what will the Holy Father do?"

"That depends upon your answer to one question." Girolamo smiled like a hunter who has finally trapped his quarry. "What are you prepared to give the pope in exchange for his unfailing support?"

"It will take a day or two for me to apprise the doge, his *Signoria,* and the Senate of your offer and to respond to your question."

"I have nothing but time. You know where to find me."

After Antonio recounted his conversation with Girolamo, Doge Mocenigo ordered the Pregadi bell rung from the Campanile di San Marco, calling the senators to the Doges' Palace. The meeting began with a report from one of the Ten.

"Duke Ercole has not softened his stand. Our spies tell us he is bent on resisting our will to the point of war. It is also our opinion that if we do not force him to dismantle his salt pans in the Po Delta, he will destroy our monopoly as our other customers flock to him to buy their salt at a lower price."

"What do we hear from the other Italian capitals?" asked the doge.

"The Dukes of Ferrara, Milan, Florence, and Bologna are all in league, arrayed against us with the King of Naples. They are waiting to see what we will do. They do not want to be seen as aggressors, for they want to attract the maximum number of soldiers to their cause when the time for war is at hand."

"And what will the pope do?" asked one of the doge's advisers.

"I can answer that," said Antonio rising to his feet. "I spoke with his nephew, Lord Girolamo of Imola and Forlì. He says the Holy Father is disposed to support us, but it will come at a price. As you know, Sixtus hates Lorenzo de' Medici and has little love for Ferrante either, whom he sees as the instigator of all this trouble."

"What does he want?" asked Giovanni Soranzo.

"I do not know what Sixtus desires. Lord Girolamo did not tell me. However, I believe that if we lavish awards and honors on his nephew, he will support us."

Antonio sat. Now it was the doge's turn to speak.

"Let us make him an honorary citizen of Venice. Better still, let us make him an honorary senator. I cannot remember when anyone else has ever been given that honor."

The thought made Antonio and most of the others cringe. He could not think of anything more abhorrent, but perhaps it would enable them to avoid a costly bribe. Money was in short supply, and much would be needed to finance the ill-timed impending war.

The doge put his proposal to a quick vote and it passed, nearly unanimously. Finally, the Senate agreed that discreet inquiries were to be made to find and hire a *condottiere* to command the Venetian army.

When he was informed he had been made an honorary citizen and senator of Venice, Girolamo beamed with joy. He had all the money he would ever need, but with this, the Venetians had bought themselves an ally. Back in Rome, he soon convinced his uncle to throw in his lot with the Venetians.

On the strength of their secret arrangement with Sixtus IV, the Venetian ambassador to Ferrara informed the duke that he would have to buy his salt from Venice. When news reached the Rialto that he refused still, the Senate levied war taxes and sent for Roberto da San Severino, Count Cajazzo, a sixty-four-year-old professional soldier of the highest repute, to lead their army. He had recently become embroiled in a failed rebellion against his cousin, Duke Ludovico of Milan, barely escaping to Genoa with a dozen of his closest supporters, including two of his sons, Galeazzo and Antonio Maria, forfeiting all of his lands and possessions.

He first made his way to Siena, where he recruited five hundred mercenaries; then he went directly to Venice, where he immediately made an agreement with the government. In return for a three-year term of service as overall commander of Venice's land forces, the count would receive an annual wage of eighty thousand florins and half of all ransom monies he could obtain.

After completing their business, the doge ordered the captain of the *Bucintoro,* his golden ceremonial barge, used exclusively for state ceremonies and special visitors, to row him, the count, and his party to Chioggia, a port just north of the mouth of the River Adige. This river marked the northern boundary of the Polesine, the band of fertile alluvial plain between the Adige and the Po. There, the doge conferred upon Count Cajazzo the rank of *nobile* of the Republic and, as a personal gift, gave him a ducal horse valued at two hundred ducats. The next day, the count and his bodyguards rode to Padua, where he held a council of war with Provveditore Antonio Loredan, the hero of Scutari, and formally assumed, from him, command of the Venetian army.

Constantine was relieved when his servants finally finished pitching his tent. The moist April air was still cold, but most of all, it felt good to be sheltered from the incessant winds that blew off the Adriatic, just fifteen miles to the east. It had been a long, wet ride from Chioggia to Padua as their horses struggled through the infernal quagmires that, in the dry summer, the inhabitants of the Veneto called roads.

The bone-penetrating rawness reminded him of those long months he had spent besieged in the bleak La Roccaforte above Scutari. It was hard to believe that eight years had passed since then. They had been good years too, bringing him a beautiful wife and two fine sons, but now he was at war again. It was time to pay for that good life he had enjoyed. This time, he thought, it would be much different. Now the Venetians would be the attackers and besiegers. He had never before fought in a field battle.

He leaned back on his camp stool and smiled as he looked at the shiny new suit of armor his father had given him before he had left Venice. Antonio had had it made in Nuremberg by the finest armorer in all of Germany. Seraglio said that the Germans had surpassed the Italians in their knowledge of steel, although Constantine did not think his new suit of armor was as beautifully finished as his last one. He reached for the cuirass and ran his hand over the smooth, shiny steel. Better to be well protected than simply to strike a dashing figure on the battlefield. There was no sense in attracting the attention of the enemy's crossbowmen. At fifty yards, their powerful bolts could pierce even this armor. It was little wonder that the pope had once tried to outlaw the crossbow on the grounds that it was too lethal.

It was interesting, he thought, what Seraglio had said about men's armor reflecting their values. The Italians sacrificed protection for beauty, while the Germans preferred protection—their harder steel was more difficult to etch with decorative markings. He wondered what kind of armor his enemies would wear.

Constantine was excited. Provveditore Loredan had chosen him to be one of his aides, a great honor, but Constantine had been surprised when he learned that Loredan would not take overall command. Too old now for vigorous campaigning, he had requested a *condottiere* be employed to command the army. Still, it would be a comfort to every Venetian soldier to know the great Antonio Loredan was with them. He was as sly as a fox.

"Signor Ziani." Elmo, a bodyguard, suddenly appeared. "Does the tent meet your approval? Niccolò and I had a devil of a time helping the servants put it up in this accursed wind."

"It is fine, thank you, Elmo."

"I was asked to inform you that there will be a council of war in Provveditore Loredan's tent after supper. Count Cajazzo and his company are due to arrive later today. He sent a courier ahead to make arrangements for them here in the camp tonight."

Elmo and Niccolò, Constantine's bodyguards, were not related by birth, but they were closer than most brothers. If they had looked alike, he would have sworn they were twins. His father had hired them to accompany him to war. Both Venetians, they were proud *cittadini* with long records of military service.

Elmo was tall and sinewy. With his bald head and diminutive chin, he was an eagle in human form. Constantine supposed that his careless sense of humor—he would speak whatever was on his mind—had gotten him into so much trouble in his life that he had learned to fight, eventually becoming a professional soldier out of necessity. Elmo was always thinking, always defeating problems with his wits. He was the optimist.

Niccolò was short and stocky, a bear of a man with deep-set, dark eyes that made him look like he had just lost a fight. But Constantine doubted that he had lost many. He was tough. Elmo had the brains, but Niccolò supplied the brawn. Just the day before, Constantine had seen him lift a wagon wheel, by himself, when it had lodged in a deep hole. Niccolò overcame problems by ignoring them, refusing to allow them to divert his attention from his aim. To him, nothing was impossible.

At first, Constantine had been indignant when his father hired bodyguards to protect him, and they had argued about it. But now, at war, he had to admit his father was right. It was a comfort to have them by his side. He would remember to do the same for his sons.

C onstantine had just finished eating his supper when he heard wild cheering outside. He rose from his table and went out. It was twilight, but in the distance he could see a party of horsemen approaching the camp up the winding road from Padua. One was carrying the Milanese flag—a white banner emblazoned with a red cross. It was Roberto da San Severino, Count Cajazzo and his troops.

He rode into camp like the *Bucintoro* rowed into the Bacino di San Marco on Ascension Day, waving to the enthusiastic Venetian soldiery, occasionally gesturing to his sons, who were basking in their father's glory as they rode behind him. The count and his men went straight to Loredan's tent, the crimson and gold Lion of St. Mark proudly flying above it.

Constantine hurried; he did not want to be late for the council of war that would, no doubt, begin as soon as the count arrived. Already he could see that the count was a man who wasted no time. Breathing heavily, Constantine caught up to them just as they were dismounting, their fine clothes spattered with mud up to their waists. He followed them into Loredan's tent and quietly took a place just inside the flaps. It was filled with about twenty men. Loredan quickly made introductions, and then the council of war began.

"Who will oppose us in the field?" asked the count.

"Being small, Ferrara will put into the field less than four thousand men, mostly garrison troops to hold their strong points near the bridges over the Adige and the Po," replied Loredan. "The Duke of Milan has sent his general, Federigo Montefeltro, Duke of Urbino, to lead his six thousand; about half are men-at-arms and the rest artillerists and infantry."

"Federigo is competent but defers too easily to Il Moro," observed the count, referring to Ludovico Sforza by his widely used nickname. "Let us hope the less experienced regent gives him plenty of advice." The count clasped his fingers tightly. "Who commands for Florence?"

"Your old enemy, Costanzo Sforza, Lord of Pesaro, will bring four thousand men-at-arms and two thousand others into the field."

The count glanced briefly to his two sons. They broke into broad smiles.

"Costanzo Sforza besieged us in Castelnuovo Scrivia after the rebellion against Il Moro failed, but we sallied forth one dark night and escaped to Genoa. He butchered those of our men who remained. It will be a pleasure to deal with him."

"Finally, King Ferrante of Naples has appointed his son, the Duke of Calabria, to lead his troops. Our spies tell us his army includes eight hundred Turks who deserted the sultan when he abandoned Otranto," said Loredan.

"So we fight the Turks? You Venetians should enjoy that. How many men will we put into the field?" asked the count.

"We have seven thousand, including five thousand men-at-arms, and many cannon for the siege. Many of the infantry are armed with crossbows, borrowed from our marines, there being no threat on the seas. The pope will field an army of about the same size as the Duke of Calabria's. He is looking for a *condottiere* to lead his forces, not wanting to entrust them to one of his nephews, who all lack military experience."

"I know," replied the count. "He tried to employ me, even offering more than your doge for my services." He smiled like a fox and turned to his sons.

Galeazzo, the elder laughed. "My father did not trust that the pope would pay him. He knew your doge was a man of his word. Better to have certain comfort than uncertain wealth."

Loredan smiled at the joke. Reputation is everything, he thought. That is why we must fight. Love us or hate us, all of Italy will know that we mean what we say.

The count continued. "The King of Naples cannot reach Ferrara without passing through the pope's lands. When the pope refuses him passage, at the very least, he will detain the Duke of Calabria for several weeks. He may even defeat him. This will disconcert Duke Ercole because his father-in-law exerts great influence on him. That leaves the two real villains in the piece, Il Moro and Lorenzo de' Medici. Forget the Bolognese. They are of no account and only fight because they are close neighbors of Duke Ercole.

"If we can quickly cross the Adige and the Po and threaten Ferrara itself, the armies of Milan and Florence will be forced to come to Ercole's aid instead of attacking toward Venice in the Veneto. I know them well, having fought many battles with and against them. Their morale is brittle. They will bluster and cheer when they are winning, but if things go badly, they will not have the stomach for a tough fight. Further, the reason the people rebelled against Il Moro was because of his rapacious taxation. He is already crushing his subjects with the highest taxes in all of Italy. Without access to gold from the pope or from Venice, he will have to pay his troops out of his own treasury. That, I promise you, he will not do for long—especially to prop up an upstart like Duke Ercole, whom all of Italy knows is in the wrong in this war."

Loredan had remained silent as the count spilled the contents of his fertile mind. Now he spoke with authority.

"Count Cajazzo, how do you suggest we proceed to bring this business to a rapid and satisfactory conclusion?"

"Tomorrow is the first of May. I suggest we march immediately. We will quickly cross the Adige and make straight for the Po, eliminating any fortress garrisons as we go, including the twin towers on the banks of the river at La Rocca di Ficarolo and La Rocca di Stellata. Then, with our rear cleared of the enemy, we will cross the Po and lay siege to Ferrara before the Neapolitan army can reinforce it. The duke will not want his beautiful city laid to waste over some salt.

"I suggest you send a small force to destroy his newly installed salt pans while you send your river galleys up the Po to La Rocca di Stellata, where the chain boom stretches across the river. We will join forces there to oppose whatever forces they array against us. Once we defeat them, we shall move on Ferrara."

"What shall we do if you have miscalculated and the Milanese and the Florentines do not march to support Ferrara but instead invade our *terra firma* lands to the north?" asked Loredan.

The count rubbed his short-cropped, tightly curled beard and smiled.

"Costanzo will take a week to pull on his armor, and Federigo would not relieve himself without first securing permission from Il Moro. In war, superior speed always defeats superior strength. We are closer to the main theater of war and will move faster, and we are nearly as strong as our opponents."

"Very well, then, Count Cajazzo. We accept your plan as our own. Let us march tomorrow. God willing, by late summer Ferrara will be invested and, to preserve his dukedom, Ercole will be begging to pay a premium for the salt he buys from us."

The count laughed loudly and slapped his thigh.

"Only the devil himself could have conceived of anything as glorious and brilliant as war. By what other means can a man turn salt into gold! Behold, my sons, a *condottiere* has greater powers than an alchemist!"

After more than thirty years, Giovanni Soranzo was not going to fight for the Republic when she was at war. Knowing this would be a conflict fought primarily on land, not on the sea, he would instead raise his eight-year-old son, Carlo, to be a man. He often thought of Enrico, now far away in Florence, under the tutelage of Cosimo, Giovanni's cousin. He wished Enrico had returned to Venice to answer her call for soldiers, but he had not come. How could he, Giovanni Soranzo, have raised a coward? Since Florence had thrown her support to Duke Ercole of Ferrara, Soranzo's arrangement with Lorenzo de' Medici had ended. Now, as part of a consortium of Venetian bankers, Giovanni loaned money to the pope to help finance the Holy Father's part in the war. When Cosimo returned to Venice, he reported that Enrico had disappeared, failing to come to work one day. Neither Cosimo nor he had heard from Enrico since. Soranzo expected that his adopted son would turn up sooner or later, when the money ran out.

Carlo was bigger than other boys his age, and what a fighter. He was everything that Enrico was not. Soranzo blessed the day that Carlo was born. If only Isabella could have seen him now. She had died four months earlier, never really regaining her health after bringing Carlo into the world. He missed his wife, but her absence only seemed to make him lavish even more love and attention on Carlo.

Before she died, she had employed the most sought-after tutor in Venice to school Carlo—her legacy to her son. The change in the boy since then had been remarkable. He was intelligent, well mannered, and, most of all, displayed courage befitting a Venetian. Someday he would be head of the House of Soranzo. Perhaps it was best that Enrico had gone. It made the future so simple to plan.

16

The Rock

onstantine was surprised when Provveditore Loredan chose him to serve as Count Cajazzo's personal liaison officer. He was thankful he would remain with the main body of the army and not go with the men who would be shivering, shin-deep in the Adriatic, as they destroyed the duke's precious salt pans.

His first meeting with the great *condottiere* lasted only a minute: Count Cajazzo visited Constantine's tent to personally deliver his instructions.

"You, Signor Ziani, are on my staff to provide me with information that will prove useful to me, when I request it, about Venetian troops. Otherwise, your role will be to observe and learn the ways of war. If you desire to engage in combat, you will do so at your own risk. I am successful in my craft because I place a greater value on preserving life than taking it. A good battle is one that results in my enemy's surrender, not his death. Corpses fetch no ransom. I have found that a man will fight more ferociously when he knows that his only alternative is death. Give him a way out—even as a prisoner to be ransomed—and he will most assuredly take it."

His sermon delivered, Count Cajazzo abruptly turned, parted the tent flaps, and disappeared, leaving Constantine alone to ponder his words.

. . .

Constantine, Elmo, and Niccolò were up at sunrise the next morning. By noon, the army had broken camp, loaded their baggage into nearly three hundred wagons and carts of every description, and begun their march to the Adige.

"An army can move no faster than its slowest wagon," sighed Elmo as he halted yet again to wait for the one ahead of them to move.

With Niccolò seated beside him, they rocked from side to side along the potholed road. It had not rained in a day, and the sun was warm, drying the road, except in the undulations wherever the column approached a stream or encountered low-lying swampy land, so common in the Polesine. Springtime had unleashed the annual torrents of snowmelt flowing down from the Dolomites and the Alps along the Adige and the Po.

Previously, Loredan had ordered the Venetian cavalry to screen the frontier, stopping all commerce from passing into Ferrarese territory. With no knowledge of the Venetians' intentions, the Ferrarese could only wait to react once the Venetians attacked.

Count Cajazzo's plan called for his cavalry to feint crossing the Adige at a bridge near the Marchesana Tower, along the most direct route to Ferrara, while his main body crossed farther to the west, over the old stone Roman bridge at Legnano and at the Polesine Abbey bridge. His plan worked perfectly, and the army met no opposition.

The next two days he devoted to building a plank road to cross the swamps between the two rivers in order to move his heavy artillery and baggage train. To defeat his plan, the Ferrarese dammed a canal between the two rivers, flooding the partially built plank road and destroying it, drowning some poor peasants and farmers in the process. Unperturbed, the count ordered his cavalry to punch a hole in the Po levee, allowing the water that had inundated the land to drain out of the swamps and back into the river. Within a week, the Venetian army had reached the Po, a few miles east of Ostiglia, about twenty miles from Ferrara, Ercole's capital city. After cannonballs rained down for two weeks on the two small fortresses there at Melara and Bergantino, the dispirited defenders surrendered.

It was then that the count learned from some prisoners that the Florentines and Milanese had moved faster than he had expected. The Duke of Urbino had sailed down the Po the week before with a fleet of river galleys and had occupied the twin fortresses at Ficarolo, on the north bank, and Stellata di Bondeno, on the south bank. As the Venetian army marched down the north bank of the Po, the count ordered raids to the east to clear the countryside of the enemy and to gather food and forage.

A courier brought news that the commander of the Venetian river flotilla had moved up the Po to a point just below the twin fortresses. He reported that Duke of Urbino had placed artillery in the bastions to defend the chain boom and had prevented Venetian ships from moving past. The count turned his attention to La Rocca di Ficarolo. Now the real fighting would begin.

T his man has boundless energy, thought Constantine as he listened intently to Count Cajazzo talking with his commanders. At sixty-four, he is older than my father, yet he still revels in the rigors of campaigning—like a true warrior.

"It is almost June and we have besieged Ficarolo for nearly two weeks. The weather has turned and the men are beginning to suffer from the heat. Soon the air will be teeming with swarms of insects, and our soldiers will begin dying from swamp fever."

He turned to Tommaso of Imola, the commander of his artillery. "What is your assessment of the situation?"

"Our enemy is strongly placed. Ficarolo is defended by about a thousand men. Who knows how many more are across the Po in La Rocca di Stellata? Under cover of its powerful guns, the Duke of Urbino is able to reinforce and supply the fortress each night without difficulty. The expert sighting of the twin fortresses, so close to one another, prevents us from surrounding La Rocca di Ficarolo without exposing our troops to a devastating flanking fire from La Rocca di Stellata, a short way across the river."

"We have nearly six thousand men under arms. Surely we should be able to reduce and storm Ficarolo," said Count Cajazzo.

"Until we complete our siege works, enabling us to place our artillery close enough to breach its walls and to prevent reinforcement and supply, in my opinion, we cannot successfully attack it."

"How much more time do you need to complete your preparations?"

"We are moving a battery of guns to the island tonight. In a week, we will be close enough to the fortress to blast a hole in it," replied the *condottiere* sharply.

He is frustrated and a little embarrassed that it is taking so long, thought Constantine.

"Very well, drive the men harder," said the count. "We must take the place before the League sends more reinforcements to Duke Ercole."

Tommaso saluted his superior and departed, obviously relieved the interview was ended. He was a proud soldier who did not like being reprimanded. When he had gone, the count turned to his sons and shook his head.

"He is a brave man, but too deliberate. This afternoon we shall visit the siege works. Then, tonight, we shall go to the island to be sure all goes according to plan."

The count turned to Constantine. "Come with us. You may learn something."

C onstantine followed Count Cajazzo and his sons, Galeazzo and Antonio Maria, as they slowly walked through the little village of Ficarolo, toward the river. In the distance, they could see La Rocca rising ominously above the trees. It was a square thirty-foot-tall stone tower, faced with hard-fired red brick. Each of its four sides was indented and at each corner, a small curved tower projected from the walls. This clever design enabled the defenders to fire down at anyone sheltering against the walls. As Constantine and the others neared it, they could see the fifteen-foot-wide moat that surrounded the fortress. The entire structure was topped by a stone roof, sheathed with lead to prevent flaming projectiles from setting it on fire. It looked impregnable to Constantine.

As they moved along the back side of a small stone house, they found the entrance to the trench dug by the engineers. They climbed down a ladder and began to move through it, passing bare-chested workers, dressed only in their pants and shoes. There was no need to keep one's head down; the trench was seven feet deep.

Constantine spotted Tommaso, who gestured to them to follow him. He had been informed in advance of the commander's visit to the siege works. They proceeded along a zigzag passage until they reached a section covered with stout planks. They were within range of the enemy's wall guns and crossbows now. It was oppressively hot, and the humid air was motionless. The trench reeked from the stench of a nearby latrine. Every few feet, a narrow space had been left in the roof to admit some sunlight and fresh air. At the end of the trench, steps led up to an observation platform wide enough to accommodate four men.

Right in front of them was the massive fortress. Constantine was so close to it, he could make out the faces of its defenders moving about inside the open windows near the top. Down below, he could see there was a single entrance to the place, only accessible across a narrow bridge over the moat and up a flight of stairs to the second level. Unless the walls were breached, there was no way to attack it. He could also see its twin, La Rocca di Stellata, across the river. The empty boats, which the enemy used each night to ferry reinforcements and supplies across the Po, were lying in plain sight, dragged up on the opposite bank. Constantine climbed down, relieved that *he* was not responsible for taking the place.

The large island of San Biagio was formed by silt deposited at the confluence of the Panaro River and the Po. It occupied an L-shaped bend in the Po, dividing it into two narrow branches, each about one hundred yards wide at its narrowest point and about twenty feet deep in midstream.

It was nine o'clock at night before the Venetians began placing their boats in the river to construct a pontoon bridge, and morning by the time they began to wheel the six large-caliber cannons across it. By afternoon, the guns were emplaced, each with an adequate supply of black powder and iron balls. The count deployed two hundred infantry to protect the battery in case the enemy made a surprise attack.

He directed Bartolomeo Falcerio, the battery's commander, to instruct his gunners to calibrate the range to a point in the river between the two fortresses, about six hundred yards away, so that they could accurately fire on the boats that the Duke of Urbino would use later, under cover of darkness, as he reinforced La Rocca di Ficarolo.

Antonio of the Marches, the army's engineer who had personally supervised the sighting of the battery, and Tommaso were there to ensure all went according to plan.

"Fire for range," ordered Falcerio.

Each gun was fired individually to allow the billows of white smoke to clear in between shots. At first, Constantine could not spot their fall. The gunners cursed as they struggled with their long wooden levers, adjusting the position of each gun while its captain carefully marked the lay of the wheels with chalk on the battery's platform. This would enable them to reset each gun in exactly the right spot after it recoiled.

As the tall columns of water rose from the river between the fortresses, one by one each gun found the range. After a few more confirming shots, they fell silent. Satisfied with their shooting, the gunners set to work, carefully measuring quantities of black powder and pouring them into sacks to ensure the amounts were the same as those used to achieve the correct range.

In a half hour it would be dark. Constantine walked a hundred yards from the battery back to where cooks were feeding the soldiers their supper of broth and bread. There, near one of the large black cauldrons, he spotted Elmo and Niccolò. He had told them they did not need to come with him to view the siege works, but they had insisted, protesting that his father was paying them to not let him out of their sight. As men of honor, they would follow his orders explicitly.

"Signor Ziani, come and join us for some supper," called Niccolò. "This cook knows how to make proper camp soup!"

Elmo handed Constantine a crude wooden bowl and a spoon. As he held the bowl in his outstretched hand, the cook dipped a big ladle into the pot and, with a chuckle, withdrew a savory serving of broth.

Suddenly his smile disappeared as a crossbow bolt seemed to pop out of his chest. Men began shouting. The unmistakable banging of harquebuses and a rousing cheer made Constantine spin around. He could see soldiers springing to action at the battery. They were under attack. Constantine drew his sword.

"Quick, follow me," shouted Elmo as he roughly grabbed Constantine's arm, pulling him in the other direction, to run with Niccolò toward the pontoon bridge.

Constantine was disgusted. Ripping his arm free, he shouted, "The battery is under attack! We must save the guns."

"Never mind that! We are lost unless we run for it," objected Elmo.

Niccolò pointed wildly toward the fighting.

Constantine turned and saw the count and his two sons running toward them over a small rise of ground. They were followed by the remnant of the Venetians' force.

"The battery is lost. Save yourselves!" shouted Galeazzo.

Constantine did not need any more convincing. He turned and ran, relieved he had left his cumbersome armor back at camp.

They all ran toward the pontoon bridge, their only escape route if they were to avoid having to swim the Po. Nearing the riverbank, he turned and saw a large company of heavily armed enemy soldiers about fifty yards behind, chasing after them in the fading light.

Constantine stumbled down to the river, sliding on loose stones and tripping over debris. The pontoon bridge was eight feet wide and about a hundred yards long. Every ten feet, the long planks were fastened to a boat by stout ropes. The bridge held together despite the Venetians' mad stampede over it. Loud splashes signaled that men were falling into the river, shot down by bolts or trying to swim to safety.

As the first Venetians reached the northern end and jumped from the bridge onto the wet sand, they formed up, aware they would be outnumbered but knowing the enemy could not cross the bridge more than three abreast. A dozen surviving crossbowmen prepared to unleash a deadly volley into the onrushing enemy.

The count barely made it, gasping for breath as his two sons, one on each arm, dragged him the last few yards. A hundred Venetians were standing together now, shoulder to shoulder. Seeing them, the enemy did not advance beyond halfway across the bridge, knowing it would be suicide. After exchanging a few crossbow volleys, they soon withdrew to the island to carry off the captured guns and unfortunate prisoners.

The Duke of Ferrara himself had led the attack. More than six hundred mercenaries and Ferrarese men-at-arms had crossed to the far southeastern end of the island, out of sight of the Venetians, and attacked the battery from the rear, slaughtering almost all the gunners and capturing Bartolomeo Falcerio and Antonio of the Marches. Tommaso and the count and his sons had narrowly escaped. Nearly two hundred men were lost. Many had drowned. The six precious guns, too heavy to move, were spiked.

Tommaso of Imola, stung by the loss but ever resourceful, found another way to use his remaining cannons more effectively. He dismantled two large-caliber guns and had them dragged up the stairs of the bell tower of Ficarolo's church. Once they were reassembled, the soldiers were able to fire at boats crossing the Po between the two Ferrarese fortresses and to rake the windows on the upper level of the fortress itself, preventing the defenders from easily firing down on the Venetian engineers. Finally, after two weeks of backbreaking work in the stifling June heat, the Venetians had dug their maze of trenches right up to the moat surrounding La Rocca di Ficarolo, barely fifty feet from the fortress wall.

C onstantine was wide awake, trying to lie as still as a corpse. It was too hot to sleep. The tent was closed up tight, blocking out the refreshing night breeze; they preferred to swelter rather than to be eaten alive by the hungry mosquitoes and painful horseflies that plagued the camp. Even if Constantine had dozed off in the heat, Niccolò's incessant snoring would soon have awakened him. Near bedtime, Constantine usually sent his bodyguard on some errand so that he could fall asleep before the man returned, only to fill the tent with thundering snorts.

"Are you still awake?" whispered Elmo, invisible in the darkness.

"If I had been killed today, hacked to bloody pieces, I think Niccolò's snoring would be loud enough to rouse me from my very grave."

Elmo laughed. "He has been my friend for more than twenty years. I guess after all that time, I have become accustomed to his snoring. Usually I can sleep right through it. I was just lying here thinking that if we could only place Niccolò next to La Rocca di Ficarolo, after two nights, I think the Ferrarese would be so exhausted from lack of sleep, they would soon beg us to permit them surrender."

Constantine snickered and then the tent grew silent again, except for Niccolò.

"Signor Ziani, have you ever seen someone and had a strange feeling that you have seen them before . . . in the past . . . somewhere else?"

"No. Why do you ask?"

"Because today I saw a man I know I have seen before. I would not have given it a thought until I observed that he was trying to avoid me, as though he did not want me to recognize him or know that he was in our camp. Unfortunately, I cannot recall where or when I last saw him. I have been all over Italy. There were just too many places and too many years."

"Describe him to me."

"Well"—he thought for a moment—"he was of average height and weight with brown hair and a beard . . ."

"Elmo, you have just described half the men in this camp. There must have been *something* that made you notice him. Think."

Constantine began to retrace his own steps that day, going over everywhere he had been, the men he had seen, trying to recall if anyone looked suspicious.

Elmo's words broke the silence. "Wait. There *was* something about him. He carried a bag over his shoulder—not a soldier's pack, more like . . ."

". . . a physician's?"

"You saw him, too?"

Constantine swung his feet onto the tent's dirt floor and pulled on his pants. "Elmo, a physician arrived in camp today. He is reputed to be a specialist in treating swamp fever."

"Who told you that? There is only one cure for swamp fever, and that is to leave the swamp. Once you catch it, there is no way to avoid suffering from it."

Suddenly it all made sense to Constantine. Count Cajazzo had told him just the other day that he thought he was suffering from the onset of what could be swamp fever. Constantine hurried out in his bare feet with Elmo close behind, leaving Niccolò undisturbed in his nocturnal rumbling.

They ran to the count's tent. Outside, a sleepy guard leaned against a small tree, tired but awake.

"Signor Ziani, what are you doing up at this early hour?"

"I must see the count right away."

"He is asleep. He had a long day. Are you sure it is wise to wake him?"

Constantine threw open the flaps and called out in the darkness, afraid of what he would find. He could hear nothing in the blackness, not even the sound of his breathing.

He turned to Elmo. "Bring me a torch."

In a few seconds Elmo returned with the flaming light. As Constantine moved it back and forth in the large tent, he saw the count lying on his stomach, motionless.

"God, no!" shouted the guard, one of the loyal men who had escaped from Milan with the count.

Suddenly the form on the cot stirred and rolled over. The count coughed once and opened his eyes.

"What is going on here?" he mumbled as he reached for a dagger under his cot.

"It is Constantine Ziani, Count. I thought you were dead."

"Dead?" he said incredulously. "Why did you think I would be dead?"

Constantine was embarrassed. The picture, so clear in his mind a moment before, had disintegrated into a confused jumble of thoughts and emotions.

"Forgive me. I was afraid that our enemies had infiltrated our camp and—"

The count suddenly held up his hand to stop Constantine. "Your instincts may have just saved my life."

He rolled over wearily, put his feet on the ground, and sat up, rubbing his eyes. He was still fully clothed.

"I was so exhausted, I fell asleep before I could take this."

He reached for a small vial on the table next to his cot, looked at it for a moment, and handed it to Constantine.

"What does this look like to you?"

"Some kind of medicine. Who gave it to you?"

"That new physician from Rovigo, the one who has come to treat us for swamp fever. He told me to drink it before going to bed, but I fell asleep before I could."

The count carefully pulled the stopper from the small bottle, sniffed its contents, and then placed it on the table. He looked at the guard and then at Constantine as he cleared his mind and began to consider what had happened.

"Florence!" shouted Elmo suddenly. "I saw that man in Florence. He is not from Rovigo—he is a Florentine."

The count looked quizzically at Elmo.

"My bodyguard thinks that physician is someone he has seen before," explained Constantine.

The count looked sternly at his guard. "Bring him to me at once. If he is not in his tent, arouse as many men as you need and do not stop searching until you find him."

While they waited, they talked about the likely plot. Had their enemies sent the physician to poison the count? Did he have accomplices? Elmo said that he had not noticed anyone with the man they suspected of being an assassin.

After a while, Galeazzo stuck his head into the tent. "We have looked everywhere. He is gone. I have dispatched *schiopetieri* on every road leading out of the camp. He could not have gotten far. We will find him."

Just after sunrise, a company of *schiopetieri* returned to the Venetians' camp. In their midst, with his hands and feet tied to his horse, was the unfortunate physician. When he saw him, the count scowled at the man and ordered him to be brought into his tent.

Constantine did not enjoy watching a man endure torture, but this time his curiosity got the better of him. He joined a crowd of about twenty men who surrounded the captive as he lay quietly on the wooden plank floor. His face was bruised and his nose bloody, but Constantine could see that he had not been too badly treated—yet.

The count pulled the vial from his pocket and held it up for everyone to see.

"You gave this to me yesterday. I believe it is poison. Now we shall find out. Hold him down," he commanded his bodyguards.

Four strong soldiers leaned hard on the man, causing him to groan with pain.

"Put a blade in his mouth to hold his tongue down. If he spits it out, emasculate him," said the count casually, almost without any emotion.

The thought made Constantine feel sick to his stomach as he struggled to hide his nausea.

The man began to whimper.

"I confess," he blurted just as Galeazzo was about to insert the blade.

"You confess quickly—too quickly. I think you are a brave man to have undertaken such a mission. I would also think you would prefer to take the poison than to endure the alternative of a slow, painful death. Why did you not choose the poison?

"Its effects are also painful, and it takes several days to die from it."

"Who sent you? Who are your accomplices?"

"I have no accomplices. I acted alone," said the assassin without remorse, his courage now evident for all to see.

"We shall see," spat Antonio Maria. The count flashed him a look of disapproval.

"I ask you again: who sent you?"

The man would not answer. As the count considered what to do next, they heard a loud commotion outside.

A guard went out to investigate and quickly returned. "They are bringing in two more men. The *schiopetieri* found them waiting with a boat near the place where the Ferrarese are encamped, downriver across the Po."

The count watched his prisoner's eyes while the guard was speaking. They betrayed surprise instead of disinterest. The flaps of the tent opened and the two were dragged in and thrust onto the floor next to the physician.

"They are all in this together," whispered Elmo. "See how they avoid looking at each other? You can always tell a guilty man when he begins to act unnaturally."

"One of you is going to tell me what I want to know. I want a confession and I am going to get it. Whoever confesses first, I will spare. The other two will hang. Now who will it be? I have all night."

The count sat on his cot and stared at the three men.

"I will bet this new golden *marcello* I have in my purse that the younger one will take the count's offer," whispered Elmo. "He has the most to live for. It is always the younger one that first takes the bait."

After just ten minutes, Elmo was proven right. The young boatman confessed. They had been hired by the physician to transport him across the river. He had paid them in Milanese lira. So they *had* been hired by the Milanese, thought Constantine.

Within a half hour, the lifeless bodies of the physician and the other boatman were hanging from an old oak tree across the town square from the church, but not before the physician had been induced to reveal the name of his employer. It was Gian Trivulzio, one of Il Moro's generals. True to his word, the count set the young boatman free.

The siege was about to enter its final, inevitable stage. Conscious of time, Count Cajazzo first ordered Tommaso to attack the fort in an effort to force the stout wooden door. That attempt failed, with the loss of 150 soldiers, but it revealed evidence that the Duke of Urbino could no longer reinforce or even support the doomed garrison. Next, the count concentrated his artillery on the point where the chain boom entered the fortress wall. After three days, a lucky shot shattered one of the links, and the massive chain slipped harmlessly into the river.

The Venetians' river flotilla moved up the Po, closer to the fortress, and poured cannon fire into it. In all, they fired more than sixteen hundred balls into the brick walls, pulverizing the structure, until finally, on June 29, the six hundred surviving defenders surrendered. It was a great victory for the Venetians, removing the last enemy force on the north side of the Po.

Next, the count placed his heaviest guns in the fortress and began bombarding its twin, La Rocca di Stellata, directly across the river. The Duke of Urbino and Duke Ercole, seeing it was now indefensible, quit the place and marched their troops south, toward Ferrara. Before their dust had settled, the count had already ordered his engineers to begin constructing a pontoon bridge across the Po at Bonello, farther downstream, nearer to the city of Ferrara.

July brought heavy rains. The downpour increased the river's flow, forcing the engineers to work in miserable conditions as they struggled, chest-deep in water, to complete the bridge across the two-hundred-yard-wide river.

Before they could complete the structure, Duke Ercole launched a surprise attack, forcing the Venetians to run for the northern shore. Eleven boats were destroyed, delaying the work. The rain unleashed hordes of mosquitoes, and soon pestilence visited the camp. Swamp fever had arrived in all its fury.

17

Bondeno

"Have you received any word from Constantine?" asked Seraglio.
"No, but Loredan sent a report to the Senate that the army, under Count Cajazzo, has finally captured La Rocca di Ficarolo and La Rocca di Stellata and was attempting to force a crossing of the Po when swamp fever laid the count low. He nearly died but is recovering in Padua and plans to rejoin the army soon. Now that he has secured his rear and cleared the enemy from the Polesine, he intends to move on the duke's capital and take it before winter brings a halt to the campaign."

"Things seem to be going more slowly than expected," observed Seraglio.

"Apparently you have not heard the news from Rome." Antonio smiled at his friend. "The Holy Father has proven to be a valuable ally. After the King of Naples learned of the pope's intention to oppose the League and join with us, he sent his son, the Duke of Calabria, to pillage the lands around the Holy See, to compel the pope to change his mind. Instead, Sixtus employed Roberto da Rimino, a *condottiere* with a reputation as fearsome as our own Count Cajazzo's."

"This pope knows how to spend his money wisely."

"Yes. Roberto advised Sixtus to raise as many infantry as he could and, when they were gathered, to bless them and send them off with a sacred commission. It was not difficult to arouse the indignation of the people, who were much angered at the duke's depredations of their lands.

"The Duke of Calabria, hearing of this, retreated a few miles from the city to Campomorto to await Roberto. The two forces were about equal in cavalry, but Roberto was superior in infantry. The son of a king and next in line to the throne, the duke could not suffer the great dishonor of refusing to fight—even if at a disadvantage. The battle lasted all afternoon. When it ended, the Neapolitan army and their Spanish mercenaries were routed. At a cost of only four hundred men, Roberto's army killed twelve hundred of the enemy and captured nearly four hundred, including more than thirty nobles for ransom. The duke escaped capture only when a party of Turks, in his pay, rescued him. Imagine that! Another two hundred men were drowned in the swamps trying to escape the pope's mounted mercenaries."

"Impressive," observed Seraglio. "But now Queen Isabella of Castile will send more men to help her cousin, Ferrante. She and her husband certainly have designs on Italy. This would give them the perfect pretext for meddling openly in Italian affairs."

"You may be right, Seraglio, but they are still occupied trying to take the last Moorish stronghold in Spain at Granada. Of more immediate concern to us is what happened after Roberto's great victory at Campomorto."

Antonio's expression became taut, his voice more subdued.

"Unfortunately, when Roberto returned to Rome to claim accolades for his great victory, he was thirsty and suffering greatly from the heat. After drinking much water, he was seized with the flux and died soon afterward. His death, I am afraid, does not bode well for the pope or his steadfastness in supporting us."

"Perhaps Sixtus will appoint his portly nephew, Girolamo Riario, to command in Roberto's place," said Seraglio with a broad grin.

"That would be disastrous for his cause—and ours. What is important is that the papal forces seem to have snatched defeat from the jaws of victory. If they cannot occupy the Neapolitan army and prevent it from joining with those already opposed to us, we may be incapable of quickly taking Ferrara and may slip into a protracted war. Or worse—together, they may overwhelm us."

It was past midnight when Constantine entered the count's tent. Two other men were already inside with him, Tommaso of Imola and the new *provveditore,* Giovanni Emo, who had just replaced the ailing Antonio Loredan, who had returned to Venice.

"You sent for me?"

"Yes. Sit down."

Constantine took a wooden stool, wondering what the count wanted. *Have I done something that displeased him?*

"We captured two prisoners tonight who revealed, under extreme duress before they expired, some very interesting information."

Constantine studied their faces. The men looked anxious, but their eyes radiated optimism. The count was a lion anticipating the hunt. Tommaso was leaning forward, looking dangerous, like a famished wolf. Still fuming over the loss of 150 of his men, killed when the count ordered him to storm La Rocca di Ficarolo, Tommaso was eager to hear what the count had to say. Emo, a Venetian, looked like a panther, leaning back on his chair, listening intently, as hungry as the others but more thoughtful.

"Duke Ercole's *condottiere*, Antonio Bevilacqua, is spending the night in the village of Bondeno."

"But that is only two miles from here," observed Constantine. "Why would he take such a risk?"

"Only one reason," interjected Tommaso. "He has an incurable itch that must be scratched regularly."

"And tomorrow he will find that he has spent the night with a very expensive woman indeed. He will fetch a fine ransom—his family is wealthy."

Emo broke his silence. "Tommaso and I, along with two hundred handpicked men, will leave camp three hours before dawn so we will be in a position to grab him at sunrise, when he leaves to make the eight-mile ride back to Ferrara. Constantine, you will come with us to help capture him."

"How many bodyguards will he have with him?"

"The prisoners said there would be about fifty. We shall have more than enough men to take care of them."

Constantine sat back and shook his head. It all seemed too easy. "How do we know for sure that the prisoners were telling the truth and that Bevilacqua is not merely the bait in a trap the duke has set for us?"

The men exchanged glances, revealing that many words had already passed between them concerning that very question.

"We must take advantage of every opportunity presented to us," said the count. "If we can deny Bevilacqua's services to Duke Ercole, it will weaken his ability to hold out long enough for the Neapolitan army to come up and reinforce him."

Tommaso nodded in agreement, but Emo did not. *They disagree on strategy,* thought Constantine as he rose to leave.

"Be ready to ride three hours before sunrise. Leave that expensive armor behind," commanded the count. "You will not need it. You will need speed more than strength."

"And bring those two ruffians with you," added Tommaso as he left the tent.

Constantine let Elmo and Niccolò sleep until a few minutes before it was time to assemble. When he told them about the mission, they responded predictably. Niccolò had been spoiling for a fight ever since their disastrous defeat at San Biagio and their ignominious retreat in the face of the enemy. He reached for his heavy sword and began sharpening it as soon as he heard the news. Elmo was more circumspect. He asked the same question Constantine had asked.

"I tell you, we are taking a risk," he said. "Duke Ercole has proven himself to be as wily as a fox. Mark my words: this is a trap if ever I smelled one."

"Shut up and get ready," hissed Niccolò. "Stop your carping. Constantine here is going, so we are going too, and that is all there is to it."

Elmo continued muttering to himself as he pulled on his chain mail. When they were fully dressed and armed, the three walked out of their tent to the area in camp where they would assemble. The entire force was mounted. Tommaso's company numbered about 160, along with Emo's personal bodyguard of forty crack Venetian cavalry.

Constantine and his companions rode with Emo. They maintained a steady clip until they reached a low ridge on the outskirts of the little hamlet of Bondeno and strategically occupied a position between the town and Ferrara. Bevilacqua would have to pass through there on his way home. As the main body dismounted and watered their horses, Tommaso ordered some of his scouts to fan out and cover the other roads out of Bondeno in case their quarry took a more circuitous route. Their preparations finished, they settled down to wait for sunrise. After a short while, Emo and Tommaso waved to Constantine, inviting him to join them.

"Here is my plan," Tommaso began. Even though Emo, the newly arrived *provveditore*, outranked Tommaso, he deferred to the experienced *condottiere*, who had been fighting the Ferrarese for months and whose men made up the greater portion of their force.

"Signor Emo, you will take half of my force with your own, dispatch his bodyguards, and capture Bevilacqua while I provide a protective barrier around the town in case any more of the enemy show themselves. Once you snatch him, head straight back to camp. Do not turn back, no matter what. We can take care of ourselves."

Emo, Constantine, and the Venetians found a place where the road wound through a grove of trees on the reverse side of the ridge. Hidden from the town, it was a perfect place for an ambush. They dispersed on either side of the road, hiding in the trees. Their twenty crossbowmen climbed the branches and hid among the lush green leaves. Finally, Emo detailed two scouts to ride to the crest and give a warning when the enemy was near.

The wait was long and uncomfortable as the chirping insects confused the sounds, making it difficult to hear horses approaching, and the Venetians' chain mail began to heat up. The sun rose, and still there was no sign of the Ferrarese *condottiere*.

"Where is he?" hissed Niccolò through his clenched teeth.

"He is not coming, I tell you," countered Elmo.

"Wait, I hear horses approaching. Shhh."

It was Tommaso. He and about twenty men rode up, all covered in dust, their horses lathered from a spirited ride.

"There has been no sign of him," said Emo, anticipating his question.

"He must have slipped through our cordon by keeping off the roads and cutting through the woods," replied Tommaso. "He could be miles away by now."

Tommaso looked at Emo impatiently. His horse was circling, still full of vigor, like him—not ready to give up.

"You wait here while I take my men and search the village."

"No," replied Emo. "Our orders were to take Bevilacqua on his way to Ferrara, not to take the town. If the enemy is strongly posted there, you could become trapped, with no way out."

"Provveditore," responded Tommaso respectfully, "I personally extracted the information from one of the prisoners. They both told the same story, even though they were kept separate from each other. I tell you, he was here last night. He is probably still here, and I am going to take him."

Emo looked at Constantine and sighed. "All right, but we are going to circle around the village and wait for you on the road back to camp. I do not want to be cut off."

Tommaso smiled, turned his mount around, and kicked his spurs into his flanks. The stallion took off toward the town with his men close behind.

"An impetuous commander is a dangerous commander," said Emo.

"That sort of recklessness could get him killed," added Constantine.

"That sort of recklessness could get us *all* killed."

.   .   .

The ancient village of Bondeno, a hundred yards long and three streets wide, lay on the west bank of the Panaro River. It comprised perhaps sixty houses made of stone and wood and half a dozen larger structures. A fine little church dominated the central square. Its modest houses backed up to one another, sharing yards, mostly planted with bounteous vegetable gardens. The town was surrounded by olive and fruit orchards and undulating fields of wheat, interrupted by small patches of woods.

Armed conflict in Italy rarely spilled into the small towns. Battles were generally fought in the open fields, and it was the larger cities that were normally besieged. In war, property was valued more than human life—except in the case of ransomed prisoners. As long as the townsfolk stayed out of the way, they knew that they would not be molested and could resume their normal lives once the battle was concluded and the few unfortunate dead were given a Christian burial.

Tommaso and eighty heavily armed soldiers approached the village from the east along the Ferrara road, crossed over the old stone bridge spanning the Panaro, and, turning right, filed onto the main street. They rode silently, with swords drawn, two abreast. Although it was a workday, they found the streets and yards empty.

The horses pranced nervously, sensing their riders' uncertainty. About halfway down the street, Tommaso spotted the village stable, where they would find Bevilacqua's horses or evidence indicating whether he had been there or not. Fifty horses would have left a stinking mess on the straw-covered floor that would be collected later and used to fertilize the fields.

As they neared it, Tommaso held up his hand, stopping his parading troop. He slowly scanned the street. Every building was shuttered. It was as if the villagers had *known* they were coming . . .

"Damn!" As he turned to give a command, a loud crack shattered the calm. Tommaso rolled off his horse and fell onto the dirt street, wounded in the shoulder by a harquebus's ball that penetrated his chain mail, driving pieces of metal into his flesh. Lying in the dust, gasping for a breath through his pain, he heard the shutters clattering open and men shouting. Suddenly his proud column disintegrated in a fusillade of crossbow bolts and balls, ten men falling in the first volley.

Two resolute cavalrymen hurriedly dismounted, grabbed Tommaso under his armpits, and threw him, like a sack of grain, over the neck of a big charger. Bleeding from his shoulder, he lost consciousness. Along with a few other survivors, they galloped up a side street, away from the ambush, toward the north end of town, as enemy soldiers poured out of their hiding places and into the street, compelling Tommaso's wounded comrades to surrender quickly.

When the four survivors and their unconscious leader reached the northern edge of the village, they halted. More than a hundred enemy infantry blocked the road back to camp. As the little company turned right, crossbow bolts whizzed past, catching one soldier in the thigh. They pressed on.

A loud cheer erupted as some Venetian cavalry appeared behind the enemy infantry. It was Emo's men. Though the Ferrarese infantry outnumbered the Venetians, they ran for their lives, most of them reaching a wooded area where they knew the cavalry would not fight them. In a few minutes, with the chase over, the Venetians joined Tommaso's remnant.

"Is he dead?" shouted Emo.

"Not yet, but he is severely wounded."

"What happened?"

"We were ambushed. There are hundreds of them back in the village."

Emo cast a disgusted glance at Constantine, careful to hide it from his men. The men looked intently at their leader as he weighed his options.

"Enemy infantry!" shouted Elmo, pointing south at a crowd charging out of the village. "Cavalry!" shouted another Venetian as they turned to see a horde of men-at-arms bearing down on them from the east.

"The road to camp is clear now. Follow me. Do not stop for any reason." Emo kicked his horse and, with his cavalrymen close behind, dashed northward up the road they had just cleared of enemy infantry. A few spent crossbow bolts fell harmlessly around them. As long as no enemy soldiers blocked their way, they would be safe, but soon, a few hundred yards behind, Constantine spotted a horde of Ferrarese heavy cavalry, bearing Duke Ercole's personal standard, riding hard after them. *Without armor, we should be able to outrun them.* Suddenly Elmo rode up alongside him and pointed.

"Tommaso's rider is falling behind. With the extra weight, his horse is done for. With your permission, Niccolò and I will pick him up, or else they will capture him."

Constantine turned in his saddle to look back. Elmo was right. In another two minutes, the duke's company would overtake them.

"Do you think you can make it?"

Elmo grimaced. "It doesn't matter. We have to try."

Constantine had a sinking feeling in the pit of his stomach, but what could he do? They could not allow Tommaso to be taken. The man was from Ferrara, and he would be treated most harshly by the vindictive Duke Ercole, who regarded him as a traitor.

"Go, and God be with you both."

Constantine's horse had slowed to a canter. The rest of Emo's company were now far up ahead, unaware of Tommaso's danger. Overcome with guilt, Constantine decided to try to help his protectors any way he could and chased after them.

Elmo and Niccolò reached the frightened soldier carrying Tommaso and transferred the wounded leader to Elmo's horse, which was the stronger. Then the three riders instantly began to flee toward Constantine. Once joined, they all took off after the dust cloud that signaled the direction of the Venetian cavalry.

Behind them, they could hear clanging metal and a horn blowing the charge. However, the duke and his men had come all the way from Ferrara, and their horses were tired. They began to fall behind Constantine and his little company.

Up ahead, Constantine could see a narrow bridge and the last of Emo's force filing over it. They were now less than a mile from camp.

Niccolò shouted, "Soon they will have to stop chasing us."

But as the words left his lips, Elmo's mount stumbled and fell in the road with a thud, throwing his rider and the still bleeding but now conscious Tommaso to the ground. The others reined in their horses and dismounted.

Tommaso, who was in a state of shock, was no worse for the wear, but Elmo had shattered his ankle. White bone protruded from his torn flesh. Unable to walk, he looked up at Constantine and shook his head.

"I am finished. Now go chase after the *provveditore* and leave us."

"I am not leaving you."

"There is no time to argue, Constantine," shouted Niccolò, raising his voice to him for the first time ever.

Tommaso of Imola lay in the road, half dead and ashen-faced from loss of blood. His man was standing beside the fallen leader, sword drawn, in a futile attempt to receive the impending charge by the duke's men-at-arms and to defend his overlord alone, to the death, if he must. Constantine turned to Elmo and Niccolò and was struck by their pose. Elmo was also down and in pain, and his lifelong friend, Niccolò, was standing guard over him too, also ready to die for him. Constantine did not know what to do. He was speechless, overcome with emotion. Compared to these stark sacrificial acts, anything he could do or say would be almost contemptible.

"Surely, they will hold all of you for ransom," he ventured.

Niccolò just smiled and turned away to face the enemy, now just a hundred yards away and coming on fast.

"Constantine . . ." Tommaso struggled to speak. "We are about to die. Give us . . . a small victory, . . . will you? Now go and save yourself . . . Go."

Constantine stood there, silent, and tried to preserve the noble tableau in the most sacred recess of his memory; two brave men willingly laying down their lives for their friends. Then, with an aching heart, he mounted his horse, turned away from them, and, in a shower of dirt and loose pebbles, darted off toward the Venetian camp and safety. After riding a short way and feeling ashamed that he had abandoned them, Constantine had to turn around one last time. In the distance, he could see two men with their swords drawn standing beside their fallen comrades just before they disappeared in a storm of swirling dust, flashing steel, and thundering horseflesh. He would miss them terribly.

Elmo and Niccolò had taught him how to be a soldier, but most of all, they had taught him about camaraderie. Men did not die for their flag, they died for their comrades. For the first time, he really understood the powerful bond between his father and Seraglio.

18

Argenta

Constantine rolled over on his side, alone in the pitch-black darkness. Shivering, he pulled his sheepskin blanket up to his chin to ward off the damp October chill. His tent, so filled with life when Elmo and Niccolò occupied it with him, felt as cold as a mausoleum, its silence a cruel reminder that those happier days were gone forever. He ached to hear their voices, arguing like children and swearing like soldiers.

It had been more than three months since Bondeno and not a word of them from the enemy camp—except that Tommaso of Imola had died of his wounds. There would be no ransom for Elmo and Niccolò. They were most likely dead. He wiped a tear from his eye at the thought of such an inglorious end for those brave souls.

Though Constantine had suffered the loss of his two companions, the Venetian army had fared well in the months that followed the ambush at Bondeno. After repairing the bridge across the Po, the Venetian army had finally crossed into Ferrarese territory. Setting up camp on the other side, they used the navigable river as a supply line to build up their strength before making a final push to take Duke Ercole's capital city of Ferrara.

The Venetians' prospects were steadily improving. The victory in August by the papal forces had shattered the Neapolitan army, preventing their intervention in the fighting around Ferrara. Count Cajazzo had recovered from his bout with swamp fever, and now spies reported that the enemy was demoralized and in considerable disorder. The Duke of Urbino had suddenly fallen ill and had been taken to Bologna, where he had died a few days later. His loss meant that the Milanese, the strongest contingent of enemy troops, were now leaderless.

When the first rays of sunlight danced through the slit in his tent flaps, Constantine had been awake for hours. Haunted by memories of his dead comrades, he had not been able to sleep. He decided to walk down to the river, wash, and get something to eat. When he stepped outside, a few men were milling about, but most of them were still asleep. Rumors had been circulating for days that the army was about to break camp and march on Ferrara itself. They were enjoying the rest before the hard marching would begin again.

As he stumbled along, rubbing his tired eyes, he pulled his grimy shirt over his head. Then, after laying it on a nearby rock, he dropped to his knees and, spreading his hands apart in the wet gravel, bent down low, pushing his face into the cold river. The icy shock restored his vitality. Cupping his hands, he drank deep, sweet draughts and then rinsed his mouth. He had chosen a place far upstream from the camp to avoid encountering any headless brown fish, the kind that had floated in a thousand rivers next to a thousand camps since the dawn of war. He smiled just thinking about the day Elmo had taught him about that.

Pulling his shirt back on, he headed toward the officers' mess. As he neared it, the smell of hot bread baking in the ovens and savory meat turning on the spit made his stomach churn. Suddenly, he spotted Count Cajazzo's son Galeazzo emerging from the large tent and waved to him. Galeazzo stopped and, recognizing Constantine, walked purposefully toward him.

"You are up early this morning." Constantine smiled.

"Better get something to eat fast. My father wants to see you. He sent me to fetch you, but the smell of that bread diverted me from my mission. Hurry. I will wait."

Constantine quickly ducked into the tent and cut a large piece of bread, stuffed a generous slab of meat into it, and hurried off with Galeazzo.

"What is going on?" he asked between bites as he gnawed his breakfast. "We are breaking camp. In two days, we will be at the gates of Ferrara."

Constantine sat silently on his horse and looked at the long rows of grim men-at-arms and *stradiotti* arrayed in long lines, respectively, to his left and his right. They were hidden just below the wooded ridgeline, out of sight of the enemy. He could feel their immense power even though they were motionless and silent, like figures in a painting.

He remembered how terrified he had been in his first real battle. He had run for his life over the pontoon bridge when, without warning, the Ferrarese had attacked the Venetian battery on San Biagio, putting them to rout. He remembered how impotent and ashamed he had felt as he rode away, leaving Elmo and Niccolò to perish. He had been unable to save them, barely able to save himself, but he was no longer afraid. He was bitter now, and for the first time in his life, he longed for revenge.

Count Cajazzo had pushed his vanguard south to within ten miles of Ferrara. His scouts had discovered the duke's army, drawn up across a narrow valley on the other side of the ridge, a half mile away. Constantine had heard the report as he sat on his horse next to the old *condottiere*. The enemy was in strength, with ten squadrons of mounted men-at-arms, about six hundred strong, and more than two thousand infantry. Opposing them, the count mustered three hundred men-at-arms and three hundred light cavalry, eight hundred infantry and twelve hundred elite reinforcements, battle-hardened marines from Alvise Valaresso's river flotilla, which had sailed up the Po from Venice.

The count's plan was simple. He would march his eight hundred infantry over the ridge and along the road into the valley, appearing oblivious to the danger posed by the enemy hidden in the woods on the opposing ridge. The mounted *stradiotti* would cover their flanks. Then he would pray that the enemy commander would launch an attack on the irresistible and outnumbered bait, smelling an easy victory.

Constantine turned in his saddle to watch as the two Brandolini brothers led their infantry up the road and out of sight. The *stradiotti* split into two equal-sized bands and rode the short way up the ridge on oblique paths that carried them away from the infantry column and out onto its flanks. As the crimson and gold banners disappeared from sight, all that remained was the amber dust, thrown up by the marching men and horses.

The count dismounted and motioned for his sons to follow him as he crept up the ridge to see what would happen next. Constantine did not wait to be asked. He was, after all, a member of the count's staff. He found it harder than he thought it would be to climb the short distance in his heavy armor. Even though it was November now, he was perspiring, so he removed his armet and one gauntlet and wiped his brow with his hand.

Peering over the trunk of a thick tree, felled by the count's party to serve as an observation post, Constantine could see the Venetian column winding its way down into the valley. There was a small cluster of houses nestled at the bottom in the center.

"If they march too far beyond those houses, they will be cut to pieces before we can come to their aid," observed Galeazzo as he pounded his armored fist against the tree.

"The Brandolini know their business. Their orders are to set up camp in the village and invite an attack. There are only about two hours of daylight left. Our enemy will oblige us by attacking within the hour."

The count was one of those men who spoke as though God himself had whispered a vision of the future into his ear. It was unthinkable to doubt what he said.

The sun was slowly sinking in the west but not fast enough to conceal the flashes sparkling from the enemy's arms and armor as they waited in the trees on the opposite ridge. Constantine could see the *stradiotti* slowly moving toward the village now, adding to the illusion that the Venetians were going to encamp in the village for the night.

"Galeazzo, go tell Captain Valaresso to form up his men. And be quick— it is almost time," ordered the count abruptly. Then he looked directly at Constantine. "Go tell Captain Secco to make ready to attack when he hears the trumpet sound."

As Constantine turned to carry out his order, the count grabbed his arm.

"Signor Ziani, you no longer have bodyguards, and I have promised your father-in-law, the doge, to keep you out of harm's way . . ." Constantine could not easily read the count's expression. He did not know whether to protest or silently obey his superior, so he decided to speak from the heart.

"Count Cajazzo, I did not come all this way to sit on a ridge, the only man-at-arms to miss the battle."

The count frowned. "Very well, but stay close. Do not allow yourself to be separated from the main body. When a man-at-arms is alone, he is vulnerable. Whatever happens, do not become unhorsed, or some peasant will drive a spike into your armpit or groin with his mallet." He broke into a wide grin through his silvery beard and added, "The doge would never forgive me for making his daughter a widow—or you a eunuch."

Constantine did not wait for the count to reconsider. He quickly turned and made his way back down through the trees in the fading light. He mounted his horse and then informed the commander of the men-at-arms, Niccolò Secco, of the count's orders. Everything was ready. Now all they could do was to wait for the signal.

Dry autumn leaves rustled across the ground as a mild breeze began to swirl. He looked up at the darkening sky, now a deep grayish blue. A lone hawk circled above, lazily going about his business, searching for a squirrel. Fifteen minutes passed.

Constantine had been ready to exact retribution from the enemy for his lost comrades, but now he began to play out the coming fight in his mind's eye. He nervously placed his gauntlet on the pommel of his heavy sword. A quick glance at the men on either side of him portrayed the two faces of battle.

The man on his left was a few years older than Constantine. He was short but muscular and built for fighting. His klappvisor was up, exposing the fear in his eyes. His horse nervously bobbed her head up and down as he tried to steady her. She could sense the danger and uncertainty he felt. The other man to his right softly patted his mount as he stood stolid as a statue— a killing machine, sinewy and gaunt, frustrated by the delay.

Constantine turned to look behind. The marines, clad in gold breeches and crimson shirts beneath their chain mail, stood at the ready, clutching their fearsome swords, axes, and halberds. About two hundred were armed with deadly crossbows; a score with harquebuses, which could penetrate any armor—even German steel.

A screaming trumpet shattered the quiet while Secco shouted, "Forward men, to the top of the ridge!"

The well-formed line quickly unraveled as they rode to the top of the ridge, with the marines rushing up behind them.

What a sight greeted their eager eyes! Sprawling before them was the patchwork valley, now bathed in shadows. The enemy's line, two thousand strong, was coming on, an irresistible, scythelike wave curling around the small hamlet. Like guardian angels, the Ferrarese men-at-arms were posted to their rear, content to let the infantry do the work while they kept their eyes on the *stradiotti*. To oppose them, the Venetian infantry had turned the hamlet's buildings into a fortress, piling furniture, some wagons, wood from demolished outbuildings, and even corpses, shot down with arrows, to construct barricades. Crossbowmen and harquebusiers in the buildings fired from the windows at the enemy that was more than double their number. It was easy to see that, in twenty minutes, the

Ferrarese would completely surround the beleaguered defenders and over-whelm them.

"Now we have them!" hissed the count. He turned to the commander of his mounted men-at-arms.

"Captain Secco, you will split your men into two wings and, together, attack the enemy's cavalry on their flanks. Captain Valaresso, you will take your men, rush straight down the road, and relieve the infantry in the ham-let. Then, after our men-at-arms have defeated theirs, you will impale the enemy infantry on our wall of horse.

The two men obeyed instantly, knowing their comrades' lives depended on them promptly executing the count's orders. Constantine rode amid the company on the right. They would be charging with their backs to the sun—Elmo had taught him that was the best position for an attack. It was difficult for crossbowmen to judge distance when looking directly into the sun.

The Venetian men-at-arms on the right rode at a steady pace diagonally down the ridge heading southwest. The enemy infantry did not see them. They were occupied with defeating the Venetians in the hamlet. He could hear the sound of metal crashing on metal ringing through the valley. More than a thousand men were locked in their struggle for life or death. Shouts and screams assaulted his ears as men were hacked to pieces or suffered hor-rible wounds from the crossbowmen, shooting at close range.

Suddenly Constantine saw the big Venetian battle flag, streaming over the head of his column, veer off to the south and head across the valley. Captain Secco, out in front, wearing his distinctive white plumed armet and mounted on his black charger, raised his hand and urged his men forward. The men in front of Constantine accelerated to a trot. To his left, he could see the backs of the enemy infantry. To his front, the *stradiotti* formed a screen between them and the Ferrarese mounted men-at-arms.

The trumpeter sounded a short blast, then four more. The two men rid-ing beside Constantine drew their heavy swords and pulled down their klappvisors. He drew a deep breath and pulled down his. Through the eye slits, he could momentarily see Secco point his sword at the enemy men-at-arms as his white plume fluttered behind him. The column's pace quick-ened to a gallop. A great cheer rose up in every man's throat.

"For St. Mark and Venice!" they shouted. "For St. Mark and Venice!"

The noise was deafening. In front, the *stradiotti* parted to permit their column to pass through. They returned a wild cheer, saluting Secco and his men as they rode by their less heavily armed comrades.

About a hundred yards away, the startled commander of the enemy's men-at-arms tried to wheel his men around to meet the onslaught. No sooner had they begun their maneuver than they froze as the other Venetian wing, bearing down on them from the east, appeared. Totally surprised, they panicked, with almost half of them fleeing for their lives. The remainder of the heavy cavalry, now hopelessly outnumbered, grimly prepared for the shock of the Venetians' attack. There was no time for them to gather enough speed to counterattack.

Twenty yards from the enemy, Constantine clenched his teeth and gripped his sword tightly in his left fist.

"For St. Mark and Venice!" he shouted one last time.

The Venetian men-at-arms crashed into the Ferrarese. Their momentum knocked horses and men to the ground. Just ahead, Constantine could see swords swinging through the air. He heard men scream, the rattle of death in their throats. Steel clanged against steel, the ringing made all the louder as it echoed through his armet. The column began to lose its formation and spread out as each rider pushed to join in the fight.

A horse in front of Constantine rose up on his rear legs and threw his rider to the ground. Across the empty saddle, he could see an enemy soldier raise his sword as he searched for his next victim.

"Bastard!" screamed Constantine as he pushed the riderless mount away with the point of his sabaton.

The man swung his sword at him, but, anticipating the thrust, Constantine kicked his spur into his horse's left flank, instantly sidling his horse to the right, away from the blow. Now he swung his sword backhanded with all his might into the man's left shoulder armor, toppling him to the ground.

With barely time to think, he searched, wide-eyed, for another target. He spotted one, already engaged with a Venetian, and moved in behind him. Whipping his sword over his head to generate maximum force, he slammed the heavy blade into the back of the man's armet, knocking him forward, off balance. The other Venetian instantly shattered the man's shoulder with a blow from his heavy axe that struck the poor devil in his shoulder joint. His shattered arm dropped limply to his side. A second vicious axe blow dented his armet just above the klappvisor, tumbling him off his mount.

A loud cheer rose as the few remaining Ferrarese men-at-arms abruptly turned and fled for their lives. The engagement had taken little more than five minutes. More than one hundred of the enemy horsemen were on the ground when the *stradiotti* rode up, sprang from their horses, and, demanding that they surrender at once, began to plunder their purses. If a man refused or was too stunned to comply, they stabbed him with their sharp stilettos in between the armor plates in their greaves, behind their knees, crippling them but sparing their lives, to be ransomed later.

On Secco's command, the victorious cavalry wheeled their horses around to face the hamlet. Occupied with the enemy men-at-arms, Constantine had almost forgotten about the Ferrarese infantry. Now all the Venetian men-at-arms reunited and formed up in a line, facing the village. Ahead, he could see the tough marines climbing over the barricades and chasing the enemy infantry up the slope toward them.

With one more trumpet blast, the company of horse sprang toward the enemy infantry. Realizing that the horsemen were not their guardian angels but were instead Venetian men-at-arms, they began to throw down their arms and surrender. In a few minutes, the battle was over.

The Venetians had lost fewer than thirty men, plus about one hundred in the defense of the hamlet, but they had inflicted grievous losses on the enemy. More than one hundred men-at-arms were captured, including seven of the fifteen enemy nobles on the field (two others were killed outright and three more were seriously wounded). In addition, more than five hundred infantry were killed or captured.

The Venetians had routed the Ferrarese force. Its survivors, streaming away to the south, left the valley littered with their dead and wounded and the shattered remnants of their once-proud army. All that remained was to take their capital.

As Constantine rode over the field, he found the man he had unhorsed with a blow from his sword. Two menacing *stradiotti* were dutifully guarding him, awaiting Constantine's return. When the prisoner, who was not badly wounded, recognized Constantine, he waved.

Constantine dismounted and asked the man's name.

"I am Antonio Farina of Rovigo, at your service, and who, may I ask, are you?"

"I am Constantine Ziani, of Venice."

"It appears, Signor Ziani, that you have gotten the better of me today. I can assure you that my family will pay my ransom promptly. Of course, *you* will need to pay off these two gentlemen who have so graciously spared my life today."

Constantine looked at the two rough-hewn, smiling men, with no more than ten teeth between them, eagerly anticipating a generous reward.

"How much do you want to release the prisoner into my keeping?"

They looked at each other, afraid to set their price too low or too high.

Curiously, war made for strange bedfellows. The two nobles were now united in their desire to pay off the *stradiotti* quickly and send them on their way.

"Ten ducats should do nicely, signore," said the tall one.

"I shall give you twelve if you can recover this man's horse," replied Constantine.

"You are most kind," complimented Farina.

"I am certain you would do the same for me if our positions were reversed."

"It is that one, the chestnut mare, over there," pointed the prisoner.

As the two *stradiotti* mounted and rode off to retrieve the horse, Constantine turned to Farina and smiled. "Tell me, why did you stand and fight? Why did you not flee like the others?"

"Because I am a man of honor," he replied with a serious frown. "I am from Rovigo, in the Polesine. I stand to lose everything—my lands, my purse, a hefty ransom. But one thing I will never lose is my self-respect."

"But you could have been killed," countered Constantine.

"Young man, I have fought in more than a few battles. I have been captured twice before, and I myself have captured and ransomed more than a dozen men-at-arms. Not once has death interfered with the business of war. I have learned that the best way to be killed is to lose the respect of your enemy. Brave men are ransomed, cowards have their throats cut. That is the way of war. Do not ever forget it."

Constantine nodded thoughtfully as he considered his prisoner's words. For the first time since he had gone off to war, it was all clear to him now.

"Signore, a year ago, I would have accepted what you have said without question. But in my brief but sad experience, I have found that it is the rich who are ransomed and the common soldiers who have their throats cut. I can assure you, Signor Farina, bravery has nothing to do with the matter. Two of the bravest and most noble men I have ever known were butchered by your comrades because they wore simple chain mail, instead of expensive armor, betraying their station as commoners. So you see, it is your fine suit of armor plate, not your valor, that has saved you this day."

19

The Betrayal

A ntonio shifted his weight on the hard wooden bench. He had arrived early at the Doges' Palace to be sure he could get a seat close to the raised dais at the end of the chamber where Doge Mocenigo and his *Signoria* would be seated. His hearing was not as good as it used to be, and he knew that the doge would be reporting on the progress of the war. Rumors had been sweeping the city that the army had crossed the Po. He knew from experience that Count Cajazzo would engage Duke Ercole and his allies in a final, decisive battle somewhere between the Po and Ferrara. Perhaps the battle had already been fought. He was worried about Constantine's safety but not nearly as much as his wife and daughter-in-law were.

The benches were quickly filling up with senators and various other officials, resplendent in their simple yet expensive garb. In ten minutes, when the meeting would begin, more than 150 of Venice's leading citizens would be gathered there to receive the news. Powerful men huddled in small groups as they greeted each other, talking excitedly about how the war was going and what the doge might say.

Antonio knew more about the situation than most of the men in the room. Venice was fighting the war with Ferrara and her allies on two fronts, as she always did. One was fought in the open, on the field of battle, deploying soldiers and marines with swords and crossbows to vanquish her dangerous foes. The other was fought behind closed doors, in the halls of power, relying upon her diplomats' and spies' persuasion and guile.

Antonio was worried. His letter to Girolamo Riario had gone unanswered. More than enough time had elapsed for a response. Since the pope had won his great victory over the Neapolitans at Campomorto in August, he had not followed up his victory. Even though his commander, Roberto da Rimino had died shortly afterward, the pope had plenty of money to hire another competent commander to replace him. Something was wrong. It was as though Sixtus had satisfied his need to punish Venice's opponents and was now content to be a spectator from the comfort of Rome.

The room quieted when the doge and his entourage entered. They quickly took their places in their high-backed chairs, speaking to no one, conveying the seriousness of the meeting. Antonio studied the doge's face. He knew him well enough to detect from his forced smile that he was unsettled, even nervous. Antonio was not alone. Other men began whispering, sharing similar observations.

"I have good news," Mocenigo began, surprising his audience, including Antonio. "Count Cajazzo has confirmed our faith in his military prowess. He has led our troops to a great victory over our foe at Argenta, just south of the Po. They have destroyed a large part of the enemy's army, killing or capturing more than six hundred. Now nothing stands between us and Duke Ercole's capital."

"What about our losses?" called a high-pitched voice from among the rows of highly polished wooden benches. Every head turned in his direction.

The doge acknowledged the reasonableness of the man's query.

"We have not yet received an official report of the dead, but I am told they number no more than thirty men-at-arms and about a hundred infantry."

A pair of hands began to clap slowly and deliberately, as if to make a profound statement. Some more hands joined in. Then a few men stood, clapping too. Suddenly the room broke into pandemonium. Rarely in the thirty-four years since he had first joined the Great Council, at age twenty-five, had Antonio seen such a breach of decorum in the ornate Sala del Senato. The exception was when Sultan Muhammad II died. The crowd of Venetian luminaries were hugging and dancing like children at carnival time. Four or five sprang forward and embraced the doge as his two bodyguards eyed each other nervously, unsure what to do.

Only a few men seemed to be detached from the raw emotion that swept the room. One was Doge Mocenigo, another was Antonio.

Antonio was not interested in the rest of the proceedings that night, having to do with conferring praise upon the army and its various commanders, especially the *condottiere*, Roberto da San Severino, Count Cajazzo. With victory secured, he only wanted to hear news of his son.

A ntonio carefully surveyed the doge's face. Gentile Bellini, Venice's greatest living painter, had recently painted his profile, capturing him perfectly. Five long, deep parallel lines cut across his forehead as they bent around his thick eyebrows. His tight, straight mouth and thin lips were pasted onto his full, pale leathery jowls like an afterthought. Clean shaven, his face begged for a beard, if only to obscure the sadness it conveyed with uncustomary starkness. This day, it was his eyes that revealed his thoughts. No one in Venice should have been more jubilant about the great victory over Ferrara and her allies than Giovanni Mocenigo, but those windows into his soul betrayed his anxiety. He looked as though he had not slept in days.

Antonio thought that the seventy-four-year-old looked as if he had aged ten years since becoming doge just four years before.

"I must say that I am not surprised you sent for me," said Antonio.

"Why do you say that?" the doge replied almost impatiently. Conscious that three ever-present *capi* sat stoically behind him, he was trying to keep the conversation formal despite their familial relationship. "Now that victory seems to be close at hand and it is time for Pope Sixtus and his nephew, Girolamo, to stand and deliver, I find their recent silence most concerning."

"I have had the same thoughts," added Antonio.

"How long has it been since you last heard from our most illustrious citizen?"

"Too long," replied Antonio instantly, asserting himself. "More than a month ago, I sent him a letter by ship via Ancona and have heard nothing from him since. I should have received his reply nearly two weeks ago."

The doge rubbed his chin and looked at the man seated next to him. Antonio recognized him as Signor Molin, the head of the Republic's vast network of spies.

"Please tell Signor Ziani what your people in Rome have heard."

"The news is bad," he began, shaking his head ruefully. "One in our pay is the secretary to Cardinal Rispoglio, the Holy Father's adviser in secular affairs. In this capacity, he is a trusted functionary responsible for making all official and unofficial appointments for the cardinal. He knows who is trying to influence the cardinal and even the Holy Father himself."

Antonio prepared to hear the news as he studied the doge's face. Mocenigo looked as though he had a broken heart.

"About two weeks ago, the cardinal received three visitors, all separately,"

said Signor Molin. "The first was the ambassador from Florence. I hardly
need to state his purpose. The second was the ambassador from Naples, no
doubt making amends for attacking papal territory in August and inciting
the notorious Colonna family to ravage the pope's lands, depriving him of
much prestige and income and compelling the Holy Father to ally with the
equally notorious Orsini."

"Ever since I can remember, Rome has been plagued by those two brig-
and families," interjected the doge. "One is as bad as the other."

"The most concerning visitor was the third," continued Signor Molin.
"It was the imperial ambassador. Frederick, the Holy Roman Emperor, who
is old and harmless and well disposed toward us, is under increasing pressure
from his ambitious younger brother, Maximilian, who is no friend to Venice.
A source in Germany has told us that he has persuaded the ailing emperor to
place on the agenda of a council, scheduled to convene next week in Basel, a
call to end the wars in Italy and to hold us and the pope responsible, brand-
ing us as the aggressors. Scores of cardinals, in open revolt against the pope,
support the measure, as do several of the electors. No doubt Maximilian is attempting to gain favor with them to ensure he is Frederick's successor."

"And, of course, he would like to buy his salt from the Ferrarese as well,"
interrupted the doge, "saving thirty percent compared to the price we are
charging him."

"It goes beyond profit," replied Molin. "There is a power struggle
within the Church. Sixtus has dangerously exposed himself as a friend of
Venice—hardly a popular position these days. Worse, he has allowed the favoritism he has shown his nephews to create a gulf between him and his
cardinals. Now, it appears, these men may have allied with Maximilian to
turn the Holy Father against us in our moment of triumph."

They sat, reflecting, thinking. Finally the doge broke the silence.

"Antonio, I want you to go to Rome. Signor Molin will arrange several
meetings, the first with the cardinal's secretary, so you can receive his latest
report personally. Then, with Lord Riario, to find out whether we can still
count on the Holy Father's support or if he will defect to our enemies. You
will have official ambassador status, authorizing you to meet with the pope,
but only see him after you have met with the other two."

"When can you sail for Ancona?" asked Molin.

"Not until tomorrow night, with the evening tide. It will take that long
to outfit one of my ships and round up the crew. The ship I have in mind
was not scheduled to sail for another week."

"Good. A packet will be delivered to you tomorrow at noon with your
instructions for the meeting with our man," said Molin.

"What is the man's name?"

"Ronaldo Zappile."

The doge rose to his feet, as did Molin, indicating that the meeting was over.

"One more thing, Doge Mocenigo." Antonio narrowed his gaze. "If the list of the dead at Argenta arrives after I have departed, and Constantine's name is on it, please do not forget to comfort his poor mother. Only your daughter loves him more than she."

20

The Spy

They reached the outskirts of Rome after an uneventful nine-day journey. Antonio and Seraglio purposely delayed their arrival in the city until just after sunset—about five o'clock, in early December. They eschewed the Venetian ambassador's residence since the street it was on would be crawling with spies and informers. They were determined to avoid any contact with their fellow Venetians until after they had finished their business with Cardinal Rispoglio's secretary.

Instead, they went discreetly to the home of Señor Alvarez, a Spaniard and an old friend of Antonio's who had once been the House of Ziani's agent in Valencia. When they appeared at his door, he gladly invited them to share his fire and his food and to stay as many nights in his house as they pleased. Antonio told him they were in Rome on secret business and easily secured the man's agreement to tell no one of their presence.

After a light supper of sausage, bread, and tomatoes, they borrowed the man's carriage and driver and went to their prearranged meeting place, just off the Lung Vaticano, near Castel Sant'Angelo, on the banks of the Tiber.

On the way there, one of the horses broke a trace. It took the old driver about twenty minutes to repair it, making them late for their appointment. Now at the appointed place, the driver slowed the horses to a walk as they searched for a window with two candles. As the street curved along the riverbank, they could see the Ponte Sant'Angelo ahead on their right, across from the mighty fortress.

"There!" Seraglio pointed. His sharp eyes had spotted two lights faintly flickering in a third-floor window about fifty yards from the bridge.

"Stop here and wait for us," ordered Antonio.

The driver nodded as he shifted nervously in his seat. "It is not safe for gentlemen to be out at night in this neighborhood of the city, signore. There are many robbers about these days—some of them are most desperate."

Antonio discounted the man's warning, blaming him for not checking the trace ahead of time and causing their tardiness.

Seraglio was already standing on the doorstep by the time Antonio crossed the street. The front door was locked.

Seraglio rapped loudly until a shuttered window finally burst open above them. Out popped an old woman's head, her silver-gray hair spilling out from beneath her white nightcap.

"Go away. People are trying to sleep," she hissed down at them.

"We have an appointment with Signor Zappile."

The woman smiled a toothless grin. "He is a popular one tonight." She laughed. "He has already gone."

"When did he leave?"

"Not more than five minutes ago. He went off with two men in a carriage."

Antonio and Seraglio looked at each other, surprised.

"That strange little man"—she shook her head—"I pity poor Cardinal Rispoglio."

They looked up at her. "Why is that?" asked Antonio.

"Well, one would think that a man who is responsible for setting a cardinal's appointments could keep his own straight."

"What direction did he go—with the two men?"

"Over the Ponte Sant'Angelo." She pointed across the river.

"Thank you, signora."

The old woman shook her head and shuttered the window with a bang. Antonio and Seraglio ran back to their carriage and roused the sleepy driver.

"Take us across the Ponte Sant'Angelo as fast as you can."

"Antonio," protested Seraglio, "how do you expect us to find him?"

"I fear foul play. Worse, our mission is compromised."

"I agree. This is too much of a coincidence."

The driver turned the carriage onto the bridge and crossed over the river, heading southeast toward the ancient ruins.

Antonio stuck his head out of the window. A cold wind slapped him hard in the face. He struggled to peer through the fog. Some lanterns glowed ghostlike up ahead.

"I see a carriage, maybe two."

"Faster!" shouted Seraglio, his blood now up as he stood on the seat and poked his head out of the other window.

They were steadily closing in on the lights.

"Antonio," shouted Seraglio. "I am concerned."

"Do not worry. We have nearly overtaken them."

"But *that* is what I am worried about. We would hardly be able to subdue his captors."

Antonio pulled in his head and sat on the seat. Seraglio quickly plopped down opposite him. They looked at each other and both smiled.

Antonio burst into laughter. He was right, by God.

"Driver, keep your distance. Follow that carriage but do not get too close."

"Yes, signore," he called back, much relieved.

A few minutes later, the phantom carriage slowed and disappeared down a side street on their right.

"Stop here, at this corner."

Antonio and Seraglio exited the coach.

"Remain here, ready to depart at a moment's notice. We may be a while," said Antonio.

"There, up ahead, see the lights?" Seraglio pointed.

A big black carriage was stopped in front of a three-story stone building, its lanterns blazing amber light through the mist. They walked along, keeping in the shadows of the buildings. Soon they could see the driver's back. He was slumped over, as though he were sleeping. As they came up on the carriage, they quickly glanced inside. It was empty.

Seraglio tapped Antonio on the arm and pointed to an open door. They drew their daggers and tiptoed into the house. The entrance was dark, but a glimmer of light cascaded down the stairway at the end of the hall. As they neared it, they could hear faint noises from somewhere above.

"Discretion being the better part of valor, I think we should go get some help."

"There is no time, Seraglio. No, we have to see what this is all about."

Antonio began to ascend the narrow stairs, stepping lightly as he tried unsuccessfully to prevent the wooden boards from creaking. Seraglio followed close behind, scared to death.

Reaching the first landing, Antonio suddenly put up his hand and stopped. He could hear men talking but could not distinguish their words.

"Go up to the next floor and see if you can hear what they are saying."

Seraglio's wide-open eyes begged him for a reprieve. Understanding, Antonio explained further.

"Your light steps will not make the floorboards creak so much. I will be right behind you."

Antonio knew his friend would obey, but he also knew it would take all of his courage.

Seraglio crept along the wall to lessen the squeaking. It worked. Soon he came to a door emitting a carpet of soft yellow light across the floor. Carefully he cupped his hand against it.

He could hear men inside talking and waved to Antonio to listen.

Two men were arguing in loud voices, confident they were alone.

"How much longer do you think it will take him to come to? It has been fifteen minutes, and he is still unconscious."

"How should I know?"

"You hit him too hard, I think."

"We do not get paid to think. We only get paid for information."

"Well, at this rate, we are not going to get paid at all for our work tonight."

"I will have to arouse him. Go down and get my instruments from the carriage."

Antonio and Seraglio instinctively ducked into the shadows at the end of the hallway. No sooner had they disappeared than the door opened and a short man emerged, shut the door behind him, and walked loudly down the stairs, oblivious to their presence.

"Our enemy has divided his forces," whispered Seraglio.

"Quick, we'll take him on the landing below."

Seraglio followed Antonio down the stairs.

"Wait here on the stairs and surprise him when he returns. While he is occupied, I will take him from behind," Antonio whispered.

A minute later, the man returned, panting slightly as he climbed the stairs to the first-floor landing. As he turned to ascend the next flight of stairs, he suddenly spotted what looked like a sleeping boy, lying sprawled on a step.

"Out of my way, you little beggar!" he snarled.

He lashed out with his boot, catching Seraglio squarely, taking his breath away. Antonio sprang at him, incensed. He smashed the hilt of his dagger into the man's skull, crumpling him to the floor.

As Seraglio gasped to catch his breath and rubbed his painful groin, Antonio tied the man up with his sash, gagging him by pushing his glove in his mouth.

"Next time, I would appreciate it if you would strike first, before I am reduced to a eunuch."

"I am sorry, old friend, but the years have slowed me down just a bit," replied Antonio as he gazed down at his victim. "What a detestable-looking character he is!"

"Yes, it must be the ugliest face in all of Rome. He looks like a pig with the pox."

"What 'instruments' does he have in his bag?" asked Antonio.

Seraglio opened the small sack and carefully arranged its contents on the floor. They were the terrifying tools of torture—a brass thumbscrew; a hammer and a dozen long, thin nails; and worst of all, a razor-sharp flaying tool, the kind used to slowly peel off a man's skin—as well as assorted lengths of cords and gags to restrain and silence a victim.

Repulsed at the sight of the cruel implements, Antonio looked up toward the landing above and whispered, "I will knock. When he opens the door, grab his leg. I will hit him with this hammer. Quickly."

Seraglio smiled approvingly, still rubbing himself to be sure his jewels were where they were supposed to be. They climbed the stairs to the landing and tiptoed down the hall. Antonio rapped twice. As soon as the door opened, Seraglio grimaced and dove for the man's leg as Antonio pushed with all his weight, slamming the door hard into the surprised man. In a few seconds, he was lying unconscious on the floor, his head split open like a melon, streaming blood. Seraglio rushed to Zappile, who was lying bound to a crude cot. He was still unconscious but breathing and apparently all right.

"Another half hour and our man here would have spilled his guts out," observed Seraglio as he tried to revive him by pinching his cheeks.

"When we reach the street, you will need to distract the driver while I carry him."

"Leave that one to me," replied Seraglio confidently.

He quietly opened the door and stole a quick glance at the street. The driver was perched on his carriage seat, like a man impatiently waiting to be paid. Seraglio quickly decided that he was not in league with the two abductors—just a simple carriage for hire.

He waited until the man was not looking in their direction. Then he quickly crept behind the carriage, hoping not to rouse the slumbering horses. Standing up, he began to whistle as he passed on the other side, into sight. The man gave him a startled stare and then shifted nervously on his seat. By the time he looked back at the door, Antonio had carried the secretary out and into the shadows behind the carriage. In ten minutes, they were in their coach, and in another twenty, safely back at the home of Señor Alvarez.

The angry purple cherry-sized lump on the back of Zappile's head was easily visible through his thinning hair. As Seraglio rubbed some ointment on it, Zappile winced with pain as he gradually regained his senses.

Suddenly frightened by the unfamiliar surroundings and faces, he shuddered. "Who are you? I have done nothing wrong. Please let me go free," he implored.

"Fear not, friend. We are your employers. We saved you from men who abducted and intended to torture you. Tell us what happened," said Antonio.

The man was incredulous; he was obviously still terrified. "Who are you?" He still trembled.

"I am Antonio Ziani, and this is my friend Seraglio. We were sent by the doge to meet with you." He smiled to reassure the frightened secretary.

Zappile shook his head. "I do not understand. If *you* are Signor Ziani, then who were those other men?"

"Impostors, no doubt in the pay of the pope or the League."

Zappile turned toward Seraglio and smiled. Then he looked humbly at Antonio. "Thank you for saving my life. They surely would have killed me."

"For sure," agreed Seraglio as he handed him a glass of wine.

"Did you tell them anything?" asked Antonio.

"Nothing. I met them at the door, thinking it was you." He took a small sip from the glass. "I had not gone three steps when they knocked me on the head. The next thing I remember was riding in the carriage on the way here, with you."

"We regret the ill treatment you have suffered, Signor Zappile but time is short. Tell us everything you know. We need to meet with Lord Riario in the morning."

The man looked at Antonio quizzically. "That is impossible. He canceled his appointment with Cardinal Rispoglio just two days ago and left Rome that afternoon."

Antonio shot a quick glance at Seraglio. "Do you know where he went?"

"I do not keep Lord Riario's calendar, only the cardinal's."

"Who shall we meet with, then?" asked Seraglio.

Antonio could feel his stomach tighten. He would see Pope Sixtus by himself if he had to. He had to find out what the pope would do. Anything less would be failure. He temporarily pushed the vexing problem from his mind and turned back to Zappile.

"Now take another drink of wine and then tell us what else you have learned since your last report."

. . .

F ortunately, Cardinal Rispoglio trusted Zappile completely, not knowing that he was in Venice's pay. As a consequence, the secretary was aware of who had attended the many meetings on the cardinal's schedule, but unfortunately, he did not know the subjects of their discussions or the outcomes.

Zappile recounted the discomforting events he had observed over the past few weeks. When he had finished his report, it was clear that Pope Sixtus had been in conversations with Venice's enemies, including the Holy Roman Emperor and representatives from Florence, Milan, and Ferrara—all in secret.

After advising Zappile to return immediately to Venice and providing him with the necessary papers to conceal his identity on the journey back, they left him. In the privacy of their room, Antonio and Seraglio formulated their plans for the next day, which they agreed would be their last in Rome.

21

The Pope

Sixtus IV sat in his chambers, patiently waiting for his lunch, before meeting with the Venetian ambassador. Already knowing what he would say to the ambassador, the pope turned his thoughts to all he had accomplished and smiled to himself. Surely the people would fondly remember him for all his good works.

Born a peasant, he had been sickly for most of his childhood. At nine, he was sent to a Franciscan convent to receive a proper education. Excelling in every field of study, he became a tutor to the powerful Della Rovere family, taking their name as his own. After teaching at Pavia and Bologna, he went on to the university in Padua, where he got his first taste of Venetian culture as he taught thousands of students there. Then, there was little to indicate that beneath his professorial demeanor were an iron will and a prodigious constitution.

Cardinal Francesco della Rovere had been elected pope eleven years earlier, in 1471. Now an old man of sixty-eight years, he had lost none of the fire that had burned in his belly from the time he had assumed the pontificate. Though he was short and heavy, his face was finely sculpted, like a Roman emperor's. He was nearly bald, and his nose curved down toward his thin lips like a scimitar. His strong chin jutted forward, discouraging disobedience. A famous man of letters, he spoke with clarity and charm. He was almost always the most learned man in the room.

After his election as pope, he had brought order to Rome and its environs, controlling the rampant brigandage and winning the respect and love of the people. He ordered the Acqua Vergine rebuilt to provide Rome with clean water, an alternative to the filthy Tiber River that had sickened city residents for years. He also restored or rebuilt dozens of Rome's decaying or abandoned churches, adding seven new ones.

He had transformed the Vatican by sponsoring the Sistine Chapel, hiring the renowned artists Botticelli, Perugino, and Roselli to decorate it. The people rewarded him for his visionary accomplishment by insisting that the chapel bear his name. He enlarged the Vatican Library. He also built the Ponte Sisto, the first new bridge across the Tiber since Roman times, and the Via Sistina, a new road leading from the Vatican to Castel Sant'Angelo, connecting the Vatican to Rome for the first time.

More than a steadfast patron of the arts, he had beautified Rome, widening its streets, paving them for the first time since the Romans, and cleaning up many of its miserable neighborhoods.

The eighteen voting cardinals had elected Sixtus for his intellect and integrity, but the demands of the job quickly transformed him from teacher to politician and soldier. As a sculptor carefully chisels away a block of marble to reveal the figure imprisoned within, so the hand of God had broken away the pope's academic façade, revealing a true titan who was resolved to strengthen the papacy at the expense of the temporal rulers who had selfishly and destructively ruled Italy for more than two hundred years.

Since then, Sixtus had relied upon his many Della Rovere and Riario nephews to extend his power and amplify his ability to accomplish his many aims. However, that approach had won him as many enemies as admirers. Most recently, his decision to support Venice had angered many of the cardinals, despite the fact that he had personally appointed most of them. He was also under great pressure from Frederick, the Holy Roman Emperor, and from most of the Italian city-states to shift his support. He still chafed at the insolence of Louis XI of France, who insisted that most papal decrees needed royal assent before they could be enacted in France, undermining the pope's power in Europe's most populous state.

Three days before Sixtus's meeting with Antonio, the pontiff's nephew, Girolamo Riario, had informed him that the Venetian army had won a great victory at Argenta and was now encamped just four miles from Duke Ercole's castle in Ferrara. Even the duke was down with swamp fever. Venice had outdone herself in this contest. She was not as exhausted by her wars with the Turks as the pope had thought and was now one siege away from the victory he had helped to make possible. He could not help admiring the Venetians and all they had accomplished.

As he sat eating his light noonday meal—a single apple, some cheese, and a piece of unleavened bread—he contemplated his awesome power. After all these years, he was still amazed by it. Although his once-prodigious appetite had waned considerably, his desire to have his way had grown stronger—inversely proportional to his remaining days. More than any mortal, he could change the world with his words.

Sixtus wondered what the Venetian ambassador would have to say. He looked at the piece of paper on the table. Antonio Ziani was his name. He was the same *nobile* who had sponsored the pope's nephew to become a Venetian senator less than a year before. No wonder Girolamo had asked to go hunting, leaving his uncle to meet with the man!

A ntonio arrived alone at the Vatican fifteen minutes early. He had faced many things in his life—imprisonment, death, ruin, failure, and all kinds of treachery—but he had never done anything like this before. He was about to meet the Holy Father, God's servant on this earth; the pope, head of His apostolic church. He would much have preferred to confer with Lord Riario first, as disgusting as the man was. Knowledge was power, and Antonio had little doubt that he could have profited from the exchange. Always pragmatic, Antonio could only regard Riario's ill-timed and unexpected absence as deliberate—a bad omen to be sure.

He also wished Seraglio could have come with him and contributed his keen powers of observation and penetrating analysis, but the pope received only duly credentialed ambassadors, never their proxies or assistants.

Two Swiss guards searched Antonio for weapons and then ushered him into the pontiff's private quarters, where he was met by the smiling Cardinal Rispoglio.

"Ambassador Ziani, we were surprised to learn that Ambassador Contarini had been recalled and that you had been named in his place. He has served Venice well for the last four years here in Rome."

"Yes, he has, but he desired to live again in Venice, so he did not seek a continuance of his appointment."

"I can hardly blame him for wanting to return to your beautiful city. I remember many joyful days there myself, when I was a student at Padua."

Rispoglio paused and smiled, as though awaiting a return compliment about Rome. Antonio decided it was time to find out what had happened to Girolamo Riario.

"I was surprised that my meeting with Lord Riario was canceled. Is he ill?"

"Hardly. He has been dispatched by the Holy Father to France to meet with the king."

"I suppose I cannot feel slighted by that," quipped Antonio.

The cardinal simply nodded without comment. With their niceties exchanged, the air in the room turned frigid, the silence almost unbearable. After five minutes, a guard came in and whispered in the cardinal's ear.

"Please excuse me, Ambassador Ziani. The Holy Father will be here shortly."

No sooner did the door shut behind the departing cardinal than another opened and Pope Sixtus IV entered, flanked by four guards, each carrying a halberd and wearing a long sword at his side.

"Welcome to Rome, Signor Ambassador," greeted the pope, an engaging smile on his face. His distinct syllables proclaimed his skill as a rhetorician.

"Your Holiness," replied Antonio as he knelt and kissed the emerald ring that encircled the middle finger on the pope's outstretched right hand.

"Please sit. When did you arrive in Rome?"

"Last night."

"You must be tired from your long journey."

"I am a merchant and a soldier. I am inured to arduous travel and hardship."

"Are not we all, we men of action?" The pope smiled again. This time he showed his yellowed teeth, and his wrinkled, clean-shaven face seemed to ripple as he allowed himself a modest laugh. "How goes the war with Duke Ercole?"

"We have defeated him south of the Po, and now the army is encamped near his capital. Thousands of his countrymen have sought refuge within the town, which was already overcrowded with the remnants of his defeated forces. Now the siege will begin."

Antonio reached out his hands in a gesture of respect. "Doge Mocenigo wishes me to congratulate Your Holiness on your great victory at Campomorto and to thank you for preventing the Neapolitans from intervening."

The pope nodded. "Surely you did not come all this way just to tell me that."

"No." Antonio tried to suppress the lightness he felt in his head.

"Holy Father, we are in the process of teaching Duke Ercole a lesson he will not soon forget. We estimate the siege may last up to two months. Are you prepared to continue to prevent reinforcement by Naples by denying them access through papal lands? In a word, will you honor your solemn pledge to Venice?"

"Those seem like strange words, coming just after congratulating me for rendering Venice such a great service. What makes the doge feel that he must ask?"

Antonio decided it would be best to be direct. "We have heard that Milan, Florence, Ferrara, Naples—even the Emperor Frederick—have been beating a path to your door, entreating you to call us off before we have finished off Duke Ercole."

Antonio leaned forward, his face barely three feet from the pope's. The nervous guards gripped their halberds with both hands and moved closer, even though he had already been searched and disarmed before the meeting.

Sixtus slapped his thigh and laughed.

"You Venetians have always been rumored to have the best spies in Europe. What else have you heard?"

"That you are in a quandary about whether to continue to support Venice."

The pope leaned forward, his smile melting into a frown. "Ambassador Ziani, it is time for peace. I have decided that I must think of the interests of the entire Italian Peninsula now. Ferrara and her allies are defeated. You have won—with my help, I might add. Now it is time to end this war between Christians."

"Are you suggesting that we stop, in our moment of victory, laying aside the Venetian lives and treasure we have expended in our righteous cause?"

"Precisely," the pope replied, crossing his arms in a gesture of finality.

"But why would we do that? It would only encourage Duke Ercole and many others to defy us in the future. Venice would appear to be no more than a barking dog chained to a stake, unable to pursue his tormentors."

"That is one way to see things, but it is not how I see them. We must maintain a delicate balance here in Italy, and you have destroyed it with your brilliant victories over the duke and his incompetent allies."

Antonio's worst fears were now a reality. Sixtus was abandoning the field, daring Venice to fight on alone. He might even be prepared to join in the League with Duke Ercole to force the Republic to see things his way.

"What do you propose to make this bitter medicine more palatable to us?"

"I have not failed to anticipate your distaste for my wishes, but I assure you, the taste in your mouth is no worse than the one that was in Duke Ercole's a year ago, when I threw my support to Venice."

The pope stood, indicating the meeting was ended.

"Tell your doge and Senate that I have signed a five-year treaty with Milan, Florence, Naples, and Ferrara to mutually defend the Italian Peninsula against any and all invaders. I want Venice, with her economic and naval power, to join this league. Of course"—he smiled slyly—"its members cannot be at war with one another.

"Tell your countrymen that they have only two options, both nonnegotiable. The first is to cease hostilities immediately, sparing Ferrara a destructive siege, and withdraw your forces back beyond the Po. In return, Venice can retain the Polesine; Duke Ercole will forfeit any claim to the territory north of the river, giving you sole control of Rovigo. Further, Duke Ercole and the rest of Italy will resume buying salt from Venice, and he will not rebuild his salt pans. In recognition of this, Venice will sell salt to him and the rest of Italy at prewar prices."

The pope paused, as if to gather his thoughts. With the carrot revealed, Antonio prepared for the stick.

"If you refuse these generous terms, negotiated on your behalf with some very angry and powerful people, including the Holy Roman Emperor and the King of France, here is what will happen: I will immediately join the League arrayed against you, bringing my forces and King Ferrante's into the field, compelling you to abandon your siege. Further, Milan and Florence, relieved of the need to help defend Ferrara, will attack you in the Veneto, laying waste to your *terra firma* lands, all the way to the lagoon. Further, we will rebuild Ercole's salt pans in the Po Delta and replace Venice as the supplier to the rest of Italy. You will also permanently cede the Polesine lands to Duke Ercole. And just in case you are thinking of choosing this option, despite these terms, let me add one more thing, just to convince you it would be a terrible mistake to defy me. If you refuse, I will lay an interdict on Venice.

"This interdict would exclude all people in Venetian territories, whether citizens or not, from participation in the liturgy and, in general, all acts performed by clerics, including the sacraments. No legal baptisms, weddings, final unctions, or burials. No communion and, finally, although I doubt it would concern you Venetians, no forgiveness for confessed sins."

The pope's steely gaze pierced Antonio like a sword. There was nothing to clarify; the pope had made himself deathly clear. To negotiate would be pointless and, worse, would intimate weakness.

"When does the Holy Father want our answer?"

"If you go no further in pressing your siege against Ferrara, I will give you two weeks to reply. If you do not withdraw, I will consider that to be your answer!"

With that said, the pope stood and walked out, followed by three of his guards. The fourth closed the door behind them, walked to another exit, and motioned for him to follow. Antonio felt as though a barrel of black powder had just exploded in his face.

On the carriage ride back to Alvarez's house, the pope's devastating words stuck in his memory. It was undeniable: Venice had been outmaneuvered by her enemies. The meeting with the pope had turned out to be nothing but a *fait accompli*. He wondered what the Senate would do. No doubt it would be split: one group would want to fight on, and the other would want to accept the pope's humiliating terms. Sixtus's perfidious betrayal would lead to a bitter fight within the Republic's leadership, making an effective response difficult—either decision would lack consensus.

22

The Choice

ntonio and Seraglio reported the disastrous news to the doge and
his *Signoria* as soon as they arrived back in Venice. Mocenigo immediately called for a meeting of the sixty-man Senate, doubled in size
by a *zonta*—an additional sixty members of the Great Council who were
added when the most important decisions were to be made.

As Antonio took his place in the Senate chamber, he knew that Venice
had not faced a more dangerous decision since it had voted to support the
Byzantine emperor Constantine XI against the Turks before the ill-fated
siege of Constantinople. That vote had triggered a monumental conflict
with the Ottoman Empire lasting almost thirty years, wrecking Venice's
economy, and weakening her so, that she now faced the prospect of a war
against virtually all of Italy. She was like a wounded stag, and the ravenous
wolves were gathering, about to move in for the kill.

Antonio looked at the men seated around him. He knew them all by
name; many were close friends and business associates. What would they do?
He thought about the vote so many years before. Then, the question had
been whether to send reinforcements to Constantinople. Some wanted to
leave the city to its fate. Most voted to support the Byzantines, despite the
many disputes with them in the past. After all, they were fellow Christians,
threatened with attack by the Turks. He doubted that many senators would

have voted the way they did, had they known what their vote would have reaped.

This time, they were not fighting a horde of infidels. They were fighting fellow Christians, and now the pope intended to defect and join them. Even more sobering was the fact that the enemy armies were only a week's march from Venetian territory and La Serenissima's breadbasket in the Veneto.

The doge abruptly entered with his entourage. The senators quickly ended their conversations and waited respectfully for him to call the session to order. When news of the victory at Argenta had been announced less than two months before, the senators had been jubilant, but no one was smiling now. Even Antonio felt depressed, as if he were attending a funeral service. As Doge Mocenigo called the meeting to order, no trace of emotion was evident on his face.

"We have received grave news from Signor Ziani, our special ambassador to the Holy See. The Holy Father is concerned that our victories in the Polesine and at Argenta have altered the balance of power in the Italian Peninsula. Faced with pressure from his flock of cardinals, from Emperor Frederick, and from our enemies in Florence, Milan, and Naples, he has informed us that we have two choices. We must now make peace, giving up all of our hard-fought gains, or he will change sides and join the League. I do not have to tell you that we would be hard-pressed to resist the forces ranged against us.

"What shall we do in the face of this treachery?" The doge raised his voice, catching the senators by surprise. Senators began to argue, shouting at those who disagreed with their impassioned speeches—an uncustomary breach of decorum.

The doge called for order, banging loudly on the arm of his ornate chair with a heavy gold ducat. With order restored, he continued.

"Here are the decisions we must make. First, which course to take, submission or defiance, in the face of this overwhelming force? If we vote to submit, we must agree on what terms are acceptable. Surely we can obtain a more favorable peace than the one the pope is offering if we pick one of our enemies and negotiate a separate peace, breaking up the League as they degenerate into recriminations and mistrust. If we vote to resist, we must find a new ally to offset the effects of the pope's defection.

"We must also advise Count Cajazzo of a new strategy that reflects our decision. He and the army are encamped a few miles outside the walls of Ferrara, awaiting our orders to begin a siege of the place. It is winter. They can no longer live off the land around the city, as they have depleted the countryside of food and forage. It is costing us a fortune to supply their needs all the way from Venice. The question is, do we lay siege to Ferrara, locking our main army in place, possibly leaving the Veneto virtually undefended? Or do we assume a defensive posture and await the League's attack, surrendering the initiative and any chance of taking our main adversary's capital?"

A senator rose to his feet. "How likely is an attack in the Veneto if we proceed with the siege?"

"It is our opinion that, given this sudden change in the political weather, all of our *terra firma* lands could be lost and our army isolated in Ferrara without taking Duke Ercole's capital. Sieges can take a long time to complete."

A long debate followed. Three hours passed as each senator spoke his mind, some controlled and thoughtful, some passionate, even inflammatory. In the end, it was obvious to everyone there that the vote would be close. One side, war weary and driven by pragmatism, expediency, and a desire to appease the enemy, argued to accept the pope's terms, with minor improvements. The other side, energetic, motivated by patriotic zeal, and aware of the long-term danger of making peace under these circumstances, argued to fight on. They believed that if Venice capitulated, her prestige would be mortally wounded, and she would be dogged by her enemies until her eventual demise.

It was nearly midnight when the debate ended. A count of hands showed that, by a slim margin, the Senate had voted to fight on. As soon as the doge officially announced the result, the discussion quickly turned to the siege. It took only a few minutes to decide to forgo the siege and pull the army back to the Po, where it could be more easily supplied by the river galley flotilla under the command of Antonio Justiniano.

Finally, the Senate ordered Venice's ambassadors and its extensive network of spies to find an ally to come to the Republic's aid, sparing no expense for bribes and other inducements.

The meeting finally over, Antonio walked home, wondering how the army would react to being restrained in its moment of victory. Would the soldiers' morale suffer? At times like this, he was concerned that Venetian troops were under the command of a foreigner, even one so distinguished as Count Cajazzo, instead of a Venetian whose loyalty to the Republic was unquestionable.

Following the fateful Senate meeting in January, the government officials feverishly prepared for the onslaught they knew would come in the spring, when Venice's enemies would leave their winter quarters and resume the campaign. They reinforced Count Cajazzo and the river fleet, put a small army in the field to protect the Veneto, sought allies, and continued their negotiations, by letter, with Sixtus IV.

Venice's enemies were busy, too. In March, Sixtus ordered Lord Riario to march to Ferrara with his force. The larger Neapolitan army would follow, a week behind them.

In order to conduct the war more effectively, with a unified strategy, the League assembled at Cremona. Consumed with their hatred of Venice and convinced that they finally had the power to defeat her, they considered Lord Riario's proposal to attack on two fronts: he and Duke Ercole would defeat Count Cajazzo's army on the Po while an equal-sized force under the command of Ludovico Sforza and Lorenzo de' Medici would attack from Milan, moving across the Adda River into the weakly defended Veneto with the object of ravaging Venetian lands all the way to the lagoon.

However, Sforza was reluctant to divide the League's forces, fearful of provoking a Venetian attack into his own territory. He convinced the rest of the League to combine all its forces and concentrate on destroying Count Cajazzo's formidable main army. There was, however, one more action to undertake in order to bring about Venice's downfall—a papal interdict. This, Sixtus ominously announced on May 25, a few days before the thirtieth anniversary of the fall of Constantinople.

In an effort to insulate the people from the effects of the pope's attack on their souls, Venice's government employed every obstacle to delay its communication. First, Venice's representative in Rome refused to pass along the official papal bull. When Sixtus's special envoy tried to deliver it to the Patriarch of San Marco in Venice, the cleric claimed that he was too ill to receive him. Finally, when the Ten were informed, they responded by ordering all churches and priests to continue to administer the sacraments, as usual. They also decreed that no official was to admit to the existence of the interdict, although they knew that rumors of it would soon sweep the Rialto.

23

The Sforzas

nrico Soranzo lay in his warm bed and thought about how oddly his
life had unfolded since he had left Venice. At his angry father's command, he had obediently gone to Florence to see his cousin Cosimo.
There, he had engaged in the boring business of banking, looking after the
needs of rich Florentines who, for one reason or another, preferred not to
do business with the Medici or the other Florentine banks.

As the months wore on, Enrico increasingly felt that his life in Florence
was unbearable, depressing. Each night he would drag his tired body home,
exhausted from struggling over columns of numbers and squinting at lengthy
contracts written in almost indiscernible script. He no longer seemed to have
time for women or drink—not like he did when he was a carefree young man
living in Venice. Though he often thought of the city of his birth, he tried
hard not to think of his father.

Eventually, a thought penetrated his mind, an idea that, in time, gave
birth to a dream. His father had sent him away from everything he loved, to
slave away like a pathetic clerk, under the stern and unrelenting oversight of
his dour cousin. Why should he suffer this humiliation? For what purpose
did he labor, day and night? Why should he not free himself forever from his
father's domination? Finally, one day, he decided that it was time to escape
his miserable life once and for all.

He smiled as he lay there, recalling that day when he withdrew five hundred ducats from the House of Soranzo. Cosimo had taken an infrequent day off to assist his shrewish wife in the care of their sickly children. Enrico had carefully forged his cousin's countersignature on a draft and concocted an elaborate story about a trip he had been ordered to take to Turin. But that had all been a ruse. Enrico had taken the money, purchased some new clothes, and boarded a fast coach bound for Milan. There, he had decided, he would pursue a life more to his liking.

He lazily rolled over in his comfortable bed and laughed out loud. For the first time in his life, he was truly free, no longer starving for his father's reluctant approval, like some beggar in front of a church hoping for a morsel of bread. Here, in Milan, there was no one to obey, no one to please, no one to fear.

There was much to commend this new life, he thought. He was unmarried, with plenty of ducats, living in an exciting city obsessed with money. Milan worshiped wealth even more than Venice because the Milanese had less of it. Best of all, Enrico had found a way to cast off his past, a life filled with disappointments and failures. Now the tales he had spun passed for the truth. All that was required to live in his fantasy world were a creative imagination and a good memory. Out of necessity, he had developed both.

Whenever asked, he attributed his fortune to his family's wise investments and to his own prowess in war. No longer merely a sailor who had missed the famed Venetian defense of Scutari, the new Enrico *had* been there, in the thick of the action. As he spun tales of his daring exploits, all told in gripping detail, the ladies would swoon. With his good looks and confident air, the silly women he pursued would usually end up in his bed, loving him long after he was finished with them. For months, he had played at this delightful game of seduction, but recently he had begun to notice that potential new conquests were becoming more difficult to find.

Recently a friend had told him that he was considered little more than a rake and a lecher by the upper crust of Milanese society. Now his reputation preceded him. Even so, like an actor, Enrico reveled in his newly created role. This would have been unthinkable back in Venice, but it seemed so natural here in this place—this strange new world.

Now, the women who still played the game with him were in it only for sport—to use him as he tried to use them. They were mostly cute, coquettish maidens, darting out from under their mothers' protection to flirt with danger for a few moments, like frightened but curious kittens. They only wasted his time and money.

Lately he had been attracted to more experienced women, mostly unmarried daughters of down-on-their-luck nobles. These were callous men, spending their children like his father spent sailors and marines to win a battle, hoping that their comely daughters could somehow entice and marry men as wealthy as they themselves used to be.

As he lay there thinking about what he would do to idle away the hours before night fell and the games began anew, his musings were interrupted by the sound of heavy footsteps ascending the stone stairs. He sprang from his bed and pulled on his pants. As he reached for his shirt, a loud knock rattled the door. Slipping it over his head, he opened the door. An officer and three soldiers stood in the hallway.

"You are Signor Soranzo?"

"Yes."

"You are to come with us at once to the ducal palace."

"The duke wishes to see me?" He was stunned.

"Not the duke. He is only fourteen years old. We have been sent by his uncle, Ludovico Sforza. I suggest you put on some decent clothes," said the officer in a monotone voice, as though reading the words from a paper.

Enrico quickly washed his face and hands, brushed his hair, and dressed in his new black robe, the one with scarlet piping. The day before he left Florence he had purchased it from a robe-maker who catered only to the nobility. He could confidently wear it in the presence of the regent. Lastly, he placed his favorite red hat on his head, careful to avoid the usual rakish tilt, and followed the soldiers down the stairs and into the street.

In minutes they reached the Castello Sforzesco, the ducal palace and fortress that dominated the city center, just as the Sforzi had dominated all of Lombardy since Francesco Sforza, the first duke, seized power from his employers, the now extinct Visconti, former dukes of Milan, in 1447. Even the Sforza name was meant to terrify—it was derived from the word *sforzare,* to exert force. The castello had been built by Duke Francesco with the help of Cosimo de' Medici, his close friend and ally. It was an impregnable fortress and, to everyone, a constant reminder of his family's unassailable strength.

After seizing the throne, Francesco I consolidated his hold on power by quickly making himself absolute ruler of Milan, cowing the merchants and petty nobles who had helped to overthrow the Visconti and had supported his accession. Always the consummate politician, Sforza rewarded their loyalty by annexing sickly Genoa, in 1464, increasing their wealth. Bled white by centuries of conflict with Venice, the once proud city-state had been unable to resist Sforza's naked aggression. This provided Milan with a valuable and long sought after seaport and access to the Mediterranean.

The Sforzas had also suffered. On the day after Christmas in 1476, while attending mass in the Church of Santo Stefano, Francesco's successor and son, Galeazzo Sforza, who had ascended the throne in 1466, was assassinated by three nobles who bore grudges against him. One had lost considerable land when the duke ruled against him in a dispute with another noble. Another's sister was rumored to have been deflowered by the duke. The third, an idealist, believed the dukedom should be replaced by a republic. While the three men knelt at the duke's feet, paying homage to him, they concealed daggers in their robes. Suddenly they sprang at the defenseless duke and stabbed him in the chest and groin, killing him instantly. Gian Galeazzo, his seven-year-old son, inherited his dukedom, but the murdered duke's younger brother, Ludovico, became regent until the boy attained majority. The virtual ruler of Milan ever since, Ludovico was known as Il Moro (The Moor), due to his dark complexion and darker demeanor.

Enrico and the guards turned a corner and entered the Piazza Castello. There was the redbrick and stone fortress. Enrico had seen it many times before, but now it looked sinister, more foreboding. Ahead were the main gate and its central tower, flanked by fifty-foot-high walls extending far in each direction, terminating in a massive cylindrical tower at each end. As they approached, Enrico could feel the power emanating from the place and radiating throughout the city. If stones could speak, every brick and block would shout in a chorus, "Here lives the duke of Milan. Enter at your peril!"

Enrico wondered what this man could want with him. *Am I in danger? After all, I am a Venetian, and Milan is at war with Venice.* He glanced at his escorts. They were grim-faced and determined; every inch, soldiers. The officer looked at him with a trace of sympathy but refused to engage him in conversation. Enrico wondered if he would ever leave the place.

They passed two more heavily armed guards and went through a large stone portal into the vast brick-paved Piazza delle Armi. A splendidly uniformed officer met them and motioned to follow him through a door and up a broad staircase, past more wolflike guards, and down a well-lit hallway, where he stopped and pointed to a chair.

"Sit and be patient. The regent has visitors. You will have to wait."

For the first time since he had awakened, Enrico allowed himself to think about food. He was famished. His stomach protested, rumbling as he sat there alone, facing two menacing guards, each brandishing a halberd, as they stood silently beside two tall, elegantly carved wooden doors that led to what he supposed was a reception room.

Time crept by slowly. Initially, Enrico mulled over the sins he had committed since arriving in Milan. He could not think of any that constituted a crime, at least none that would have concerned the regent. Despite his precarious position, he was becoming angry, but he was careful to conceal his feelings from the guards, who eyed him continually, for he was their only escape from the monotony of their duty.

Finally, the great doors slowly and silently opened on their well-oiled hinges. Three finely dressed men emerged, whispering intensely among themselves as they hurriedly disappeared down the long hallway. One guard signaled for Enrico to enter. He rose, took a deep breath, and walked alone into the unknown.

The cavernous chamber was illuminated by daylight that streamed through the large windows lining its two exterior walls. Seated on an ornate, thronelike chair, upholstered in regal blue and golden cloth, was Ludovico Sforza. Two of his ministers stood at attention, flanking him. His family's coat of arms, with its silver bascinet and golden lion on a field of blue, hung behind him, above his head.

"My lord, this is Signor Enrico Soranzo, the one I told you about."

Il Moro smiled and nodded politely. He is about the same age as I am, thought Enrico, slightly disappointed, as he bowed. He had expected a much older man.

The demands of his regency had aged Il Moro far beyond his thirty-one years. Actually, he was seven years younger than Enrico. He had been severely tested by constant battles with his nobles as he struggled to retain his authority to rule Milan as *de facto* duke until his nephew reached manhood. He had already squelched several intrigues to push him aside, ruthlessly dealing with the plotters.

Ludovico sized up his quarry through his bright brown eyes, which seemed to peek out from under his drooping eyelids. His long, straight black hair, parted in the middle, fell onto his shoulders. A broad, hawklike nose left little room above the thick lips that were the most remarkable feature of his noble face. His mouth was formed in a straight line above his prominent chin. A thick crease extended down each cheek, framing a constantly leering expression. Not a smile, not a frown, it conveyed self-satisfaction at all he had accomplished in his short life, but most of all, it betrayed his guile. It was a face created to make lies ring true and the truth to seduce like a well-told lie.

"Have you been in Milan long?" Ludovico asked in a mild, pleasing voice.

"Nearly a half a year," replied Enrico to the easy question.

"Why are you here and not serving in the army? Are you Venetians not at war?"

Enrico thought for a moment before he answered. "I have already raised my sword for Venice. I fought at Smyrna and Scutari, where I dipped it in Turkish blood. I have no need to prove myself in battle again."

The regent looked at the man who had told him about Enrico and smiled approvingly. Then he turned back to his visitor and slowly rose to his feet.

"I could have you thrown into prison as a Venetian spy and let you rot in obscurity. Not a soul would ever know what happened to you."

Enrico could feel the blood rush to his cheeks. He shifted his feet uneasily. "Would the great Ludovico Sforza, ruler of Milan, stoop to such an act? I am no threat to Milan. Though my country is at war with yours, I am a simple émigré who merely desires to be left alone and live in peace in your city, one that rivals, I must admit, even Venice in her majesty."

"Your flattery will not help you now. There is no depth to which I would not sink to preserve this dukedom, Signor Soranzo."

Enrico's mouth went dry. He did not like this dangerous turn in the conversation. "What do you want with me?" he responded bravely, almost defiantly.

Sforza cast a glance at his ministers. Then, turning back to Enrico, he descended the three steps that separated them and placed one hand firmly on his guest's shoulder. "I want you to help me make peace with Venice." He uttered these words with such sincerity, such ease, that Enrico was spellbound. *But what could I, a refugee from Venice, do to help make peace between these two bitter rivals?*

"The pope has thrown in his lot with the league arrayed against Venice even though this war was caused by the Duke of Ferrara and his father-in-law, the King of Naples."

"But the pope is fighting *alongside* Venice." Enrico was confused. *Is this some joke or perhaps a ruse?*

"He *was*, but all his diplomacy in this perfidious peninsula is directed at maintaining a sort of balance. The treacherous pope has now, after solemnly pledging to defend her, singled out Venice for destruction."

"I can hardly believe what you are saying, though I know you would not lie."

"Listen well, my Venetian friend. The pope is a true rascal. Only five years ago, he gave the word that launched the Pazzi and their conspirators at the Medici. They butchered my dear friend Giuliano de' Medici on the most blessed of all days, Easter Sunday, in the house of the Lord, no less." Il Moro said this in a voice filled with anger.

"He was pierced nearly twenty times by daggers as he shielded his brother Lorenzo, the current duke. Just before he died, he shouted for Lorenzo to run and save himself. Lorenzo hid like a common criminal in his own church, wounded and hunted by priests and murderers! But"—Il Moro smiled broadly for the first time—"the Florentines, who loved him, rose up and resisted, and then defeated the conspirators. He laughed at Sixtus when the pontiff laid an interdict upon Florence." Sforza turned to his counselors. "Instead of despairing, Lorenzo laid one on the pope as his reply.

"And now, Sixtus shows Venice the same sort of papal goodness. Do you not see? I cannot let the pope defeat Venice. For if he does, who will be next? Ferrara? Bologna? Florence? Milan?"

Enrico looked into Sforza's blazing eyes, filled with unrestrained passion, the kind that exceeds even love in its fury.

His rant finished, the regent regained his composure, walked back to his chair, and sat down with his folded arms across his chest.

"I am considering signing a separate peace with Venice to offset the weight the pope has added to the league ranged against La Serenissima. I need someone to inquire of the doge and his counselors, to ascertain if they will accept my terms. I have chosen *you* to be the bearer of my offer."

"Why not send someone else? I doubt the doge would believe me."

"You are the son of a powerful noble, a war hero," countered the regent. "You *are* a member of the Great Council, are you not? Besides, I will pay you a substantial reward for your services." The jingle of golden florins rang in Enrico's head. He had exhausted more than half of the money he had taken from his father's bank on that last day in Florence. *Is there a better way for me to return to Venice than as the bearer of such good tidings?*

"What details can you tell me about my commission?"

A minister stepped forward eagerly. "You will leave for Venice immediately. We will supply you with a document that will prove you are acting with the authority of the Duke of Milan. However, it will contain no terms. You will memorize those in case you and the document fall into the wrong hands. This way, we can both deny the true purpose of your mission. You can say that you were seeking only to arrange a prisoner exchange. The document has been written in a way that it will support such a claim."

The minister smiled at him. "Is this sufficient for you to accept?"

"You have forgotten one important detail," reminded Enrico.

The other man now spoke. "For your services, you shall be paid one

hundred ducats—a large sum for such an agreeable task. You will be celebrated as a hero by your countrymen at the same time that you are rewarded
by their enemy."

This is too good to be true, thought Enrico. Surely there must be others
who could have merited such good fortune.

"You still have not told me why you have chosen *me*."

The three men exchanged glances. Then Sforza himself answered.

"Because if my allies somehow hear about your mission, they would never
believe I would have trusted someone like you to carry out such a plan."

Enrico smiled politely and bowed to his new employer. The regent had
insulted him, but his offer was lucrative. As the first minister led him from
the room, he felt a strange sensation filling him up until he was intoxicated
by it. For the first time in his life, he was important. He had a mission. No
other man on the face of the earth had the singular purpose that he did at
this very moment. Finally, he was going home a hero.

Later that afternoon, the regent's foreign minister detailed the conditions
by which Milan would abandon the League, which had sworn to defeat
Venice, and sign a secret, separate peace with her. There were three conditions.

First, Venice would pay an indemnity—a bribe, really—of ten thousand
ducats directly to Ludovico Sforza. These funds would be deposited into a
bank in Paris to avoid detection by Il Moro's erstwhile allies.

Second, Venice would return all Milanese war prisoners, asking no ransom.

Finally, to provide cover for Sforza's treachery, Venice would shift her
operations from laying siege to Ferrara to launching an attack on Milan.
This would give Sforza a pretext to sue for peace with Venice in order to
avoid the invasion. The regent knew that Venice could not sustain the siege
at Ferrara. With the pope now in her enemies' camp, strong reinforcements
would soon come to Ferrara's aid before the city could be starved into submission. Venice would need to pull back her army and shorten her supply
lines in the face of her more numerous foes.

As a final inducement, the regent promised to desist from war with
Venice for ten years from the date of the treaty, which he agreed to sign in
Milan as soon as practicable following Venice's acceptance of the regent's
terms. Under no circumstances would any details be revealed. The last thing
Il Moro wanted was the reprobation of his former allies. He knew that he
could not depend on Venice to come to his aid if they decided to destroy
him in their fury.

Enrico returned to his apartment with two soldiers and packed his belongings. After nearly a year, he was going to return to Venice, but this time, he would return as a man who mattered. For the first time in his life, he could stand face to face with his father as his equal because of what he was about to do.

In the quiet of his private quarters, Ludovico Sforza knew he had made the right decision. Only a few weeks before, he had enthusiastically pledged, on his honor, to fight Venice with the other members of the League. Now he was about to betray them and sign a separate peace with the object of their collective hatred. There could be no moral considerations when the survival of his regency was at stake. But as he sipped his wine, a nagging thought entered his mind, one he could not quiet. *What if I have simply exchanged the enmity of Venice for the enmity of virtually the whole of Italy?* He hoped the Venetians' attack on his territory would be convincing.

24

The Heritage

The shadows in the third-floor room stood like silent towers against the whitewashed walls. A single large window drew the last of the fading afternoon light through the green-painted slatted shutters, filtering the narrow bands of light onto the center of the wall, illuminating the clouds of dust that hung like mist.

The two eight-year-old boys sat on their beds, their backs propped up against the wall, motionless, waiting for their grandfather to begin. Though he was just sixty years of age, he seemed old as he sat in the room's single wooden chair, at the foot of their beds.

Antonio cast a loving glance at his twin grandsons. Their eyes met. He had climbed the stairs to the boys' room to give them their history lesson. Tired, he did not really feel like teaching them today, but he had so much knowledge to impart and he was already older than his father was when he had died.

He wiggled his finger, signaling for them to come closer. Obediently, they both crawled over their blankets to the foot of their beds. Antonio leaned forward, gently patting them on their light brown hair, and smiled approvingly.

"So, do you want to hear more about our glorious past?"

They both nodded enthusiastically. They were always interested in what their grandfather had to tell them about Venice and her history. It was a family tradition passed down from generation to generation for centuries— grandfathers instilling Venice's rich history in their grandsons. It was the Zianis' way to ensure that their sons would make any sacrifice, no matter how great, to defend and glorify La Serenissima.

The boys looked at their grandfather with pride. He told his tales of old with great drama and in colorful detail. It was their favorite part of the day. While other children played or worked at their studies, the Zianis drank in all the history they could. To them, their grandfather was a hero. He had fought courageously in the great siege of Constantinople.

"Grandfather, there are many other islands whose people have been invaded. Why has Venice not suffered the same fate?" asked Tommaso as Sebastiano looked on expectantly. Tommaso had already learned to approach conversations with his grandfather as if he was fishing: he would put some bait on his hook, ask a good question, and then wait to see what he would catch.

Antonio's eyes lit up. He had a wonderful tale to tell. They needed to hear stories that taught them about the value of courage, the kind that Venice depended upon, if they were to grow up to be men capable of ruling their family and its affairs.

He looked at them and thanked God for giving him such fine grandsons. Antonio stretched out his arm, clasped the boys' hands together, and began to speak slowly, with his majestic voice that seemed to defy his age.

"That is a thoughtful question for such a young boy," said Antonio. "There are two reasons. First, we possess a proud naval tradition. We are the greatest and most prolific shipbuilders in the Mediterranean. Our galleys are usually able to defeat our enemies before they can come near our islands. Second, Venice is situated in shallow water, in a vast lagoon at the head of the Adriatic Sea. Other islands, such as Malta, Cyprus, Crete, or Sicily, can be approached through deep water. Ships can approach Venice safely only if their captains know the secret ways through the shoals and into our anchorage. In times of danger, we remove the markers that show the way through these shoals, making a safe approach impossible."

"But experienced captains would surely learn the way over the years, even without the markers," observed Sebastiano suspiciously.

"Ah, but that is the beauty of Venice. God is always shifting the sandy shoals and their passageways. They never remain the same and must be continuously dredged and marked as old ones disappear and new ones are created. The sea is our greatest ally."

"That is what Seraglio says," said Sebastiano with a broad grin.

Antonio smiled approvingly at his intelligence. He was the smarter one and destined to walk solidly in his father's footsteps. Antonio hoped he would live long enough to see that day.

It is time to begin the lesson.

"Do you know how St. Mark the Evangelist came to be our patron saint?"

The boys looked at each other, wide-eyed, with blank expressions on their faces.

"No, Grandfather," replied Sebastiano. Tommaso echoed his denial.

"Well, today I am going to tell you the story about how it came to be." He drew a deep breath and continued.

"There is an old tale that when St. Mark was traveling from Aquileia to Rome, his ship stopped at some islands at the northern end of the Adriatic, which were then uninhabited. There, an angel appeared to him and blessed him with the words '*Pax tibi, Marce, evangelista meus. Hic requiescet corpus tuum.*' Translated from Latin, it means, 'Peace be unto you, Mark, my evangelist. On this spot shall your body rest.' Mark later became the archbishop of Alexandria, Egypt, and remained there until he died.

"One day, more than six hundred and fifty years ago, two Venetian merchants went to Alexandria on a mission. This is the story of those two Venetian merchant traders. Now close your eyes and I will take you back to a day in 829 . . ."

The brothers leaned back onto their beds, with eyes shut, and listened intently.

Their galley was running with the wind. The air was filled with the sweet, earthy smell of vegetation. A few land birds circling overhead argued loudly with the seagulls. After a three-week voyage, the last half out of sight of land, the walls of Alexandria were a welcome sight to Jacopo, a Venetian merchant, and his son, Giovanni. No doubt the captain would be looking for a bonus for providing such rapid transit; normally the voyage took four weeks. They could see him on the deck, standing by the tiller, beaming, but the rowers were even happier. Below, nearly one hundred rowers were resting on their oars as the billowing canvas sails did the work, propelling the ship. In times of peace, Venetian war galleys were used as fast merchant ships.

Alexandria, Egypt—named for Alexander the Great, the Macedonian warrior-king who conquered the Egyptians in 332 B.C.—was, next to Rome, the greatest city on earth in the days of St. Mark. It boasted two of the Seven

Wonders of the Ancient World. One, the Lighthouse of Alexandria, built by Ptolemy II, towered four hundred feet above the harbor, throwing its light miles out to sea for many years, until a violent earthquake toppled it into the harbor.

Even more famous was the city's Great Library, which at one time housed one-quarter of the Western world's thoughts in thousands of ancient scrolls, books, and manuscripts. Learned men flocked to the city, to study and live in the library. But Alexandria ceased to be the world's center of thought, science, and technology when the Great Library burned in a disastrous fire, destroying thousands of years of human trial, error, and discovery. Certain medicinal remedies that were known to the ancients have never been rediscovered.

Jacopo was a prosperous merchant who traded salt and fine manufactured Venetian goods for ivory and other oriental luxuries. He traveled to Alexandria once a year to buy ivory from Arab traders, who shipped it across the desert and down the Nile. Its origin was with the Nubians, a mysterious race that sold their own people as slaves to the Mediterranean peoples.

Jacopo had always pondered the paradox of slavery. He could not understand how people could sell another member of the same tribe when those would-be slaves had done them no wrong. Pride welled in his chest as he thought of the rowers below—all free men. Other rowers might cower like dogs from whips and sadistic overseers, but not his crew. They rowed for Venice.

"Father!" Giovanni shook Jacopo's shoulder. "Those must be the remains of the great lighthouse you told me about."

"No, my son, the lighthouse fell into the sea after a violent earthquake and was completely lost. Stones from the Great Library were reused to build the city walls."

Jacopo had brought Giovanni with him on this voyage so that his son would learn more about the great Egyptian city.

"Those walls must be forty feet high," marveled Giovanni.

"Yes," replied Jacopo. "They took many years to build."

"Why are there no city walls like these in Venice? Surely we could afford to build them." Giovanni peered over the side to get a better look at the massive masonry sea wall that seemed to grow in size, by the minute, as they sailed closer.

"Our walls are made of water. We use finely hewn stone to build our churches and *palazzi*. Stone is far too valuable to pile up into useless walls."

"But how can we depend solely on the water to keep out our enemies?"

"My son, nothing is more unconquerable than the sea—or more unpredictable. It is our best defense. The closest land is over two miles away, a distance far greater than an arrow flight or even the range of a great siege engine."

"But how can we be sure that will never change?" asked Giovanni.

"Our navy will see to that," replied Jacopo confidently.

A ntonio paused to explain.
      "Like all great maritime powers, Venice relied upon the sea and her fleet to provide protection from her enemies, but ships had to be built, manned, and paid for. With such a small indigenous population, Venice could not hope to provide the manpower or raw materials herself that she needed to construct her war galleys and merchant ships. Only by developing robust trade could she hope to create this capability.

"Trade is the great multiplier of wealth. Even in the ninth century, buying cheap and selling dear was the way to accumulate wealth and, in Venice's case, the means of her very survival as well. Jacopo and his son were serving the Republic in the great tradition, roving the known world to find goods at advantageous prices and then taking advantage of Venice's superior shipping capabilities to bring those goods to markets that would pay dearly for them. On this trip, they were trading salt for fruits and ivory.

"Salt is the only practical means by which people can preserve meat. Ice is too difficult to use, even in northern Europe, for most of the year. Ice was unheard of in Egypt. But salt, rubbed on fish or meat, could keep foods edible for more than a year. Salt also makes it possible to eat slightly spoiled food.

"The islands in the Venetian lagoon were flat then, only a few feet above sea level at their highest points. The ebb and flow of the tides created many tidal pools. Our ancestors built small earthen dams to prevent the resurgence of water at high tide. The pools quickly dried up in the Adriatic sun, creating thousands of tons of sea salt every year. This salt was more highly prized and much cheaper to produce than salt mined from the earth, which had to be crushed into powder after mining. Venice also had the advantage of producing salt in the same place where her shipping was located, further lowering her costs.

"Jacopo and Giovanni were your ancestors, engaged in the Republic's most revered profession, as our family still is to this day. In time, their descendants would produce two men who would become doges. But these two traders were going to produce something for the Republic that was even more important. They were going to bring back something infinitely more valuable than ivory or fruit—or even jewels. This time they were going to bring back something so priceless, its value was beyond comprehension."

Antonio continued . . .

Now the deck of the galley was alive with the hustle and bustle of docking activity. As the captain carefully eased the vessel alongside the long stone quay, sailors and dockworkers exchanged thick hemp lines to secure the ship. A dozen languages punctuated the air, which had become noticeably warmer.

"Never has a ship made this voyage so quickly. Only three weeks!" boasted the self-satisfied captain.

"Never has a ship made this voyage for such an exorbitant price—over fifty ducats!" Jacopo shot back, wiping the grin off the captain's face.

"Well, the expenses today are outrageous, and the—"

"Captain, how would you like to make a bonus of another fifty ducats?"

"You have my rowers' attention; you have my officers' attention. By God, you even have my attention, but a man like you does not overpay, even for his daughter's wedding festivities. This sounds very illegal, Jacopo."

"It *is* . . . in Alexandria," he replied with a chuckle.

They pushed their way through the narrow streets, teeming with people. "Alexandria has the strangest smell, Father," said Giovanni as he wrinkled his face and squinted. "It has an odor like . . ."

"Garbage," interrupted Jacopo. "You smell a mixture of heat, spices, sweat, and puke. Too much cheap wine, smuggled in by the sailors, mixed with bad stomachs. It is illegal to produce or sell wine in Islamic lands, but sailors and smugglers ensure it is always available if one is willing to pay the price. In this cosmopolitan city, Christians and Jews are permitted to practice their faith alongside the more numerous Muslims."

They entered a little inn through a wall of stringed beads. It was so dark that they struggled to adjust their eyes to the dim light. Jacopo could see a short man in a caftan and a turban seated at a secluded table in a back corner.

El Hassan ibn Mustafa was rich, and that made him famous in that city, filled with so many beggars. He was obsessed with wealth, but unlike most other wealthy men, he was also devoutly religious. He believed in the superiority of his God, his religion, and his judgment. And this day, he was going to cheat these arrogant Venetians with a plan he had been patiently cultivating for three years, from the very first time he had met Jacopo. It is not that he did not respect the Venetian or even that he did not like him—he did. He just could not accept that these lions from the north were traders of such renown that their reputations preceded them. How could they out-haggle a Saracen, a son of Islam?

Islam had been around for less than two hundred years, and already its believers comprised an area larger than all of Christian Europe. As El Hassan saw it, the greatest difference between the two religions was that Saracens killed Christians and Christians killed each other. At this rate, it was only a matter of time, he reasoned, before there would only be Saracens left in the world. Allah be praised!

They walked over to El Hassan's table and stood before him, saying nothing. El Hassan looked up and cracked a broad smile as he motioned for his big, muscular eunuch to leave them. As the man brushed past, he scowled at both of them with eyes that seemed to say, I may not be a man like you, but I have *killed* many and I will kill *you* if you attempt to cross my master.

"Jacopo, my Venetian friend," El Hassan blurted in fractured Greek.

"It has been too long since I have been in Alexandria," replied Jacopo, "but the winds and currents were unfriendly this spring. Giovanni, kiss the hand of a great man."

Giovanni, somewhat unsure of himself, seized the little man's hand and quickly kissed it, casting a worried look at his father, unsure if he had done it properly.

"Sit down, my friend. Sit down and join me."

"Tell me, how is the ivory business?" inquired Jacopo.

"It is hardly as prosperous as the salt business, I regret to say. If only we Egyptians could make our own salt, but alas, the prevailing winds here in Alexandria drive all the waste from our city back onto the shore. No one could eat salt made here. Venice has even the winds in her favor."

"Yes, El Hassan, and because that is true, it will probably take us five weeks to make the return voyage as we row against those same winds."

The preliminary conversation stopped. Both men stared deeply into each other's eyes. They slid their stools closer together on the dirt floor until their faces almost touched. Giovanni knew he was about to learn the real purpose of their trip.

El Hassan whispered slowly, in perfect Greek, "Now, my friend, do we have an understanding? We can wait no longer. My partner is leaving Alexandria next month, and with him, this opportunity will be gone forever. The Islamic authorities are growing impatient. There is talk they may order it destroyed."

Jacopo leaned back slightly on his stool and gazed at the ceiling for a long time. Abruptly he said, "There is a problem." After a long pause he continued, "How can I be sure?"

"Sure it will succeed? Because I guarantee it!" El Hassan boasted, slightly insulted and a bit concerned by the Venetian's reluctance.

"No. How can I be certain that it is really what you say it is? After all, as I must rely upon your word, you also must rely upon another's. Neither you nor I have ever seen it. How can we be sure?"

"Jacopo, the guards are Christians. It is in their interest for our little plot to succeed. Besides, it is in my interest as well. You see, I am not undertaking this dangerous enterprise only for the money. Of course, I would be a fool to take such a risk without the assurance of a profit equal to that risk. But as you know, I am also a true believer in Allah and his prophet, Muhammad. I believe that the whole world will one day pray only to Allah. Until then, I am called to do anything I can to rid the world of relics of the old, failed religions—and to risk my life to do it, if necessary."

Jacopo took a long drink of juice from his cup and looked at his son, not as a father but as a partner. Giovanni had begun to notice this tendency lately. It made him feel like a man, but it also made him realize how difficult it was to be a man and make the weighty decisions a man must make, often with scant information.

"What do you think, my son? How can we determine if a relic is genuine?"

Giovanni slid some juice down his parched throat and put the cup down slowly. "That would depend."

"On what, my son?"

"On its condition and on the looks in the eyes of the men who guard it, when they tell us it is genuine."

The three men were only inches apart. No one spoke. Sensing the tension, El Hassan abruptly leaned back.

"He is a smart young fellow," he said, slapping his thigh.

"There is one other very important question," said Jacopo, ignoring his patronizing compliment. "How will it work?"

"There will be time for that, but it must be done no later than tomorrow night. Torches will be too dangerous, and the moon will be full. The next day, the tides will permit an early departure," whispered El Hassan under his breath. "Meet me here tomorrow after evening prayers and I will reveal every detail to you."

Jacopo stood, instantly followed by Giovanni. He and El Hassan embraced. Giovanni imitated his father's farewell. Then they left the inn.

"Father, I do not trust that man."

"I would sooner trust a pirate before I would trust that infidel," spat Jacopo.

"But you will learn that business must go on regardless of one's distrust. Trust is a bonus. If you find it where you do not expect it—it is a treasure. If you expect it and it deserts you, or worse, it was never there in the first place—you are finished."

"Still, how will we know? How can we keep him from cheating us?"

Jacopo tugged at his beard. He stopped walking and faced his son. The street was almost deserted now, as it was nearly prayer time.

"My son, have you ever noticed that men fear most in others what they give others the most cause to fear in themselves? What does El Hassan fear most from us?"

Giovanni thought for a moment. "He talked, at times, as though Saracens are inferior to us Venetians. I think he fears our superiority." He thought some more. "I suppose his greatest fear is that we will not act by tomorrow night."

"You are very observant," said Jacopo. "He is trying to make our judgment fall like sand through an hourglass. He wants to cause us to be careless by trying to convince us that he is not as smart as we are. He did not give us details because he does not want us to have time to discover if his plan is true—that it will work as he says. But we have an advantage."

"What is it? We cannot succeed without him."

"Our advantage is that we know that we cannot succeed *with* him," replied Jacopo with authority.

"Return to the ship and tell the captain that we sail tonight. Hand him this. It contains fifty gold ducats. Tell him to be ready to sail when the wind is dead, two hours before sunrise. I cannot tell you any more about my plan. I can only tell you that tomorrow we will be famous . . . or we will be dead."

It was well past dark when Jacopo, standing silently in the shadow of a wall, squinted to see down the narrow street. He could not make out the man's face, but he knew it had to be him. No one else in Alexandria was that tall.

Like a phantom, the man began to move toward him. Jacopo's heart was racing. The giant stopped twenty feet away. He was more afraid at that moment than at any time since he had fought in battle more than twenty years before. The man whispered, long and low, "Jacopoooooo . . . Is that you?"

"It is I," he replied softly. "Is everything ready?"

"Yes," replied the giant.

They walked the short distance to the shrine and entered. It was not as

Jacopo had remembered it. It seemed smaller and less impressive at night. They quickly found the undercroft and descended the narrow, winding stone steps. At the bottom, a single torch lit the damp chamber. He could see two men waiting there, holding stout wooden levers.

At the giant's signal, they inserted the levers and began to heave at the massive stone sarcophagus. They had scraped away the mortar seal, so only the stone's weight still prevented them from shifting it. Jacopo and the giant bent down and pushed hard against it with their shoulders. The stone slid sideways in a bumpy motion until they exposed the hole beneath. At the bottom was a bundle, wrapped in a dirty, musty, yellowed cloth sack, barely visible in the dim light. The odor of spices overpowered them as the two helpers leaned over to look at it more closely.

Jacopo felt faint. He was disoriented, as though he had entered another world. Perhaps he had. He bent down, ignoring the stiffness in his fifty-three-year-old legs. He was shaking as he peered more closely into the pit. The two men lay on their bellies and reached their hands under the coarse cloth sack. They carefully rolled it over. The bottom side was white, but soiled with earth. Suddenly, a large scimitar flashed in the giant's hand. With a single, slow stroke, he slit the sack lengthwise. Then the two men carefully pulled it apart. Inside was a tightly wrapped bundle, five feet long and covered with muslin strips. As Jacopo turned away from the hole, they lifted up the body and laid it alongside the hole. Just then, the giant appeared carrying another bundle of muslin that was about the same size.

"Allow me to introduce you to St. Claudian," the giant croaked as he placed the second corpse alongside the first. The three men quickly inserted the new corpse inside the shroud of the first, sewed it up, and then carefully lowered it back into the pit. Finally, they slid the heavy stone back over the hole.

"Do you have the basket I asked you to bring?" hissed Jacopo.

"It is here," whispered the giant. "Do you have the gold?"

Jacopo reached into his shirt and found the small sack. He tossed it to the giant, who immediately opened it and examined its contents.

"We agreed the price would be one hundred ducats! What is this?"

The others stopped and gazed uneasily at their leader, reaching for their daggers.

"I will pay you an additional fifty ducats for a small favor," said Jacopo with a wry smile. "I was forced to send my helper back to the ship. I will need someone to carry the basket to the pier."

"I will do *that* myself," said the giant as he placed the relic into the basket.

The four men quickly left the shrine, the giant carrying the basket on his broad, muscular back. They hurried silently through the narrow labyrinth of streets until, after a few minutes, Jacopo abruptly held up his hand and motioned for them to stop.

"Here," he said, turning toward the panting giant.

As if prearranged, the giant said to the two other men, "Leave us. Go back to the shrine and reseal the sarcophagus with mortar. When you have finished, meet me at my house and I will pay you." The two men immediately left them. When they had gone, Jacopo opened the door. He recoiled from the overpowering odor of rotten meat, but the giant gritted his teeth as he stifled a mighty laugh.

"*Kanzir,*" he said, as he went inside, opened the lid of the small basket, and inspected the vile contents. "You Venetian bastard! I was wondering how you were going to do it. Those Saracens will not go near *this!*" Even the customs inspectors will avoid it.

Holding their breath, they dumped the contents of the smaller basket on top of the bundle in the larger one, completely covering it with rotting pork. Then, shutting the door, they quickly covered the remaining distance to the docks.

C ome aboard, Abdul. We have nothing in the hold but ivory, fruit, and a bit of rotten meat for a few slaves we have bought," said the captain brusquely.

The two officials climbed the gangway and went immediately to the entrance of the stairway that led down to the hold. As they descended the steps, they began to wretch from the putrid odor that assaulted their nostrils. It was then that they noticed all the rowers had covered their mouths and noses with scented cloth.

"What *is* that horrible stench? I thought you Venetians were shrewd businessmen?" Abdul mocked. "You must have purchased your provisions from El Hassan. He is the only one I know who would dare to sell such rotten meat."

The customs inspectors weaved their way through the benches of oarsmen and into the storage area of the ship's hold. They were talking to each other in Arabic and laughing at the foolish Christians' poor bargain.

Jacopo, who had followed them at a respectful distance, called out, "Slaves in Venice prefer rotten meat to starvation."

The officious inspectors continued laughing as they walked over to the large basket resting against the forward bulkhead.

"What is this?" asked Abdul as he casually removed the cover. At the sight of the rotting pig parts, the two men put their hands on their heads and screamed, *"Kanzir, kanzir."*

They beat a wild retreat down the narrow aisle between the banks of oarsmen, tripping over outstretched legs and oars and scuttling up the ladder. They did not stop running and shouting until they were safely back on the stone quay. The captain and his two employers laughed uncontrollably as they watched from the deck. As the commotion continued on the pier, the captain quickly gave his orders to the crew.

"Throw that stinking meat over the side as soon as we get under way. Do not touch the contents under it. Then wrap the basket in canvas and hoist it up the mast, as high as you can, away from the deck."

Then he turned to Jacopo and said, "You gave me your word that you would unravel this mystery for me once we were under way. By God, I know you did not pay me fifty ducats just to carry some damned fruit and ivory back to Venice."

"Captain," Jacopo said slowly, "you should not use such language in the presence of St. Mark the Evangelist, who is coming home to rest in Venice!"

The captain removed his hat and crossed himself as he dropped to one knee.

"Poor El Hassan," said Giovanni. "I do not think he will ever recover from the shock when he discovers our deception."

"Even worse, El Hassan cannot tell the Saracen authorities about what we have done without the guards from the shrine implicating him as a conspirator in the plot to steal the relic," said Jacopo. "In a few months, his anger will diminish. In a few months more, our business will go on as before because he knows that he is better off trading with us than not. He will admire our courage and fear our guile, and because there is nowhere else he can obtain salt at such a price, he will do business! But there is one thing I know for certain. You and I can never set foot in Alexandria again as long as we live."

Tommaso giggled. "What a story!"

"It is funny, but do you see the significance of what your ancestors did?"

"I think so, Grandfather," replied Sebastiano.

"Tommaso?" challenged Antonio.

The boy nodded, but his eyes betrayed his lack of understanding.

"It shows that you can accomplish virtually anything you set your mind to if you have courage and if you use your brain," admonished Antonio.

"It taught me that you must be careful who you trust," added Tommaso.

"You have to out-think your adversaries," warned Antonio. "And because our ancestors did just that, their deeds changed Venice forever. Do not ever forget that."

25

The Offer

E nrico waited until early evening to cross the lagoon from Mestre, so that no one would tell his father that he had returned to Venice before he had a chance to confront him. With his hat pulled down low over his brow, he walked from the landing on the Fondamenta Nuove, through the narrow streets, and over the wooden bridges that spanned the dark waters of the canals, running like black ribbons between the stone houses. As he walked, he thought about what he would say. Despite his theft of five hundred ducats from his father's bank, Enrico was not fearful. Instead, he was eager. Now he held in his hands something that all of Venice would surely embrace, but would it make his unrelenting father forgive, if not forget, his past transgressions?

He turned a corner and, finally, the Ca' Soranzo loomed darkly up ahead. He ran to the door and pushed it open. Venetians had no need to lock their doors; crime was almost nonexistent. He crept inside. The atrium was dark, but there was a light at the top of the marble staircase. He bounded quietly up the steps and paused on the landing. A lamp spilled amber light into the hallway outside his father's library. Enrico's heart pounded as he passed through the open doorway.

"You!" shouted his startled father as he rose from his paper-strewn table and pointed an accusing finger at him.

"Villain, have you already spent the five hundred ducats you stole from me?" He walked toward his son, his fists in tight balls and fire blazing in his eyes.

"Father, give me one minute and I will explain everything. That is all I ask."

Without warning, Soranzo struck him hard on the cheek, causing him to stumble backward to maintain his balance. The blow left a stinging red handprint on Enrico's beardless face.

"I want no explanation from you," Soranzo spit. "Your actions have spoken louder than any feeble words you could invent to defend your treachery now."

Recovered, Enrico stepped toward his enraged father. The two men faced each other, inches apart, neither prepared to give way. Without taking his eyes from his father's, Enrico reached for the commission he had received from Ludovico Sforza.

Soranzo's hand suddenly shot out and locked his son's wrist in an iron grip, but Enrico ripped his arm free and, stepping back, pulled the parchment from his robe.

"What is this?" asked his father, eyeing the official-looking document.

"When I left Florence, I went to Milan. A week ago, I was called to the palace—"

Soranzo impatiently snatched the document from Enrico's hand. As he perused it, he began to shake his head slowly. When he finished, he frowned at his son.

"Do you expect me to believe that Ludovico Sforza chose *you* to deliver a peace offer to the Republic of Venice?"

"It is true, Father. I swear it."

"You swear it," he mocked. "How could I believe an oath sworn by a man with so little honor that he would steal money from his own father?"

"Forgive me . . . please, Father, forgive me. I made a terrible mistake. But every word I say now is true. Look, this document bears his seal. He told me that the pope has abandoned Venice's cause and has thrown in his lot with the League to fight against us. Can the government afford not to believe that he wishes to make a legitimate offer?"

Soranzo scratched his beard thoughtfully, and then he began to nod his head. A laugh pierced the silence.

"Damn, Enrico, I believe you are telling the truth about this."

Suddenly, his brow narrowed and his smile disappeared.

"This simply says that you are empowered to deliver a proposal from Il Moro. There are no terms contained here. What does he propose?"

Enrico described the regent's terms in great detail, having committed them to memory before he left Milan. When he finished, Soranzo grabbed his shoulders.

"Do you realize what this means? The League is beginning to unravel, and while ten thousand is a princely sum, it is worth every last ducat to preserve our *terra firma* lands, which will surely be lost if this war drags on into the spring.

"It has been dark for an hour; that makes it about eight o'clock. The doge does not go to bed for at least another hour. If we hurry, we can tell him the news tonight."

Soranzo had no trouble convincing the guards to take him to his old friend, Doge Mocenigo. After a short wait, they were ushered in to meet with the doge and a few of his counselors who were working late. When Enrico finished his story, they agreed unanimously that they would call for a Senate meeting to be held the next day. Enrico's triumphant return had exceeded his expectations.

The next day he told his story again, only with greater flair, as the doge and the sixty senators listened, awestruck. Il Moro had provided them with an excellent and unexpected opportunity. When he had finished, a short debate ensued. The doge called for a vote. By a large majority, the Senate voted to accept Ludovico's offer and to issue new orders to Count Cajazzo to quit Ferrara.

The count had already begun preparations to besiege Ferrara when the Senate suddenly ordered him to leave the place, abandoning all of his diligent work. His orders were to retreat to the Po, where he would receive new instructions. He was disgusted.

The next day, the army grimly packed up camp and wearily began their march back to the River Po. Soon, however, their morale plummeted as doubts began to creep into the minds of the officers and their men. What did we fight and bleed for? they asked. For what purpose did we endure the hardships of camp and field? they grumbled. For what did my friends give up their lives? How could the politicians back in Venice, so quick to shout for war, now just as quickly lose their nerve? What have we gained by all of this sacrifice, all this suffering? they wondered.

Poor weather added to their misery as spring downpours turned the dirt roads into a morass. The horses in the light cavalry vanguard churned every thoroughfare into mud. The infantry, following them, had to slog through foot-deep brown muck that sucked at their shoes, making every step a wearisome struggle. It held the army's heavy wagons in its viselike grip as cursing teamsters beat the frightened oxen and horses senseless in an attempt to extricate their precious cargo from the quagmire. Many wagons were simply abandoned. Soldiers threw away equipment, carrying only food, water, and their weapons.

The Duke of Ferrara, reinforced by the King of Naples and Pope Sixtus, had initially kept his distance, allowing the Venetians' hard march to reduce their numbers, but now he decided to take the initiative. While the count's troops had trudged on up the miserable roads toward the Polesine, the Ferrarese and their allies had spread out and marched along parallel, drier roads to the west, leaving only cavalry to harass the Venetians' rear. This enabled them to outpace the weary Venetians, reaching the Po two days before Count Cajazzo's vanguard.

They fell upon the unsuspecting Venetian flotilla that had been guarding the Po near the twin forts of La Rocca di Ficarolo and La Rocca di Stellata. By the time the Venetian commander, Antonio Justiniano, realized the danger, it was too late. Two thousand men-at-arms and six thousand infantry overwhelmed the Venetians, destroying their flotilla of two hundred small river galleys and capturing its humiliated commander.

When the tired Venetian army finally reached the Po, Count Cajazzo ordered a day of rest. His grateful soldiers fell to the ground, exhausted, but when he heard the disastrous news, Count Cajazzo reacted with his usual industry. He deployed his artillery to command a narrow point on the Po, downstream from the place where the flotilla had been destroyed, and then ordered his sappers to quickly throw a pontoon bridge across the river, under cover of the protecting guns. In two days, the last of his men had crossed over to the safety of the northern bank.

26

Lombardy

A courier has arrived from Venice with new orders."
Count Cajazzo's son, Galeazzo, handed him the folio. The count immediately broke the wax seal that bore Doge Mocenigo's crest and slowly read its contents. He carefully considered each word, weighing its meaning, seeking the intent behind the words. There could be no doubt about his instructions. His face betrayed to his son that he was surprised. Though he tried to hide it, they knew each other too well for him to conceal his feelings.

"What does it say?"

"We are to march at once for the River Adda, cross it, and invade Lombardy, with the object of taking Milan. We are to encourage the people to rise up and depose the young duke and his puppeteer, Ludovico Sforza."

"Damn," replied Galeazzo, "revenge at last!"

His father placed the orders on his table and cast an angry glance at his son. "We must put aside any thoughts of revenge for what Ludovico did to us. We are in the employ of the Venetians now and must diligently execute the doge's orders. That is all. If this means we injure or kill some of those who have injured us, so be it, but that must not be our sole aim. Do you understand?"

"Yes, Father," he replied, unable to resist his father's icy stare.

"Now tell all the officers to come to my tent and receive their marching orders."

In a half hour, all the high-ranking officers in the army assembled in the count's tent. An aide-de-camp, Constantine took his place among them. Guards were placed in a cordon around the tent to prevent common soldiers and camp followers from hearing what was said inside. The count spoke quietly, just loud enough to be heard.

"We are to march west along the north bank of the Po until we reach its confluence with the Oglio River. There, we shall turn north until we reach the bridge at Orzinuovi, where we shall cross and march west with all haste for the River Adda. From there, we shall drive on Milan and take the city.

"It is my opinion, being from the place, that our approach will cause the unhappy Milanese to revolt and depose the duke and his regent. This will eliminate one of the states arrayed against us and seriously weaken the resolve of the others. This strategy also has the advantage of placing our army between the enemy and *terra firma* lands in the Veneto. Now I will answer any questions."

"If we march to the west, what force will stand between the Duke of Ferrara's army, encamped not ten miles from here, and Venice?"

"The Senate had provided for that," replied the count. "They have retained the services of the Duke of Lorraine and a body of mercenaries under his command. As we speak, they are marching from Padua. I will leave a third of the army here, to join with the duke and watch the Ferrarese and their allies. This force should be adequate to prevent them from invading north of the Polesine until we have captured Milan."

Constantine scanned the faces of the haggard, dirty officers. The vermin-infested foot soldiers looked worse, like scarecrows. The whole army was exhausted and confused about their purpose. The last time he had seen faces like this was at Scutari. Then, the army could not have fought on for another day. Now, this army was going to attempt something he thought was impossible. They were to march more than a hundred miles, cross two major rivers, and attack a fortified city, all while watching their backs. Constantine had little faith in mercenaries. Now a force that was half foreigners—and Frenchmen, at that—would cover their rear! The count outlined the order of march for the next day. There being no questions, the council ended.

Later that evening, the troops that were to join the Duke of Lorraine stoked the campfires, while the bulk of the army marched away, under cover of darkness. Their aim was to put enough distance between themselves and the Ferrarese to make good their escape. Count Cajazzo deployed a cavalry screen to the southwest to prevent the enemy from determining his line of march.

The next morning, as the army prepared to resume the march, Constantine was summoned to Count Cajazzo's tent.

"I am placing you in command of a troop of light cavalry, under Captain Morosini."

Constantine had not commanded anyone since Scutari. Now he would be in charge of more than fifty men. Although he was pleased to be given such a great responsibility, he was uncertain whether he could discharge his duties to the high standards of Captain Morosini, known throughout the army as a stern disciplinarian and an exacting commander.

"What happened to the man I shall replace?"

"I do not know. He never returned from checking on his roadblocks last night. He was probably captured. Do not allow the same fate to befall you." The count smiled. "You will find Captain Morosini in his tent, awaiting you. You have served me well all these months. Thank you for your loyalty."

After shaking the count's outstretched hand, Constantine lingered.

"Is there something else?" asked the perceptive count.

"I . . . I do not know if I am qualified to assume this command. I—"

"My son, you have earned it. If someone asks by what right you assume command, say that Roberto da San Severino has given it to you. That is enough. Now go, and God be with you."

Constantine bowed, grateful for the count's words, and walked out of the tent.

C aptain Morosini was tough but fair. *What more could a junior officer desire?* Morosini knew and respected Constantine's father. This established their relationship on solid ground and, of course, the captain had heard of Constantine's exploits at Scutari. This, more than anything, made the men accept him as their commander. He quickly learned that his predecessor was beloved—he had big shoes to fill.

After a few days, the light cavalry was able to confirm the Duke of Ferrara's intentions: along with the pope's troops and those of the King of Naples, he had decided to pursue the main Venetian force, headed for Milan, instead of attacking the Duke of Lorraine and his covering troops in the

Polesine. By forced marches, every night for three days, the Venetian army opened the distance between them and their pursuers. Further, as the leader in the race to Lombardy, the Venetians were able to strip the land of food and fodder, leaving little for the enemy.

As the weather grew warmer, the Venetians trudged on, driven by sheer determination and the irrepressible spirit of their commander, which infected every man with optimism. Finally, however, the heat began to take its toll.

Constantine easily settled into his new command. The men accepted him as their leader, and he found them to be first-rate soldiers, though he had not seen them in battle yet. There was only one thing he could not get used to: light cavalry wore only chain mail—no steel armor, except for a light helmet.

They had crossed the River Oglio the previous day and would reach the Adda by evening. Morale had improved markedly on the march. The men found good food, it being springtime. They roasted pigs and chickens on their evening campfires and ate plenty of fresh bread each day. As always happens when the land is bounteous, the army's momentum slowed. Soldiers would rather eat than march. Constantine's company, in the vanguard, was the eyes and ears of the army. It was just after noon when Constantine spied his commander at the head of his column.

"Captain Ziani, reporting as ordered." He saluted his superior officer as he wheeled his horse around to face him.

Morosini was the second son of an old patrician family that numbered three doges among their ancestors. A short man, he was built like a bull. Constantine had no doubt that, if unarmed, Morosini would try to chew his adversary to death rather than surrender. He wore his hair uncustomarily short under his helmet and, having virtually no neck, he looked almost comical. But woe to the man who mistook his strange appearance for anything but that of a coldhearted killer.

"Captain Ziani, you will return at once to Crema to cover our rear. You must delay the Ferrarese army that is pursuing us, any way you can. Due to the indiscipline of the troops, our lead over them has been reduced to no more than half a day. We must widen that distance. Tonight, the rest of the army will force march until dawn. If you are successful in executing your orders and if the weather holds, by tomorrow we will again be more than a day ahead of them. That is all we need. By tomorrow night, after you have succeeded, you must come up with us and resume your position in the van after we cross the Adda at Lodi. Do you have any questions?"

"No, Captain Morosini, no questions."

"Good. Take Lieutenant Dona's company with you. He is gravely ill, down with the fever and not fit for duty. I am placing you in command of his men. This will give you nearly one hundred and twenty altogether. That is all I can spare. Now, do your duty—for St. Mark and Venice!"

27

The Ruse

As Constantine rode back to rejoin his company at the head of Dona's men, he wondered what he could do to delay the enemy. Try as he might, despite the hour-long ride, he could not think of anything. He spotted his own company up ahead, dismounted and resting in a grove of shade trees. He ordered them to mount up immediately for the ride back to Crema. The usual complainers observed they would have to retrace their march at the height of the afternoon sun, but Constantine ignored their insubordination. Once the column was on the road, headed back east, he called for all the officers to dismount, leaving the troops in the care of their battle-hardened sergeants.

"We have been ordered to delay the enemy's advance to give our main body time to open up more distance from them. I have a plan to accomplish this, but before I reveal it, there is another matter of great importance I want to discuss. This will be a dangerous mission, in close quarters with the enemy. I need to determine which one of you should take command if I am killed or captured. Since we have not all served together as a single company before, I do not know which of you should command if I am no longer able to lead you."

He smiled and pointed at each man in succession.

"Who will be the first to guess my plan? That man shall be my successor."

His officers, animated by the challenge, began to talk among themselves. He desperately hoped one of them would have a good plan. One stood to begin the contest.

"I say we should turn the road signs around to confound our enemies and make them lose their way as they pursue us!"

"But what if they see the dust from our horses?" said another. "Remember, some of our pursuers are Milanese. They will surely know the way to the bridge at Lodi."

Another rose to speak. "Let us chase away the inhabitants of several towns along their march route. The empty houses will encourage the enemy's vanguard to plunder them and drink themselves into a stupor, slowing the entire column."

"But we have already drunk all the wine between the Oglio and the Adda," the first man replied, triggering laughter from everyone.

"I will tell you how we will do it!" said one of Dona's men. "Let us tie branches to our saddles and, from behind a ridge, create a mass of dust to their front. They will think our entire army has turned on them, and they will deploy to prevent us from attacking them when they are vulnerable in marching order. Then we can ride away, leaving them to take time to reform and resume their march."

Constantine liked the idea, but it was not enough.

"That might work, but who can think of something better?" he taunted the men.

"Lieutenant Ziani," said one quiet man. "I came to Venice from a place near Crema, so I have an advantage because I know the terrain around here well. A few miles to the east of Crema, there is a small village, on the main road to Lodi, where a bridge crosses over the Serio River. Being summer, the river will not be too deep now, barely more than a stream, but our enemies will still not be able to cross it with their cannon and supplies unless they use the bridge there. We can burn it. The Serio's steep embankments will even be a considerable obstacle to their cavalry and infantry."

"But there must be other crossings over the Serio. How would we prevent them from using one of them?" Constantine looked at his officers, challenging them to think harder. Their lives could depend on it.

One of Dona's men spoke. "We could convince them that, while there are other bridges that span the Serio, the one on the main road to Crema offers them the greatest advantage."

"We could circulate a rumor that there is a brothel in the village there," said another man. "That should surely convince them to fly to the town. The Duke of Ferrara and the King of Naples would be the first to arrive in the place!"

As the officers exploded into laughter, Constantine quickly held up his hand.

"What if they thought there was gold in the village?" a voice chimed in.

"Why would they think that? That is always the first rumor a soldier hears, and never stops hearing, but it is nearly always just a rumor."

A young man, the only officer who had said nothing until then, spoke. "If they capture an officer who tells them it is so, they will believe it."

"Are you crazy?" laughed one of the others. Two more nodded agreement.

However, the officer was dead serious. He stood, challenging the others with his eyes. Constantine could feel a plan coming together.

"But that would mean certain torture and probable death for the man who spreads such a rumor," he protested.

"Maybe, Signor Ziani, but many of us will die anyway. Can slow torture and a quick death be worse than suffering horrible wounds and a slow death? Would not the first require the greater courage and be infinitely more glorious?"

Constantine marveled at what the man said. "How would your plan work?"

The rest of the company of officers grew somber as he spoke slowly and clearly.

"One of us could carry a cache of ducats and a note ordering him to deposit them at the army's treasury train in the village. When our enemies discover this information, they will head straight for the village to raid our pay wagons. By the time they reach it and realize we have burned the bridge over the Serio, it will be too late in the day to march to another crossing. They will be forced to rebuild the bridge in order to bring their cannon and supply wagons across, losing many hours."

The quiet man, whose family was from near Crema, now spoke.

"The land beyond the town, toward Crema, is gently rolling hills all the way to the Adda. Why not combine the ruse of the treasury gold with the one he suggested?" He pointed to the man who had proposed using branches to stir up a cloud of dust. "Once our enemies repair the burned bridge and finally cross the Serio, we can further delay them by making them think the whole Venetian army has returned to the village, mad as hell, to recapture their plundered pay!"

Constantine congratulated himself on his own successful ruse, which had elicited such good plans, and said, "We will combine both deceptions to delay the enemy." Then he stoically asked, "Now, which of you will volunteer to be captured?"

Three men raised their hands. Constantine announced they would choose by lots. The same officer who had suggested the gold ruse in the first place was chosen. They filled a small sack with as many gold ducats as they could collect, about forty in all. Every man gave all he had. Constantine, who had contributed most of the gold, wrote the note in his fine script and sealed it with his ring. The man galloped off on a circuitous route to the south that would be certain to bring him into the hands of the enemy. The others, each relieved that he would not be the one captured, rejoined the column.

By afternoon, the company reached the village east of Crema and laid their trap. They burned the bridge and collected every nail they could find in the town, along with any tools that could be of use to the enemy. Then, retreating behind the first ridge, a mile west of town, each cavalryman dismounted and tied pine tree branches to the sides of his saddle. Constantine posted lookouts to advise him of the enemy's progress and waited with his officers on the crest of the ridge, east of town, for the enemy to appear.

It did not take long for the brave young officer to fall into enemy hands. He attempted to eat the note and discarded the bag of gold, but he did not fool his captors. He quickly spit out the paper when one of them held a razor-sharp dagger to his throat. A quick search in the tall grass along the roadside turned up the sack of gold ducats. The men who had captured him were not Italians but Spanish mercenaries in the pay of the King of Naples. Smelling more gold, they brought him to their captain, who interrogated the helpless prisoner. At first, the brave officer protested that the note was a ruse, designed to fool the Venetian army's pursuers. After a few punches and kicks failed to produce the "truth," the captain became impatient and angry. The Spaniards knew how to torture a man. They had perfected that knowledge during the Inquisition, when they had become expert at separating many a man from his gold. In minutes, driven to the edge of insanity by the horrific pain inflicted by his captors, the young man quickly broke, whimpering that the note was indeed genuine.

The Spaniard was finished with his prisoner. He had no reason to disbelieve his prisoner's pain-wracked assertion that the Venetians' treasury wagons were parked in the village just east of Crema, guarded only by a small company of Venetian light cavalry. He could see no purpose in ransoming the prisoner. He preferred the thrill of pillaging the Venetians' gold to wasting time torturing him further. He nodded to his sergeant, who returned a knowing smile.

As the company of Spanish cavalry dashed off toward the village, the sergeant and four soldiers threw a stout cord over a limb and hoisted the Venetian's wriggling body, with legs kicking wildly in vain, six inches from the ground. Then they rode off, leaving him hanging from the tree. Not one cared to look back as their victim breathed his last. As death mercifully released him from his suffering, he managed an ironic smile through his gritted teeth as he thought of his tormentors' surprise when they found that the forty ducats they had taken from him would be all the treasure they would find.

The Spanish captain dispatched several of his men to find the Duke of Ferrara and the King of Naples and inform them both of his discovery. Then, with his duty done, he drove his men hard for the bridge over the Serio to get to the gold first. However, it did not take long for the news to spread through the League's army. When the duke learned of the cache of gold reported to be near Crema, he rode straight for the town at the head of a body of men-at-arms. Soon a large part of the army was attracted toward the bridge over the Serio like metal to a lodestone, as they followed their speeding commanders, ignoring the other crossings over the river. Nothing attracts an army like gold, not even the prospect of victory.

As the Spanish cavalry galloped down into the defile across the river from the village, they could see commotion and confusion among the few Venetians there. They could also see the wagons Constantine's men had commandeered from the townsfolk. Finding the still-smoking bridge in ruins, they rode upstream as the duke and his Ferrarese men-at-arms, not far behind them, turned and rode downstream, both troops searching for a place with banks low enough for their horses to negotiate. The Ferrarese cavalry won the race to cross the river first and began their dash toward the town, three hundred yards away.

On a prearranged signal, the twenty Venetian cavalrymen still in the village abandoned the wagons and rode for their lives up the road to the low ridge to the west. As they expected, the Duke of Ferrara headed straight for the wagons, ignoring the retreating Venetians. Not far away, south of the village, the Spanish cavalry finally crossed the Serio and were riding hell-for-leather toward the village.

The Spanish cavalry, more lightly armored, made up their deficit quickly. As it happened, both bodies of horsemen arrived at the village simultaneously. They leaped from their saddles, many falling to the ground in the dusty town square, and scrambled up into the wagons. The first men to reach them began to fight each other with fists, sword hilts, and the flats of their blades. As soon as their officers arrived at the scene, they shouted, ordering their men to stop and quickly restored discipline.

"Bring me the gold," ordered the Duke of Ferrara as the Spanish captain, who had discovered the gold in the first place, rode up with a scowl on his face. His horse was covered with lather, completely blown from running the longer race.

A giant cavalryman, the first to clear his wagon of other pillagers, now dejectedly but dutifully carried two heavy sacks to the duke and lifted them up high with his massive arms fully extended. The duke placed both sacks on his horse's saddle and, removing a dagger from its scabbard, sliced a cord on one of the sacks in one easy motion. Then, removing his armored gauntlets, he greedily plunged his hand into the bag to remove its valuable contents; three hundred gold-hungry soldiers leaned forward in their saddles in eager anticipation, hoping the duke would share some of the bounty with them.

With a mighty shout, the duke suddenly threw the contents into the air, showering the Spanish captain and the obedient giant with human feces and stones.

More sacks were quickly slashed open and their disgusting contents verified at sword point. The warriors flew into a wild rage.

As he tried to wipe the filth from his resplendent uniform, the duke called to the giant, "Go tell His Excellency, the King of Naples, that the Venetians seem to be out of money. Their treasury has been depleted, so they are now paying their soldiers with the *dogaressa*'s dowry!" Then he shouted angrily, "The rest of you, search the town. Kill any Venetians you find—after you make them eat this!" He pointed to the contents of the opened sacks strewn in the dust at his horse's feet.

"Report back to me as soon as you have finished!" Finally, he turned to the Spanish captain and said, "Señor, I suggest you have your men search for some wood, tools, and nails and begin repairing that bridge."

Fearful soldiers scrambled in every direction. As he rode off to do as he had been commanded, the Spanish captain thought about the Venetian officer he had tortured and hanged.

"If he were still alive, I would pull out his tongue," he said to his aide.

Then, admitting to himself that the prisoner had bravely sacrificed himself, he whispered softly, "What courage! Who can contest with men such as these?"

Before long, the enemy's footsore infantry began to march up, only to see the lone bridge there destroyed. Their officers made the easy decision to rest while sappers repaired the bridge. They knew their men could not march another mile in the heat; they fell out in heaps along the riverbank, exhausted by their rapid march.

It took twenty minutes to search the village. They found no Venetians. Not long afterward, the King of Naples arrived at the head of a large body of infantry. On hearing the news, the dour Duke of Ferrara went to meet his ally. With his treasury depleted from the costly war, the duke lamented his bad luck, desiring the Venetian gold more than a victory. The king, who already possessed more gold than he could spend in his lifetime, laughed at the cleverness of the Venetians' trick and suggested to the duke that the cavalry attack toward the Adda at once. On the king's orders, his infantry were already fording the river, as he was unwilling to wait for the bridge to be repaired.

As the two thousand cavalry and infantry formed up for battle, it was already late; only an hour or so remained until sunset. On the duke's signal, the force began to move along both sides of the road toward the low ridge a mile ahead. Three hundred cavalry advanced on each flank, slowly walking their horses to stay even with the fourteen hundred exhausted Neapolitan infantry in the center. All the men had marched through the day without wearing their heavy steel breastplates and helmets. Now, expecting a fight, they donned the metal armor. Hot, tired, miserable, and disappointed that the rumors of Venetian gold had proven false, they grimly advanced.

Constantine and his men had seen the two bodies of enemy cavalry search for a crossing over the Serio and then speed into the village. They had all laughed together as they thought of their rapacious enemies digging their hands into the bags of "gold" they had bravely captured. The officers had all taken a turn describing what they thought the pandemonium had been like, laughing, as each description was more outrageous than the last. But Constantine did not laugh. He was thinking of the poor dead officer whose noble self-sacrifice had made the ruse possible.

Now, like angry bees whose nest had been smashed, the enemy was advancing toward the low ridge. When they reached a point halfway from the village to the crest, Constantine waved his hand. A series of men, each in turn, relayed the signal all the way back to the hundred men waiting a half mile to their rear. In minutes a great cloud of dust began to rise as the Venetian cavalry advanced up the road three abreast toward the ridge where Constantine sat on his big gray horse.

Within five minutes, the enemy had closed to three hundred yards, their line now concave as the horsemen on their flanks inevitably began to outdistance the infantry. Suddenly they spied a great cloud of dust cresting the trees on the top of the low ridge, signaling a large body of men to their front.

The Duke of Ferrara, spying the telltale sign, stood in his silver stirrups to see as far as he could. They were coming closer. He quickly turned around to see what troops had come up behind him, in the second line, to support him.

"Damn that Ferrante!" he muttered under his breath. He looked back at the billowing clouds of dust that surely indicated a force much larger than his own and suddenly reined in his horse. Perspiration dripped down his face in dirty rivulets as he took off his bascinet. Now others hesitated. They could sense the indecision on the part of the duke. The attack began to falter.

A man shouted, then three more. A nervous horse whinnied and stood up on his hind legs, sensing his rider's fear. They were now close enough to see a few Venetian cavalry on the ridge, sitting, watching, unafraid. Tired, hungry, and unsure of what was coming toward them on the other side of the ridge, they began to break. In minutes, the two thousand men had turned into a disordered mass, too fearful of the Venetians to advance and too afraid of their officers to run away. Many slowly began to back away and then, turning around, headed for the rear. Some began to shout.

"We are lost! It is a trap!"

"Look, the Venetian army is here!"

"It is another ruse, like the gold!"

"Save yourselves! We have been betrayed!"

All the protestations a soldier could conjure up now spewed forth from hundreds of mouths. The Duke of Ferrara began to strike nearby fleeing men with the flat of his sword, but even some of the officers had begun to melt away with them. It was no use. He turned his big warhorse around and slowly cantered back to the Serio, turning occasionally to be sure he should not gallop.

Thanks in part to the Venetians' clever ruse at Crema, their army crossed the Adda two days ahead of their pursuers. As they moved through Lombardy, like a horde of locusts on the way to Milan, they raised the cry, "The duke and Lady Bona." This was intended to incite the populace to oust the regent, Ludovico, in favor of the young duke and his mother, Lady Bona of Savoy. At first, the Milanese were inspired by the Venetians, but soon the army's unavoidable depredations, caused by the need to feed so many men and animals, began to tell. Within days, the Milanese rallied to Ludovico and patriotically responded to his call to arms.

Facing increasing danger, Count Cajazzo wisely canceled his attack when his cavalry confirmed that sixteen thousand men-at-arms and cavalry and seven thousand infantry—more than twice his number—opposed him. This host was composed of Milanese, Florentines, and Neapolitans. It did not even include the Ferrarese, who had gone back to their own territory to attack the Duke of Lorraine.

Back in Venice, the government recognized that Ludovico's offer to sign a separate peace would be meaningless as long as Lombardy was swarming with the League's forces.

Late that summer, after more than a year of constant campaigning, the League had now seized the initiative from the Venetians. La Serenissima, with her treasury depleted after more than a year of war, her army in retreat, and her arrangement with Ludovico Sforza no more than a worthless scrap of paper, prepared for the worst.

28

The Rialto

In mid–September, the Venetian army grudgingly retreated, trading territory for time. They burned bridges and ravaged the countryside, slowing the League's progress to a snail's pace. As happens with alliances, they wasted much time and suffered many delays because of their endless councils of war. Soon the onset of winter would bring an end to the campaigning season. The League had retaken all of Lombardy and had seized the cities of Bergamo, Brescia, and Verona. Their next objective would be to invade the Veneto as soon as winter turned to spring. Time was running out for Venice.

Count Cajazzo, by employing rapid marches and staging sudden demonstrations, had been able to concentrate his inferior numbers to prevent his more numerous enemies from compelling him to fight a pitched battle. To the south, the Duke of Ferrara had retaken most of his territories, sweeping aside the weak force that opposed him, commanded by the Duke of Lorraine. Back in Venice, in the hallways and chambers of the Doges' Palace and in the streets and inns, people were despondent. The war with the League was bleeding Venice of her bravest sons and her gold.

Antonio and Seraglio had just returned from a walk, the day being the warmest in a week. They had stopped for a glass of wine in their favorite

café in the Piazza San Marco. It was buzzing with bad news. A messenger
from Count Cajazzo had arrived in the city that morning, announcing that
Verona had agreed to surrender to the League its strategic bridges over the
Adige in return for a promise to refrain from sacking the city. Now the rest
of Venice's *terra firma* lands would be more vulnerable to invasion. The government had failed to foresee that the Veronese, tired of war, would uncharacteristically choose to save themselves at a cost of imperiling the rest of the
Veneto.

On the way back to the Ca' Ziani, they discussed what the government
should do. As they entered, Antonio's faithful servant greeted them. He
seemed nervous.

"There is a woman here to see you, Signor Seraglio."

"Who is she?"

"She told me to tell you that she is an old friend of Constantine Ziani's,
from Naples."

Seraglio was stunned. "Did you tell her Constantine is not here?"

"Yes, signore, but she would not go away. She insists upon seeing you."

Suddenly a young woman appeared in the atrium. It was Estella Carboni.

"Signor Seraglio! I have come a long way. It is good to see you again."

"Signor Ziani, allow me to present Signorina Estella Carboni."

"That will be all. Leave us," commanded Antonio, turning to the bewil-
dered servant.

"What do you want with us?" asked Antonio gravely.

"I am from Naples. My father was the man who was hired to kill your
son. Instead, he ransomed him back to you. Later my father was brutally tortured and killed when the man who hired him discovered that your son was
still alive." She began to tremble. "Not long after that, at my father's funeral,
I met this man"—she gestured toward Seraglio, who nodded.

"He told me he could bring to justice the man who murdered my father,
if I would only supply him with the man's identity. I am here today because
I know the name of this man."

Antonio's muscles tightened. "How did you discover his identity?"

"The murderer had an accomplice, a Neapolitan."

She sighed and looked directly into Antonio's eyes. She was not an attractive woman, but there was dignity in her bearing that transcended her
physical appearance. She acted like a beautiful woman and spoke like one,
too.

"We Carboni are a large family, with many aunts, uncles, and cousins,
Signor Ziani. For years, we looked in vain for this man until we realized that
he had probably left Naples forever. We had all abandoned any thought of

finding him. Then one day, about a month ago, this man made the mistake of returning. You can imagine my surprise, but also my excitement, when I spotted him in the marketplace by the docks. I could never forget his face."

She began to cry. Tears streamed down her olive cheeks as she convulsed with emotion. Antonio pulled her tightly to his chest. After a while, she regained her composure and continued.

"He revealed the name of my father's murderer after two of my cousins laid rough boards hard upon his shins in a most horrible manner for nearly two hours. Even after he revealed the name, they beat him some more, just to be certain he was telling the truth."

"Where is he now?"

"He is dead. Once he gave us the information we sought, my cousins gave me the honor of slitting his throat. Imagine that I, a young woman who had never before thought of killing another human being, felt pleasure as I cut into his throat with the dagger."

"And what is the name he revealed to you?"

"Before I tell you, will you honor Signor Seraglio's pledge to give me justice?"

"Yes. Tell us the killer's name."

"Enrico Soranzo. He is the beast that pushed a serpent into my father's mouth as he begged for the same mercy my father showed to your son. But what reward did he receive at the hands of Soranzo? A horrible, painful death as the snake chewed at his innards. A villain who kills like that does not deserve to live," she snarled.

Antonio squeezed his hands into fists. He wanted to hold her in his arms and tell her he was sorry. He wanted to destroy this man who had brought such misery to his family.

"By God, he will pay for his crimes," he said. "But Enrico Soranzo's father is a rich and powerful man. Signorina, have you spoken to the police, here in Venice, about this?"

"No, I have come to you first, hoping that you will help me."

"The police would never take your charge seriously, against Soranzo's denial. You must depend upon me. Say nothing to the police, or else I will not be able to help you. It will take a little time for me to deal with this."

"I will say nothing, I promise," said Estella as she made the sign of the cross.

Estella looked at Antonio and then at Seraglio as she wiped away her tears.

"I must go now. I will remain in Venice until I hear from you. Each day, at noon, I shall be on the Rialto Bridge. You can find me there. I beseech you, do not make me wait too long or I fear I shall go mad."

She lowered her head and walked through the still-open door.

Alone now, Antonio looked at his old friend, his eyes filled with anger and pain.

"Oh Seraglio, when will this vendetta ever end?" he lamented. "For thirty years, I have contended with Giovanni Soranzo, mostly defending myself and my family from his designs, though sometimes we have fought together, as at Smyrna." He shook his head, searching for words to describe his feelings.

"His cousin, Vettor, surely helped to cause the death of my brother. Now I have proof that his adopted son tried to kill Constantine. How long can Venice survive if her *nobili* act toward one another with such malice? Old friend, what can I do?"

Seraglio gazed at Antonio, who looked tired and spent. *He is truly at his wit's end. Perhaps his age had begun to weaken his iron will. I must help him.*

"Antonio, the city is set to explode like a powder keg. Every day I hear recriminations about the war and our dire situation. The last thing Venice needs right now is a revelation that one of her *nobili* tried to have another murdered. It would be a blow to morale, but worse, it would make the *cittadini* wonder who and what they are fighting for."

Antonio knew that Seraglio spoke the truth. But what was he to do? He had given his word that he would deal with Enrico Soranzo. He had to do something. The bastard had tried to kill Constantine, and yet Antonio could do nothing, at least not now.

"I must wait until Venice is at peace before I act. In the meantime, Seraglio, what can I do about Estella Carboni?"

"Leave her to me."

29

The Encounter

Sitting in his friend's lush rooftop garden, Enrico had just finished his lunch of savory roasted chicken and delicate pastries. Though the man implored him to stay and drink some more wine, Enrico decided to go for a walk and bask in the contentment of his recent success. His return to Venice had been triumphant beyond his expectations. The Senate had reacted enthusiastically to Ludovico's peace offer, and he had finally placated his angry father, nearly repairing their tumultuous relationship. It was as though he had never left Venice and, best of all, his father had sent Cosimo to Paris, far away from the Rialto.

It was late summer, and though the air was still quite warm, he continued his aimless rambling, eventually ending in the Piazza San Marco. It was teeming with men taking a break from their busy day. Most were government employees who worked in the state buildings that rimmed the vast rectangular expanse. Their wives, sisters, and daughters strode through the many shops filled with exquisite items imported from the corners of the world, or they just lounged outside, drinking wine or picking at the remains of a midday meal.

Enrico had been with a few women since he had returned to Venice, but he did not care for any of them. Each one was only a pretty perfumed vessel to enjoy for a moment's pleasure, only to vanish from his mind the next morning, like a pleasant thought.

He headed for the shady south side of the piazza, found an empty table outside the Café Leone, one of his favorites, and sat facing the piazza. As the crowds passed by, he focused on the young women, enjoying the view. He ordered a glass of wine from a comely maid and sucked in a deep draught of salt-tinged air. Closing his eyes, he was more contented than he had ever been in his thirty-eight years. He had finally attained respectability.

The sounds of the people enjoying life's pleasures, despite the war, filled his ears. A few minutes passed as he listened intently. He slowly opened his eyes to let the light reveal a panorama of colors and motion. As they focused, something intriguing caught his attention.

A crimson dress flashed among the yellows, greens, and blues of the ladies and the omnipresent black robes of the *nobili*. Her dark hair cascaded from under her wide-brimmed hat and spilled down over her shoulders. He admired the delicateness of her lily-white hand, clutching a small package she had purchased from one of the shops. He could not take his eyes off her. Swallowing his half glass of wine, he rose, dropped a coin on the table, and headed in her direction as she drifted away through the crowd.

As she walked west, away from the Basilica di San Marco, he hurried his pace, afraid he would lose her in the crowd that funneled into the narrow street at the end of the piazza. When she disappeared around the corner, he began to run after her. He did not care what other people would think of a black-robed *nobile* running like some base *cittadino*. Bumping and pushing those coming and going in front of him, he quickly reached the point where she had turned. She was already halfway down the narrow passageway. There were fewer people now. He guessed that she lived in one of the *palazzi* along the Grand Canal. Dressed in such finery, she was obviously a woman of means, no doubt the daughter of some rich *nobile*.

He decided to take a parallel street and cut in front of her to *accidentally* meet her. His blood was up. For the first time in years, he was excited about meeting a woman—and he had not even seen her face. *What if she is plain? She cannot be. She must be beautiful. She must!*

As he rounded the last corner, he took a deep breath. *What if I have miscalculated? What if she is not rich? What if she only lives in one of the mean little houses in this* cittadini *neighborhood?* The street was empty. His heart sank, but just as he was about to turn away, she miraculously reappeared. He still could not see her face, under her hat, but her shape was divine and her walk spoke volumes—confident and proud, with her femininity thrust out for all to see.

She was only yards away now, and he trembled with excitement as he smiled broadly.

"Good day, signorina," he said loudly, ensuring no retreat from his bold greeting.

Her red hat tipped back, revealing her sublime face beneath, frozen with surprise. She was no cute young signorina; she was Venus, mature and dazzling. She was Maria Mocenigo.

Old memories, long suppressed, exploded in his mind like magma from Vesuvius. Delightful anticipation turned to painful recollection. He was naked, exposed, the long-nurtured scab ripped from his heart in an instant. *What could be worse?*

"Are you speaking to me?" she replied, a confused look on her face as she looked around and noticed there was no one there but the two of them. Her expression suggested to Enrico that she did not recognize him. It was the moment of truth, a last chance for him to beat a hasty retreat.

"Signore, please allow me to pass," she curtly insisted, her eyes imploring him.

"Maria! Do you not recognize me?"

"Enrico Soranzo!"

"Yes. I . . . I have not seen you in so long . . . years."

"What are you doing here?"

"I was on my way to the Piazza San Marco."

"But you do not live near here. This is not the way from the Ca' Soranzo," she observed.

"I . . . I was visiting a friend," he stammered, caught in his quickly expanding web of lies.

"You have a friend who lives here, in this neighborhood?"

His eyes begged her to stop, to show him some mercy—not like their last encounter.

"Signor Soranzo, I am a married woman. I am Signora Constantine Ziani. My husband is in the Veneto, fighting with Count Cajazzo's army, defending La Serenissima." She scowled.

He wanted to flee, but his feet were rooted to the paving stones. He was speechless.

"Do you think I do not know what you are about? You are a rake, signore. You are a disgrace to your family. I saw you sitting by yourself outside the Café Leone not ten minutes ago." She was spitting her words angrily now. "I think you have stalked me like you would hunt some animal in the woods."

He began to shake his head to object, but she was right. It was as though she had some magical power to know his innermost thoughts. In an instant, she had demolished his resurrected spirit. He exploded.

"You think you can talk to me like that? Like I am some child to be scolded!" Spittle ran from the corner of his mouth as his head trembled with rage.

Every wrong ever committed against him now welled up and ran together into a torrent of pain and anguish. She became the cause of his failed life, the source of his misery.

"Let go of me!" she shouted. "Wait until my husband hears of this."

He looked down. In his anger, he had unconsciously grabbed hold of her forearm. He wanted to break it. Leering at her, he recalled the pleasure he had felt as he had killed the Neapolitan brigand who had defied his order to kill her husband. He increased the pressure on her arm.

"I will kill him," he said quietly, without emotion.

"Let go. You are hurting me!" she begged as she began to cry.

Her terrified face made him feel powerful, like a man.

"May I be of assistance?" a man's voice interrupted.

Enrico spun around to see two *cittadini* standing next to him.

"Yes," replied Maria, wiping the tears from her silky cheeks.

"Is this man hurting you?" asked the other stranger.

She pulled her arm free as Enrico relinquished his grip.

"Will you deign to walk me home to my *palazzo*? The streets are not safe here."

She pushed past Enrico and held out her delicate hand for one of them to take. Then the three walked away down the narrow street, leaving Enrico alone to contemplate the fullness of the disaster he had just created.

"I live in the Ca' Ziani." Her words echoed from the fascias of the stone buildings as the trio disappeared around the corner.

Will these Zianis never cease to plague me?

Antonio walked through the narrow streets on his way to the Doges' Palace. He gazed up at the stars, twinkling like so many candles in the night sky. The sea air smelled fresh and sweet. He missed the bracing feeling of standing on the rolling deck of a sleek galley.

A member of the Senate, he had executed several important diplomatic missions for the Republic. Now, in time of war, his days and nights were increasingly devoted to affairs of state. Further, his unique relationship with Doge Mocenigo had become very close in the years following his son's marriage to the doge's daughter.

This evening he had received a message from the doge to come at once and attend a special meeting of the Senate. He knew it must have been prompted by events pertaining to the war. He prayed it was not more bad news. Ever since the pope had changed sides and laid the interdict on the Republic, as he had promised Antonio he would do, things had deteriorated. Less than a year after Venetian forces had won impressive victories, they were retreating everywhere—even conceding Verona, part of *terra firma*.

He reached the broad expanse of the Piazza San Marco, glowing in light provided by the many iron lanterns that ringed the great square. The dark form of the Basilica di San Marco loomed at the far end of the piazza, its many domes glistening gray in the yellow moonlight. He turned in front of the church and headed toward the Doges' Palace. The large windows above the loggia, facing the Piazzetta, were dark. He entered through the Porta della Carta, where the alert guards instantly recognized him, and walked across the darkened courtyard. It was after nine o'clock when he passed through the doors into the Senate chamber on the third floor.

Giovanni Soranzo was about to respond to the question he had just been asked when he caught a glimpse of his old rival entering the room. Ever since the battle of Smyrna, when Antonio had saved his life, Soranzo could never again hate him as he once had. Now, as he contemplated the grave circumstances confronting the Republic, he was glad to have a man with so much experience serving at his side.

Antonio found an empty seat in the middle of the room, on one of the long benches that ran perpendicular to the dais reserved for the doge and his *Signoria* at the far end of the room. Every member of the Senate was dressed in his fine long black robes. He greeted the men sitting next to him but did not feel like engaging in idle chatter. He was worried about Constantine. The decisions made in this room, this night, would have a profound effect on the army and, ultimately, on his son's safety. It was a heavy burden for him to bear.

A door opened and Doge Mocenigo, robed in his ceremonial gold brocaded garments, walked purposefully into the chamber. He was followed by his counselors, dressed in scarlet robes, and the Ten, in black. All being present, the doge called the meeting to order. After a few welcoming words, he announced the purpose of the meeting.

"I have called you here this night to discuss the current military situation. I invited Count Cajazzo to attend, but he did not think it wise to leave the army. He has sent his elder son, Galeazzo, in his place."

The doge nodded toward his secretary, the *cancellier grande*. He was the only man in the room who was not a patrician. Appointed for life by the

Senate, he occupied the highest position open to a *cittadino*. As proof of his status, he was the only man who was not required to remove his hat in the doge's presence.

The secretary walked to the door and opened it. Through it strode a young man dressed in chain mail and dirty boots. The guards had removed his sword from its scabbard. Spontaneous applause arose from the senators. Obviously moved, Galeazzo da San Severino acknowledged the recognition with a polite nod as he remained standing, there being no place for him to sit. From across the room, Antonio was reminded of his own son—they were about the same age. He decided to ask Galeazzo for news about Constantine when the meeting ended.

"Thank you for coming tonight," said the doge. "When you return to the army, please express the Senate's appreciation to your father for his loyal service."

Galeazzo smiled gratefully and again nodded but respectfully remained silent.

"Now," said the doge, "please tell the Senate the state of affairs in the Veneto."

"Signori, the enemy's army is hungry and exhausted. We have stripped the countryside bare and marched them into the ground as they pursue us in vain, trying to bring us to a decisive battle. My father does not believe they will advance beyond Verona before they must retire into winter quarters.

"Our army is also exhausted, but it is capable of opposing the enemy if they press on before winter. In a matter of weeks, we will know for sure if the fighting has ended for the year."

Galeazzo paused; his eyes swept the faces in the room. The senators absorbed his words as a dying plant absorbs life-giving water. The army had apparently succeeded in preventing the loss of *terra firma,* at least for the time being.

"How many men are fit for battle?" called out a senator.

"About nine thousand. The enemy force opposing us is nearly fourteen thousand."

Hunger, disease, and desertions have reduced both armies equally, thought Antonio.

"What plan does the count now recommend to us?" asked the doge.

"There are three options that he proposes to this Senate. First, sue for peace before our enemies, with their superior numbers, overrun the Veneto in the spring. Second, raise more men and arms during the winter respite and resume the fight in the spring. Third, renew the fight but convince a powerful new ally to join our side first, improving our odds of achieving victory."

Galeazzo measured his audience. He could see a variety of reactions to what he had said: surprise, fear, anger, and resolve.

"Which of these does the count recommend to us?" asked one of the Ten, his voice betraying some impatience.

"He believes the third to be the best option, the second to be the worst."

Antonio was not surprised. Given the progress made by the League, there was no way the Venetian army could prevent the loss of all Venice's *terra firma* lands in the coming year.

"Thank you, Signor da San Severino. Now if you will wait outside, we will debate the options you have presented and advise you of the Senate's decision."

No sooner had the door shut behind the soldier than the room erupted into a score of heated discussions. Senators hissed their opinions at one another, some nodding their heads in agreement, others vehemently opposed. The doge, now an old hand at this sort of thing, after wearing the *corno* for five years, allowed these conversations to continue for a long time before he stood and asked for silence. The room quieted down as if by magic.

"Who shall begin?"

One old senator majestically rose. He turned around, his face taut with anguish. Antonio recognized him as Agostino Barbarigo. The previous year he had been critical of the decision to go to war. *Now he is going to carp at those who favored attacking Ferrara.*

"The situation is bad. None of these options is good." He shook his head, waving it from side to side like a man about to faint.

"How did we ever let things get this far?" He looked directly at the doge and pointed his finger at him, a gesture of supreme contempt. Even in the dark days at the end of Doge Francesco Foscari's rule, Antonio had never seen such an insulting display toward a doge.

Doge Mocenigo seemed to recoil from the silent rebuke. Several of his supporters in the *Signoria* sprang to their feet and began to protest, but it was not about the point Barbarigo had made, only his disrespect for the head of state. Other senators began to shout, some agreeing, others disagreeing with Barbarigo, who remained standing, still as a statue. Finally, he slowly lowered his arm and turned to face his fellow senators. The room fell still.

"There is no point in arguing about the past. We must decide tonight which of the three courses of action is best, so we can end this infernal war once and for all."

Near Antonio, another senator and a supporter of the doge's policies now stood.

"I say this to Signor Barbarigo and all who would agree with him.

Events are not as grim as you portray them. We know that Ludovico Sforza would like to withdraw from the League. If we can induce another power to join us, as Count Cajazzo suggests, we may be able to convince Milan to sign this separate peace, decisively reducing the League's strength, making further hostilities pointless for them."

Now Soranzo stood and the room went quiet again.

"I suggest we invite King Charles of France to join us. He has a claim to Naples through his ancestor, Charles of Anjou, whose descendants received it from the pope and possessed it until 1432, when it was seized by the House of Aragon. Further, his cousin, the Duke of Orleans's mother, was a Visconti, and she sat on the throne that Francesco Sforza stole and that Ludovico now covets. I have no doubt that Ferrante and Ludovico would quit the League at once if their own thrones were threatened by the French claims."

Antonio was mortified, as were a few other older senators. *What was Soranzo saying? If the French army invaded Lombardy, there would be hell to pay.*

Seeing the folly of Soranzo's suggestion, Antonio was compelled to speak.

"I would caution this body most strongly against inviting Charles into the Italian Peninsula. It would be like inviting your neighbor into your home to settle a family dispute. Once he looks around at your possessions, you can be sure he will covet what you have."

Many in the chamber voiced their agreement.

The doge held up his hand for silence.

"Signor Ziani may be right, but what other choice do we have? Who else could strike fear into the hearts of our enemies like the French? They are powerful, and the mere threat of her involvement in what, up until now, has been an Italian affair will strike fear into the hearts of Milan and Florence, our two enemies closest to France, geographically. Further, King Charles's claim on the throne of Naples would add no little terror to King Ferrante's thoughts. I am in favor of the proposal."

The room exploded into loud arguing. Finally, the doge called for a vote to make overtures to Charles. It narrowly passed. There being no other business, the meeting ended. Soon only a handful of senators remained, talking idly.

Antonio sought out Galeazzo and found him conversing in the hallway.

After a moment, he asked, "Signore, can you tell me how my son, Constantine, is?"

"He is well, Signor Ziani." Galeazzo remembered Antonio's face. "He performed prodigious acts that benefited our army when he commanded our rear guard at Crema."

Antonio smiled, filled with a father's pride.

"Is the count going to grant leave to any of his officers once the army goes into winter quarters and there is no threat of attack?"

"That, I do not know. Do you have a message you would like me to give to your son?"

Antonio thought for a moment.

"Tell him that his wife and children are well but that they miss him terribly. Tell him that his mother and I miss him too and hope to see him soon."

Galeazzo shook his hand, turned, and walked down the hall to the golden staircase.

Antonio went back into the Senate chamber to see if Doge Mocenigo was still there, but he had gone. Only a handful of men remained. One was Giovanni Soranzo, the architect of what Antonio believed was a strategy that Venice would regret one day.

"Signor Ziani, we were on opposite sides tonight," observed Soranzo, a chill in his voice.

"Yes, and someday you will be remembered as either the man who won this war or the man who lost all of Italy to the French."

"Strong words. Do *you* have a better solution to our difficulties?"

Antonio hesitated. *He has a point.*

"Would you suggest that we do nothing of substance and merely continue bleeding in the spring until we lose all of our *terra firma* lands?" prompted Soranzo.

"Signore, the Milanese and the Florentines will forgive our harsh dealing with the Duke of Ferrara, although I suspect *he* will carry his grudge to the grave. However, they will never forgive us if Charles enters Italy at our request, with his army of cutthroats and mercenaries. Such men do not wage war as we do."

Soranzo laughed. "You mean the French actually try to *kill* their enemies?"

"Yes, and they mercilessly sack their cities, too. And I will tell you this. If Charles sends his army to fight here, the Spaniards and the Swiss, with their fierce pikemen, will not be far behind. They will be unable to resist meddling in our affairs as well. The Italian city-states are the finest examples in the world of concentrated wealth. To outsiders, we look like gold coins on the floor of a treasury, just waiting to be snatched."

"Well, Signor Ziani, it matters little what you think now. The decision has been made."

"Yes. All I can do now is pray that Charles will be occupied with affairs in France or with the English. I have heard that he has finally thrown them out of Calais, their last foothold on the continent . . ."

Just as Antonio was about to finish the thought, he heard a shout from the hallway. Suddenly an excited guard rushed into the room, wild-eyed and hatless.

"The palace is on fire!" he shouted.

They ran after him toward the end of the palace that housed the doge's apartments. They could see smoke billowing from under a door at the far end of the corridor. More guards rushed toward the smoke, carrying buckets of water, while others removed their capes to beat down the flames.

It had been centuries since the last fire at the Doges' Palace, which was decorated with irreplaceable works of art by the likes of Bellini, Tintoretto, and the greatest Venetian painter of them all, Titian. It was unthinkable that these masterpieces might be damaged or destroyed.

They ran to the end of the hallway. Someone had thrown open the door. Thick black smoke roiled from the room, stinging their eyes. Antonio instinctively dropped to his stomach, then crawled into the room. Soranzo and a handful of others followed him.

Antonio took a deep breath. *I must get to the doge's apartments.* He shut his eyes and stood up, fumbling blindly for the door handle. Finally, he found it and pulled the door open. Inside, the smoke was so thick, it would be suicide to enter. They retreated. Now, with Soranzo in the lead, they ran through the blackness back into the corridor. They turned right and opened the door to another room. They could feel the heat emanating from somewhere in the building. Luckily, there was little smoke inside.

"The doge's apartments are through that door," shouted a guard, pointing to the other side of the room. "Quick! We may not have much time."

They rushed in. It was hot, but the smoke was more like thick fog than what they had encountered earlier. Suddenly Doge Mocenigo appeared in the doorway, dressed in his nightclothes, coughing as he leaned against the doorframe.

"It is my fault. It is all my fault!"

"What happened, Giovanni?" shouted Antonio over the tumult, dropping formality.

"A candle must have fallen and ignited the carpets. Now people will ransack my rooms!" He grabbed Antonio's robe, a wild look in his eyes. "You must not let them. They have no right to come into my rooms!"

Antonio could not believe his ears. "What are you saying, Giovanni?"

"Not to worry. I have locked the doors, and now that you are here, we can all go in and fight the fire together." He produced an oversized iron key and smiled like a man possessed.

Antonio glanced at Soranzo and the disgusted guards. *You risked the total destruction of the Doges' Palace and its irreplaceable contents just to save some sticks of furniture worth a few hundred ducats?"*

"Come on," screamed Soranzo, "we must save the palace." He ripped the key from the doge's hand and quickly unlocked the door. This time, sooty black smoke billowed out from the chamber within, burning their eyes and filling their mouths and nostrils with its acrid taste. Guards formed a line, heaving buckets, kitchen pots, and even helmets filled with water. They could see the orange and yellow flames licking at the walls and ceiling. Ancient wooden rafters and beams crackled as they turned into red-hot embers. It was like hell on earth.

"Did you also lock the door on the other side of this room?" shouted Soranzo.

The doge's eyes betrayed his answer: his dull, lifeless stare suddenly turned to brightness as he realized his terrible mistake. Soranzo knew what he must do. He grabbed two guards by the arms and shouted above the tumult.

"Take off those cloaks, soak them, and put them over my head!"

Antonio could see what he was about to do.

"The fire is too advanced for you to attempt to open that door!"

Soranzo spun around, his fierce eyes, stabbing Antonio with anger.

"Will you go in my stead, or shall we stand here and do nothing?"

Antonio stood, transfigured. *No one should attempt such a foolish thing.*

"Once you risked your life to save a man—a single *nobile*. Now the Doges' Palace is threatened. Shall I risk less than you did?"

He turned aside and nodded to the two guards, who immediately threw their dripping wet capes over his head. Without another word, Giovanni Soranzo ducked his head and disappeared into the conflagration. Antonio tried to hold him by his sleeve, but Soranzo tore loose, leaving only a scrap of cloth between his rival's fingers. One of the two guards placed a hand on Antonio's shoulder.

"God help him."

"Yes, yes," said a voice. It was the doge. "God help him. He is a brave man."

30

The Lodestone

The stench of ruination wafted through the city on pungent, smoky feet, creeping under doors and through shutters like a phantom. It carried with it the odor of death—not of burned flesh but the acrid smell of an old hearth. It portended that something terrible had happened. That Sunday night most Venetians had gone to bed before the fire broke out. Now, at first light, thousands of workers awakened as usual to the ringing of the *basso* voice of Il Marangone, the massive bronze bell in the campanile, summoning them to the Arsenal.

They dressed, and as they gnawed at their dried fish and bread, they sensed that something was wrong. Soon they walked silently through the streets en masse, as though they were on a pilgrimage to a place they feared to go. From north and west they came, drawn to the source of the smell like pieces of iron to a lodestone. They filed past the unscathed edifice of the Doges' Palace; the telltale gray smoke drifting in the sky behind it indicated there had been a large fire. From the east, Arsenal workers delayed the start of their workday and walked toward the palace. Curious people by the thousands filled the Riva degli Schiavoni to gawk at the smoldering corpse that was once the pride of Venice.

The golden morning sun threw its rays above the city's red-tiled rooftops, revealing the extent of the damage. The southeast corner of the ancient building was in ruins. They could see the hazy smoke still drifting out of the empty windows of the doge's apartment—the glass had melted in the heat. The pink, gray, and white bricks were burnished sooty black. The once-magnificent building seemed to cry out in pain to the people. Many shook their heads in disbelief. How could this have happened?

The inevitable rumors began percolating through the crowd. *It was the Ferrarese. The pope's agents did it. God did it to punish Venice for ignoring the Church's interdict.* However, officials sent to control the angry crowd told them the fire had started in the doge's apartments. Late for work, the Arsenal workers who comprised more than half the people there began to disperse, their mood as dark as the soot on the walls of their beloved palace.

Workers had already begun to throw charred remains out of the windows and into the black waters of the Rio di Palazzo. There, men in boats with wooden boards lashed to their prows pushed the floating debris into the Bacino di San Marco.

The disastrous fire could not have happened at a worse time. Venice was embroiled in a war that had begun with such high hopes, but the odds had turned heavily against her. Fortunately, winter would provide a respite for her armies in the Veneto and the Polesine, but the fire had shaken the doge. He had narrowly escaped death. Some superstitious members of the government believed the fire was a bad omen, a portent of doom.

The ducal apartments were completely gutted. Most on the Great Council did not think it wise to spend the more than six thousand ducats— the estimated cost of repairs—on the palace. They thought the money would be better spent on the army. One patrician, Nicole Trevisano, proposed a plan to purchase all the houses opposite the palace (across the canal) as far as the Calle delle Rasse and build a new residence for the doge there. It would have a large garden and be joined by a stone bridge to the Sala del Collegio in the old building, which would be restored and used solely for governmental purposes. In the end, it was decided that the original palace would be rebuilt just as it was, but its priceless artwork had been lost forever.

There was little time for the doge and his counselors to lament the loss. There was much work to be done. To his credit, Doge Mocenigo recovered quickly, ignoring his personal loss, and set himself to making overtures to the King of France.

Antonio was not surprised when the Senate chose someone else, besides him, to go to Paris to try to persuade Charles. Others knew the ways of the French better than he did and, more important, they were in favor of the plan.

· · ·

S eraglio had told Antonio that he would wait up for him in the library, no matter how late it was when he returned from the Doges' Palace. The clock had struck midnight only a few minutes before Antonio finally pushed open the door and strode quietly inside the Ca' Ziani. Despite his friend's pledge, Antonio was surprised to find Seraglio sitting in his chair, dutifully awaiting his arrival. Normally Seraglio went to bed at around ten o'clock.

Antonio looked more closely at him and smiled. Seraglio's short legs jutted straight out from the broad seat; he was too short to bend his knees toward the floor. His chin rested at a painful angle on his open palm, propped up by his rigid forearm. His breathing was heavy, though he was not snoring. *He has just dozed off.*

Antonio walked over to the chair and touched him lightly on the arm. Seraglio snorted once and shifted uneasily. One large brown eye fluttered open and seemed to drift lazily as it tried to focus. Then, as if he were a sentry caught napping by his superior officer, he sat bolt upright with both eyes opened wide, an embarrassed look etched across his face.

Now fully awakened, Seraglio slid off his chair and came to attention. After all these years, he still paid Antonio the little marks of respect he had always shown to his mentor. His pained expression melted away into one of eager anticipation.

Antonio thought for a moment, saying nothing.

"Seraglio, you and I are going to get drunk."

"Tonight?"

"Tonight—and we are not going to stop drinking until the sun's rays penetrate *that* window."

He lifted his friend's chair, carried it over to his table, and placed it opposite his own.

"But that window faces west," protested Seraglio.

"Exactly. That will give us more time to drink."

Seraglio watched as Antonio flopped unceremoniously into his red leather upholstered chair. His face, weathered by years of bracing sea air, normally looked older than his sixty-one years. But tonight Antonio's face looked older still, worn out by the rigors of his life.

"I tell you, it was a depressing meeting. Do you remember when, all those years ago, you first saw Venice? You related to me how, as a Greek, you experienced the city through your five senses and described each one in detail."

Seraglio nodded, fondly remembering that wonderful day when Antonio had taken him on his first-ever tour of the city. He had told Antonio then how La Serenissima smelled, felt, tasted, looked, and sounded to him, a stranger who had never partaken of her before.

"Well, allow me to describe the Senate meeting in the same Greek way. First, though, we must arrange for some wine."

"Yes, yes, an excellent idea," replied Seraglio, rubbing his eyes.

Antonio rang the bell, summoning his personal valet. When the tired servant came, Antonio told him to bring five bottles of the finest Sangiovese from his well-stocked supply. When the man closed the door behind him, Antonio continued.

"The smell was overbearing. I could not put aside the thought that God had burned the Doges' Palace to send Venice a terrible message that he was displeased with our war, perhaps with our very being. The only good thing about the stinking air in the place was that, despite the interminable length of the business and the bombastic blathering of some of the senators, one could not doze off."

"And what business *was* conducted, Antonio?"

"Kindly indulge your old friend." Antonio smiled. "Allow me to finish."

"The cavernous Sala dei Pregadi is still filled with residue from the fire. The doge said that it was thoroughly cleaned only this morning, but the fine sooty mist that fills the room simply settled back down, coating every surface. It turned our black robes gray. The doge's gold brocade was fairly ruined."

Antonio shook his head. "It is filthy in there, two days after the fire."

The faithful servant returned, uncorked a dusty black bottle, and filled one of the fine Murano glasses he had placed on the table. Antonio tasted the wine and pronounced it good. After the man poured a glass for Seraglio, he looked expectantly at his master. Antonio nodded and the happy servant departed, his labors finished for the night. Finally alone, they raised their glasses in a timeworn salute and each drank half a glass in one long gulp.

"Even now, as I drink this wine—wine that I love—I can still taste that damned soot. Antonio wiped his mouth and tongue across his sleeve with a grimace.

Seraglio laughed. "Now you have smudged your cheeks with the soot from your robe."

"Damn! And all this from a single candle left burning near a window curtain fluttering harmlessly in the night breeze."

"So tell me about the sounds," prompted Seraglio, eager to hear more.

"Not yet. Allow me to describe the scene in the room. The faces of the doge and his counselors revealed the result of the ambassador's discussion with the French king even before they opened their mouths. It was a complete failure."

Antonio rose to his feet, animated.

"As you know, I did not think it was wise to invite the French into the peninsula to meddle in Italian affairs. As badly as we Italians deal with one another, at least we fight our wars in a civilized manner. We go out into the fields, kill a few men on each side, capture some of the enemy, and then sort out the ransoms to determine who won."

Antonio's eyes were filled with passion.

"That most certainly is not how the French make war. They do not fight to possess; they fight to destroy—lives, property, even whole cities. The last thing we need is mercenaries ravaging our cities like the barbarians of old, for it is mercenaries who comprise much of their army.

"I tell you, Seraglio, it was disgraceful. They never should have invited Charles to enter this fight. But then, having committed that grievous mistake, they did not even convince him to come. That created the worst of all outcomes for us."

Seraglio slowly nodded, understanding completely.

"If the League discovers that the Republic tried to entice the French to depose Ferrante and Ludovico and annex Naples and Milan, we will be pariahs. An interdict will seem like small punishment when laid against what could befall us in the spring."

"We have made ourselves a hostage to King Charles's dubious discretion. Now he can use our overture as a way to blackmail us in the future. What a bloody mess they have made of it. At least our ambassador had the good sense to make our offer orally, eschewing a written proposal."

"What reason did Charles give for refusing to come to our aid?"

"He said that he was not interested in contending with the King of Naples for his crown, as he had to keep his eyes on the English. It seems their new king, Richard III, the one they call 'Crookback,' has sworn to retake Calais back from the French. The Duke of Orleans was also too busy to claim the throne in Milan. But mark my words: one day we will regret planting such an idea in Charles's mind—suggesting that the French are justified in claiming these rights of inheritance."

"So what will we do when spring comes? We cannot hope to hold back our enemies, all acting in concert against us."

"We shall do what we have always done." Antonio winked. "If our army can no longer fight, we will employ our considerable diplomatic skills, complemented by spies and bribes. If our diplomacy fails, as it surely has this time, we will rely on our most decisive weapon."

Seraglio smiled and leaned forward. "The fleet?" he whispered.

"The fleet," confirmed Antonio. He looked at the two empty glasses and filled them up. Seraglio reached for his glass and continued.

"So what is the plan? Of all our enemies in the League, only Naples has a fleet. Are we going to attack the Neapolitans, then?"

"Nothing escapes you, my friend."

Antonio's mood changed suddenly. A wistful expression made his eyes droop. His gray beard nearly dipped in his wine as he bent his head, as though in a moment of prayer.

"What is it, Antonio? Tell me."

"Oh Seraglio, I have been in much danger in my life. Much of it you yourself have witnessed, but this time, I have bad feelings about the future."

Seraglio thought he could see a trace of dampness glistening in his friend's eyes.

"I have something that I must confess to you."

"Before you do, let us have another glass together."

This time Seraglio lifted the nearly empty bottle of wine and poured all of its contents into Antonio's glass. Antonio opened a second bottle and placed it on the table, not bothering to first determine if it was good.

"The reason I was so late is that, after the Senate meeting, I spoke privately with the doge—or should I say, the doge spoke with me."

"Surely you cannot mean privately. Were the three *capi* in attendance?"

"Of course. He is never permitted to speak without them present."

"What did he tell you?"

"He said that lately his motives have been questioned by some of his powerful political opponents. They have spread rumors that he favored the war with Ferrara in order to increase his personal wealth. They say that his family is making huge profits by supplying the means of waging war. And since Constantine is married to his daughter, this includes us."

"Who else would they expect to purchase these materials from? The House of Ziani has been providing the Republic with war materials for centuries."

"The point is, Seraglio, he feels the need to demonstrate that he is willing to take personal risks to carry on the fight—that he, too, is willing to make a sacrifice."

"And what might that sacrifice be?" inquired Seraglio, beginning to suspect the worst.

"He informed me that since he has no son, he must send an order to Count Cajazzo, instructing him to detach his son-in-law to fight with the fleet, as a marine."

Seraglio leaned back as he swilled the fine mellow wine around in his mouth, thinking.

"So Constantine, who has given so much already, will be asked to give even more, putting himself at risk as a marine, something he has never done before."

"Yes, and I confess that I do not know whether to be proud or afraid, but in either case, I am not embarrassed by my feelings."

Antonio drank the contents of his glass and poured another for both of them. Seraglio felt a buzzing in his head. His diminutive size had always limited his drinking capacity.

"What did you say to the doge?"

"What could I say? I agreed with him. Constantine is a man now. Besides, I knew that he would want to go."

"It must be hard to contemplate him in harm's way while you remain here in the safety of your *palazzo,* spared from the danger and the privations of shipboard life."

"Yes, Seraglio, it would be most difficult. A naval battle is different than one fought on land. It is more savage, bloodier, and a man stands a much greater chance of being killed."

Seraglio reached out his gnarled hand and seized Antonio's wrist, nearly spilling his friend's glass on the table.

"You said it *would* be most difficult. Tell me now that you are *not* going, too!"

Seraglio had never spoken to Antonio in that tone before. He immediately released his grip. Their eyes locked, neither giving an inch.

"I must go."

"Why? You did not see the need to accompany him on the campaign in the Polesine."

"That is because I sent two bodyguards with him."

"Why not send four this time and trouble yourself no longer?"

"Because the commander of the fleet shall be Vice-Captain of the Gulf Soranzo." Antonio leaned back, reached for his half-empty glass, and drained it in one gulp.

"I see," replied Seraglio quietly. "*That* is something to consider."

He drained his glass too as he mustered his courage. "Well, old friend, you will both be in need of a bodyguard, and I shall be that man," he loudly proclaimed, saluting with a flourish.

Antonio controlled his urge to laugh. Seraglio was not a brave man, but he had offered to risk his life to protect Constantine and him.

"I would be honored to sail with you."

Seraglio's bravado now retreated into rational fear. "What will be your command?"

"I will have no official role. I am getting too old to swing a sword or axe.

The first Neapolitan seaman I encounter would run me through faster than a Turk can skewer a chicken. I shall be a supernumerary on the *San Marco*, which I am placing at the disposal of Vice-Captain Soranzo under the command of my cousin Andrea."

Seraglio reminded himself that, next time, he would be more careful about what he asked for. Antonio had duped him into begging to do what he hated most—to fight. He swore he had shrunk an inch and his hands were so crippled now, he could barely hold a dagger, let alone a real weapon. What could *he* do to fight?

"When does the fleet sail?"

"In three days. We are to attack the Neapolitan ports of Bari and Brindisi, in Apulia."

"After that nasty business a few years ago, when all of us were almost killed in the inn at Mesagne, you swore you would never go to Brindisi again as long as you lived."

"Ah, but this time, *we* shall be the intruders. Our spies have reported that, any day now, the Aragonese fleet based there will sail back to Spain for the winter, leaving the Neapolitan fleet to fend for itself. As you know, they do not have a seafaring tradition like ours."

Seraglio smiled at the thought of the Venetians catching that fleet alone.

"But what about Constantine? How will he join the fleet if we are to sail in three days?"

"Some of Count Cajazzo's men will serve as marines on some of the ships. We will embark them at Chioggia and then sail straight for Bari."

"There will be hell to pay to those Neapolitan bastards!"

"It is our chance to convince them that they no longer want to fight us," replied Antonio. "If we can knock them out of the fight, we can make the odds more favorable. Without the Neapolitans, the League's remaining forces in the Veneto may not be strong enough to defeat us. Tomorrow I will go to the Arsenal to make sure the workers have finished scraping the barnacles off the *San Marco*'s hull. She will need all the speed she can make."

Antonio knew the ship well. He had fought upon her decks at Smyrna, eleven years before when she had been named *The Republic*. Then, he had left Constantine, who was just nineteen, at home despite his angry protests. Seraglio had remained with Constantine, to console him.

"So, for the first time, the three of us will be off to war together," observed Seraglio.

"Yes. I just wish I felt better about it all. For some reason, I fear the future."

"Antonio, you worry too much. Have you not exposed yourself to dangers a hundred times? And yet here you are, unscathed, not a cripple, not an invalid. Why cannot three of us survive this test? Surely the odds are in our favor. Would you rather be fighting the Turks?"

"No," replied Antonio thoughtfully. "As usual, you are right. The odds are in our favor. We will have the element of surprise, and without the Aragonese, we will outnumber them."

Antonio poured another glass, emptying the bottle. He immediately opened a third.

"If the truth be told, the principal reason I fear for the future is because Soranzo will be in command. I will never forget, as long as I live, watching his ship sail out of the Golden Horn at Constantinople, leaving us behind, dooming us to certain capture—perhaps even death—at the hands of the Turks."

Through his wine-induced haze, Seraglio recalled that fateful day when he had saved Antonio's life, changing his own forever. If that day had not happened, he would never have come to Venice. His inhibitions collapsed, as so often happens whenever two old friends imbibe the fruit of the grape. He wanted to tell Antonio, this night, how much he loved him and Constantine, to express himself in a way that was superior to any way he had ever told him before.

They talked for hours until the first rays of daylight began to intrude on their sanctuary.

"Your honor, and I say that most humbly," he began, "no matter what happens to us, I want you to know that a man never had a better friend than you. And a man—you, I mean—never had a better son. And for a man who never had a son, I could not have had a better young man to love like a son of my own."

Frustrated, Seraglio knew as soon as the words passed his lips that they did not come out quite right, but he was too spent to try to improve upon them.

Antonio placed his glass on the table and slid it over to Seraglio's, touching it lightly.

"You are truly the finest, most loyal friend a man ever had."

He took another sip and continued.

"I confess that when I first met you all those years ago, I was embarrassed even to be seen conversing with you. I thought you were grotesque and of no account. How wrong I was. I should have known that you cannot judge the contents of a crate by merely observing the kind of wood it is made from or the markings that denote what is contained within."

Seraglio took another drink, already beyond his limit.

"I, too, have a confession: I was looking to separate you from your ducats.

It was only after you showed me that, contrary to the poor image of Venetians I acquired in school, you were indeed an honorable man. And then, all those months we spent together in captivity . . . well . . ." He could not focus his brain well enough to continue.

Antonio rose with his glass and walked around to the other side of the large wooden table and, dragging his heavy chair on the floor, placed it right next to Seraglio's.

"Remember the look on the governor's face when you showed him the superiority of our religion to his?" Seraglio laughed.

"Remember when you and the Spider saved the army at Corinth?"

Seraglio slapped his thighs with both hands. "I nearly died of fright in that tunnel."

They both became silent. The sun had now risen in its full morning glory, bathing Antonio's library in radiant light. All that remained of the wine was little more than half a bottle. They could already hear sounds echoing through the Ca' Ziani as the servants started to prepare breakfast. The night was over. Their heads ached and their mouths tasted of stale wine and too many words. Their eyes burned from lack of sleep.

They both stood and faced each other.

"Seraglio, I am old and now I have only one desire. I want my son to survive this coming battle and carry on my family's destiny. He must live so that his sons, Sebastiano and Tommaso, will grow up to be true Zianis, ensuring our survival for another generation. Promise me that you will do all in your power to make this so." His eyes narrowed. He gripped his little friend roughly, almost hurting him. "Swear it to me now."

"You have my word, Antonio. I swear it."

Antonio let go of him, conscious that he had crumpled Seraglio's shirt.

"And in return, you must pledge something to me as well."

"Ask."

"You must look out for yourself. I confess that I do not worry much about Constantine. He is strong and smart, but you . . . you sound too much like you have resigned to die. You are the glue that holds this family together. I would be but a poor substitute for Antonio Ziani as Constantine's counselor. Live—live and return when the battle is done. Promise that!"

Like a thief caught in the act, Antonio stared at Seraglio. *He has divined my innermost thoughts.* The truth was, Antonio did not care anymore what happened to him. He had completely transferred his life spirit to his son and grandsons. They were all that mattered to him now. They alone would complete his unfinished work on this earth. A man cannot live forever.

His eyes surveyed the face he had seen ten thousand times before, but this time Seraglio's eyes seemed to penetrate into his very soul. There was still amazing power in this little man with the giant heart. They seemed to will an answer. They would not let him escape without one.

"Very well, I promise."

"Good. Now let us go to bed."

31

The Fleet

The fishing village and small port of Chioggia loomed in the distance. Antonio leaned on the ship's rail and squinted into the fading sun, setting in the west. He could barely make out the new stone tower, built just before the war. To the right of it, the River Brenta lazily deposited its silt into the lagoon.

"We have not seen Constantine for nearly a year and a half. I wonder how he has changed," thought Seraglio aloud.

Antonio seemed not to hear. He was intently focused on the quayside, where they could just make out the forms of soldiers lining the pier. Progress had been slow; the rowers had already been at it for several hours. At least the air was cool, even if there was not a trace of wind. The *San Marco*'s mainsail hung limply from the spar; her huge crimson and gold Venetian battle flag drooped straight down, its tendrils nearly touching the waves.

The *Veneto*, Vice-Captain of the Gulf Soranzo's flagship, led the long single line of nineteen war galleys. Along with the *San Marco*, she was one of the largest ships in the fleet. Each Venetian ship had a complement of one hundred or more oarsmen—all volunteers, paid with the spoils of war.

It did not take many sailors to handle a galley, but in time of war, additional crew members were assigned to each ship to compensate for casualties. A galley's two principal weapons were a sharp prow, used to ram enemy ships, and marines, who would deliver the *coup de grâce* in a fight. Half of the ships had embarked their company of sixty marines in Venice. The *San Marco* was to pick up hers in Chioggia. Antonio had arranged for Constantine to be assigned to his ship.

Each galley was also equipped with several small cannon to sweep the enemy's decks with grapeshot, and to split their masts and tear holes in their sails with round shot. They were also capable of firing loads of flaming pitch at close range, to set the enemy's sails on fire.

Andrea Ziani, captain of the *San Marco* in peace and war, addressed his older cousin.

"We will anchor in the harbor in twenty minutes. We have orders not to leave our formation. We will not be loading any supplies."

"I want Constantine to share my cabin."

"As you wish. I shall arrange it."

The minutes dragged by as the big ships slowly turned to port and anchored in a long line along the pier. Even before the last anchor had crashed into the blue-gray lagoon, small boats loaded with troops began to make their way out to the ships. The crews cheered the marines, their protectors in battle, and the marines cheered the crews on board the ships.

Finally, the moment for their reunion had come. Constantine climbed up the small rope ladder and alit heavily on the deck. He was dressed in full armor, unusual for marines, who typically wore chain mail to avoid drowning in the heavy steel plate.

"Father!"

"Son, let me have a look at you."

Antonio hugged him and then held him at arm's length. His son's beard was longer than when he left and in urgent need of a good trimming. He looked as though he had not bathed in weeks. Antonio could smell a generous amount of camp perfume—a homemade solution of mint oil, rose essence, and fortified wine—coming from Constantine's direction.

Constantine kissed his father on both cheeks, then began his own inspection. Antonio was a sight to behold. His old chain mail shone, and the sunlight glistened from his polished, battle-scarred bascinet. A bushy blue ostrich plume completed its decoration.

"Have you forgotten your old friend?"

"Forgive me, Seraglio. I did not know whether you would be sailing with the fleet."

"And why not?" replied Seraglio with mock indignation. "Did you think I would allow you two to fight without this?" He brandished his old rusty dagger.

They all laughed.

"That is so dull, you could not slice a tomato with it," teased Andrea as he observed the joyous scene.

"Andrea, it is good to see you again."

"Who else would be able to take orders from so many commanders?" He waved his hand toward Antonio and Seraglio and bowed ceremoniously. Then, standing erect, he became serious.

"How many marines did you bring with you?"

"Fifty-six," answered Constantine. "I have served with all of them in the cavalry. They are tough, and I would place my life in their hands." He looked back at his company, already forming on deck. "I already have several times, but I will tell you more about that later. First, I would like to feed them. We arrived in Chioggia three hours ago after a long journey. We have not eaten."

"My men have set up some food at the stern." Andrea pointed toward a makeshift table—two barrels with planks laid across them—that was bending under quantities of dried fish, bread, and raw vegetables. A large basket of apples sat nearby, and beside it was a cask of wine.

"With your permission, Captain Ziani, I will see to my men," said Constantine as he turned and walked to his men, now standing quietly in ranks, eyeing the food.

"He is the picture of an officer," observed Seraglio.

"He is your son, Antonio," added Andrea.

"I must say, it feels strange to be standing here on this deck, knowing that my son commands the marines who will protect us. If only Giorgio could see him."

When he was young, Constantine had followed Antonio's younger brother around like a puppy, enamored by his martial bearing and zest for life. Antonio suddenly felt a chill as he recalled that fateful day, so long ago, when Giorgio had fought the Turks at Corinth, never to return to Venice. He wondered whether he and his shipmates would be so happy in a week, after they had engaged the Neapolitan fleet.

Up ahead, on the *Veneto,* Vice-Captain of the Gulf Soranzo watched the boats rowing the marines out to his fleet. His ship had sailed from Venice with her company of sixty veteran marines. He estimated that, in an hour, the fleet would be ready to sail.

"Captain, I am going to review my charts. Notify me when the loading is finished."

He ducked his head as he entered his cabin. There was Enrico, tucked in his bunk, under his blanket, sleeping. The very sight of his son relaxing like that made him angry. Enrico had not wanted to come, but Soranzo had insisted. He clenched his teeth and pushed him with his foot. Enrico cursed and then stirred. The covers fell away as he turned his face toward his father.

"Why did you wake me?"

"It is time for you to get dressed. We have arrived at Chioggia and are taking on the rest of our marines. Soon we will weigh anchors and make for Bari. Once we set sail, I will be too busy to speak with you again today. I need to talk to you."

Enrico sat up, rubbing his bloodshot eyes. His uncombed hair fell wildly to his shoulders.

Suddenly he rose and splashed some water on his face and hands. Sufficiently awakened, he stared at his father, a confused expression on his face.

"What is there to talk about? I did not see the point in coming along. You insisted and I obeyed, as usual. What else do you want from me?"

"You have been awake for less than five minutes and already you irritate me," spat Soranzo, trying to control his temper.

Every man encounters someone in life who has the uncanny ability to anger him simply by opening his mouth. Soranzo would have never thought it possible that *his* tormentor would turn out to be his own adopted son. *This time, I must find a way to get through to him.*

"Enrico, listen carefully to what I say. Your life may depend upon it. At the very least, your fortunes as a *nobile* will."

Enrico stiffened, his face flushed.

"Ever since the day I ordered you to leave Venice, after you were involved in that stupid attempt to kidnap Constantine Ziani, I have been trying to find a way to make you understand what it means to be a man."

Defiant, Enrico tried to ward off his father's stabbing gaze.

"When you stole money from me, your own father, I was incensed, ready to disown you. But did I not show patience and listen to your story about Ludovico's offer? And then, did I not arrange for you to meet with the doge and his *Signoria,* to bask in glory as you told them all about it?"

For an instant Soranzo's expression lightened. Then, just as quickly, he scowled. "I am ready to give you a chance to redeem yourself for all of your past mistakes."

"I cannot live out my life craving your approbation, Father. I must live for myself."

"Even so, do you not want to redeem yourself in your own eyes?"

Enrico remained silent, refusing to give his father the satisfaction of an answer. Sensing his thoughts, Soranzo continued.

"Very well, I am going to give you an opportunity to earn the respect of other men, to be a credit to your late father and a credit to the Soranzo name. If you succeed, I shall forget all that has separated us in the past."

The words seemed to reach Enrico as he sat up straight, interested.

"And if I do not succeed?"

"Then you will no longer be my son. You will be disinherited as surely as the sun rises, and banished from my sight forever."

The silence in the tiny cabin was broken by the sound of thumping feet on the wooden deck above. Enrico was stunned. *This time he really means it. What does he want me to do now?*

"You shall serve as my personal bodyguard. I will be in the thick of the fighting, I assure you. There you shall be also. I want you to fight for something besides yourself, Enrico. I want you to fight for something worth dying for, and the only thing I can think of that you would value as much as your life is your inheritance. Once you discover the glory of putting your life on the line for something, I pray that you will find that there are other things also worth dying for, such as your family, your friends, your country, and your honor. Will you commit to fight for your inheritance?"

Enrico was too selfish to say no, but he could not admit, even in the privacy of his innermost thoughts, that his father was right. He desperately wanted to respect himself more than he did now. But how could he admit that his whole life up to this point had been misspent—wasted—in the pursuit of base things like women, money, pleasure, and stolen glory—the kind that was never earned but only claimed?

Soranzo awaited Enrico's answer, standing there like a rock, though his heart was screaming for his son to fall on his knees and beg forgiveness. He studied Enrico's face, searching for a clue as to how he would answer. Suddenly he detected a trace of emotion, something he had not seen since Enrico was young.

"Father, I know I have disappointed you. Ever since Carlo was born, I have felt like an outsider, not entitled to the respect given freely to a son by his father. Instead, I have had to earn your respect, like some base employee. You never showed me how to care about anything. Now, that emotion is not to be found within my heart."

He placed his hand on his father's shoulder. "You have my word, as a Soranzo, that I will defend you with my life, not only to preserve my inheritance but to do my duty. I will do it because I want to prove to myself that I am not the man you say I am."

"I care not what your reason is. I care only that you do as I ask."

Enrico held out his hand. Soranzo grasped it. Their eyes met in a way they had never met before—as two men, equal in stature, each wanting desperately what the other had always withheld. Now, perhaps, things would finally be different. Only time would tell.

32

The Voyage

Shortly after the Venetian fleet sailed from Chioggia, the wind picked up, but it was no help. For four long days, the galleys struggled against the unpredictable, mostly contrary breezes blowing up the Adriatic from the coast of Africa. Soranzo, intent on saving his rowers' strength for the battle, was determined to use only his sails. To avoid detection from the lookout towers that dotted the coast, he charted the fleet's course just over the horizon, out of sight from the land to the west. The few unfortunate fishermen who sailed far enough from shore to encounter the fleet were made prisoners and their little boats smashed and sunk.

Finally, they sighted the Tremiti Islands to starboard. This isolated archipelago lay approximately twenty miles east of Termoli and ten miles north of the Gargano Peninsula, the "spur" on the east coast of central Italy. These dry rocks, mostly limestone bluffs broken up by sections of heavily wooded land, afforded the Venetians a perfect spot to wait for their straggling galleys to rejoin the fleet. Careful to avoid detection and in no need of fresh water, Soranzo chose to anchor in a sheltered V created by the tiny rock of one of the Tremiti called Pianosa. It was the farthest of the islands from the mainland.

Soranzo used this pause to call his officers to join him on the *Veneto* and reveal to them his plan of attack. He ordered signal flags raised to announce his intention. In two hours, all of his captains and marine commanders assembled on the *Veneto*'s deck.

T his war that the army prosecuted with so much skill and valor when it first began has gone decidedly against us. You are all aware that earlier this year the Holy Father, seeing the success of our arms, ignobly changed sides. Now nearly all of Italy is ranged against us as we stand alone.

"The Senate has determined that our only hope of success lies in selecting the weakest of our enemies and convincing him that he no longer wishes to fight.

"The Senate has ordered us to attack the Neapolitan Adriatic fleet. It should be anchored at either Bari or Brindisi. If it is not, then it will surely be wintering in its principal base at Taranto, on the western coast of Apulia. If we can destroy it, we can ravage Naples's trade and quickly cripple her economy. We judge that the people will rise up and demand that King Ferrante withdraw from the League, offsetting the pope's intervention. We believe Ferrante is the one ruler who is vulnerable to this strategy, since the others do not derive nearly as much benefit from trade, not being maritime states. As the lone wolf seeks out the hobbled old stag, so we have found our prey."

The officers already knew all of this from the scuttlebutt they had heard before leaving Venice. A few of them, like Antonio, as members of the Senate, had been among that select body that had ordered the fleet sent on the mission. He was reminded that it was impossible to keep such things secret in war.

"My plan is to sail to a point just over the horizon from Bari. From there, two hours before dawn, I will dispatch our fastest galley to reconnoiter the harbor. This old sailor can feel a cold bora wind on its way from the north. If I am right, that galley can run before it all the way to Bari, have a good look around, and then return to the fleet. If the enemy is there, her captain will raise her battle ensign as a signal. We shall attack immediately with the bright morning sun at our backs, blinding the enemy. With fresh rowers and a stiff breeze, we will be on them before they can form up. We shall advance line abreast, blockading the port and preventing their escape to the south."

Most of the officers voiced their approval of the orthodox plan. It is what most of them would have done if they had been in command. When Antonio turned to Constantine to comment, he saw that his son did not have his gaze fixed on Soranzo. It was riveted, instead, upon another officer.

"Enrico Soranzo," his son muttered, just louder than a whisper.

"I had hoped that he would not sail with the fleet," quietly added Antonio.

"Someday I will kill him for what he did to Maria," Constantine whispered.

"Do not even utter a thought like that. I should never have told you," admonished Antonio.

Constantine sat with his arms folded on his chest and scowled at his enemy.

Soranzo continued. "If Bari harbor is empty, we shall sail for Brindisi and employ the same plan of attack there."

"How many enemy galleys do you expect to oppose us?" asked one captain.

"Our spies tell us that they have fifteen, but some are hardly comparable to ours, being of older designs and no match for our ships."

"Show me one Neapolitan galley that is a match for any one of ours, and I will show you one built in the Arsenal and purchased from us!" shouted another officer.

"And bought at a dear price!" shouted a third.

Everyone laughed, breaking the tension.

"Some of their galleys may have been built in Venice," continued Soranzo, "but their sailors and, most important, their officers were not built there. They were, instead, built in the deepest dung hole in all of Italy."

"That would be Naples, where they were fathered by that old bastard king and his whore," interjected a marine.

Soranzo silently tolerated this last crude outburst.

"Captain of the Gulf, what news do you have of the Aragonese fleet?"

"We have heard that King Ferrante has ordered it to return to Valencia, apparently believing it is too late in the year for a sortie by our fleet."

Like a pack of hungry wolves, veteran officers exchanged grins, anticipating an easy time of it, facing only the Neapolitans, who had a reputation for avoiding battle.

Despite the importance of what was being said, Antonio noticed his son continued his trancelike fixation on Enrico Soranzo. *I had better keep these two apart.*

One of the captains who had been quietly leaning against the ship's rail stood up and walked confidently across the deck to Soranzo.

"My ship is fast. I ask for the honor to scout Bari harbor."

Soranzo smiled and shook his head.

"Captain Bragadin, I am sure you would perform that duty with great skill and courage, but I have already selected another ship."

Completely surprised by the rebuff, Bragadin quickly backed away, embarrassed.

"Captain Ziani, you will go and see if the enemy fleet is at Bari; if so, you will raise your battle ensign as a signal to begin our attack."

Soranzo's words caught Andrea off guard. Recovering quickly, he bowed respectfully, acknowledging the order. Then he cast a quick glance at Antonio and Constantine, whose eyes were wide open as they looked at each other, speechless.

"Now," finished Soranzo, "it is time to return to your ships and get some sleep. Tomorrow will be a long day."

Soranzo's intuition had been correct. The bora began to bluster down the Adriatic from the mountains to the north, propelling the fleet on its southeasterly course. The Venetians sailed all day and through the night until they neared Bari. After midnight, lanterns began to flicker from the stern of each ship in succession, signaling Soranzo's order to furl sails and await the *San Marco*'s return after she had inspected Bari harbor.

Andrea Ziani skillfully maneuvered the *San Marco* to within five miles of Bari, close enough to see in the early dawn's light. The sun had not yet broken the horizon. The port was empty. Before the few small fishing boats there could sail out for their daily catch, he was already over the horizon, hurrying back to the fleet. The *San Marco,* giving no signal, rejoined them, taking her place directly behind Soranzo's flagship.

The Venetians continued on their way, headed for Brindisi and their almost certain rendezvous with the enemy. By late afternoon, they had reached a point twenty-five miles northeast of the port, at the head of the Strait of Otranto, at the mouth of the Adriatic. The fleet furled sails and drifted as the blazing red sun set in the west, a portent, many thought, of the sanguine day that would greet them tomorrow.

Andrea Ziani and his tired crew ate their evening meal and, except for those assigned to the first watch, retired and tried to get some sleep. Meanwhile, as Antonio and Seraglio talked quietly in Antonio's cabin, Constantine conversed on deck with some of his marines who also could not sleep. The hours passed slowly as the October night winds chilled the sea air.

Antonio awoke to the ringing of four bells and the changing of the watch. With his eyes still closed, he surveyed the painful stiffness he now suffered daily in his limbs and back. The moist sea air always seemed to make the pain worse. He had almost forgotten how cramped sleeping accommodations were aboard a ship. *I am getting too old for this.* The rocking motion told him that the *San Marco* was under full sail, headed for Brindisi harbor. His eyelids fluttered open as he looked over in the darkness to where he could hear Constantine lightly snoring. He rolled over, sat up, and slid his feet onto the floor. Then he leaned over and reached out for his son.

"It is four o'clock," he said softly as he shook him, "time to get dressed."

He fumbled for a match to light the single lantern that hung from the low ceiling. Now, illuminated by the flickering amber light, he could plainly see his son as he pulled on his pants and boots.

"Last night, I could not sleep, no matter how hard I tried," Constantine complained. "I could not stop thinking about the battle. I have never fought as a marine before. You have fought on land and sea. What is the difference?"

Antonio had thought about that question before.

"Marines fight until the enemy is dead or he surrenders. There are no prisoners until all the fighting is finished. Do not be concerned with ransoms—survival is all that matters. Do not forget that. There is no place for chivalry when you are a marine."

Constantine nodded like a student acknowledging his teacher's wisdom.

"We are sailing for Brindisi. Andrea will be on deck. I must go now and speak to him. Join us as soon as you are finished dressing."

Constantine nodded and reached for his shirt.

"Should I put on my armor?"

"Have you no chain mail?"

"I brought only the fine German plate you gave me last year."

"Very well, but be careful. If you are knocked overboard, you will surely drown with all that extra weight."

Antonio closed the door behind him. Constantine pondered his father's words. *He is right. I would never be able to remove my armor in time if I fall in the water.*

Andrea Ziani stood on the poop deck, by the tiller, conversing with his officers. Antonio wearily climbed the four steps and joined them. Standing up higher now, he scanned the horizon to the west. Land was barely visible just over the line where the dark gray sky met the slightly darker gray sea. A patrol of seagulls cried and shrieked as they dove at the *San Marco*'s wake, looking for breakfast. The sea smelled strong in his nostrils, filling them with the same aroma he had loved all his life.

"Look, Antonio!" shouted Andrea, pointing to the lighthouse.

There it was. Far in the distance, he could just make out the faint orange light, flickering on the horizon. *How could I have missed it?*

"I make it about ten miles distant."

"Yes," agreed Antonio, still struggling to see it as it faded in and out of sight. "How long will it be before we are able to see if any ships are in the harbor?"

"An hour, maybe less."

"With this wind, we will not need to wake the rowers," observed Antonio.

"I have given the order to let them sleep a little longer. They will need all their strength later for the battle."

"Do you think the enemy fleet will be there?" called a familiar voice from the deck below. It was Seraglio.

Antonio turned and smiled at his friend. Dressed in only his pants and shirt, he wore no armor or chain mail. He did not even have a helmet.

Although the sun was not yet visible, its rays had begun to stream across the surface of the sea. On deck, marines were beginning to join their comrades in small groups. Many were already dressed for battle. Rolling gray waves were now clearly recognizable to the east.

Twenty minutes passed as the *San Marco* sailed on, cutting through the three-foot swells, pushed on by a fresh northeasterly breeze. They looked intently at the gradually expanding shoreline. The lighthouse keeper had extinguished his fire and gone to bed. The town's fishermen would be walking through the streets on the way to their boats. The rest, except for the bakers, would still be asleep, unaware of the speeding attackers.

Now, just beyond the low jetty, as their line of sight moved farther into the port, they could make out ships' masts rising above a low fortress wall. Antonio, Seraglio, and Andrea remembered the layout of the town from the time when their ship had been driven there by the gale, eight years before. Nothing had changed. As the interior of the harbor unfolded, they counted the enemy vessels. There were eighteen in all, a few more than their spies had predicted.

"Some may only be merchant ships," observed Antonio.

"Yes," replied Andrea, "but they will fight to protect their livelihood."

"Come about hard to starboard and set a new course east northeast!" commanded Andrea. Then he turned to the others and said, "Time to rejoin the fleet."

The *San Marco* began to heel over to port as the ship's hull strained against the sea. Though the day had dawned, there was little sign of activity in Brindisi. No doubt they had been spotted by someone, but it was unlikely that an alarm would be raised quickly. After thirty minutes, the harbor was little more than an interruption on the horizon. Now their attention shifted back to the east.

"Raise the ensign!" shouted Andrea.

A minute later, a sailor emerged from below deck, carrying a large bundle of crimson cloth. Another assisted him in hooking it to the halyard. Suddenly it seemed to burst into the blue morning sky, an explosion of crimson and gold as they hauled it aloft. The golden Lion of St. Mark, sword in hand, seemed to be searching ruefully for their comrades, somewhere out there in the distance. The flag's tendrils fluttered and cracked against the cloudless sky. It was a glorious sight.

Constantine thought he saw his father wipe a tear from his eye. He felt a lump in his own throat as his attention shifted between the flag and his father. Seraglio, who never missed anything, smiled and then turned and saluted the flag, as did all of the sailors and marines.

Suddenly the captain raised the centuries-old battle cry—"For St. Mark and Venice. Come on, men. For St. Mark and Venice!" A wild cheer rang out all along the deck, now crowded with the rowers who had left their benches below and joined the men on deck. In all, more than two hundred men repeated the chant, over and over: a solitary company of warriors, alone in the vastness of the sea. Not just native Venetians, the crew comprised Slavs, Spaniards, Germans, and Hungarians—even a few Englishmen. Venice had always attracted the most skilled seafarers with the lure of better pay and conditions.

Antonio surveyed the scene and beamed as though it were all his own creation. And, after all, who could really say that it was not? The *San Marco* was *his* ship, paid for with *his* ducats. The captain was a Ziani. The marine commander was a Ziani—his own son, offered without condition to the Republic, even to be sacrificed if necessary. Were not the rowers *his* rowers? Did *he* not pay for the powder and balls and the food and wine? *And I have willingly given all this to repay the Republic for all she has given to me.*

Seraglio, more than any other man on that deck, understood what it meant to be a true Venetian. It was easy for a man born of privilege and instilled, from childhood, with her ways to love Venice. That kind of love was formed in the womb and woven into the soul of every Venetian. But Seraglio had come to love Venice in a different way. For him, it was a choice—not a birthright, a duty, or some kind of repayment. He ventured his life willingly, and by his very presence on board the ship, he proclaimed that he was willing to die for Venice. This, he thought, is what made Venice unique. This is what would make *them* victorious this day—that a man who was not born in Venice could love her as much as a man who was.

Suddenly a loud cheer brought Seraglio back from his thoughts. Off in the distance, a long row of galleys in line-abreast formation was bearing down on the *San Marco*. Between the *Veneto*'s starboard side and the port side of the galley next to her was an open space, obviously intended to be the *San Marco*'s place in the attack.

The rowers hurried to take up their oars, three men to a bench, arranged in twenty rows on either side of the ship—120 in all. They quietly laid their swords, axes, and spears at their feet as they awaited the order to begin rowing. The cannoneers began loading their weapons with long-range shot.

Constantine deployed his marine company into lines along each rail at the ship's bow. His twelve crossbowmen, each armed with forty deadly bolts, carefully selected their firing positions.

Andrea turned the ship 180 degrees and trimmed his mainsail, slowing the *San Marco*'s progress and allowing the fleet to close up quickly. When the nearest ship was three hundred yards away, he ordered full sail, increasing her speed.

Five miles away, tucked into his plush canopied bed in Castello Alfonsino, the Neapolitan admiral sat bolt upright and cursed the loud banging on his bedroom door.

"I will cut off your balls, you who have awakened me. Enter if you dare!"

"Admiral Coppola, the Venetians are coming!" quavered a voice through the heavy wooden door. The speaker was not foolish enough to identify himself.

"What?" The admiral jumped onto the carpeted floor and hastily began to dress.

"Admiral, Venetian galleys are bearing down on the harbor. We are lost!"

Growing more excited, Coppola struggled to pull on his boots and cursed angrily as his nervous fingers failed him. Suddenly, a comforting thought struck him. *It is probably the Aragonese fleet returning from their mission to Messina.*

King Ferrante had ordered them to bring food to the starving Sicilians, whose crops had been ruined by a long, dry summer. Now, fully awake, he laughed loudly and shook his head. *How can they expect me to command such rabble? They are idiots, every one of them.*

He had just begun to climb back into bed when another, more assertive voice penetrated the door.

"Admiral, you had better come quickly and look out the window to the east." The officer threw open the door and faced his commander.

"Are you certain it is the Venetians?"

"They are but five miles away, who else can it be?"

"The Aragonese, you fool! They are due back any day now."

"Those ships are not Aragonese."

The admiral froze. This was the *one* man whose judgment he could trust as his own. He pushed his subordinate aside and ran down the hallway to a room on the east end of the fortress. He threw open the door and gazed out at a panoramic view of the harbor and the sea beyond. Men were streaming onto the decks of his galleys while their crews struggled to raise sails and haul up the anchors. He looked down at the street below. Frantic people were running in all directions. Soldiers, sailors, and common civilians alike seemed to be in a state of panic. He took a deep breath and gazed far out into the Adriatic. They were galleys, all sailing abreast of one another. Only an attacking fleet would be such a formation.

"Quick," he barked, "tell the governor of the fortress to call every man to his duty and to prepare for battle. I am going at once to my flagship. Meet me there after you have warned him."

He hurried back to his room and shouted for his servant. After he had finished putting on his uniform, he dashed down the stairs and out through the fortress gate. Followed by his excited retinue, growing behind him, he ran along the quayside to the pier where his flagship was moored. Her captain had not dared to cast off without the admiral of the fleet.

As Admiral Coppola flew up the gangway, he shouted for him.

"Admiral, I am here," the captain shouted back from the poop deck.

"Cast off immediately! I am going to put on my armor. There is not a moment to lose. We must clear the harbor."

"Yes, Admiral. We have been awaiting you," he spat, knowing they had lost precious time waiting for the overfed nobleman.

N̄ow at his place on the highest deck, Coppola peered out directly into the morning sunlight, his hand across his eyebrows to cut down on the glare.

"Damned sun! Eighteen . . . *nineteen!*" He turned to the captain. "And we are but sixteen." He shook his head. "We will be outnumbered three to one in fighting men once the Venetian rowers engage us. We are lost unless we can make a run for it."

He looked up at his admiral's pennant, indicating that the *Vesuvio* was his flagship. It was fluttering in the strong breeze, clearly indicating the wind was blowing ashore at an angle from the northeast. The Venetians had the weather gauge. His captain had made the same observation twenty minutes before. They could not outrun the Venetians.

"Damn," spat the admiral. "Well, Captain, we have three options. We can fight in the harbor, under the protection of Castello Alfonsino's guns. We can sail out to meet them, with a quarter of our marines and sailors still asleep in the brothels—"

"Or," interrupted the captain brazenly, "we can abandon our ships and save our men, fighting the enemy from our land fortifications."

The admiral slashed him with his angry eyes.

"And have the king hang me for cowardice?" he snarled.

Coppola's ferretlike expression betrayed that he was deep in thought.

"Today we are going to fight like men, and though we may die like men, I will be damned if I am going to run like a coward. Besides, perhaps the Aragonese fleet will return before the battle is over. If they do, we may yet turn defeat into victory."

Disgusted by what he heard, the captain felt the bile rising in his chest. *This crazy fool would sacrifice all these men just to protect his own reputation with the king.*

"What are your orders, Admiral?" he said, not disguising his contempt.

"You think I am wrong, Captain?" he snapped.

"May I speak frankly?"

"Of course."

"If we sail out to meet them, we will be slaughtered and all of our ships taken as prizes or sunk. But if we can deny them entry to the port, we can prevent them from burning our ships *and* the port. I think the only sensible thing to do is to abandon the ships and man the fortifications."

The admiral stared at him. Then he turned to the captain's second in command.

"Take this coward below and chain him to an oar. You surely must have an empty bench for him. Congratulations on your promotion, Captain."

The surprised officer stole a piteous glance at his former superior as he saluted and called two marines to execute the admiral's order.

"Now let us make haste!" shouted the admiral.

The Neapolitan fleet slowly assumed the posture of a fighting force. One by one, the galleys, with their useless sails furled, rowed out of the harbor, into the wind, past Castello Alfonsino. A few of the captains had even cut their anchor cables in their haste to get under way. Two of the ships collided, causing minor damage to each other. More than four hundred marines and sailors were left behind, unable to make it back to their ships before they sailed. Only a handful of young well-born officers who had never before tasted battle were eager to engage the Venetians. The rest of the Neapolitans cursed their bad luck and set themselves grimly to their work.

An hour after the Venetians were first sighted, the Neapolitan fleet was in the open sea trying in vain to duplicate the Venetian's formation. Only a mile separated the two long rows of galleys now.

I would have defended the harbor from within its defenses," observed Antonio.

As he watched the enemy galleys row out of the harbor, he counted them again.

"Sixteen. We will have at least twice as many fighting men," calculated Seraglio. "Why would the Neapolitan commander risk meeting us on such unequal terms?"

"Because he is either uncharacteristically brave or a fool," replied Andrea.

Antonio looked down at Constantine, huddled with his marines near the *San Marco*'s bow. Then he looked to port. The *Veneto* had fallen behind slightly. The galley to their starboard side had fallen even farther behind—three ship lengths at least. He looked at Andrea. Their eyes met and his cousin gave him an understanding smile.

"When the *Veneto* signals to begin rowing, wait until I give the order to begin," commanded the captain. "We need to let them catch up a bit, eh, Antonio?"

He nodded. Andrea was the best galley captain he had ever seen.

The two fleets were now only a half mile apart. The Neapolitans were arrayed in a ragged line-abreast formation, their oarsmen, who were all slaves or convicts, were rowing hard, under the lash. Sailing toward them, the Venetian ships were in perfect formation. Their freemen rowers, aided by the following wind that filled the galleys' large lateen sails, made their speed triple that of the enemy's.

Soranzo cut an imposing figure, standing under his distinctive red-and-white-striped awning on the *Veneto*'s poop deck. He liked what he saw. He had caught his adversary napping. His decision to attack at dawn had given him every advantage.

He turned to Enrico and allowed himself a smile so pronounced it fairly burst through his thick gray beard.

"The sun will be in their eyes and the wind will be in their faces, rendering their sails useless and exhausting their rowers. At this early hour, we can count on the fact that a fair number of their seamen and marines did not make it back to their ships before they sailed. Now their stupid commander is sailing his ships out of range of the guns in the fortress. All the odds are in our favor."

Enrico gripped the rail and leaned over the water as it crashed along the
Veneto's hull in frothy white sheets. The oarsmen were pulling for their lives
now. He could feel the ship surge and glide with each powerful, unified
stroke of the oars.

"What happens now?"

Soranzo turned to his son and slammed his armored fist into his steel-
encased palm. "Now we slaughter the bastards, just like they would kill us, if
only they could."

The sheer simplicity of what he said revealed the essence of war on the
sea. The difference between it and war on land was dictated by one simple
fact: on land, once individual soldiers sensed that their side was losing a battle, they could melt away, running in every direction, using terrain for concealment. On water, there was nowhere for an individual man to run,
nowhere to hide. A ship's crew lived or died together.

Constantine, though he had never been at war on the sea, had come to
that very same realization after considering his father's words. He surveyed
the faces of his marines who were, until a few days before, all light cavalrymen. They had sustained few casualties in that war of maneuver. This day he
imagined that most of them would die. Marines were expected to kill or
defend the sailors. This meant that they would be in the forefront of any
melee. Today it would be nothing but cold steel and blood—confined, as
they were, to fight in these wooden arenas called galleys. Despite what his
father had said, he was thankful he had his full suit of armor to protect him.

33

Brindisi

Once begun, a sea battle proceeds inexorably to its conclusion. It cannot be stopped. In all, more than six thousand men were converging, the brave and the cowards alike, to meet glory or death. There are no stragglers aboard a ship.

Two enemies first engage with their eyes. The enemy ships look small and vulnerable, one's own large, powerful, unstoppable. Then the ears engage. Friendly cheers and chants easily overwhelm and drown out the enemy's distant shouts. Then the mind begins to question, to confuse, to become demoralized as the enemy ships grow larger, his shouts louder and more frightening. Soon, just before the battle is joined, it becomes a test of will, of raw courage.

"Giulio Cesare," quoted Seraglio, "said that, in battle, each side is equally fearful of the other, but the one that first sweeps away their fear takes the high road to victory! Just look at Constantine—he looks fearless. By God, Antonio, he looks like a warrior."

Antonio looked away from the enemy fleet for a moment and saw his son, gripping his sword in one hand and some rigging with the other. He followed his son's gaze skyward. Far above the deck, four crossbowmen were perched in the rigging, preparing to rain death down upon the enemy. He remembered Constantinople and the night he had repulsed a Turkish attack with Greek fire. He wished that he had some now.

"Almost time," shouted Andrea over the rising tumult.

"Time for what?" called out Seraglio, always curious about everything.

"Watch" is all Antonio said.

Suddenly the cannoneers lit their slow-burning matches. The crossbow-men placed their coronel bolts in their stocks, hardened arrows, specifically designed to punch through armor and chain mail at close range. A few terri-fied men pissed in their pants. Another difference versus land combat was that the puddles on the deck were visible, but few took notice and even fewer cared.

Constantine looked at the sharp ram, jutting like a bird's beak from the prow of the *Veneto*. He imagined the damage it would do to the wooden "skin" of an enemy galley.

Admiral Coppola now regretted his decision. As he surveyed the enemy fleet, with their marines crowded into the bows of their galleys, mak-ing full sail and bearing down on his ships with their sharp prows, he knew he had made a terrible blunder. He should have heeded the advice of his unfortunate captain, now rowing below, his tender back likely split open by the lashes of the cruel rowing master.

Coppola's only hope was to defeat the galley that grappled with him and then beat a retreat to the southeast, enabling him to catch the wind. In the confusion of battle he just might make good his escape. He grabbed an of-ficer by the arm.

"Young man! Go and cut away my admiral's flag."

The youth, no more than sixteen, looked at him, not understanding.

"Do you hear me, you idiot! Do you want to survive? They have four more ships than we do. If they see that we are the flagship, we shall have all of them on us."

Finally understanding, the boy ran to the stern, hauled down the ensign, and dropped it unceremoniously into the sea. Seeing his orders were obeyed, the admiral turned back to the business at hand, pleased with his de-cision to disguise his ship's identity. He hoped he had not thought of it too late.

Most of his captains knew their business. Their marines were armed and ready, their cannon loaded. He had only to give the order to fire, a right re-served for him on his flagship. The others would engage at their own dis-cretion following his signal.

Unlike his adversary, the admiral had narrowed his thoughts simply to surviving the battle. He had chosen the honorable course—to fight. But now, losing his confidence, he was thinking only of his own safety. With his flag gone, in the smoke of battle, his captains would not be able to tell which galley was his, and thus he would not be able to control the actions of his fleet either by using signal flags or by taking the lead.

Now, with the closest Venetian galley just three hundred yards away, he placed a woolen cap on his bald head and pulled on his bascinet. Then, snapping down his klappvisor, he drew his expensive sword and prepared to meet the Venetians.

Antonio could clearly see the enemy's faces, but before he could turn to speak, Andrea gave the order to fire. The four gunners held their glowing matches to the touch holes, and the bronze cannons exploded in a quick succession of booms, sending iron projectiles hurtling toward their target. Seconds later, three geysers rose up in front of the nearest enemy galley, but the fourth ball hit its mark, crashing over the rail and tearing into some closely packed marines, killing two instantly and wounding three others. Now guns began to crash all along the two lines, acrid smoke billowing from their barrels.

They were only a hundred yards from a big enemy galley. The Venetians shouted insults and shook their swords and axes at the enemy. Constantine knew they were close enough to use their crossbows now, but he wanted to be certain their twelve-inch bolts would have enough penetrating force to kill. A few more seconds slipped by. Suddenly someone yelled, "Down!" A hand pulled him to the deck as a flight of enemy bolts whooshed overhead. They had aimed too high. As his marines stood up again, Constantine admonished them, "See what poor marksmen those fellows are? Now, men, aim low but be careful not to kill any fish!"

He did not need to remind these veterans.

"On my order . . . Ready?"

He plunged his gauntlet down and shouted, "Fire!"

The first volley felled four or five men as the rest dropped safely to the deck.

"Prepare to grapple," shouted Andrea through his cupped hands.

This was a job for the sailors, well-accustomed as they were to throwing lines accurately. The crossbowmen were firing at will now. Cannon discharged in irregular blasts, shattering timbers and tearing apart human flesh. On every deck, marines brandished their weapons above their shoulders, shouting insults and oaths.

The two fleets came together bow to bow with little more than fifty yards separating each friendly galley. They were packed together too closely to obtain the proper angles to ram enemy ships. This day, the battle would be won by boarding and defeating the enemy. The difference between the two fleets in a boarding action was that the Neapolitan ships carried about fifty marines each, sailing as they did without a full complement. The Venetian ships each carried about the same number but could add to them all of their rowers, numbering at least a hundred men per ship. Both sides knew of this disparity. The last thing the Neapolitans could ever do was to free their rowers, all slaves and convicts, and give them arms. The only chance for the Neapolitans to win was to take the Venetian flagship, destroying their enemy's morale. The only way the Venetians could lose was to fail to prevent it.

Captain Ziani adroitly maneuvered the *San Marco* alongside the enemy galley, swerving hard to port at the last minute and fouling his prow in its rigging. Constantine watched as a dozen sailors ran to the port rail, swinging their grappling hooks in lazy circles before throwing them across the twenty-foot gap between the ships. Crossbow bolts killed two as they bravely exposed themselves, but the rest of the sailors hit their marks.

All hands heaved on the heavy ropes, inextricably lashing the ships together.

"Up and at them men!" shouted Constantine.

The Venetian marines leaned over the side. Those with long spears stabbed at any enemy marines who tried to cut the grappling lines. Crossbowmen on each side made life a lottery and death a possibility for every man on deck.

"Bring those deck guns to bear," shouted Andrea.

The gunners quickly obeyed his order. They swiveled their small bronze pieces—little more than large harquebuses, now loaded with eight to ten iron balls—and fired them into the densely packed Neapolitans.

On the *Vesuvio,* the Neapolitans prepared to grapple with the enemy ship. Admiral Coppola could tell by the red-and-white-striped awning across her poop deck that it was the Venetian commander's galley. He smiled as he thought about the nasty surprise he had in store for him. On board was a special company of one hundred elite royal marines from the naval base at Taranto. They would give him what would perhaps be a decisive advantage. Both crews were spoiling for a fight.

Soranzo gripped the rail as he watched more Neapolitan marines streaming up from below deck. He looked again at the empty flagstaff rising from the stern and turned to his captain.

"It appears that I have miscalculated the strength of the enemy. There must be more than a hundred marines on that ship!"

Enrico pulled down his klappvisor with its birdlike pointed nose. Encased in armor from head to foot, he did not fear the enemy bolts, though he should have at such close range.

"They are going to board us," he shouted through the small holes in the steel plate covering his mouth.

Soranzo heard his son's words, but he was already looking to his left, over the enemy ship. Another enemy galley had grappled the Venetian ship on his port side. It was closer than the Venetian galley. He looked to the right. The *San Marco* had grappled with her opponent, but that enemy ship was closer as well. This meant that the three closest ships to him were all enemy galleys.

How quickly things can change in war. "Captain, it seems this Neapolitan commander is not such a fool after all. Order your rowers up to help repel boarders."

The captain immediately left his post and ran down the stairs to the hold to ensure Soranzo's order was quickly obeyed. Soranzo calculated his odds. They would be approximately fifty men in his favor—not enough to ensure a quick victory. If either of the other two enemy galleys were able to disengage their opponent and grapple with him too, his crew would be overwhelmed. It was too late now to cut the grappling lines. He was committed to a fight to the death.

Admiral Coppola watched eagerly as his men stood three deep along the port side, waiting to board the Venetian flagship. He scanned the stern and spied the enemy commander. His red plume marked him as Vice-Captain of the Seas, a rank well known throughout the Mediterranean. Coppola saluted him with his sword.

Soranzo grabbed his son's arm. "See? he gladly salutes me," he said as he responded by raising his own sword and waving it back and forth. "Give me an hour and we shall see how content he is!" The duel had begun.

The *San Marco*'s swivel gunners and crossbowmen concentrated their fire on the center of the Neapolitan ship. Due to the rounded configuration of a ship's hull, this was the point where the gap between the two ships would be narrowest. Half a dozen enemy marines fell. This was the opportunity the Venetians had been waiting for. Constantine's most eager men, anticipating his order, suddenly began to stream across, swinging on ropes, while the rest jumped the few feet that separated the two ships.

Their tiny foothold began to expand. Those enemy with chain mail received wounds in the legs or neck, below the helmet. Others wearing full armor were pushed back. Constantine climbed the rail and jumped, landing hard on the enemy's deck. A hundred men swinging their weapons hacked and stabbed at each other. Man after man went down, dead or seriously wounded, out of the fight. Slowly the Venetian attack began to falter. Boxed into a small area near the rail, they fought for their lives. The marines were getting the worst of it now. One in four was down. Any man who was wounded was cut to pieces by the Neapolitans, who wanted to be certain he was dead.

"Call up the rowers!" shouted Andrea to a lieutenant.

Thirty seconds later, unarmored men dressed only in their distinctive striped shirts exploded from the hold and poured onto the deck. No sooner had they begun crossing onto the Neapolitan ship than the Venetian marines renewed their offensive with a vicious vengeance that only men who had just seen their comrades butchered could display. The enemy slowly gave way, outnumbered now, two to one.

On the *Veneto,* Soranzo ordered his men to repel boarders, knowing it would be too dangerous to attack, surrounded as he was by enemy ships. As the swivel guns and crossbowmen did their deadly work, men dropped on both ships, but the Neapolitans did not attempt to board, seeing no weak spot on the Venetian ship.

Suddenly Soranzo felt a blast on his left side. Its force staggered him. He fought to keep his balance. Enrico quickly reached out to steady him. He instinctively turned left. Two ships were grappled together, the enemy closer to him. Flames were clearly visible from the stern of the Venetian ship. Only thirty yards separated the enemy ship from the other one grappled to the *Veneto.*

"Something has happened," shouted Enrico above the roar of battle.

Thick smoke now started to billow out of the Venetian ship. Neapolitan marines were streaming back onto their own ship to escape another explosion. They were preventing the unfortunate Venetians from following them.

Phhht! A bolt struck the deck a foot from one of Soranzo's sabatons. *Phhht!* Another just missed his other foot.

"Up there!" screamed Enrico, pointing up at the enemy crossbowmen.

Three of them were in the crow's nest. They had obviously spotted the Venetian commander and intended to dispatch him with their coronels, able to pierce even steel plate at this close range.

Soranzo instantly retreated under the striped awning, obscuring the archers' view. He looked back at the action on deck. The Neapolitans were still afraid to attempt to board the *Veneto.*

Another explosion split the air. This time, its force knocked them down. Stunned, Soranzo fought to regain his senses. His face throbbed and his vision was blurred. He could taste blood gushing from his nose and into his mouth. He reached for a rail, hauled himself up, and looked in the direction of the burning Venetian galley. She was listing heavily to port.

The Neapolitans on the ship grappled to her were frantically hacking at the stout ropes that bound the two galleys together. The few Venetians left alive on their galley dove into the chilly waters, abandoning ship. Soranzo noticed that the swells had picked up and were now running about four feet.

Enrico stood up and righted himself. Suddenly a bolt crashed into the back of his cuirass. Though it did not penetrate, the glancing blow bruised him badly. He clenched his teeth, fighting the pain that radiated above his hip. He had never before been shot or wounded. Most men would have thought it bad luck, but Enrico was strangely pleased. It buoyed his confidence. *Am I not in great danger? Have I not been wounded?* He stood up straight and put his arm around his father's shoulder to turn him around. He recoiled at the sight of blood streaming out of Soranzo's helmet and down his breastplate.

"Father!" he screamed.

"I am all right."

"No, you are wounded. Take off your bascinet."

Soranzo obeyed his son. Enrico could see that he was bleeding profusely from both nostrils. He was obviously in pain.

"I must have broken it when I was knocked to the deck," he said as he cut some pieces of cloth from a dead sailor's shirt and stuffed them into his nostrils, trying to stop the bleeding. "It looks worse than it feels. I will be all right."

A loud cheer burst forth from the deck below. At first Soranzo could not tell what had prompted it. Then he stared, wide-eyed, at the enemy galley that had been grappled with the burning Venetian ship. The enemy had cut all the grappling lines, freeing her completely. Her captain was slowly maneuvering her next to the other side of the same enemy ship the *Veneto* was grappled with.

"Two to one against us now, Enrico," he shouted, spitting coagulating blood on the deck. His injury magnified his distress at how the engagement was developing. His blood was up, driving him into a rage. Soranzo put on his bascinet, pulled his sword from its scabbard, and shouted, "Follow me!"

Father and son hastened down onto the main deck and joined the marines and rowers massed there to defend against the enemy attack that would surely come, once the two Neapolitan ships' crews joined.

Admiral Coppola was elated. He did not know how or why the Venetian ship had exploded. All he knew was that now he could bring to bear two ships against the Venetian commander's one. If he could board fast enough, he just might take her, leaving the Venetians leaderless. With confidence rooted in his own self-importance, he could not imagine how they could fight on without their vice-captain of the seas.

"Captain, I am taking personal command of the *Vesuvio*. I want you to inform Captain Malatesta that he is to bring his ship alongside ours and immediately join in our attack on the enemy flagship."

The captain saluted, ran down the stairs onto the deck, and gathered some sailors to throw and secure grappling lines between the two ships.

S eraglio and Antonio watched helplessly as the burning Venetian galley slowly began to sink. It was a bitter loss in a battle that had been going so splendidly. They had shot down all of the Neapolitan crossbowmen. Constantine and his marines, reinforced by the oarsmen, were swarming over the deck of the Neapolitan galley, killing any remaining enemy sailors and marines. The ship was theirs, but there would be no celebrating. Constantine had lost nearly half of his marines, killed or severely wounded. There was no such thing as lightly wounded. If you could stand and brandish a weapon, you fought with your comrades. To do otherwise was unthinkable, intolerable.

With the lull in the action, Antonio surveyed the situation. Andrea was on deck, assessing his losses. The *San Marco* was undamaged, but her prow and ram were entangled in the enemy's rigging. It would have to be cut away to free her. Further, he would need to leave a skeleton prize crew on board the enemy ship to deal with the rowers. It was a matter of great urgency and honor to unchain any Venetian citizens they found imprisoned as rowing slaves below deck.

Finished with his assessment, Andrea bounded up the stairs to where Antonio and Seraglio stood.

"We have lost about half of our marines and a quarter of our rowers. Constantine fought like a lion and, thank God, he is unscathed."

Antonio and Seraglio were relieved, since they had not seen him for a while.

"Andrea"—Antonio pointed—"that galley is joining the other one and both will take on the *Veneto*. We must come to her aid or I fear she will be lost."

Without uttering a word, Andrea left them and went to work, deploying his prize crew, collecting the wounded, and separating the two ships. While he did, Antonio ordered the gunners to bring up more powder and balls.

To the right, all the way down the battle line, they could see ships locked together in mortal combat. The superior Venetian numbers were beginning to tell. Three enemy ships on that side had already struck their colors, indicated by the huge white flags fluttering from their staffs. No Venetian ships had surrendered. He looked left. One enemy ship on the far end of the line had slipped past the farthermost Venetian ship and was trying to escape with two Venetian galleys in pursuit. As for the rest, the huge black pillar of smoke rising from the dying galley obscured the outcomes of the other individual duels.

Admiral Coppola watched as his reinforcements climbed aboard the *Vesuvio* and formed up for the attack. From the elevated deck, he could see that the battle was going badly on his left. Time was running out. He pulled down his klappvisor, strode down the steps to the main deck, and joined the mass of sailors and marines.

"Men, the Venetian commander stands yonder." He pointed at Soranzo, no more than a hundred feet away. "Take him and victory is ours!"

Then he turned to his two captains and finally gave the order to attack. A shower of bolts and balls swept the *Veneto*'s deck, killing or maiming a dozen Venetians. Then, with a mighty shout and led by the elite marines, nearly two hundred Neapolitans began their spirited attack.

"Look!" Seraglio pointed. "They are attacking the *Veneto*."

Antonio searched for Andrea in the crowd on the deck below. He was directing a group of sailors as they struggled to free the prow. He looked over at the *Veneto*. Soranzo was not under the striped canopy where he had expected to see him. He scanned the deck. Suddenly Antonio spotted his red plume in the thick of the action, directing his marines as they doggedly sought to prevent the Neapolitans from successfully boarding.

He ran down the stairs and grabbed Andrea.

"How much longer until you can free the ship?"

"Not long," shouted Andrea. About fifteen men were chopping away at the entangling ratlines and ropes. Others were retrieving grappling hooks, trying to salvage a few in case they were needed later.

"Cut those ropes. There is not a minute to spare."

Five minutes later, they were finally free. Andrea grabbed every rower he could find and pushed and shoved them toward the door that led down to the hold. They quickly went below to pick up their oars.

"I am going to try to back the *San Marco* away and cross the bow of the prize ship. Then we can gather some speed and ram the stern of that big galley grappled to the *Veneto*."

The enemy ship was about a hundred yards away. The Venetians could see enemy marines rising up and down as they mounted the rails and jumped onto the *Veneto*'s deck. The *San Marco* slowly backed away. Andrea shouted the order to turn to port, and the oarsmen on the starboard side ran to port and picked up their fallen comrades' oars to turn the ship. Now, perfectly aimed at the side of the enemy ship, Andrea gave the order to ram. The *San Marco* shuddered as she began to accelerate through the swells.

Antonio looked over the side. He could see needles of spray blowing from the wave tops. The wind was picking up. The ship rolled nearly twenty degrees as she cut across the direction of the swells. Constantine formed up the remnant of his company of marines. About thirty were still fit for duty. Black smoke from the sinking Venetian galley towered into the blue sky. Flames quickly devoured the mainsail and rose all the way up the masts. She was done for as waves rolled over her main deck.

Two big sailors helped Coppola climb over the rail and onto the *Veneto*'s deck. His marines were pushing back the Venetians hard, pressing them toward the stern. The forward half of the ship was already theirs.

The clash of steel was terrific. The Neapolitans, all sheathed in armor or chain mail, were hard pressed to defeat Soranzo's marines, who were equally protected, but his rowers were falling fast, protected, as they were, by only their helmets and leather gloves.

"Look!" shouted Captain Malatesta as he grabbed the admiral's arm.

They could see the *San Marco* bearing down on them, fifty yards away, her ram aimed directly at the side of their stern. There was nothing they could do. The melee was so loud their orders would never be heard above it. They grabbed the rigging and held on for their lives just before the Venetian prow struck. The splintering, groaning sound as the copper-sheathed prow ripped into oak boards sounded like a collapsing building. The deck rose up as the *San Marco*'s momentum rolled the *Vesuvio* hard to starboard.

Almost every man still on the *Vesuvio* was knocked to the deck. They tumbled against the far rail and were struck by flying debris. Below deck, the prow cut a swath through the rowers on their wooden benches, smashing ribs, arms, legs, and skulls. With the hole four feet above the waterline, sea water began to slosh in with every passing wave.

The slaves went wild, fearing they were about to drown. They tore at their chains and cried out. The rusty manacles shredded their wrists and ankles as they fought their bonds in vain, unable to free themselves. Their overseers ran up the steps that led to the deck, abandoning them to their fate.

The collision spun the *Vesuvio*'s forward hull hard against the *Veneto*'s stern. The collision temporarily disoriented the combatants, making victors of some who were about to be vanquished and surprising others who had been about to defeat their opponents. It was as though the world had suddenly turned upside down.

Soranzo was felled again by the impact. Weak from loss of blood, he grew faint.

"Enrico, help me," he pleaded as he staggered backward.

His son grabbed him as he was about to fall and half dragged, half carried him back to the steps leading up to the poop deck. Enrico laid him down on the deck, where he tried to recover his senses. Soranzo could see the backs of the Venetians lined across the fifteen-foot-wide deck, four deep. Raised arms hacked and stabbed at steel-helmeted enemies. The lightly armored rowers stood behind the marines and used their long spears to poke and stab, carefully maneuvering through the arms and torsos in front of them.

Constantine and his men climbed over the splintered rails and charged onto the enemy ship. Their aim was to hit the Neapolitans from the rear, compelling them to abandon their attack on the *Veneto* and defend their own ship. Closely followed by the *San Marco*'s oarsmen, about a hundred men in all, they were more than a match for the handful of Neapolitan sailors opposing them. They quickly swept across the main deck, dispatching every enemy sailor they could find, but enemy crossbowmen, advantageously lashed to the rigging, had not been thrown by the impact of the collision. They spotted the Venetians and took a terrible toll on them. A dozen men fell to their well-aimed bolts.

When they had killed every man on the deck, Constantine detached a small party of rowers to go below to search for fugitives and to liberate any Venetian slaves they could find there. He spotted four Venetian crossbowmen who had followed him and shouted to them to shoot at their opposites above, plainly silhouetted against the azure sky. The Venetians bravely exchanged their lives for an equal number of the enemy crossbowmen. Though they had not eliminated the menace, they had reduced it. Constantine quickly shifted his attention to the *Veneto*.

A wild melee on the deck made it difficult to distinguish between friend and foe. Hundreds of steel blades rang out as they crashed into armor, chain mail, or each other. He could see no one on the poop deck. Every Venetian capable of wielding his weapon was in the thick of the fighting now, including Soranzo, his plume clearly visible as it seemed to fly from side to side as he swung his sword alongside his men. He knew it would not be long before they were overwhelmed.

If Soranzo is captured, the battle could be lost! Constantine immediately shouted and motioned for his marines to follow him one more time and board the flagship. His exhausted, bloodied company obediently rose up and began jumping over the gap to the *Veneto* to engage a score of Neapolitans who, perceiving this new threat, had lined the rail to oppose them.

On the *Veneto*, Admiral Coppola and his marines and sailors, their attention fixed solely on slaughtering Soranzo's marines and taking the vice-captain prisoner, smelled victory. In the confusion of battle, they were unaware of Constantine's attack in their rear. There were no more than sixty men left under arms from the *Veneto*'s original crew, packed into the stern.

Antonio agonized as he watched Constantine and his company take the enemy ship. He cringed as he watched him parry or avoid each sword thrust. Once, a mace blow glanced off his shoulder armor, nearly knocking him off his feet. If he were helplessly sprawled on the deck, one thrust of a sharp dagger into an unprotected joint, severing a tendon or opening an artery, would be fatal.

Antonio could not simply be a spectator while his son fought for his life.

"I do not like that look in your eye," Seraglio suddenly admonished him.

Antonio turned to him and pointed at the *Veneto*.

He was trembling with rage. "That is where the battle will be won or lost."

"There is not a minute to lose. One sword could be the difference!"

Antonio pushed past him and ran to the stairs leading down to the main deck. Seraglio knew he could not dissuade him. Antonio's eyes desperately searched the deck, looking for Andrea's helmet with its white plume. Suddenly he spotted him, organizing the last of the rowers, preparing to cross over to the captured enemy ship that was lashed to the *Veneto*. As he chased after Antonio, Seraglio reached for his old dagger, tucked in his leather belt.

Antonio saw Andrea, with his back turned to him, but he rushed past him in his haste to climb the rail and jump onto the enemy ship. He was oblivious to the danger posed by the surviving enemy crossbowmen, high above in the rigging.

Seraglio instantly recognized the great danger they posed to Antonio. He seized Andrea by the gauntlet, spinning him around.

"Antonio has gone to fight with Constantine," he shouted above the din, pointing.

"Damn him!"

"He will make a fine target for those crossbowmen up there, with his blue-plumed bascinet and chain mail as his only protection. They will take him for an officer, for sure."

Andrea quickly scanned the deck. Suddenly he spotted two cannoneers loading their swivel gun and dashed toward them.

Antonio jumped over the rail, landing awkwardly and falling to the deck. As he rose, he could see the mutilated bodies that littered the deck, their blood staining it red. *The butcher's bill is still totaled in the same way.* A razor-sharp bolt slammed into the deck not two feet from where he stood. He looked up. There, high in the rigging, he could see a man, then another, then one more. He moved out of their line of sight. The three of them were up there killing like assassins, but he could see that they were choosing their targets carefully. *They must be low on bolts by now.*

"Quick, up there."

The gunner followed Andrea's pointing finger aloft. *What a target!* He carefully finished ramming the balls on top of the powder charge. Then he pushed down on the back of the gun, raising the muzzle. Bending low to sight the target, he tried to hold it at the correct elevation, despite the rocking motion of the ship.

"Ready," he shouted to the other gunner.

The match touched the small hole in the barrel, igniting the charge. The blast sent eight iron balls hurtling toward their target.

They missed, hitting the mast below but close enough to get the enemy crossbowmen's attention. As the gunners doggedly went to work, reloading their piece, two of them took careful aim. In three seconds, both gunners were down, one dead and the other with a bolt through his hand.

Antonio ran to the rail, but he could not go any farther forward. He was blocked by a wall of Venetians finally climbing onto Soranzo's flagship, having overpowered most of the enemy sailors who had opposed them.

Seraglio had observed the contest between the swivel gun and the crossbowmen. Though they had not eliminated the danger, he bravely decided to climb over the rails and onto the enemy ship, chasing after Antonio. Andrea, his work finished on board the *San Marco,* saw Seraglio land on the *Vesuvio's* deck and ran after him.

The Neapolitans were close to pushing the *Veneto's* crew back against the stairs that led to the poop deck. Enrico grabbed his father and pointed above.

"It is time to move up there," he shouted to him.

They climbed to the top of the stairs, stepping over a wounded sailor who had been shot through the neck and past two others who had expired in pools of blood. The striped canopy was shot through with holes, but it would still provide some concealment from the enemy crossbowmen.

"I fear that there are too many opposing us," observed Enrico.

"Those marines from the *San Marco* are our only hope for salvation." His father pointed. As he spoke, Enrico's eyes were glued to a tall marine officer in the melee, viciously hacking and slashing like a madman. He drove one enemy to the deck, then delivered a killing stroke to his neck, expertly aimed at the gap between his sallet and chain mail.

Soranzo removed his red–plumed bascinet.

"Here, put this on. It will protect you better than that one you are wearing. I cannot stand the pain any longer against my broken nose."

Enrico sheathed his sword, removed his own helmet, and discarded it on the deck. Then he reached out and took his father's bloody bascinet.

"You had better cut off the plume," ordered Soranzo just before he turned back to watch the battle. Enrico pulled it onto his head and redrew his sword.

Coppola was intoxicated with the prospect of victory. No longer thinking of running, he could focus only on capturing the man with the red plume, standing no more than sixty feet from him on the deck above. It was then that he heard the shouts behind him. He quickly twisted his neck to see what it was. Venetian marines' helmets glistened in the sunlight, interposed with those of his own men. Time was growing short. The battle had turned into one big melee, with the Neapolitan force in between two Venetian mobs. All three were shrinking by the minute and compressing toward the *Veneto*'s stern, where the Venetian commander was protected by no more than thirty men still on their feet. He shouted and cursed at his men, beating the nearest ones on their backs with the flat of his sword, urging them to press the enemy harder.

Antonio called to Constantine in vain. Men packed three deep between them waited to join the fray on the narrow deck. Suddenly a light blow from behind startled him. He turned and raised his sword to defend himself—it was Seraglio!

"Go back!" shouted Antonio. "You can do nothing here."

"Nor can you!" Seraglio replied. "I shall remain here as long as you."

Antonio exploded. He swung the pommel of his sword at Seraglio's bare head, knocking him to the deck. By the time he turned back around, Constantine was gone. He began to push and shove wildly, trying to make a path through steel and flesh to reach the place where he had last seen his son.

Andrea found Seraglio crumpled in a heap on the deck and bent over him. He rolled him over and saw that he was unconscious. Seeing no blood, he jumped up and continued to push his way aft. He could see Soranzo and a dozen of his marines huddled under the canopy. They were fending off an enemy attempt to storm one of the two stairways. Six feet in front of him, he could see Antonio struggling to push his way through the crowd.

Constantine's left arm hung limply at his side. A fresh dent from a heavy axe marked the spot in his armor sheathing where the blow had struck. Right-handed, he stood back up and stepped over the giant who had wounded him. A spear-wielding oarsman had expertly skewered the man through the throat, pinning him to the deck, and was now struggling to withdraw the weapon.

Dying men screamed with pain, their lifeblood oozing from their grievous wounds. Some howled vile oaths. Others cheered on their comrades, while still others grimly dealt death to their nameless enemies, uttering nothing more than a grunt. Venetians and Neapolitans alike could sense that their fight to the death was coming to a climax.

The Neapolitan crossbowman carefully aimed at the red plume, momentarily visible through the hole in the canopy. He hated Venetians, especially *nobili,* after what one of them had done to his cousin. He squeezed the trigger. The coronel whizzed through the air so fast, he could not follow its flight.

"That one is for Ercolano," he said quickly as he placed his foot in the stirrup to redraw his bowstring.

The three-feathered bolt crashed into Enrico's armor, ripping through his steel cuirass and penetrating five inches into his shoulder muscle. He collapsed onto the deck, writhing in pain. In disbelief, Soranzo stared at his son as he lay on his back, barely conscious, still holding his sword tightly in his right hand.

Soranzo raged at heaven, beseeching God to undo what had happened. Then, desperate to protect his son from another shot, Soranzo lifted his feet and dragged him back next to the tiller. He carefully propped him up against the rail and gently removed the bascinet he had given him to wear, ripping out the plume with his hand and throwing it overboard. Enrico's eyes fluttered open. *He is in shock, but at least the bolt did not cause much bleeding.* Enrico's mouth twisted into a tortured smile. Gasping for breath, he could not speak. Soranzo had to look away.

Down on the main deck, Antonio could clearly see his old nemesis. He wondered why Soranzo's head was bare. Why was he not wearing his bascinet? With sword drawn and Andrea right behind him, Antonio pushed along the port rail toward the melee at the foot of the stairs leading up to the poop deck and Soranzo. He glanced down at the roiling sea below. The waves were getting higher as the wind whipped the water. He could see Constantine and his men fighting up in front of him. He was almost there.

Seraglio shook his head to clear his brain. He rubbed the painful knot on his head from Antonio's unexpected blow, but he was not angry. He was only more determined than ever to find him and protect him—somehow.

He stood up slowly, but it was impossible for him to see over the backs of the men in front of him. Suddenly an oarsman directly to his front threw up his arms and fell to the deck with a groan, a bolt stuck in his back.

Like a man possessed, Antonio continued to push his way ahead until he was right behind Constantine and his exhausted comrades. As he reached out his arm to make a place to fight, a powerful-looking enemy marine suddenly swung his axe directly at his son, smashing it into his bad shoulder. Stunned, Constantine flew sideways, crashing hard into the rail and flipping over it into the sea.

The cold water shocked him back to his senses. He ripped off his bascinet and began to tear at his heavy steel-plate cuirass, all the while furiously kicking his legs as he desperately fought to stay afloat. Already weak from his exertions in battle, he could feel his tight-fitting armor filling with water. He remembered his father's words and realized that, without a miracle, he would drown.

"No!" Antonio shrieked. Turning to Andrea, he shouted, "He will drown."

Andrea did not hear him. His eyes were fixed on the big Neapolitan who, flushed with his victory over Constantine, was about to swing his axe at Antonio.

"Look out!" he shouted to Antonio as he swung his sword over Antonio's bent head and hit the giant in the forearm, slowing the axe's descent. Antonio spun around and, seeing the danger, backed away. Not connecting, the heavy axe ripped through thin air, pulling the Neapolitan off balance. Striking as fast as a scorpion, Andrea thrust the point of his sword at the two inches of the man's neck that were exposed between the top of his chain mail and his bascinet. His jugular exploded, showering all three men with his blood. He dropped his axe and fell to one knee, dazed and gurgling for a breath. Antonio and Andrea finished him off with a kick to the chest and a quick slash across the throat.

Farther back, Seraglio had seen Constantine fall. He instantly ran to a corpse lying by the rail. Standing on it, he peered over the rail. He could see Constantine, bareheaded, bobbing over the swells and struggling to remove his armor. His expression told Seraglio all he needed to know. He pulled out his rusted old dagger and looked for some rigging to cut for a line. Deciding it would take too long, he turned his eyes back to the water. He spied a large half-submerged piece of burned wood. With a father's instinct, he climbed onto the rail and jumped. He disappeared under the surface, but his buoyant body quickly popped back up. Shaking water from his eyes, he struggled to get his bearings. Then he spotted Constantine about ten feet away.

No swimmer, he began to flail his arms as he frantically kicked his feet. Suddenly his left hand hit something hard. *Praise God—the plank!*

He pulled it to him, sliding his belly onto it, keeping himself afloat.

"Constantine!" he shouted.

His head spun in Seraglio's direction. One arm extended toward him, his head now half submerged. His strength was gone. Slowly Constantine slipped away, out of sight. Only his chain-mailed arm and bare hand rose above the water.

"Oh God, take me but spare *him!*" prayed Seraglio as a wave broke over him, filling his mouth with brine.

Suddenly Constantine's bare head broke the surface. Wasting no time, Seraglio slid backward from the board and pushed it toward him, hitting him in the side of his neck. Constantine looked at Seraglio, his eyes wide in horror.

As Seraglio's nose filled with water and his head slipped beneath the waves, he realized in a flash what most never understand all their lives—that God needs men to love others more than themselves to fully accomplish His purposes.

Constantine wearily slid his shiny steel breastplate along the soggy wooden plank. His throat burned as he coughed salt water from his aching lungs. He looked in Seraglio's direction, but there was no sign of the little man.

As Antonio and Andrea battled for their lives on the main deck, above, on the poop deck, Enrico lay against the rail, barely alive, while his father fought in the line like a common marine. In between them, Admiral Coppola and his men realized that, caught between a force of Venetians that would not yield and another that would not relent, they were doomed. They quickly lost heart. In the end, war is about morale and survival. They began to drop their weapons and surrender. In a minute, the fighting had stopped.

As soon as it was apparent that the battle on the *Veneto* was over, Antonio and Andrea hurried to the rail and looked over the side. There was Constantine, looking half dead as he lay shivering on his stomach, floating on his life-saving board. By now, he had removed most of his armor.

"Thank God," implored Antonio, his grateful eyes raised to heaven. "I thought he would surely drown, dressed in his armor."

Andrea suddenly grabbed Antonio's arm. "Where is Seraglio?"

Seraglio! Antonio was embarrassed. He quickly scanned the deck, but there was no sign of him.

"I will fish out Constantine while you find him," ordered Andrea.

The Venetians rounded up nearly fifty surviving Neapolitans; Admiral Coppola was among them. They quickly pushed and shoved their prisoners down into the *Veneto*'s hold to sit on the benches that belonged to their dead and wounded oarsmen.

When Soranzo finished directing his men to secure the prisoners, he turned around and hesitantly looked at the stairs. He wondered if he would find his son still alive at the top. He climbed them slowly, fearful of what he would find. As the deck came into view, he could see Enrico leaning against the stern rail. Soranzo was horrified to see the side of his face covered with blood. *What has happened?*

Moving closer, he could see the bolt still protruding through the armor covering his shoulder. *Something else has happened.* He lifted his son's slumping head by the chin, only to see it fall away, lifeless. *Can it be? Is he . . . dead?*

He gently wiped the blood from around his left eye with his bare hand. The socket was smashed. He could see and feel sharp pieces of broken bone protruding around it. His eye was gone—there was only a deep depression where it once was.

Suddenly, the head moved and a long whimpering groan escaped from Enrico's lips. *He is in shock but he is alive—barely.* Soranzo stared down at the once handsome face in horror. *What life will my son have with his arm crippled and his face disfigured beyond recognition?* The vice-captain of the gulf, commander of the Venetian fleet, hung his head and cried.

Antonio hurried around the deck, disentangling bodies, looking for Seraglio. It took Antonio only a few minutes to finish searching. He was not on the *Veneto*. He decided that Seraglio *must* be back on the *San Marco,* where he was probably in a foul mood, nursing his sore head. He desperately wanted to go to Constantine now.

He turned just in time to see Andrea and three sailors haul his son over the rail and carefully lay him out on the deck. Constantine was trembling with cold and barely conscious. Antonio ran to him, knelt, and held him in his arms. He embraced him for a long time like that, rocking him slowly on the deck. After a while, he looked down into his son's half-closed, bloodshot eyes.

"I thought I had lost you," whispered Antonio.

Someone brought a blanket and draped it over Constantine. Antonio began to rub him to put warmth back into his body. Constantine revived a little. Suddenly he opened his eyes, a grave expression on his face.

"Are you wondering about the battle, son? Do not worry, we are victorious."

Antonio gently smiled, certain his words would allay his son's fears, but Constantine's expression only turned to tears.

"You have fought bravely and suffered much this day. You have earned the right to weep. Go ahead. Do not be concerned about what your comrades will think."

Constantine began to move his head slowly from side to side. Andrea leaned closer and looked quizzically at Antonio.

"He is confused. All this has shocked him more than I would have thought."

Suddenly Constantine tried to speak.

"Armor . . . heavy . . . drowning . . . could not swim," he struggled weakly.

Antonio and Andrea looked at each other.

"Saved me . . . drowned . . . could not swim."

"He is telling us that he almost drowned in his heavy armor," said Antonio.

Constantine shook his head more violently.

"No . . . he is drowned . . . saved me."

"But you did not drown, my son. You are here—alive." Antonio felt a chill as he looked at the expression on Andrea's face.

"I will go and find Seraglio. You stay with him," said Andrea.

As Antonio watched him walk away, he thought about how hurt Seraglio would be that he had hit him. In thirty years, he had never done that before, admonishing him like a disobedient servant. *He deserves better.*

As the warmth returned to his body, Constantine slowly regained his senses.

"Seraglio . . . where is Seraglio?"

"Back on the *San Marco.* Andrea has gone to find him."

Constantine breathed a heavy sigh. "Thank God."

Antonio smiled. "It seems that we have all come through the battle in one piece."

He stood and looked down at his son. "I must speak with Vice-Captain of the Gulf Soranzo. Lie here quietly and rest."

Antonio dragged himself wearily up the stairs to where he knew he would find Soranzo. At the top, he could see a crowd gathered around a man lying prostrate on the deck. He looked into the center and saw it was Enrico Soranzo. His horribly disfigured face, cleansed of its mask of dried blood, was contorted in agony as a surgeon attempted to withdraw a bolt from his shoulder. His only succor was a piece of leather someone had mercifully placed between his teeth. *If he is lucky, he will die.* He remembered his son's oath to kill Enrico someday for insulting Maria.

He could see Soranzo standing at the rail, looking away, surveying the scene of the battle. Antonio went to him.

"Signor Soranzo, we meet again in the aftermath of another battle."

Soranzo looked at him as though Antonio was the last person on earth he expected to see at that very moment.

"We have won a great victory here today," Antonio continued.

"Yes, but at a steep price." Soranzo looked down ruefully at his son, now wincing like a child. After the surgery, he looked like a living corpse.

Suddenly Antonio heard Andrea calling his name from the main deck. He turned and walked to the rail. Andrea was signaling for him to come down.

"Andrea requires me. Constantine is there, also wounded. I must go to him."

Soranzo just nodded, having nothing more to say to him.

Antonio wondered what would have been important enough to call him away. *It is Seraglio. Andrea has found him.* He prepared for the outburst he knew would come.

He climbed over two bodies at the foot of the stairs, locked in a death embrace, enemies to the end.

Andrea was standing there, holding something in his hands. With a far-away look in his eye, Constantine sat with his back against the rail, looking more alive than dead for the first time since Andrea fished him out of the sea.

Antonio recognized the weapon—it was Seraglio's dagger. He froze. Antonio began to shake his head. He looked up to the heavens. The white clouds drifted across the blue sky in the brisk wind. He did not want to look away.

"Father . . ."

Antonio lowered his eyes, not wanting to hear the words.

"Seraglio is dead. He drowned saving my life."

Constantine recounted how he had fallen into the sea. He told how Seraglio had jumped in, not able to swim but knowing that to remain on deck would have been to abandon him to certain death.

Sometimes a man is too heartbroken to shed tears. Antonio listened in silence.

"He must have dropped his dagger just before he jumped into the water," observed Andrea. "I found it near the spot where Constantine was knocked overboard."

He ceremoniously handed it to Antonio as if it were a sacred relic, the kind that the Crusaders gave their very lives to protect.

"So this is it—all that remains of that little man with the heart of a giant." He looked at Andrea and at his son as the cruel emptiness tore at his innards.

"How can I ever replace him?"

Antonio stood on the bloody deck and dropped his old gray head as the waves of pain washed over him with the realization that he would never see Seraglio again.

Andrea, who was a religious man, more so than Antonio, recalled a simple verse.

"Greater love hath no man than he who would lay down his life for a friend."

Antonio looked up, tears trickling down his blackened cheeks. "I shall have those fitting words inscribed on his tomb."

Then he slowly turned to Constantine and held out the old dagger. "Here, this belongs to you now. He would have wanted you to have it. Cherish it always. I pray that someday you will find a friend like him."

Historical Note

By the battle's end, the Venetians had sunk or captured fifteen of the enemy's ships; only a single Neapolitan galley had escaped to the south. The price of their victory was one Venetian galley, which had caught fire, exploded, and sunk when a lucky Neapolitan crossbowman shot a flaming bolt into a keg of black powder that someone had carelessly left on deck. Though the Venetians had lost many good men, they had dealt a mortal blow to the Neapolitans, winning a crucial victory for the Republic.

This single victory triggered a series of events orchestrated by La Serenissima and her elaborate network of diplomats and spies. First, Venice blockaded Neapolitan ports, crippling her trade and, with it, her ability to finance her participation in the League. Next, she convinced Ludovico that Ferrante, whom he hated, was about to make a separate peace with Venice and offered him a last chance to make a separate peace of his own.

Ludovico was aware that the King of Naples had pledged his granddaughter, Isabella, to be Duke Gian Galeazzo's bride, and he feared that if old Ferrante made peace with Venice first, the Milanese would overthrow him as regent and his nephew and the boy's mother would gain full ducal powers. He jumped at the chance to end the war and strengthen his own position at the expense of his erstwhile allies.

In total secrecy, representatives from Milan and Venice negotiated the

Treaty of Bagnolo, which was announced in August 1484. The other members of the League, and especially Pope Sixtus IV, were furious at Ludovico's treachery. However, Florence and Naples had had enough. Privately, they welcomed an end to a war that had cost so much and gained so little. The terms allowed Venice to keep Rovigo and all of the Polesine. Without his allies' support, the Duke of Ferrara's venture in the salt business was ended. He returned to the fold as a disloyal ally of La Serenissima.

Only Pope Sixtus, brokenhearted and dying, continued to resist. When he was informed that the suspected treaty was official, with his tongue so swollen he could hardly talk, he weakly told his attendants that he would *never* give his blessing to the peace as long as he lived. The next morning he died. When his successor, Innocent VIII, lifted the papal interdict from Venice a few months later, he completed the final act of the Ferrara War.

Venice, after nearly thirty years of constant war, at home and abroad, against Christian and Turk, through force, guile, sheer determination, and some luck, had finally won peace. Little did the Venetians know that in a few years the greatest threat to her existence yet would burst onto the world stage, but that is a story for another day.